THE FUGUE

After over a decade in prison, a young sculptor, Yuri Dilienko, returns to his old neighborhood in Cicero, Illinois. He finds the town stripped of so many places he used to know, while the town's familiar streets, bricks and steeples trigger memories of his traumatic youth. To convalesce, he sculpts from collected scrap metal, but his arrival in town soon rouses a young girl, Lita Avila, to curiosity. Could this reclusive and oddly quiet man, whose art is sensitive yet intense, truly be guilty of setting fire to his parents' bungalow and burning them alive? At once an homage to the urban grit of Nelson Algren and the family sagas of Leo Tolstoy, *The Fugue* is a true epic that spans three generations and over fifty years, a major new achievement in the history of Chicago literature. It considers the effects of war and the silent, haunting traumas inherited by children of displaced refugees. Gint Aras's lucid yet lyrical prose braids and weaves a tale where memory and imagination merge, time races and drags, and identity collapses and shifts without warning.

THE FUGUE

"**A character** in *The Fugue* describes the eponymous musical form as having melodies "weave together like braids or plaits, then split up and come back together again." One of Gint Aras's many achievements in this constantly compelling novel is to propel the reader back and forth in time, encountering several generations of characters (mostly congregants and clergy at St. Anthony's in Cicero) in various permutations with each other and in relationship to a house fire, the central act of violence (and many subsidiary affronts) that bind and break them.

"Set in a community of displaced persons living just outside Chicago during the decades following World War II, *The Fugue* is partly a 'whodunit,' but is more concerned with the steps leading up to and fallout from what's been done. Aras is a master with dialogue and seemingly innocuous details, exploited here to accentuate evil and surprise us with good. Aras doesn't sugar-coat the agonies—great and small—endured and perpetuated by his cast; rather, he spices them in such a way that you feel the bite on your tongue and remain hungry for more. Amidst shattered lives, it is still possible for broken pieces to find each other and make something beautiful."

"Gint Aras' epic novel *The Fugue* is nothing less than a tour de force masterpiece. In a morality play that takes place against the bleak backdrop of Cicero, Illinois, we see the lives of an amazing set of characters, all haunted by nightmares and dark obsessions. Like a musical fugue, the complex recurring thematic materials of the story carry the reader on a nail-biting journey that sustains incredible suspense until the very end of the novel. The imagery is masterfully portrayed throughout and the deep sadness of the story is also juxtaposed with the possibility for beauty and redemption."

THE FUGUE

GINT ARAS

Tortoise Books
Chicago, IL

Contents

Dramatis Personae

Bronza Dilienko (b. 1922-1923): Husband to Gaja Laputis
Gaja Laputis Dilienko (b. 1944): Wife to Bronza Dilienko
Yuri Dilienko (b. 1963): Son to Bronza Dilienko and Gaja Laputis
Anya Dilienko (b. 1968): Daughter to Bronza Dilienko and Gaja Laputis

Benediktas "Benny" Laputis (b. 1926): Uncle to Gaja Laputis, great-uncle to Yuri Dilienko

Lars Jorgenson (b. 1920): Husband to Victoria Jorgenson
Victoria Jorgenson (b. 1924): Wife to Lars Jorgenson
Alina Jorgenson (b. 1954): Daughter to Lars and Victoria Jorgenson

Reikel (b. 1954): Alina's childhood friend

Angelita "Lita" Avila (b. 1981): Niece to Sonia Avila
Sonia Avila (b. 1954): Aunt to Angelita Avila

Monsignor Kilba (b. 1900): Pastor of St. Anthony's Parish
Father Cruz (b. 1944): Priest at St. Anthony's Parish

To Masha

Subject: Western Ukraine, February 1940

Orest managed to listen to his grandfather. "You take the infant down for the night. That's where you'll sleep. Your mother's too weak right now. Look at her." Orest stepped to the small wheelbarrow to lift his month-old brother, a light bundle of warm cloths, and strapped the sling over his shoulder. He did not glance at his mother but left the shack to have a moment alone.

He sat on a stump near a scavenged wagon, able to see the tired, frozen fields of the abandoned farm, and he lit a cigarette butt he had saved. Orest knew he should have looked at his mother, acknowledged her wounds, and let her share some of his strength. But with his infant brother bound to him, and the butt smoked down to his fingers, Orest didn't feel strong. He could go back to wish her good night before sleeping himself, but she'd see his cowardice. He only sat on the stump and smelled the cold night air, dry and crisp, the temperature falling and the wind blowing harder, and he recalled how it had last been to warm himself beside a good fire.

Orest returned to the shack and opened the trap door to the cellar, pressing his brother to himself gently as he took care down the narrow stone stairs. The cellar was the best place for the baby to sleep; wind blew straight through the shack, so many of its windows broken, the roof full of holes. The cellar—nothing larger than a closet cluttered with crates and junk—was hardly enough for one person. Orest lay down, his brother on his chest, and slept.

Gunfire woke him. It was real, not a dream. When he heard the tumbling, shouting and shuffling above, his throat and arms tightened. His brother awoke to whimper, but Orest whispered,

"Hi. Hi. Hi. Тихо тихо тихо," as the baby started to cry. Orest wrapped a palm around the infant's mouth and nose, and his entire body hardened fast. The thought "Ni" ricocheted about his thoughts, "Hi. Не роби цього!" and he did not allow a single breath to escape his brother. Furniture tumbled and shouting men dragged things along the floor. Someone fired a pistol.

He saw the last thing that would happen in his life: men knocking the trap door open to flood his eyes with terrible light. Faceless shadows moved toward him as a prayer poured from his body—he could see the land outside, the gray and brown winter plains, and the sun shimmering off the river, underwater grasses swaying in the gentle current. He saw the cherry trees that grew in his grandfather's yard and the log table where his mother sat spitting pits into a cup, her fingers purple from cherry juice.

When Orest finally came up from the cellar, dawn had already broken, the clouds red and gold outside the window. The shack's doors had been kicked down, broken furniture thrown everywhere. A bloodstain had frozen where his grandfather had been sleeping. Just beyond the threshold, his mother's black shoe lay dusted with fresh snow. No other sign of anyone remained—no track of wheels, no footprints, no direction to follow, nothing to understand.

Orest needed a shovel. He searched through the abandoned wagon and rummaged through the crates in the cellar, but there weren't any tools on the abandoned property. He first tried digging the cold ground with his hands but found it frozen hard. He stabbed at it with a small bread knife, impossible.

Eroded stones had been piled in the middle of a field. Most were round and heavy, not flat and light like he wanted, but he had no choice. While burying his brother under the stones, he promised God he'd return in the future with a shovel. One would eventually turn up somewhere. He hoped his unbaptized brother could be forgiven. Surely, an infant could be forgiven.

When he was finished, his hands numb from the cold rocks, he couldn't be sure if he was facing the morning or evening, which way was east or west. Paint strokes of gray clouds now obscured the sun, and just below, down at the horizon, behind silhouettes of low trees, the moon's dark orange sliver was either rising or setting. Orest set out in that direction, thinking only that he must find a shovel. He had strength and could walk—he knew it—very far. If he had to, he could keep walking forever.

Summer, 1994

1

The sound of freedom was a sudden and riveting release of a huge metal latch. Yuri saw a band of white sunlight fall along the concrete floor—it widened as an armored door rolled open to reveal his exit. An enormous square led to a rust-brown, fenced-in walkway, large coils of razor wire strung above and below. At the gate an officer stood holding a shotgun.

Yuri tried to keep his steps from appearing eager as a second officer followed him. At the gate they might laugh and tell him to turn back.

But the officer behind Yuri stepped past to open the lock as the one with the shotgun cleared his throat. They told him to go, and the gate clicked shut behind him as he continued down a cracked footpath to an abandoned warehouse. He rounded a corner but did not feel hidden from the prison's lookout posts and peepholes. His pace increased steadily down the neglected street and, stepping around a rain-warped cardboard box, Yuri fought the urge to look back. After a few blocks, he believed no one could see him any more.

Yuri started running. The rubber soles of his black leather boots clapped against the sidewalk and the sound echoed through the deserted street. He was already out of breath but carried on and ran through several intersections without ever looking for traffic. He soon tripped forward to catch his balance against a lamppost.

Yuri pressed his forehead and palms against the warm metal, breathing heavily, smelling the rust. He pressed fingers to feel its gritty surface. This was the first metal he had touched in twelve years that he did not hate.

The visions came immediately. With a torch or a saw, Yuri could cut the post down and sculpt a giant serpent or a pointing finger. The metal lay cut up in pieces, and he sculpted a frightened porcupine, an eyelid with heavy lashes, the narrow shoulders of a woman. Stepping back from the post, he saw usable metal all around him—hubcaps, soda cans and broken down vehicles.

He continued through the town—it was now coming to life in places, a man retracting an awning, a woman bringing letters to a mailbox—and on to the area train station, a neglected little building with a clay shingle roof. With money the officers had returned him, he bought a train ticket to Chicago.

When he saw the first skyscrapers, modest twenty and thirty-floor residential buildings somewhere on the South Side, his knees tapped together and the heels of his boots pressed hard against the floor.

He did not recognize newly remodeled Union Station. Under halogen light, people bustled through sliding green glass doors; they shouted and babbled, rushing in all directions. Yuri had no idea how to get to the "L" but followed a hurried woman walking in tennis shoes. Once he saw the city—cleaner and full of brand new buildings, medians for trees and flowers—he lost her and went to wander around.

Yuri had almost forgotten Picasso's sculpture of a black metal bird, the ribs exposed and its head like an upside-down cello. The last time he had seen it, over a decade before, the bird had looked confused and sullen, but today it looked wise, if lonely.

A Blue Line station appeared. He rode the "L" through the West Side to the Cicero Avenue stop. Wooden and yellow the last time Yuri had seen it, the station was modern now—metal painted white and gray. Newspapers and fast food bags overflowed from garbage cans. Yuri had never liked graffiti, but it was familiar and did not seem as ugly as he remembered.

He avoided walking down 49th Court, the street where he had once lived, but took 50th Avenue. The tree-lined street was like most others in Cicero: old cars parked bumper to bumper in front of bungalows and two-flats built tightly together. His destination, a shop named 14th Street Meats, was on the corner of

50th Court and 14th Street. The shop was dark and empty, but a note had been taped to the door:

Yuri,

Sorry. A things come up and be back later tonight. I know your tired so I got you twelve hours in a room at the Karavan Motel. 1620 S. Cicero Ave. I know thats a dump but the Shamrock dont got no rooms. Tell them my name and yours. Meet you there. Again sorry. I'll make it up.

 Reikel

Yuri stuffed the note in his pocket. Reikel must have forgotten that in his youth Yuri had worked for the Karavan. He knew the address and all about the cheap motel's suicides and murders. The place was a good walk away, but he went to check in because *I'll be back tonight* could mean anything coming from Reikel.

The hotelkeeper gave Yuri a key and a yellow envelope. He said, "Your place is down that way," tossing his double chin to the left.

The room smelled of naphthalene. Yuri knew motel workers sprinkled crushed mothball dust behind furniture to mask the odors of vomit and stale urine. Much of the furniture was burnt and scratched up. Large silver squares and rectangles had been spray-painted over the bathroom walls; these meant to cover, Yuri believed, suicide letters written on the plaster. The carpet and comforter, both worn and faded, were dotted with cigarette burns. Yuri touched the comforter with an open palm to see if it was damp, and finding it dry, slowly lay himself on the bed, his feet still firmly on the floor.

He tore open the envelope and found sixty dollars along with a message: *Get some chow. And maybe some temprary cloths. Reikel.*

Yuri stared at the ceiling's brown water stains, one shaped like a brain, the other a map of Ukraine, and he listened to the hard purr of a truck parked just outside his window. Stretching his arms back against the thin pillow, he felt something hard and long that he grabbed and pulled out. It was a cane, a cheap dime-store hook of pine.

2

Lita didn't realize how quickly it would be over. The doctor told her, "We're all done now, that's it," and they cleaned her up, let her dress. At the reception, the woman asked if she'd like to be billed, but Lita said she had money in her purse. She handed the receptionist a small brown envelope lined with bubble wrap where she had $243.17, three dollars in quarters, two nickels and seven pennies, one green. The woman handed over a receipt and Lita left the clinic.

She could walk. The doctor and others had said she'd be able, but Lita hadn't really believed them. Her belly felt uncomfortable, like it had been inflated, stretched to capacity, then punctured. But Lita could walk and think and feel, and she left the clinic feeling like herself.

Down the block, a white woman was handing out little red fliers. Her three children, two toddlers and a newborn in a carriage, surrounded her. Lita didn't take the flier, but the woman told her, "Jesus can forgive you. Even *you*, for killing your child. So great is His love." Lita couldn't really ignore her as she walked on to the bus stop.

Sitting in the bus shelter with two old Mexicans, she could still feel the woman's presence and attention. People were walking by with the fliers, so many of the folded red cards dropped on the sidewalk. Lita decided to get away from these people and headed to the library.

In her favorite chair, next to a large spider plant by the drinking fountain, she paged through a pop magazine, then went to the mystery section to look for a novel. She usually took murder mysteries, although sometimes Lita picked biographies of musicians.

Lita lived all the way down on 14th Street, next to the laundromat on the corner of 51st Court. Back at the bus stop with a book, she thought she felt cramps coming on and grew scared she might be bleeding. The bus shelter was crowded with old men who had come from the bowling alley, the reek of cigarette smoke saturating their shirts. One man with dry, chapped lips was looking at Lita's chest even though the loose, light sweatshirt was hiding its curves. When the bus did come, Lita didn't get on with the people, but walked to 14th, all the way to Reikel's meat shop.

The shop was closed—Lita remembered Reikel had taken her Aunt Sonia's cat to the vet. He should have been back by now, but with Reikel you never knew. Lita was standing on 14th Street with vagrants and poor women walking around, drunks without cash in front of the liquor store down the block. She blocked the way of people trying to get by with their wagons and dogs. Although it was the last place she wanted to be, Lita went home to her aunt's wooden house, letting herself in through the back door.

The kitchen reeked of fried grease. When Lita saw the used pan, cold fat, hard and ivory white, she gagged. Aunt Sonia wanted her to vacuum the front room, especially all the cat hair off the sofa and cushions, but Lita felt cramps returning. She sat at her desk and felt their little fists tightening.

She drank some pills and lay on her stomach with her face deep in a pillow. These were violent cramps and the pills barely helped. Lying down, she felt she was standing against a wall, her legs heavy and head light, and might fall backwards. Dizzy, she remembered the disgusting fat in the frying pan and finally threw up in a wastebasket. Lita opened a window, but the breeze only brought in the smell of burning lighter fluid from a neighbor's grill.

She cleaned the basket in the bathtub and drank cool water from a blue coffee mug. *I'm stronger than this*, she told herself, *and these cramps aren't so bad.* They seemed to tighten even harder once she thought this way, but Lita insisted—*I'm stronger than this. My body's not stronger than me.* Taking a comfortable chair, Lita picked up her guitar, tuned and strummed the chords of a gentle song, making up words:

That's heavy, but it's invisible.

That's heavy, I can be heavy too.
I can buy myself a brand new dress
I can change the color of my eyes.

Unable to think of more words, she hummed and wished a boy, any boy, could understand how it felt to sing a song in a soft voice while having cramps. When the pain wouldn't stop and the pills started wearing off, Lita put the guitar down and took her hitter box, hidden in the wall behind the bookshelf. She opened her second window to get a cross wind and smoked the dry, harsh grass, inhaling slowly to keep from coughing, but the old weed hurt her lungs. Still, it worked—her body had relaxed by the third hit; by the fifth, she could still feel the cramps but her mind didn't care so much about them now. She could play guitar.

It must have been after 5:00 when she looked out the window again. People were coming home from work, carrying their bundles and lunch boxes. Stoned, she could see the contradiction, how much these people wanted to be home, yet how their tired bodies and minds kept them from moving as quickly as they wished. The whole street was overcome by a languorous impatience Lita found funny.

Fuck it, she wanted to go out. Why sit around the house alone with dry weed and a bunch of sad songs? It was Friday in the summer. Lita changed out of the light sweatshirt and baggy jeans into a loose blouse and black pants. She took her set of multi-colored contact lenses from the top drawer and changed her brown eyes to blue. Stashing the set in her purse and making sure she had money, Lita left.

3

Yuri awoke with the truck still running outside his window, the wooden cane along his left leg. The sun had already set. He noticed a digital alarm clock flashing useless red numbers: 26:75. In the parking lot, a man and a woman were arguing in Spanish.

Yuri went out to see a tilted half-moon hanging above the scrap metal yard on the corner of 16th and Cicero Avenue. He rested the cane on his shoulder, like a soldier with a rifle, and set out through his old neighborhood.

He wandered right down the middle of the abandoned train tracks on 16th, littered with odd trash, refrigerator doors and rusted coils of wire. He passed the sheet metal cutting plant, the old oil works, and the empty lot on 49th Court. Against the navy sky, he could clearly see St. Anthony's church tower, a dark and domed silhouette with a spear-like point, almost like the helmet of a conquistador. Yuri headed in that direction, the way to 14th.

He was 31 years old. He couldn't remember the streets being quite this dirty when he had last seen them at eighteen. Every block had a house that had been boarded up or gutted. So many of the front lawns had been trampled down to patches of weeds in packed dirt. Children had littered them with plastic bats and pieces of broken toys, or pages of coupon books that now lay brittle against the ground. The breeze carried the scent of motor oil or some kind of mechanical grease.

It was disgusting to feel hungry while smelling oil, but he had not eaten all day. As soon as he imagined all the good places for food on 14th Street, the Polish and Italian delis, he knew they'd be gone. When he got to 14th, he found it foreign, now resembling the kind of place people called the wrong part of town. The building that used to be Sherwin's Fruit Market had become a nameless liquor store. Sherwin used to sell frozen chocolate bananas, and the old man would get excited about ripe plums, smile and show them to people. But now this liquor store looked much like a jail, bars in the window of the thick metal door. The drunks who huddled in front asked Yuri for spare change, but he passed them without a word.

He was scared to see what had happened to Carry's Bakery. A thick shadow loomed over the place where it used to stand, just a few doors from the Cicero Family Clinic.

He remembered the warm glow that used to fall from the bakery's window, a pool of soft light against the sidewalk. The old powder blue and pink neon sign that flickered through the fog on autumn mornings. The bacon buns and cheese sandwiches, napoleon tort, black currant pie, custard bismarks and raspberry panczkis, tiny Kaiser rolls taken out of the oven only moments ago, arranged neatly on a cloth in a basket. The chain-smoking old women, gossiping for hours, their coffee cups stained with pink lipstick. They were all gone. Carry's had been leveled and all that remained was an empty lot full of gravel, garbage and broken glass. Human figures had clustered together in the shadows to sit on blocks. Yuri stood there, pressing the cane against the back of his neck. The people hardly noticed him before he walked away.

He took the bus to 22nd Street where he ate two portions of fried perch in a 24-hour diner. Stuffed, his tight pants and shirt started to feel uncomfortable, and he thought he'd go to a thrift shop. There was one down 22nd, owned by an old Hungarian named Ven. Ven's ceiling and floorboards were all vintage, unchanged since the '20s—the store had a massive antique mirror with an ornate bronze frame. Yuri was sure it would be leveled, an empty lot full of human ghosts, but Vin's was there, open late as always next to a barber shop.

A grayer and balder Ven was still behind the counter, making tea on a hotplate. The shop's clothes were packed so tightly in narrow aisles that two people could not pass each other. Tired women were sorting through skirts and a man with a scar across his upper lip was trying on a sport coat. Yuri asked Ven, "Still take trade-ins?"

"Trade?" Ven rolled his r's heavily. "Vatta trade? Trade cane?"

"These clothes. What I'm wearing."

Ven looked Yuri up and down, frowning. "Not much for trade." He shrugged. "We see."

Sorting through Ven's racks, Yuri kept noticing a young Mexican girl—she couldn't have been older than fifteen—coming in and out of the "dressing room," a corner curtained off with black drapes. She seemed to know the store's aisles by heart, and Yuri shopped only vaguely while watching her. She'd disappear behind the curtain with a pile of stuff and come out in a color coordinated medley—hats and scarves, blouses and skirts, pants with heeled black boots—to pose and spin in front of the bronze-framed mirror, her tiny reflection free and light in the mirror's wide space. She matched her outfits to colored, eerily artificial contact lenses. Ven watched her turns and poses, nodding, "Very nice, this. This very nice," sipping tea and beaming.

The girl was hogging the dressing room and Yuri had to wait. She finally came out dressed in a purple wool skirt and beret, white turtleneck with a leather vest, tall boots on bare legs. Her eyes shone bright yellow, two bug lights. Yuri stared right along with Ven. "Yellow," the Hungarian said. "This new? I never see this yellow eyes."

When Yuri came out of the dressing room with his clothes, the girl had left the store. He had found a black pair of pants, a decent button-down shirt, and a very light gray overcoat. Ven gave him less than two dollars for his old clothes, but Yuri made the trade. "And cane?" asked Ven. "You need cane?"

Yuri held it lightly against his body.

"So young a man like you. You hurt? You got ankle?"

Yuri shook his head, taking his receipt. He left the store.

It was tempting to go see the place where his childhood home had been, but Yuri knew he wasn't ready. The old house had burned down. Someone had visited him in prison—Yuri couldn't remember who—and told him a new house had been built and people were living there now.

Wandering, he soon found himself amid the factories and warehouses on 54th and 16th. Graveyard shift workers were coming down from the "L" stop, walking with him along an impenetrable brick wall.

It was more difficult, he realized, to feel the pain of sadness outside prison—he had forgotten how it interfered with things like talking to strangers or buying clothes. He didn't want to be outside, among these rough faces and walls, and imagined himself alone in a garage with a blowtorch and a piece of iron that glowed orange-red like a piece of the sun.

He was in front of the Corner Billiard Club. Yuri had almost forgotten about this bar, often popular after Sunday masses or funerals. He didn't really know how to drink, but the familiar sign and building invited him. Maybe they had coffee. Or he could order a drink and stare at it the way drunks did in books.

The name *Billiard Club* was a bit of a joke. The place had one small table but only a few cues. The long room was always dim. Shaded lamps hung above the drinkers and skirts of light fell through cigarette smoke, yellow over the rows of bottles, pale gray onto a dusty painting of a small lake. Some of the seated men had now turned to look at him, and their slow silence left Yuri nervous. He stayed only because it would be rude to walk in, look at people and walk out.

The bartender was a Mexican woman in her forties. He asked her, "You serve coffee?"

"Mm." She nodded. "One a coffee?" Her accent was fast. "Milk an' a sugar?"

Yuri said, "Just black," and put his few remaining dollars on the bar. The bartender brought him a mug larger than his fist. "Careful. Is hot."

The coffee energized him immediately. He noticed a "Help Wanted" sign hanging behind the bar, so low that only people at the bar could read it. Maybe this was some kind of subtle joke, because people who sat at bars usually needed help. Yuri imagined working there. Most of the men were only drinking beer, and if they ever wanted something different, scotch and soda, Yuri was sure he could mix it.

"I'm sorry." Yuri spoke up to a bearded man. "Excuse me. I'm sorry."

The man perked up. "What for?" He lit a cigarette.

"That sign there. Below. The *Help Wanted*."

"The sign? Oh, for the job?" He rattled and stuttered: "Yeah, that's...that's for the job." The man coughed into a loose fist. "Hey, Sonia!" She stepped over from the bar's other end. "If you want the job," he told Yuri, "Sonia's gotta read your palms."

All the other men now seemed interested.

"You wanna job?" asked Sonia. "Is por bartender. We have the day position."

Yuri shrugged. "Daytime? You mean what? Noon?"

Sonia smiled at him. "I see your hands. Both hands."

Yuri hesitated. The whole bar was watching him, some of the men grinning. He wanted to take his cane and tell the people he was very sorry, it was a big misunderstanding, because he had to go. While looking at their intense faces, pockmarked skin, lopsided mustaches, Yuri felt surrounded by the most violent men—grotesque and incapable of compassion, their eyes the color of mortar. His mind began racing, as it did often when he found himself confused or surprised. Strong, hard hands grabbed at him from all around and a shiver buzzed over his entire body, electric over his chest. He was powerless and could only give in, curl up, let the blows come, let them pass, then bury rage and fear deep in his center, deep into his pelvic bones and base of his spine.

Yuri shoved his hands out to Sonia, leaving his palms open and tight.

She smiled again and put on reading glasses, a thin gold chain hanging from the frames. Sonia took his hands very gently. "Lifeline," she whispered, brushing it softly with an index finger. "So long." Looking over his palms carefully, she said nothing else.

Yuri's left palm was dotted with four flat white scars. His right hand also contained a few—the large one was actually a cluster of smaller scars. Sonia didn't touch them when she brushed her finger over his skin once more, but she pressed his thumb. He told her, "They're cigarette burns."

"I see," Sonia nodded. "I see this." She easily folded Yuri's hands into fists and gripped his wrists firmly, looking at him from above her reading glasses. It seemed she wouldn't let go of his arms. "You have hands from a berry creative person," said Sonia. "And lifeline is a good."

Yuri hid his hands below the bar. After a long pause, he said, "I'd like a glass of ginger ale. Without much ice."

Sonia was all the way at the bar's other end when the door flew wide open and an overweight man, bald and charged with energy, stormed into the Club. He set down a small cage near the beer taps. Inside was a thin, very beautiful black cat with a white patch on his chest and one white front paw. His hindquarter had been shaved and a wound stitched up.

Yuri didn't recognize Reikel until he heard his voice. "Holy cripe. Holy cripe...like you ain't gonna believe it." Reikel opened the cat's cage. "Sonia, like you ain't gonna believe what kind of day. Yeah, whiskey for me, sure, a little one. But okay, because first, it's the vet. Waiting all afternoon. Then, this damn-ass car. This damn-ass car. That guy's not fixed nothin'. He ain't fixed nothin'. And Sonia, I said, I *said* you gotta take that kind of thing to Javi. Why you don't take it to Javi?" Sonia was only shrugging. She set down Yuri's ginger ale.

Reikel was shaking his head. His eyes scanned the Club, and when he noticed Yuri his whole body slumped. "Yurs," he whispered, looking closer and wiping his mouth. "Yeah, Yurs." He took his whiskey from Sonia. "Well, here. You're *here.*"

"Hey, Reik."

After a moment, Yuri got up from his stool and Reikel approached him, almost cautiously. They hugged, holding each other tightly, Reikel patting Yuri hard on the back of the neck. "Yurs," he said. "You're here."

4

As soon as the guy with the cane moved into Reikel's apartment building across the street, Lita started seeing him everywhere. Reikel told her his name was Yuri.

She very often watched him from her porch or window. Lita had never seen anyone like him: he moved with slow precision and touched things so lightly that she feared a shopping cart or the lid of a garbage can might shatter from his touch.

He was always picking through trash. The guy would walk up and down the streets—always slowly, as if time were different for him—and pick through stuff in the gutter, in the alleys and around the dumpsters. Once or twice, she saw him standing in front of the messy lot by the Family Clinic, staring at the ground as if he had lost something. Lita wondered if he was sick in the head or maybe a little bit retarded. He didn't notice that people stared at him when he walked by, and that old Mexican women would point at him, cock their heads and shrug.

Lita very often went to Reikel's shop to chat. On a lazy afternoon, when he didn't have any customers at all, she asked him, "That Yuri. Is he sick or something?"

"Why you thinkin' that?"

"He's always staring at walls. And he picks trash."

"Yuri's a funny guy, that's all. He's a funny guy."

"Where'd he come from?"

"What you so curious about him for? He's Yuri. Was born here, before you, that's all. He does some funny stuff sometimes. Because he's confused."

"Confused?" said Lita. "I think he's depressed. Or sick. I think there's something wrong with him."

"Hm," Reikel shrugged. "Maybe."

When Lita found out from a girlfriend that Yuri had just come from prison, she started paying even closer attention to him. His crown was balding and his shoelaces were frayed at the ends. She soon understood that he didn't look for any old pieces of garbage but was always searching for metal—he picked cables, coat hangers and rusty nuts and bolts out of the soil. Once she saw him walking with the frame of a chair—another time he was carrying the bent gate of a cyclone fence. When he found the head of a hammer in the dirt, his face lit up, like he had found money or a piece of gold.

There soon came a time—it was about six days, maybe more—when she didn't see Yuri at all. Lita thought he had moved away and nobody would ever stare at him again. She'd never figure out what he had done with all that metal. Oddly, when he was gone, it became difficult to remember 14th Street without him. Sometimes she mistook other tall white men for him, and—deep down inside, a secret feeling Lita barely admitted to herself—she was upset those men weren't Yuri.

One evening, alone in the house, Lita got high by the window. She was playing guitar and the vibrations resonated in her small room. She saw Yuri walking back from someplace, a canvas sack swinging in his hand, the cane on his shoulder. He put his bundle down and searched through all his pockets for keys. Yuri couldn't seem to find them; he had patted down every part of his clothing and now stood facing the street, scratching his neck. In the bright orange light of the late evening, his shadow cast sharp down the sidewalk, he seemed taller than usual, ultra vivid, like he was standing in the middle of a painting.

The next second, he turned and swung the cane violently against his apartment window. He knocked all the glass out of the frame, threw the canvas bag inside, and then climbed up in an awkward scamper, his shoes scratching against the brick wall. He came back to board the frame up with blows that echoed down the empty street.

The next day she had to go to her guitar and singing lesson. She had not practiced and her teacher only shook his head, "Not wasting anybody's time but your own." Lita promised she'd learn everything correctly next week and went straight home, determined to play guitar for two hours before dinner. She came in through the back door, right into the kitchen where Sonia, Reikel and Yuri were discussing something at the table.

Aunt Sonia told her, in Spanish, "You're early. Did you argue with your teacher again?"

"No."

Reikel turned to Yuri. "Yurs, this is Lita," he said. "She's Sonia's niece. Lives here, too."

Yuri waved two fingers and Lita only said, "Hi there," then left the kitchen quickly, certain it had been too quick. Aunt Sonia continued her questions, calling down the hall *¿Estabas peleando con tu maestro? ¿Me estás mintiendo?*

"No. I gotta play." As she walked, Lita felt the fat jiggling on her thighs and the pimple on her lip started to hurt. She closed her door and tossed her guitar case on the bed. In the hanging mirror, her pimple looked huge, bulging out from below the foundation, and her hips were wide, hair greasy. At the end of her bed, Lita strummed away to make it seem like she was practicing, but then stopped to hear them in the kitchen. She could only hear Reikel's dominant baritone amid patches of silence or whispers.

5

Yuri was setting up his studio in Sonia's basement. She had agreed to accept a small amount of rent if he promised to run errands for her, go shopping and help with maintenance. He had to clean out the basement: it had garbage left from the time Sonia's husband, dead for eight years, had bought the place. Much of it was nasty: piles of rotting newspaper and cardboard, mice nests in a moldy recliner, and an inch-thick layer of their shit pellets by the walls. Occasionally, mice would scatter when he lifted bushels of moldy clothes and milk crates full of old magazines.

In less than a week, he had moved all the trash to the alley, saving all the usable metal and old boards and pallets to build shelves. He strung white Christmas lights neatly around the room and cleaned the swinging window near the ceiling to let in the sun. All his things had to be raised on cinderblocks in case of a flood, and he planed down the closet door so that it swung freely. Sonia couldn't believe the place. She gave him the first two months for free.

Reikel had kept all of Yuri's sculpting tools and fuel tanks in the attic of his house—Yuri needed three long trips with a shopping cart to get it all down to the basement. He had a small forge, torches, two anvils of different size, all sorts of files and tongs, etching tools, hammers, a large vice and a few old sculptures. The basement was big enough for all of it and Yuri found the perfect places to arrange his studio the way he liked. Before he knew it, everything he needed was in place. He could sculpt.

At home, he boiled eggs to take to work. Yuri had turned down the Corner Billiard Club, because the job required too much talking. Instead, he worked night shift at the Cicero Stadium—it was really an after-school children's club, much like the YMCA—where he cleaned the toilets and showers, and waxed the floors and basketball court. The only other people working at night were a fat security guard and a Mexican woman who cleaned the offices. She didn't speak a word of English and was so burned out that she could hardly ever muster a smile. The guard spent his whole shift watching a small TV and got pissed if anyone bothered him. The job paid seven bucks an hour and was perfect.

Yuri wrapped the hot eggs in paper towels and packed them with a can of ginger ale. With two hours before his shift, he grew apprehensive. Why? Yuri poured ginger ale into a coffee cup and sat to know his feelings. And he knew this feeling: guilt—a kind of wonderful guilt he had not felt since before prison. It was the guilt he felt whenever he had time to sculpt but wasn't sculpting.

Drinking ginger ale, Yuri sat with the feeling and paid attention. For the first time since his release from prison, Yuri looked around his apartment, a sparse room with only a mattress, and realized he lived there. No police were coming to take him. There wasn't anyone in the next room who could take his pencils and throw away his drawings. This beginning was wide open and huge, yet unfamiliar and frightening.

Besides his sculpting tools, everything else he had owned before prison was in the blue milk crate left by the door. It was a box of memories Yuri wasn't sure how to sort through. Should he just throw them away? Of course, he couldn't, but what part should he look at first?

Yuri knelt down by the crate, soon sitting on his heels. He removed old Russian books, a Lithuanian version of the Old Testament, his tobacco pipe and holder, a notebook of sketches and writings, and a bunch of dusty votive candles. At the bottom of the crate lay some old Christmas ornaments he had sculpted back in high school. His battered notebook, with its flattened, straightened spiral, smelled like old paper, a bit like the prison library.

He used to have two notebooks. The one he would have liked to read the most had been confiscated for evidence during the criminal investigation. The one that remained hadn't mattered to them. Yuri gently paged through entries written in his loose, teenaged hand:

There Lars was playing the piano and I got so excited to hear that beautiful one he had composed, the one that sounds like two strands of the cleanest light wrapped around each other. It's like a rope and if you climb it then you get to understanding and a place where you're invited. That's the kind of music he played just a short moment ago out in the garage, and it sounded like the invitation. Right now I got that weird feeling right after the music is over when you have hope but it slowly slowly slowly fades away before you get back to regular life.

Yuri found another passage, written in purple pencil:

When the skin on my hands gets callus dry and chapped it hurts and there's this buzzing around the scars for some reason, like they become aware of themselves in this sensitive way. It can feel like a dying fly got stuck under my skin, or somebody lit a sparkler right there and it's fuzzing, it's making that fffffffff shower of sparks inside my hand. (In Lithuanian, mama used to call sparklers "Cold Fire".)

I remember mama's hands—one time they were so chapped, bleeding a little around her knuckles on the top of her hand, and it was winter when the house used to get so dry. One time she rubbed butter on her hands. I tried that but it didn't work which proves she's crazy.

Yuri couldn't read anymore. He was embarrassed by the juvenile ideas and feelings and took the notebook to put on top of his small European-style fridge. When he sat on his mattress to drink the ginger ale, he saw that pieces of paper had fallen from the spiral—or maybe from the Russian books? Somehow he hadn't noticed. Some of them were just little papers with messages, phone numbers and names. But three photographs had also fallen to the floor. All three of them, as if on purpose, lay face down, daring him to see what they were.

Yet Yuri knew exactly which photos they were. He didn't need to look at them and could pack them away someplace, back to a book, or in an envelope to tuck under his mattress. He wasn't looking at them now but could see all three pictures, side by side, like they had been glued into an album.

The first one, colorful and crisp: his family and some friends standing by a Christmas tree. Yuri clearly remembered the day his father had taken it. Papachka had stepped into a bowl of beet salad someone had left on the floor and everyone had laughed. In the photo, the faces, four adults and three children, still showed signs of that laughter, candid smirks, flushed cheeks. Yuri, only six years old in the front, could smell the Christmas glug: red wine mixed with orange juice, spiced with cinnamon. He remembered all the dry evergreen needles fallen in to the rug and how they poked through his socks when he walked around.

Besides Yuri, only two people in the picture were still alive. His father and mother had died in a fire. His sister Anya choked in her sleep when Yuri was twelve—she had gone to bed with a piece of food in her mouth. Of the family friends, Victoria Jorgenson— an elegant lady, she spoke Russian so beautifully, and the way she moved her head like a ballerina—she was killed by a car while waiting for a bus. It was easy to remember the photograph's dead faces because Yuri didn't have any questions left about them. If he did, answering them wouldn't change anything.

But the faces of the living, the teenage girl and her dad— Alina and Lars Jorgenson—Victoria's daughter and husband. He had not heard from either since his conviction. They were somewhere outside of Cicero, impossible to find, by this time completely disinterested in his release. It was best to forget them.

But now memories of Lars Jorgenson's music crept up on Yuri. Lars had been a composer, pianist, the church organist and Yuri's piano teacher. The music was so close, so alive Yuri felt the sound was about to tap him on the shoulder. For the rest of the night and all through his shift at work, while waxing the floors and mopping the showers, Yuri couldn't get the music out of his head.

Just before Yuri's arrest, Jorgenson had composed a fugue...he simply called it *The Second Fugue*. It was a madman's rant, frightening, full of demented jealousy and pride but also terrible passion. Music always had one powerful effect on Yuri: it filled his mind with visions. If he heard that fugue, he always saw multiple bands of metal...bronze, steel, brass, aluminum, copper...a choking nest of bent and cut metal, still hot and glowing orange. A living creature kept struggling through the madness, thrashing to get out of that nest, but the metal kept growing, choking everything inside.

When his shift was over, Yuri walked east on 14th, daylight breaking in front of him, *The Second Fugue* still weaving through his thoughts, now only as a quiet shadow. He thought he'd pass out immediately in bed, but those pictures still lay on the ground in his room. He tossed around, his body tired, yet curiosity and longing were electrifying his mind.

Yuri took the photos to the bathroom where he had more light. He set aside the Christmas picture and, sitting on his toilet, put the other two photographs on his knees. Both were pictures of Alina Jorgenson, one a studio portrait, her blond hair held back with a hair band, green eyes shiny from the electric flash. In the other she was being pelted by snowballs, prepared to throw one herself at the cameraman.

He thought seeing Alina in a photograph would move him somehow, break into a part of him he couldn't control. But this was not Alina anymore. The pictures showed a young girl who'd be different now, wherever she was, all grown up and impossible to recognize.

In the family picture of Christmas, Lars was a middle-aged man, drunk from scotch and cognac. Today, Lars would be 74 years old. Yuri could feel, deep in his center, that Lars was still alive. And it made no sense to understand that all those other people could be dead, but that Lars, after all this time, after all the abuse he put himself through, alcohol and raging music, was probably playing piano somewhere. If he wasn't playing, then a stream of music was carving a valley in his mind and keeping him from sleep. Or it could be one note played again and again. An F-sharp, *ping*, like a pick stabbing *ping ping ping* into the soft flesh of his imagination, at the most tiring hour of night, when all he wanted was rest.

6

Lita was listening to Father Cruz, the pastor of St. Anthony's Church, mumble a sermon at the podium. Washed by a bright spotlight, he kept repeating about St. Paul's message, his conversion, and the will of God the Father. The only thing Lita liked during church was playing guitar with the other musicians and singers. The rest of it, especially sermons and readings, bored her so terribly that she often thought about sex and drugs on purpose.

She had once confessed to Father Cruz, "Father, I think really dirty stuff in church. Like swimming naked with guys or doing cocaine." He had forced her to read the Sermon on the Mount with him, then spoke for a half-hour about how sinful it was to lose control of thoughts. That whole speech had been worse and more boring than anything he'd ever mumbled during mass.

Father Cruz was Mexican, but his Spanish could occasionally sound Colombian...*fake* Colombian. Lita couldn't understand how people didn't see through it. Aunt Sonia always said that Father Cruz was a very educated priest, cultured and cultivated, and that Lita should look up to him. The pastor had definitely traveled a lot and he spoke English better than most gringos. But Lita couldn't take him seriously when he said things like, "The Virgin Mary helps us when we pray passionately," and "Christ will return to Earth, not when we expect Him, but when we least expect." How the hell did he know?

After mass, Lita and Aunt Sonia always went to the school hall to eat at the parish breakfast and to gossip with neighbors. The hall would be especially packed after the eleven o'clock

Spanish mass; sometimes dozens of people had to stand by the windowsills to eat. Aunt Sonia always wanted to hurry over and grab a place at one of the front tables where Father Cruz might sit. If Lita dragged behind after playing the final procession, Sonia could get bitchy. "Now look where we have to sit! Three tables over! Why can't you ever hurry up?"

This Sunday, Aunt Sonia was very pleased to be sitting right next to Father Cruz, who had found a place directly across from Lita. So many people complimented his sermon, and then they talked about the good food. The conversations meandered and Cruz was eventually talking only to Lita.

He asked her, "How's school?" Lita and Father Cruz almost always spoke English.

"School? It's summer."

"Aren't you repeating algebra?"

"No. That was a false alarm. I ended up with a D."

"A D? Well...but even so. If I were you, I'd repeat anyway. Don't you think you can do better than a D?"

Lita shrugged. "I wanna concentrate on guitar this summer."

Cruz nodded, chewing his food slowly. "Anyway, I heard you have a new neighbor." He smelled his coffee before drinking it. "A sculptor. He's going to be using your basement."

"I don't know," Lita said. "It's this guy. Yuri. He's weird. He walks around with a cane on his shoulder."

"A cane, yes." Cruz set the coffee down. "What do you know about him?"

Lita grew skeptical. "I don't know. He was in prison or something. You're worried that an ex-con's in our place?"

Cruz shook his head. "I'm really curious because I used to know Yuri. And, in fact, I used to know his whole family, his mom and dad, when he was a boy. When I first came to St. Anthony's, and..." He stirred the coffee even though there was no milk in it. "This is...of course, you know...I started in this church before you were even born." His bushy eyebrows narrowed. "And I visited Yuri when he was in prison. I only did it twice. But I did visit him."

"Really?"

"Has he told you why he was in prison?"

"No," she said. "I mean. It's not like...we don't like talk or anything. He's always picking garbage. And he messes around in the basement, that's all."

"Maybe Reikel's told you?"

Aunt Sonia had started listening in on their conversation. Cruz topped off his coffee from a white pitcher, this time adding cream. He watched it mushroom and cloud. "*Señiora Avila*," he told Sonia, continuing in Spanish: "I don't think Yuri will ever come to see me. But please let him know he's welcome in the church and in the family of our parish. If you speak to him, let the boy know he can come to the rectory. To talk. Or just to show his face. See what's changed."

Cruz cupped a tight hand around the coffee and held it, smiling. "If you could tell him...I'm looking forward to seeing him. And I'm very sorry about everything he's been through." Cruz sipped. "Just let him know, if you could. I don't want to preach to him. It would just be great to see the boy again."

7

The heat and humidity hung still and thick on Tuesday morning. Yuri rolled up his shirtsleeves and tore a strip from a green tablecloth to tie around his forehead, but the sweat was still dripping into his eyes before he had come to the end of the block. It was his day off and he really needed to have a look around for more pieces of metal, but searching in the heat soon left him lightheaded and thirsty. He cooled down in Sonia's basement where he could sit, drink seltzer and sketch.

Yuri had already sculpted one piece, titled *Open Bird*. It was soldered together out of cut and folded aluminum triangles from soda and beer cans. The bird looked cubist, like a nude descending a staircase, one wing possibly broken, the other pressed hard against the triangular feathers, the pointy and thin pieces prickly sharp. He didn't really like the bird and was embarrassed that he couldn't think of a better title. But coming up with ideas for aluminum cans and junk from the street turned out to be harder than he had thought.

He had to cut and flatten a bunch of pipes and a radiator cover. Yuri wanted to make ornaments for his apartment's walls, designs of broken, wounded swirls. He had an idea for one ornament, spiral arms radiating from an arthritic hand he could flatten and lay on the floor beneath a coffee table. Even though Yuri didn't have enough of the right kind of metal for any of those ideas, he put on his goggles and heated a pipe till it glowed orange hot. Then he beat it against the anvil, bringing the hammer down with solid force.

Lita was always fascinated by the precise, controlled rhythms of Yuri's banging. She listened often from her room, directly above his studio. One, two. Rest, rest. One, two. Rest, rest. He could carry on that way for fifteen minutes at a time. It hurt her shoulder and elbow just to hear him endure it, although the sound often hypnotized her into weird daydreams about being lost in a maze of Cicero's alleys, or of blacked out streets, nothing but a cluster of ambulance lights way down at the end of 14th. Yuri had another rhythm: one, two—one, two—one, two. Rest, rest. One, two—one, two—one, two. Rest, rest. She never dared play guitar to it, although she imagined many chord combinations.

None of them could ever end up in pleasant summer songs or ballads. The clang of Yuri's metal made her want to plug into an amp and thrash recklessly with massive distortion, waste every house clean off the block. Even though Yuri's rhythms were restrained, every single blow released something red and heavy. She saw sharp, pointy shards of broken bricks scattered over asphalt.

She felt mildly guilty for going down to the basement at times when he was away. His studio was the most orderly space, a room from somebody else's house. And the sculpture of the bird was the most seductive thing she had ever seen.

Before he had soldered it together, it had been a bunch of aluminum triangles arranged on a table according to color and shape. Then—it couldn't have been more than three nights later— she came down to find a bird that looked like music. It seemed to be captured in flames. She wanted to take it up to her room or photograph it to glue in her diary, but Lita didn't have a camera. She tried to memorize how it looked, but away from the basement she remembered more clearly how the bird made her feel. Dissonant. Broken but healing. A prickly shield defending a warm, soft place somewhere deep below. Lita wished she could play guitar that way.

In a few minutes, she'd have to leave for lessons. She had been practicing and her teacher would be pleased, but Lita really had no interest in pleasing anyone. She didn't care about scales and complicated melodies, but wanted to thrash, rain red paint all over the town.

After the guitar lesson, Lita went for a walk. With the low sun casting long shadows, she walked home in a wide arc, all the way to Cicero Avenue, past the Karavan motel and the scrap metal yard, then down an alley to the sheet metal cutting plant. There she saw something extraordinary leaning against the wall of a sagging wooden garage.

An old black bicycle. One wheel was missing, and the frame had been bent. The handlebars were all scratched up and the wheel didn't have a tire. Lita glanced up and down the alley for people and then peeked into the gangway. Strapping her guitar tighter on her back, she lifted the heavy bike and carried it to her backyard where she left it against the porch.

Yuri was still in the basement. He wasn't banging the hammer anymore, but from her room she could hear him tinkering around, probably cleaning up to go home. She had thought it would be easy to knock on his door and tell him about the bike, but Lita had grown bashful. She left the bike in the yard for Yuri to discover himself.

After three days he still hadn't taken the bike. Lita always had to hide it from Aunt Sonia, stashing it between the garage and fence, then leave it out again for Yuri. He only went to the yard once to take out a bag of trash and didn't even stop to look at Lita's gift. Did the idiot think that busted bike was hers? Did he think she and Aunt Sonia were slobs?

Moving the bike back and forth soon grew tedious. Lita thought about leaving him a note or telling Reikel about it. But all of these options were copouts. Finally, with Yuri working quietly in his studio, she found the courage to bring the bike to the side door of the house where a stairway led down to the basement. It would be obvious she had left the bike there.

But if he found it now, he'd think she was afraid to talk to him. Lita wasn't afraid—that wasn't her problem. As carefully and quietly as she could, she carried the bike down to the basement door and stood there.

Yuri was silent inside. She wiped her face. Lita couldn't knock on the door like this. What would she tell him? Yuri had never even spoken to her. Now she heard him moving around, his feet shuffling.

The knob turned. Yuri cracked the door open and peeked out. Lita waved and said, "Hi there," her body twisting side to side. He stared at her, uncertain, and she repeated, "Hi." Yuri finally opened the door and put on a light. "Sorry," he said. "I was sure the noises I heard out here were in my imagination."

"I found this," Lita said, pointing with a thumb. "It was in an alley."

Yuri glanced at the bike only quickly. He nodded but then concentrated on Lita's face, his eyes huge and cloudy. A pinky stuck out of his loose fist to point at her forehead. "You've got some stuff, some dirty. It's bike grease or something."

"Oh—*I've* got?"

"On the forehead. Your forehead." He pointed closer and Lita pulled away slightly. "It's from the bike."

"Yeah...well, I'll go clean up. I'll go." Lita's shoes clapped against the wooden stairs. She was looking for the key to the kitchen door. "Eh, fuck it." She trotted back down. "I'll clean up later. I don't care. I don't care what's on my face."

He was holding the bike's frame. "Yeah?" Yuri shrugged. "This here. Pretty serious bike. Got hit by a car." Yuri touched the bend in the metal. "Look, you see that right there?" He spoke slowly, lugging through words. "That's an accident."

Lita sat on a stair.

He looked at the bike patiently and Lita could feel him thinking, imagining, caught in a daydream. She noticed his wet shirt and the beads of sweat on his forehead, some suspended in his eyebrows. He must have been sanding metal because a brownish dust had collected in his cuticles. And she could smell his body, the sweat, which smelled like salt water, the way people smelled in Mexico after ocean water had dried on their bodies.

Yuri fell out of his daydream gently and said, "Wait." He wiped his hands with his shirt. "Wait. *You* found this."

"Yeah. In the alley."

"And you're bringing it?" He lifted the bicycle an inch and put it down. "It's for...for what? What's it for?"

"You can have it," she said. "You're supposed to take it."

Yuri was rubbing his wrist. He smirked, his eyebrows rising, and he reached out to hold the handlebars again. "This is good," he said. "It's usable. It's really usable."

"Should I help you carry it in?"

"No no." He waved his hands around. "No. I got it." Yuri lifted the bike effortlessly and carried it to his studio. Lita followed him. She asked, "Do you know what you want to make out of it?"

He wiped his mouth, forehead and neck with a paper towel. "I'm." Yuri hopped up to sit on an old table. "I'm a bit...I kinda worked hard today, so I'm kind of fucked up right now. Don't think right, not when I'm tired." Yuri kept looking around him, although Lita knew there was nothing that he needed; he knew exactly where everything in the studio had been left. He said, "It's really a good bike."

"When you make something out of it, let me know. Okay?"

"Sure. Sure, I'll let you. Should I just...should I just, when I see you around? Or, maybe." He seemed extremely confused. "You know, actually, do you need something to drink? Right now I have some seltzer, but it's flat and warm. But should I get more?" he asked. "Do you need some seltzer?"

"No, thanks."

"No. Then...how about at the bakery? I can get you something from the bakery, bring it back. What do you like from the bakery?"

"What bakery?"

Yuri brushed a hard thumb against his eyebrow. He looked around himself again and lifted a pair of pliers to set next to the anvil. Then he got off the table and stood under a frosty white light bulb. "I used to really like the Kaiser rolls. And the poppy seed cake."

Lita nodded and shrugged at the same time.

He asked her, "What do you like?"

She wasn't prepared for this question. Lita said, "Music," but Yuri didn't respond and hardly moved. She muttered, "Clothes," and felt the futility of liking clothing. "But I like art, too. A lot." It sounded like a lie.

Now Yuri sat on a milk crate. He reached out and gripped the bike's warped spokes. "It's great how you found it by accident. After it got in an accident."

"Does that...like...does it bother you? That it got hit by a car?"

Yuri shook his head. "It's just interesting." Now his head turned. She was not prepared to feel his eyes looking straight into her, boring down in a way none ever had in her life, with effortless intensity. Lita could never have known how it would make her feel. She wondered if he was he seeing parts of her that she barely knew herself. Something clear to him but invisible to her.

Yuri asked, "Do you know if the bakery burned down?"

"I've been here since I was ten," she said. "Here with my aunt. But they never had any bakery around here."

"That's true." Yuri nodded and rubbed his hands together. "Some things disappear. Before we get to see them."

Lita was quiet.

"When I was a kid, I never had a bike. I don't even know how to ride one, really." He took a gentle step to the corner and packed a red plastic bag with some things—his cup, the leftover seltzer, a notebook. "I never asked for one, though."

"Was your family really poor?"

Yuri shook his head. "Not really." He swung the bag over his shoulder. "But I have to go across the street now."

"Yeah...yeah, sure."

Yuri held out his hand for Lita to shake. "I'm happy about the bike." Lita smiled and they shook, his hand warm and loose, callused in places but terribly soft in others. Yuri said, "It's a really great accident."

8

Father Cruz finished saying the final prayers, and the small group of people backed away from the casket. Two of the cemetery's groundskeepers twisted a few latches, released the green belts they used to lower the casket into a vault. Father Cruz silently spoke a special prayer of forgiveness as a woman tossed one last flower. Cruz watched them all slowly disperse and head back to their cars or to other parts of St. Anne's Cemetery.

Cruz liked the cemetery very much, especially its entrance: a gated archway under a gorgeous brownstone tower on the corner of 22nd and Cicero Avenue. The tower looked much like the turret of a palace or an English mansion, and the tall brownstone walls that enclosed St. Anne's created a quiet refuge. Near the entrance, the landscapers had planted rows and clusters of flowers around a shrine to St. Anne, her statue gleaming white. The pathways that wound through the cemetery really did encourage peace of mind and, after funerals, Cruz often strolled around for a few minutes, remembering and praying for all those he had buried.

He was not far from a gravesite he visited often. It was just behind a trio of birch trees fused together at knotted and strong roots. A lamppost also stood there and, further to the east, an old wooden bench, left over from the days when the cemetery had been open to the public at all hours.

Cruz was surprised to see a taller man standing there, dressed in dirty black slacks and a wrinkled white shirt. He had leaned a cane against one of the headstones, something Cruz didn't like at all. "Excuse me," he said politely. "Excuse me. Did you know these people?"

Yuri immediately recognized Father Cruz. The priest had grown a potbelly and his hair was graying above his ears. He wore a modest gold ring on one hand, and his patent leather shoes were polished to gleam like obsidian. Yuri just said, "I knew these people." He took the cane away from the headstone. "This one's my sister. Here's my great uncle Benny. And here's my mom."

Cruz hesitated. He gripped his prayer book tightly. "Hello, Yuri," he said, lifting one hand. "How embarrassing. And a coincidence, like this."

"Hello, Father." Yuri nodded to Cruz, then sat in the grass. From a plastic bag, he took out three small potted flowers along with a hand trowel. Cruz watched him plant one flower, first at his sister's grave, his long fingers pressing deep into the black earth. "You know," said Cruz. "They actually discourage people from planting that way. It's better to leave the flowers potted. The ground staff will take care of them."

"I got permission," Yuri mumbled.

"Yuri, I don't think that's true. I know the men here and they don't really allow..." Cruz shut himself up. "But it's fine, of course. It's fine."

Yuri stood. "Father Cruz. Aren't those people over there? The bereaved. From your funeral mass? Aren't they going to have a lunch?"

"Well...yes. Yes."

"Most of them are gone. Won't they be waiting for you?"

Cruz's heels came closer together. "Now, Yuri. I didn't want to get off on bad terms. Of course...under the circumstances, and this odd coincidence..." It was rare for Cruz to stutter in this way. "These are unfortunate circumstances. And the way things turned out. But, please. I'm sorry. You should know I'm very glad you've been released. Really and truly, I am very happy that you're out. And I hope you'll come to the rectory, perhaps. Perhaps to talk—"

Yuri interrupted. "About what?"

"Well, why would you be like that? So adversarial? I feel nothing but respect and happiness for you. When I learned they were letting you out, I thanked God."

Yuri smiled. He stood, took the cane and pressed it against the back of his neck. "Did you thank God also when they were putting me in?"

Cruz sighed. "Now, that's unfair. You're being unfair."

Yuri crouched down in the grass again. He looked across the cemetery to the gravesite Cruz had left. "Those people are all gone. There's just one car. And your limousine. Is that your limousine?"

"Of course not. It's the funeral home's."

Yuri dug another hole with the trowel. "I guess I never got to thank you," he muttered. "For helping make sure my mother's remains got a proper burial. Thanks, then, for making sure. And for taking care of the gravesite here when no one else was around." He stuck the trowel into the ground and looked up at Cruz. "But now there's someone around. I'm around. And the funeral home's limo is leaving. It doesn't seem like we have very much time to talk."

Cruz stood stoic. He said, "You'll always be welcome in the church." He raised a hand slightly before turning to go. While stepping along the curved footpath, his heels clicking, Father Cruz did not look back and walked with the most extreme restraint. Yuri sat to watch the limousine slowly pull away and drive out of St. Anne's.

9

Reikel was swatting flies when Lita came into his store. It was the hottest hour of midday and the meat shop was one of three places on 14th with normal air conditioning. Lita's honey brown skin glistened. She had braided her hair, something Reikel had not seen in a few years; instead of jeans or shorts, she wore a yellow and white sundress. The girl sat on the tiled windowsill and pulled a book from her backpack. "Mind if I cool down for a while, Reik?"

"Go on." He waited for a fly to land. "Your friends came by here a minute ago. Those two girls, and with their ma. Which one's the oldest? Claudia or some' like that?"

"Yeah."

"Well, that one and her sis." Reikel swatted a fly against the glass of the display case and wiped the splat quickly with Windex. "Lit...just cuz there's no customers don't mean I ain't got nothin' to do."

"You're swatting flies. You need help?"

"It's just one swatter in here. But broom and mop in back. Dead flies all over the floor. And look—some guy brung in footprints."

Lita casually swept and mopped. Reikel was whistling the whole time—she was always impressed by his clean pitch. After some time, when no customers had come in, she whispered, "Reikel?"

"Mm?"

"Did you know Father Cruz knew Yuri?"

"The pastor? Yeah, Lita. Anybody who's lived here since back when Yuri got in trouble, they know Yuri. Or they know *about* him. Definitely, Cruz knows him."

Reikel washed his hands at a small white sink. He and Lita exchanged eye contact in a mirror. Reikel said, "You're bein' pretty curious about Yurs the last while. Why's that?"

She shrugged. "Dunno. Maybe 'cause everyone's so secret about him."

Reikel turned around, crossed his arms and gripped the straps of his apron. "Secret? Who says so?"

"I mean...he can't talk. He talks, but—" Lita returned to the sill. "He thinks there's a bakery on 14th."

"Well, it used to be. Across the street." Reikel leaned half his behind against a large wooden block. "You're probably figurin' it out. How Yurs ain't all right in the head."

"That's not it. That's not what I mean."

"Look at it this way, Lit. Let's say...what if tomorrow, out of nowhere, you get locked up for crap you ain't even done? Though everybody says you did." Reikel paused. "Back then, everybody taught he did it. And I mean everybody, the whole town, except maybe a coupla people. But that's it."

"Why'd he get locked up?"

Reikel smirked. "Guess no one's told ya, kiddo?" He wiped a knife and attached it to the magnet strip. "What'd he say?"

"How'm I supposed to ask him that?"

"Doncha read the papers? Was in the local paper."

"I...no. No, I didn't."

Reikel brought a stool and wiped his hands in a soft, white towel. In a blunt, surprisingly short story, he told Lita everything he knew. Nothing Reikel said shocked her, although she couldn't believe anyone who knew Yuri even slightly would ever accuse him of killing people. She could see him breaking things or hurting himself, but Lita couldn't imagine him setting a house on fire. She asked Reikel, "Did you believe he did it?"

Reikel grabbed the straps of his apron again. "I don't know."

Lita picked nail polish from her thumb. "Do you think that's why he makes those things out of metal? Because they're all cut up. He made this bird. It looks like it's burning."

"His statues..." Reikel moved the stool away. "I don't know nothin' about them statues, Lita...why he makes them or what. Yurs ain't completely right in the head. He's probably got past stress disorder, and maybe somethin' else on top of it. Though Yuri always used to make them statues...it was like some kind of sickness with him, even when he was really young."

"A sickness?"

"Nobody gets them, what they're supposed to mean. Maybe he puts all his taughts in it. Because a lot of the stuff what's happened to him, if you ask me, he don't understand himself." Reikel folded up the towel. "He ain't being secret. He ain't ashamed to tell nobody nothin'. He just don't talk unless someone's talkin' to him."

Three women came into the shop, bringing a steamy-hot draft with them. Reikel waited on the customers and Lita zipped up her backpack. She said "Bye, Reik," and went into the sweltering day.

At home Lita took a phone call from Claudia. Someone was throwing a party later that night. Lita pretended to be really excited about it but knew she wouldn't go. After Claudia hung up, she sat at the end of her bed with the guitar and looked out the window.

The street was full of traffic, not even the slightest breeze to cut the heat. A group of boys walked by, moving from the west end of 14th, probably from the Laramie bus stop. One of them was the guy who had gotten her pregnant.

Her skeleton turned to electric steel, her insides hot while a chill shivered her. The guy didn't just keep walking but the whole group stopped right in front of Yuri's building, seven lanky high school boys with peach fuzz mustaches and tipped baseball hats.

Lita pulled deeper into the room, closer to the far wall. She wanted to draw the curtain but didn't dare come any closer to the window. The boy could see her. Definitely. Right through the window, even through the wall—they must have heard her guitar. He had found out she was pregnant and learned where she lived. He wanted to find out about the kid, or to take it away, because everybody had learned it was his. Lita was holding the baby tightly, trying to quiet it down. The whole street could hear it crying. And the father—Lita realized, ashamed, that she couldn't remember his name—he was coming up to the house, walking up the front stairs, the wood of the porch bending under him. She tucked the little head into the curve of her neck. The father opened the front door and stepped into her house, releasing pressure that billowed all the curtains.

Lita sat up straight. When she looked out the window again, the boys were gone, wandered to the end of 14th, more than a block away. In their place, right in front of his building, Yuri was holding a shovel and a pillowcase full of laundry. He was wearing new clothing, a white tee shirt and faded, baggy jeans.

Lita laughed. Then a bomb of tears exploded from her and she grabbed a pillow to muffle her sounds. Aunt Sonia was home, and Lita *never* cried—the only time Aunt Sonia had heard Lita cry was when her dad had been killed. She waited for the sound of Sonia's footsteps, and for her gentle voice—*¿Que tienes, mi-ja? ¿Que tienes?*—but the house was quiet. When Lita listened carefully, she heard Sonia and Yuri talking in the gangway, their voices fading out as they moved to the back yard.

Running mascara had stained her pillow. Lita wiped her face with tissue and hid the pillowcase at the bottom of the laundry hamper. Looking to see if anyone had entered the house, she hurried to the bathroom. Lita stripped, opened up the cold water and sat in the shower to let the hard and icy needles rain over her neck and back. Soon her skin was rough with goose pimples and her toes and fingers numb. She could barely feel her hands when she adjusted the water temperature, shivering while washing her hair, scrubbing her face with Aunt Sonia's soap. Lita only patted herself dry and combed her hair through with a wooden comb.

The sundress stuck to her wet skin. She lay on the sofa and tried to watch television, but the talk show with fat girls screaming about some guy made her feel foolish and wrong, similar to them. She wanted to smoke cigarettes. Without any real place to hide from Aunt Sonia, Lita took a cigarette from her secret pack and went down to Yuri's basement.

He had just left. The orderly studio was cooler than the house and Lita could breathe easier, although she smelled a faint hint of propane. That shovel he'd been carrying now leaned against a wall. Lita giggled when she remembered Yuri standing in the middle of 14th, but the memory also pushed warmth out from behind her eyes and they watered. He had left a bottle of seltzer on his worktable, and she drank it from a dusty teacup. She had forgotten her cigarette lighter. Too lazy to go back, she sat on a milk crate and felt the comfort of the studio.

Yuri had made a sculpture from the bicycle—Lita saw it in the corner, hidden in a gray shadow. It was another bird, some kind of eagle, with the wheel spokes wrung together and flattened as wings. Its warped and jagged body was suffering from open wounds and splattered with tear shaped drippings of metal. Despite the broken parts and dissonance, every part flowed together, like a composition Lita wished she could write. She heard a cinder-red, prolonged note of a violin somewhere deep in the city's center, in the place where homes get abandoned after they burn down.

She was daydreaming now, as she often did, of running away, packing a tote bag with only a few items, some clothes, a book, a bar of soap and a bottle of shampoo. With her guitar on her back, Lita walked in some direction out of Cicero. She could see cornfields and tight roads with only two lanes, deep ditches full of rainwater, and streams of thin clouds reaching out into the distance. In one part of the daydream, she was heading towards Mexico—she could make a living playing guitar for tourists. In another, she headed to Canada and walked along a road that followed the coast of Lake Michigan. Along the coast, on top of a dune, flames poured out of a cabin's narrow windows, and the roof collapsed to send sparks swirling against the deep night, before a moon white as a hunk of ice.

Lita didn't know how much time had passed when Yuri came to the door. Her hair was still damp, but her skin was dry and cool. She didn't get nervous but sat calmly when he came in with a bag full of glass bottles. Without noticing her, he set the bag down by the table and plugged in the Christmas lights. Yuri went back out and returned with a black iron fence and some grates from old grills. He leaned the metal against the wall by the shovel, then sat on his stool to flip through sketches.

Yuri only sensed that something was different when he smelled girl's shampoo. He glanced to notice Lita sitting by the eagle. Her damp hair wavy, she was pressing her knees together oddly, her hands flat against her tummy. Yuri said, "Lita," and stiffened for a moment. Her sallow expression struck him, all the color gone from her cheeks and eyes.

She said, "You said you'd say when you finished the bike."

Yuri mumbled, "Yes, only. I'm not sure. I mean, I wasn't completely finished." He drank from the seltzer. "I wanted to get you. I didn't see you around."

"You were supposed to get me. You made this bird," she said. "Didn't you want me to see what you made?"

"I really did," he said. "I really wanted you to see it."

"Well," she sighed. "I got to see it, anyway. It's another bird." Lita sat for only a moment longer, then walked up to the kitchen, her bare feet light on the stairs.

Yuri could hear her footsteps above his studio. Her awkward flop into bed always creaked the ceiling heavily and scattered dust from between the planks. He didn't know if he should invite her down again, if that was what she wanted—he couldn't tell if she was angry with him or only using him to express anger about something else.

Yuri just wanted to concentrate on sketching—he had a plan for the window he had shattered with the cane. But now, following Lita's disturbance, he could only doodle. Sweat fell from his chin onto the paper. Yuri went home and slept near a box fan before heading to work.

He saw Lita only a few times during the next several days. In the public library, she was reading a newspaper by the spider plant, right by the drinking fountain. He had no way to approach her and only looked from afar. Another time she was walking towards him along the sidewalk, probably on her way to Reikel's shop. Lita's blouse accentuated the full form of her breasts, and he knew she caught him staring. It was blatant—more blatant when he tried to look away at the last second to pretend it had been an accident.

Yuri worked hard each day to replace the pane he had broken. It took a long time to fuse glass from beer bottles into a crude stained glass window, and he made many mistakes. Posts from the iron fence made a frame—smaller pieces and strands from the grates kept the glass together. The window's bumpy surface resembled a pattern of green and brown elm leaves fallen among pointy shards. Satisfied, he could mount the new window on hinges so that it swung out into the street.

Lita was watching him do it from her room, paying attention to the details of his movements. He waved to her, and she raised a quick hand.

Yuri did not glance her way again, but felt her careful attention on him the whole time he worked, up until the time he shut the window.

The time soon came for him to sculpt something from the shovel. He had removed the cracked wooden handle and set it to the side. Over several days, he sketched more than twenty ideas: some abstract shapes, half a Roman helmet, a slit that looked like a pussy but could have been the mouth of a cave or a wound hacked into the bark of a tree. None of the drawings were any good.

One afternoon he finally decided, fuck it, he would stop sketching and start sculpting. Down in his basement studio, Yuri held the spade tightly with tongs and let the blue flame glide over its surface. He flattened it with a hammer, keeping his rhythm, pausing to heat the thing whenever it cooled. He was going to sculpt Lita's portrait.

He imagined Lita posing, illuminated by a bright lamp closer to the far wall. Patiently, Yuri considered the details of her face, the few dark hairs that bridged her thick eyebrows, the small scar on her chin, the slope where her jawbone curved back to her neck. She had a small forehead, rich black hair and puffy flesh over her cheekbones. Her brown eyes, hard with longing, contained little green slivers, the shards of shattered bottles.

Yuri worked on the portrait for several days and didn't realize how quickly he had finished it. He came down one afternoon to touch it up but saw that he could let it go. He mounted the portrait onto a broomstick and attached it to a stand so that it stood upright in the middle of his studio. Content, Yuri cleaned up to go home.

He walked by as Lita and Claudia were talking on the porch. Claudia was petite, peroxide streaks in her jelled, mop-like hair. She wore a half-shirt, tons of bracelets, several gold chains and jeans so tight that a small roll of fat oozed over her belt. She had three hickeys on her neck, smeared purple bruises. Claudia asked Yuri, "Hey, what you beating up in there all the time? So loud, man."

Yuri said, "It was a shovel."

Claudia rolled her eyes and Lita giggled. "A shovel?" asked Claudia. "What's up with that? Why you beating up a shovel?"

"To make something," Yuri shrugged. He crossed the street with brisk steps and the girls watched him.

From inside his room, he opened his new window, swinging it out and keeping it in place with a long hook. He could see them peering into his room but couldn't hear them talking.

Claudia asked, "Lita, what's his window all about, girl? That's what he made?"

Lita nodded. "You should see the stuff he makes. It's like, freaky."

"Like what?"

"Like cut up birds and these messed up things to hang on the wall. And he draws all the time. Like, really messed up."

"Lemme see."

"No. We can't go down there."

Claudia grabbed Lita by the arm. "I wanna check it out."

Lita could have pretended she didn't have a key, but Yuri had left the basement open. His portrait of a woman stood in the middle of the floor. Her face had been etched and beaten into the spade, the edges flattened and cut to look round. Broken, asymmetrical cheeks and a small chin grew from her bumpy, tired skin. The dense, meshed-together and wavy hair was woven from a cyclone fence and spray-painted black. The woman's eyes weren't round but broken from sharp pieces of glass. One was a slanted and scratched brown square, green slivers forming a maimed pupil. The other eye, a curved green triangle, had brown slivers; they formed an oval that reminded Lita of stitched fabric. Even though the woman was deformed, she seemed delicate and sad, beautiful somehow.

Claudia said, "That's fuckin' horrible."

Lita nodded.

"This guy's really fucked up."

Lita's silence always meant that she agreed with Claudia.

When Claudia had left to go home, Lita looked under Aunt Sonia's bed to fish out Chango, the cat. Chango had long since healed from his operation and was starting to let people touch him. The tom rested his head on Lita's shoulder and she sat on the floor against a wall, petting him lightly and feeling him purr.

Who was the woman he had sculpted? She was someone Yuri had known before prison. Maybe a relative, an aunt from Europe or a grandmother. Lita couldn't believe anyone would sculpt a relative with so much tender but strange pain. It was probably a girlfriend or an ex-wife. It was possible Yuri had kids somewhere. His wife had abandoned him because she thought he was a murderer, and Yuri still loved her and was hoping to find her.

The telephone rang and Chango slithered away. Lita didn't bother to get up but listened to Reikel mutter into the answering machine about a transmission and a clutch.

She closed herself in her room and listened to her favorite CDs—she had all sorts of music. At first she played pop discs, standing in front of a mirror with a make-believe microphone and a massive stadium crowd in front of her.

Lita must have imagined herself this way thousands of times, but now it felt different. Moving around, staring into herself with intense, seductive eyes, Lita noticed two people in the mirror. There was a person on the outside, a body with big tits, dark brown eyes, long hair and chubby legs. Behind her was another person, an invisible one that Lita could only *feel*. She liked that girl so much more even though she could at once seem as foreign as she was intimate.

Lita searched through her discs for more music to play. All of the music she had was full of feelings that came from the body. Lita wanted feelings that came from that true girl without the body.

The recordings her guitar teacher had given her were all organized on the bottom shelf. There was one special recording, a disc Lita rarely listened to that her teacher really wished she would love. It had been written by a guy named Lars Jorgenson, a composer who had actually lived in Cicero. Aunt Sonia hated the music because it was frightening—the disc could shake Lita up. But Lita set *The Fugue* into her player and lay back on her bed.

Lita knew what a fugue was, a composition of usually two strands—voices—of music that borrowed short melodies and phrases from each other. It was like a game where melodies played side-by-side and pretended to be each other, or sometimes even became one another. They could weave together like braids or plaits, then split up and come back together again.

The Fugue's first innocent notes struck her with powerful irony. Lita's teacher had taught her how to tell the composition's two voices apart, one limp and gimpy, the other virile and violent. He had said they were extreme opposites that came together perfectly, the way a sharp knife could enter flesh and leave a perfect cut, the slice beautiful and clean as the flesh stained the blade.

The music grew and progressed quickly but patiently. Lita saw herself combing the hair of a doll with a wire brush. The hair came out in bunches, massive nests of blonde fishing line, and the doll was balding. Lita wanted to stop ripping at the hair but couldn't because a force was acting on her. When the doll was bald, she tore its arms out of its sockets, bent the legs back and twisted the head off.

In the music, Lita wanted to put the doll back together, and she gathered all the limbs, the mess of hair, but they didn't fit together anymore.

Her child's father came in and saw all the doll's parts. Lita felt his strong, masculine hands tightening around her nape. He held her down, the entire weight of his body on her throat and she struggled with him, sick from the smell of his cheap cologne and sweat. When the music surged, Lita broke free, now impossible to defeat. She tied him up with rough rope, his ankles to his wrists and told him his kid was dead. Lita repeated it, making sure he knew, but the boy didn't care. He just wanted to be untied so he could fuck another girl at the next party. She saw him fucking that girl on a rug in the middle of a bedroom, in a house where she had never been before, friends outside the room laughing at her for finally fucking someone. When the father fell away from her and lay on the side, Lita easily pushed a long, sharp knife into the soft flesh of his stomach where it left a perfect, beautiful wound.

Seeing Yuri standing in her doorway scared the shit out of her. His face was pale white, almost chalky, and he seemed taller than usual. Yuri barely paid any attention to Lita and only pointed to the CD player. The music was almost over, the notes settling down. When *The Fugue* had ended, Yuri mumbled, "Where'd you get it?" his eyes wide and wet.

Lita couldn't really speak.

"Where!" He raised his voice. "Where!"

She sat up straight. He was nervous and agitated, deeply confused. How had he come in without a sound?

"Lita, I want to know. How? That music...where's it from?"

"It's just a CD." She showed him the case on top of the player and Yuri grabbed it aggressively, tearing the notes out. He knelt on the floor to read them. "Lars," he said, stabbing the picture with his finger. "This is Lars."

"Yes," she whispered. "Jorgenson. Yeah."

"Who told you about this?" Yuri tossed the case onto her desk. "Who!"

"Don't *shout* at me." She didn't want to yell at him. "I mean, you're in my room. Don't *stare* at me like that." He stood to tower above her. She got up to put her disc on the shelf.

"You tell me where you got it," he said. "You have to tell me now."

"From a store, okay. Where do you get CDs? In a store."

Without asking Lita, Yuri pulled the CD from the shelf and looked at the notes one last time.

In the constricted room, she sat on the floor with her back against her desk, and she sighed. Yuri muttered, "I knew Lars Jorgenson." Lita knew he wasn't speaking to her when he said, timidly, "I'm sorry. I'm so sorry." He tried to slide the notes back into the case but couldn't.

Yuri handed her the case and leaflet and stroked his hair. For a moment, it seemed he had just woken up in her room with no memory of how he had come over.

He left without another word. Yuri walked to the pay phone and called in sick for the night. They thanked him for calling but said he wasn't on the schedule until tomorrow.

It was true, Yuri thought, I'm sick. He had to find a way to calm down and went home to smoke. He needed a long walk but was afraid—it was irrational, he knew, but it didn't matter—to leave the apartment. When he tried to sleep, Yuri could only hear Jorgenson's sounds.

The memory of the music was like his memories of the photographs. Played live, the music shone clear and vivid, but his memories had yellowed and faded.

He imagined walking up the stairs to the choir in St. Anthony's church where Lars was sitting at the organ, wisps of his blond hair flailing about as he played.

Later, Yuri would go to Carry's and talk about the music with Alina. He'd say, I can't listen to it, but I can't stop listening. It's like burning up and seeing yourself burning, watching yourself as you set yourself on fire. Whenever I hear it, I can feel the house is about to light up. Not the moment when it's burning, but the moment it's about to burn and you can't do anything to stop it.

Do you understand me? Alina?

Had he dozed off? Yuri was lying in bed, a bit sweaty, his cup tipped over next to him and a small wet spot on the sheet. Night had already fallen.

Yuri opened his window and let in the mild summer breeze—the air smelled fresher than usual. Drunks were laughing and pestering each other, swearing and breaking bottles on the sidewalk. Yuri could hear sounds from someone's Spanish TV show—he smelled *molé* and a neighbor's fried beans. Hungry, he decided to dress and go out for a bite.

Someone knocked on his door while he was looking through his shirts. Probably a neighbor. The knock came again, a bit less timid. After the third, Yuri peeked through the hole, but someone was covering it with a finger. He heard Lita's voice. "I know you're there. The damn light's on. Open the door."

Lita must have come from Ven's. In the corridor, she wore a long, '50s style green dress, and had let her hair down to hang over her shoulders. Using her colored contact lenses, Lita had given herself one playfully artificial, bright green eye, but had left the other alone. She smiled and said, "Hi there." Yuri nodded and stepped back into his room, giving Lita space to come in.

His place smelled of cheap pipe tobacco and old laundry, but it was just as clean and orderly as the studio. Flat metal ornaments hung above his mattress and a shelf. The cane was left on a hook soldered to a swirling design near the window. Spiral arms reached out from underneath a coffee table he had hammered together from particleboard. Yuri gave Lita his only chair while he sat on the mattress. "Do you want something to drink?" he asked. "I got ginger ale. Can make tea."

"Sure. Tea."

They waited for it to boil, their silence surprisingly comfortable. He made them Earl Gray and she held it warm in her lap. "This room is really neat."

Yuri set his tea on the table.

"The cane. Is it a decoration too? Or just where you hang it?"

He shrugged. "It reminds me of someone, so I leave it there."

"Lars Jorgenson didn't use a cane. Did he?"

"He's an old man now. I haven't seen the guy in over a decade." He slurped his tea. "You've got a green eye," he said.

"Yeah." She paused, one corner of her mouth smiling. Lita looked at him intriguingly. Didn't he understand? Couldn't he tell? She said, "I got the idea for this outfit from you."

"From me?"

"Your woman with two eyes. The sculpture. One brown and one green. I thought, what the hell? It's a pretty cool idea."

"*My* woman?" he asked, nodding. "You like that idea."

Lita lifted one loose shoulder. "It's cool. I mean, she's like deformed. I'm not trying to be deformed or anything. Just, tonight I got two different eyes."

Yuri covered his cup with a saucer. They listened to the sounds of the street, a car's bad muffler and the drunks causing a racket. Lita said, "You know why I came over?"

Yuri glanced at her.

"When you come over my place, and sometimes when we talk together, or when we pass each other in the street or something. I don't want it to be secret all the time. I want it to be open, you know. Because I." She paused. "I talk to Reikel a lot. He told lots of stuff about you."

"I know."

"He told me. I found out about your hands, the scars, also from Sonia. About the burns. What used to happen to you. When you were a kid."

Yuri breathed quietly. He opened up one palm, the one with the cluster of scars, and let her see. When she touched the white scar, Lita's finger was warm from the hot cup. She said, "I know you didn't burn down your parents' house. I know you got released early because they figured out it wasn't you."

"I'm glad somebody told you."

"When you come to visit." She put her dripping tea bag onto a small plate. "Don't you think...don't you think it feels secret all the time? I hate that. Don't you hate it?"

"I don't have any secrets, Lita."

"I don't mean that. I heard about your mom. And what that priest did to her. You know, I went to the library and I read the old newspapers about your trial. And new ones, about how you got out. I read all the articles about that priest, that monsignor."

"Monsignor Kilba."

"Because I was curious. So I read about that."

"Do you believe what you read?"

"I mean. When I found out about your hands, I think I understood why you make the sculptures like that. And I can see why everyone thought you torched your folks' house. But I didn't think you could kill anybody."

Yuri took out a small box where he kept his tobacco, and he packed his pipe. When Lita saw him do it, she took out cigarettes and they smoked together. She thought it was hilarious, completely unexpected that Yuri smoked a pipe. He didn't look like a wise man but like a boy at camp who smoked to feel he was breaking a rule. When they finished their tea, Yuri made more and Lita kept talking. "Anyway, I think it's unfair," she said.

"What?"

"I can go to Reikel. But there's no place where you can go to talk about me. Because nobody around here knows anything. I go over to Reikel's shop and he tells me. But who'll tell you?"

"You want to tell me something?"

"Not some *thing*." She started rattling and Yuri finally realized she was really high. "It's because I was saving money. From Christmas gifts and birthdays and stuff. I was saving money because I wanted to buy an electric guitar and an amp. Did you meet Claudia? What do you think of Claudia?"

"Your friend? With the bracelets."

Lita blew smoke to the floor.

"I don't know," said Yuri. "She wears a lot of perfume."

"Claudia and all my friends. They used to make fun of me since the beginning, since grammar school. They all called me *virgin* and *church girl*. Not because I go to a Catholic school...Claudia goes to one, too. It's that I didn't fuck guys. Because they fuck guys all the time. So...at parties, you know, I just started fucking. Picking them up. Like they do it, without rubbers. They're like, because it *feels better*. Man, you fuck with a *rubber*? You don't want to let them raw dog?"

Lita paused to see Yuri's reaction. He was listening carefully, neither shocked nor upset. She continued, "I'm like, I don't care. I can do anything. I don't care. Not even Claudia knows I did it in the bathroom at school one time. But I know *exactly* which time it was. It was the fourth time, just at the end of the school year, when I got pregnant. This total idiot who walks around on 14th. He got me pregnant."

Yuri had inched slightly closer to her.

"And the money for the guitar," she said. "I used the money from the guitar. Because I hated that guy. And I didn't want him inside me anymore, or around me my whole life, or inside another human being who never asked to be made out of his garbage." She waited, swirling the tea around in her cup. "Aunt Sonia, she would beat my ass if she found out. Throw me in the street. She would beat me if she found out about the guitar money, too. She'd tell Father Cruz. I know it. And he'd put me in a convent or some crazy shit like that."

Yuri sat still for a moment, looking at her green eye. Casually, he opened up one fist and showed Lita his palm. She knelt down by the coffee table to see it up close and touched a smaller scar. Yuri said, "That was the first one I got."

Lita's shoulders straightened and she pulled her hand away gently. She asked, "Do you think I'm a whore?"

Yuri leaned towards the table. He turned his teacup round and around. "Did you ever think you were a *church girl*?"

"I mean. No."

"So why did it matter then, what someone else thought of you? What name they had for you? And why would it matter now?"

"Because." She had never thought about it that way. Lita didn't speak for a long time. "Sometimes I feel disgusting. Other times, it's like I got tricked."

Yuri went to sit on the sill of his window. One leg was dangling outside and the other was on his floor. He asked, "Which feeling is better?"

Lita didn't know. They were both fake. And in Yuri's room, surrounded by the metal he had shaped, her hands on the table he had built, neither feeling mattered very much.

Yuri was facing the west side of 14th. A figure lumbered through the fluorescent haze falling from the windows of the laundromat. Yuri recognized Reikel's gait and round body. He seemed to be rushing, maybe even a bit nervous, and soon Yuri understood that he was coming over. Reikel saw Yuri from a distance and raised his hand rather meekly, although he didn't slow down. He stopped in front of the building to stand awkward, unsure. "Hey, Yurs," he whispered.

"What's the matter, Reik?"

"It's happened. Sooner than me and you taught."

"What?"

"I just got a phone call. Monsignor Kilba."

"What?"

"They just told me he's got a stroke. Dropped hard, they said, was almost instant. Just an hour ago, maybe. A really bad stroke."

Passage: Monsignor Kilba's Birthday,
February 25, 1970

Monsignor Kilba would have to wait until after one o'clock for his first snifter of cognac. Traditionally, the children from St. Anthony's school invited their pastor to the school hall on his birthday—they sang songs, gave him drawings and cards, and the school always presented gifts, useless junk for his office: letter openers and paperweights of saints. Couldn't they leave him alone today, make an exception for a seventy-year-old man who only wanted to have a drink and listen to the famous arias from Carmen?

Eventually two eighth graders came over to the rectory and invited him to the hall.

Whenever he got cranky about formalities and "sincere" events organized by the school's nuns, Kilba could forget how much he enjoyed spending time with the children. Their songs, even the stuffier ones...*God Shines Bright on You*...pleased him. He'd smile, drinking tea while listening.

Some of Lars Jorgenson's private students played him piano. Yuri, only seven years old, made a ton of mistakes during *For He's a Jolly Good Fellow*, but Kilba shouted "Bravo!" when Yuri bowed.

When the music was over, every single class presented Kilba a shoebox full of cards. Then volunteer moms brought out a buffet of food, a medley of Slavic and Mexican dishes but also cupcakes.

During the meal Yuri sat right next to the Monsignor. Kilba watched him unwrap his cupcake neatly, careful to let his crumbs fall only on the plate. Kilba asked him, "Is it good?"

"Mm."

"Even if it tasted bad, it's better than sitting in class. Right?"

"Yes," said Yuri.

"What were you learning today?" Kilba asked.

"We read a play. It's called *Stone Soup*."

"I know that one. Those two hungry soldiers...they trick a whole village into making them soup. That's a funny play."

Yuri said, "And then we had Catechism."

"Oh, yeah? What did you memorize?"

Yuri shrugged. He put another piece of cake in his mouth and chewed patiently. Then he asked, "Monsignor Kilba. What did you want for your birthday?"

"Me?" His wiry eyebrows rose. "Honestly?"

"Yes."

Kilba tapped his long thumbs together. "I think I'd like a time machine." He chuckled to himself. "Go back in time about ten years. But only ten. No more than that."

"I wasn't even born."

"Yes. But I'd take you with me. Wouldn't it be fun to see how it all was before you were born?"

Yuri seemed to agree.

"Of course it would," said Kilba. "But what I'd really like...and I'll be honest. I want one whole day of nothing but quiet. And fresh air with light temperatures. And a good book, a beautiful piece of music. One whole day when nobody dies and nobody gets married and nobody gets sick and no babies are born. And a day when nobody comes to church at all. That would be exactly what I'd like."

Yuri picked the cupcake apart and toyed with the pieces on his plate.

"You don't seem to think it's a good thing to want."

"I don't know," said Yuri. "It's really horrible to want something. To really want it very much. It's a sin. Jesus doesn't like it."

"Oh, really?" Kilba's face softened, but he could not hide his annoyance. "Did Sister teach that?"

Yuri nodded.

Kilba whispered, "*Vaikut*," and glanced to see where Yuri's teacher, the nun, Sr. Beatta-Marie was sitting. The Monsignor spoke in heavily accented and broken Lithuanian: "I tells you. Nobody know what Jesus want. Nobody. You heard? Most person who teach these things, they tells you what they want, not what God want." Kilba couldn't continue embarrassing himself and changed to English. But he whispered, leaning close to Yuri. "Of course, don't be selfish, but don't torture yourself. You can want a toy for your birthday. Or a piece of cake. Don't let anyone make you feel guilty."

Yuri thought quietly and finished his cake. Soon, Sr. Beatta-Marie raised her voice to tell the children it was time to say good-bye and clean up. Kilba stood to thank everyone for the beautiful music and said he couldn't wait to read the cards. A few older boys helped carry the shoeboxes to the rectory, all the way up to Kilba's third floor study.

He drank cognac by himself and listened to selections from *Carmen, Il Trovatore*, and a good recording of Bach's cello suites. When the last suite had ended, the cognac was relaxing him pleasantly. Kilba now looked through the shoeboxes. He opened up the cards from second grade and searched through to find Yuri's. He must have mistaken the grade because the card wasn't there. Kilba checked again and read the names in every single card.

He finally found it. Yuri's card was blank on both sides and only contained a message, the handwriting slanted and oblong, but symmetric:

Dear Monsignor Kilba,

Happy Birthday! I'm sorry if I made mistakes in For He's a Jolly Good Fellow. I wanted to draw you a portrit of you and the way the music sounds coming from deep inside the piano where the hammer hits the strings but I didn't draw it. Please have a most happy Birthday and best wishings.

> *Your friend,*
> *Yuri Dilienko*

Advent, 1975

1

Walking through the rectory, Lars Jorgenson dipped his forefinger into a glass of scotch and rubbed the alcohol into his temple. He coughed heavily from a four-day-old illness and stumbled down the corridor, a narrow, curved passage with a low ceiling, which connected St. Anthony's rectory to the church. He bumped his knee hard against a radiator and almost fell down but caught his balance on a windowsill. The glass of scotch fell to the floor. It didn't break, but the whiskey was gone and Lars damned it to hell.

In the cold church, he could smell the pine wreathes and boughs and the hot candle wax. Lars sat at the grand piano off to the side of the first rows of pews. The keys were cool when he began one of his shorter compositions, titled *Woman at the Window*. Lars had not played it since well before Victoria, his wife, had died four years before.

His drunken hands couldn't play with any nuance. But Lars saw Victoria writing by the window. Her elegant hands and white fingers held the journal's page down, kept it from flipping on its own—her pen moved easily, leaving Russian words he couldn't understand. He heard the pen scratch the surface of the paper, and she was breathing. Lars only saw the back of her head, thick black hair in a tight bun. She stopped to think, took a deeper breath, and Lars heard her fingernail scratch the skin on her neck. Then she wrote the final words, tapped a full stop into the page and all was silent.

Lars played *Woman at the Window* one more time, now louder, but an attack of coughs kept him from finishing. He started from the beginning, missing notes. He played in a cycle, never stopping at the end, but simply taking it again from the top.

The sounds were carrying down the corridor into the rectory. Father Cruz, reading in the small library, could no longer bear the repetition. The wooden floor creaked as he walked along the corridor where the glass and stain in the red carpet frustrated him. "Drunk idiot," Cruz thought, picking up the glass.

He came to Lars and gently touched his shoulder, careful not to startle him. Lars took his hands from the keys and turned his head. "My friend," said Father Cruz. "Do you have any idea what hour of night it is?"

2

Monsignor Kilba, hung over, was listening to the church tower's chimes while he lay warm under his goose down comforter. After the short, pleasant melody that signaled the top of a new hour, the tower bell struck one. Kilba waited. He kept waiting—it couldn't be true. It was already one o'clock? He was terribly late.

The monsignor rolled to his side, letting the weight of his legs help him sit up. His wind-up alarm clock should have been on a bed stand next to the message, *Set the alarm, old man*, but Kilba found the clock on the floor at the foot of his bed. He rubbed his eyes to check the time and found he had only a half-hour before he had to be in a confessional, listening to confessions.

Kilba rushed through his routine—after a quick shower, he put in his dentures, sprayed his mouth with an antiseptic and combed down the two puffs of hair on the sides of his head. The network of thin red vessels in the skin of his nose and cheeks disgusted him. Rushing to shave stubble from his chin, Kilba cut himself twice.

The rectory's kitchen was warm and full of sun when Kilba showed up, still in his bathrobe. Father Cruz, already in his vestments, stood at a window overlooking the churchyard and convent beyond the small, snow-covered lawn. Water was boiling for tea and Cruz had left out teabags and milk.

The Monsignor took some hair of the dog, a touch of Black Label at the bottom of a snifter. The scotch cleared the pain in his head and warmed his chest, but it also had him burp and Kilba feared he might get hiccups. He prepared some light tea and sat at the kitchen table to wash down a few water crackers.

Cruz's stiff posture made it clear, Kilba knew, that he did not like the mess left on the kitchen table: oily smoked fish on wax paper and dry crusts of black bread. Cruz said, "Our organist stayed here last night. Very late."

"I was with him," said Kilba.

"You were not. You had already gone to bed."

"Lars stayed around, then?"

"I couldn't get very much sleep with the amount of laughing, and with all that opera playing so loud. We're liable to break the stereo if we treat it that way."

"What was Lars doing?"

"It was already 5:30. I had gotten up to pray, went to read. Lars was in the church playing the side piano. Terrible, absolutely terrible and embarrassing sounds. A drunk at a piano. Had he been on the pipe organ all of Cicero would have heard."

"Are you angry?"

"I'm exhausted with no sleep. And I have to listen to confessions."

Kilba smiled. "You should thank God you're exhausted from lack of sleep and not from confessions," he said, raising his palms up to the ceiling the way he did when saying Mass. "I'm sorry we got carried away last night. You're not the first priest to join our parish and wonder about Lars. Or, for that matter, to wonder about me. Last night doesn't happen very often. Believe me. He usually has a birthday only once a year." The Monsignor washed his hands at the sink and dried them against his bathrobe. He said, "I'll have to vest quickly. If you'll excuse me."

In the church, Father Cruz took his place in the confessional on time. Many people were already waiting in long queues—most parishioners at Cruz's confessional were Mexicans. Yet many more people, of all available ethnicities and ages, even those whose English was limited, patiently waited for Kilba to come out. He was ten minutes late, cup of tea in one hand and a pillow for the hard wooden seat in another.

Kilba always drank tea while listening to confessions, nodding his head without ever closing his eyes or, like other priests, covering his mouth with a tight forefinger. Parishioners knew that Kilba was rather lax in giving out penance. Stolen items did not have to be returned to their rightful owners but could be dropped in the poor box. Wives and husbands did not have to fess up to their spouses when they cheated for the first time, but had to promise God, right there in the confessional, that they would never commit adultery again. On occasion Kilba asked what good deeds parishioners had done since their last confession and wanted to know about events that had made them feel closer to God. He praised people for spending time with their families, working hard and saving money.

This morning Kilba heard about fistfights at the bar and a woman who had lied about her friends. A vindictive business owner had fired his ex-wife's cousin and a young boy had stolen his father's *Playboy*.

Moments after the steeple bell had rung two o'clock, Lars started playing the organ. He wasn't supposed to play during confessions, and from the amount of mistakes Monsignor Kilba understood he was still drunk. When the music stopped in the middle of a piece, he guessed Cruz had gone up to the choir to get rid of him. Kilba said a prayer for them both.

Now the door to the confessional opened and someone entered on Kilba's left, his better ear. The Monsignor slid the window open to expose the screen and waited for the confessor to begin—he heard breathing that could have been from crying. It was a coughing, congested boy. The boy blew his nose and then his voice, as thin as air, whispered, "Bless me, Father..." and stopped. The coughs that followed were muffled by the sleeve of a coat or scarf. "Bless me, Father, for I have sinned." Kilba strained to hear the faint whisper. "It has been twenty-five minutes since my last confession and these are my sins..."

Kilba waited and finished the last bit of his already cold tea. He heard the lightest whisper, although it might have been nothing at all. His ear was practically touching the confessional screen when he nodded and said, "I'm listening."

"I told it."

"What did you tell?"

"To the new priest. To Father Cruz. I told it to him."

Monsignor Kilba recognized Yuri's voice. "What did you tell him?" asked Kilba.

"I told the secret only God knows about."

"The secret?"

"Yes, Monsignor. And the devil knows it too. It's the devil's secret."

Kilba was now certain that Yuri was not only crying but had caught a bad cold. He paused before asking anything more and hoped Yuri would speak on his own, but the boy knelt quietly in the dark chamber, occasionally drawing air through his stuffed nose. "So," said Kilba, "It's a secret you couldn't tell."

"I can't tell it."

"Why?"

"I'll be punished."

"God will not punish you for telling your sins. He'll forgive you."

"No. I'll get burned...God knows I get burned. And if I tell anyone..." Yuri's words trembled and he inhaled air in quick staccato gasps. "I'll die like Anya. And then I'll be with her in hell."

"What is this, Yuri?"

"Monsignor Kilba. Please help me."

"Why would you die, Yuri? Who's frightening you? Tell me what's wrong."

"Anya died because she told the secret."

"Yuri, your sister died in her sleep. She went to bed with food in her mouth and choked. You know that."

"That's *how* she died. Not why. She told the secret. And now *I* told the secret."

Kilba pressed a knuckle hard against his forehead and, his mind still cloudy from the hangover, did his best to concentrate. "Yuri..." he whispered. "Please help me understand. Twenty-five minutes ago, you went to confession?"

"Yes. I told Father Cruz."

"So this is your second confession today?"

"Yes."

"All right. And you told Father Cruz your secret?" He paused to think. "Now I...I still don't understand. Why are you confessing a second time?"

"To get forgiven. For telling it."

Kilba leaned even closer to the screen. "You want God to forgive you for confessing?"

"I don't want it to happen."

3

Lars got up from the organ, took his winter cap and stepped down the choir's spiral staircase. Cruz followed him down, babbling and complaining, "I'm keeping parishioners waiting. Do you think it's pleasant?" but Lars ignored him. Outside, he was certain to walk only where rock salt had melted the ice. He had lost his coat and his pocket flask was now empty, so he grew very cold waiting at the bus stop.

Lars lived several miles from St. Anthony's in a brick garage behind the two-flat house he owned. He had once lived in the top flat with his family but had moved out shortly after his wife's death. The garage had been expensive to remodel—it had insulation, running water, a kitchenette, an antique chamber pot—and Lars had furnished it with the necessary comforts: an upright piano, recording equipment, original paintings and a bed that automatically adjusted into reading position. Except for the cold floor, the garage was comfortable.

At his desk, he tried working on a composition-in-progress but only needed a second to realize that the whole thing was shit. Lars flapped the papers to the floor and went to his fridge. The bus ride and cold weather had sobered him and he took a quick shot from his stash of Wisconsin shine to help him sleep. Falling into bed, he passed out.

He couldn't hear Alina shouting, "Dad, open up. It's cold." She knocked on the door again. "Dad, come on. It's cold out here."

Alina put her ear up to the door's chipped paint but heard nothing. The garage windows were frosted over and she tried to scrape a patch to peer through but then remembered the key taped to the underside of the outdoor grill's lid. There wasn't any need for it—her dad had left the door unlocked.

The garage stunk from a pile of nasty socks and an old cigar left in an ashtray. Lars lay in bed with his mouth wide open and the whites of his eyes showing. He was still wearing shoes—salt and dirty snow had stained his comforter, and his right pant leg was dried up with blood around the knee. "Oh, for fucking stupidity," shouted Alina. "God! Just God dammit. Happy birthday to you, dad!"

She threw her father's birthday card at him. It bounced off his chin and landed on his chest. "That's your fifty-fifth year come around. Fifty-five candles burnt down to the frosting." Alina turned on the heat. "Burning down because no sad bastard, wasted in the afternoon, can't get off his ass to blow them out."

She tried to pull the pant leg up to see how badly the knee was hurt, but the pants were too tight. She took his shoes off and brushed some of the salt off the bed. "If you knew how sorry people get about you." Alina felt her father's hot forehead with the back of her finger. "Fever. What did you do to yourself? If mom saw you like this..." She slapped his cheek lightly and in a moment of panic felt to see if he was breathing. "See how paranoid you make me?"

Alina had to take his pants off to check the knee. She straddled him, covered his middle with the corner of a loose bed sheet, and worked underneath it. "What did you do?" She unbuckled the belt, slid her hands under him and pulled, as hard as she could, at the back pockets. After a struggle, she had the trousers down far enough, but the polyester had stuck to the wound. Alina carefully pulled the material from the skin and ruptured the scab—a bulb of dark blood oozed from the knee, swollen blue. There was no puss and the wound did not need stitches, but it was dirty with lint.

She washed and bandaged him, then wrapped him in wool blankets. There wasn't any thermometer in the small cabinet above Lars' sink—Alina only found heartburn pills, some canned food and a bottle of vitamins full of rolled hundred- and fifty-dollar bills.

The hidden money left her laughing and she sat at his desk. "Such a clown. Such a lunatic." He'd left out the jar of shine and Alina poured a touch into the small glass. She swirled it around and inhaled its smell of hearty bread. "Here's to you, dad," she said. "Here's to doing things your way."

Alina wore a silver ring she had made herself—it was a spider-like flower centered with a tiny emerald. Whenever she got nervous, she turned the ring around her finger, pressing it down against her knuckle so that the spider's legs dug into her skin. She was trying to remember a phone number—Alina hadn't needed it since her mother's death. Taking the phone, she held the receiver against her cheek lightly but then slammed it into the cradle. "God dammit! Why do you have to be sick? Why do I have to stress out about this shit?"

Lars didn't wake. His chest was rising slowly.

Alina took the drinking glass off the desk and threw it over her father—it landed and broke in the sink. The phone number climbed out of her memory's basement when she set her finger in the dial.

A woman's voice answered, "Cicero Family Clinic."

"Hello. Yes. I need Dr. Dilienko for a house call."

"He has appointments at the clinic for another half-hour. May I ask your name?"

"Alina Jorgenson."

"And the doctor would see you?"

"No. Lars," she sighed.

"Oh, of course. Sure. What's the matter with him?"

"I don't know. I think he fell...He has a fever."

"Is this an emergency?"

"Look, can Dilienko come or not?"

The receptionist remained polite. "He should be finishing up with his final patient shortly."

"Can he come or not?"

"Miss Jorgenson, please calm down. Are you sure he does not need emergency care?"

"No. Just get Bronza over here..."

The receptionist paused. "I urge you to call for an ambulance if you feel he needs immediate care. It will be twenty minutes here, perhaps longer."

"Fine. I'll wait. That's fine."

4

After his last appointment, Bronza Dilienko went to the back room to smoke by himself. It was a tight and gray space with a few lockers and folding chairs. A window faced the alley, and Bronza blew the smoke out that way. He kept a small radio in a drawer and often listened to music or news between appointments.

He wasn't sure where he would go or what he would do with the rest of the afternoon. Since his daughter's death, he'd been working incessantly. Whenever he finished work in the clinic, he'd visit hospital patients who were fine, in some colleague's capable hands. Coworkers in the clinic urged him to take a break, but he'd smile, his eyes confident, and reassure everyone, "I'm well. I need work."

The little room's door opened and the receptionist entered. "I'm sorry," she said.

"What's the matter?"

"I got this a short while ago," she whispered, handing him a note. "It's Lars Jorgenson's address. I think his daughter called. She claims he fell."

"Fell?"

"There was something peculiar about her."

"Call her now, say I'm coming."

Bronza drove his brown Buick rather quickly down the unplowed streets. He left two footprints on the stairs leading up to Lars' front door before remembering the guy had moved into his garage. He found a message taped to Lars' garage door:

He's sick. I'll be back right away. He's got a fever. I went to the deli to get hot soup. ~~There's a key~~ Door's unlocked. ~~Leave whatever~~ If I don't come back, write instructions, leave whatever prescriptions I'll need. There's a vitamin bottle full of cash on dad's desk. Take how much you need. (if I don't come back before you go)

Alina

Bronza found Lars tucked in, his head deep in a large pillow. He picked up Alina's card from the floor, still sealed, and put it on the piano, recalling that Lars' birthday was probably around the corner.

Bronza was struck by his red complexion and slightly swollen eyelids. He searched through his instruments for a thermometer—when he loosened the blanket around Lars' neck, he became alarmed; Lars was very warm. Holding the thermometer under an armpit, he felt for a pulse and found Lars' heart racing. When he read the thermometer, he tossed it onto the bed and picked up the phone.

5

Gaja Dilienko sat praying in one of St. Anthony's front pews. Her hand stuffed in the pocket of a coat, she held a scapular tightly, its band woven through her fingers. Gaja focused her gaze on the massive crucifix above the altar, looking mostly at Christ's gentle face. For the time being, she had forgotten about Yuri—he was around, in the confessional or praying his penance somewhere.

Repeating the *Our Father* over and over in her heart, she kept retracing the steps she had taken that day. Gaja's morning tea had not soothed her. The Lithuanian radio program had played stupid, idiotic music. She had failed to find a new dusting of snow on lawns calming while walking to church with her son. Bickering sparrows had her clench teeth, as had the distant chimes, the squeak in the church's side door, the scratching shuffle of people's feet against the marble, the crack when someone flipped a misalette in the back pew. Gaja was having one of those days— their frequency seemed to be increasing—when no matter how she tried to distract herself, the memory, the feeling, wouldn't leave her.

She exited the pew and thought about praying at the statue of the Virgin, but Mary had not been helping her recently. Gaja knelt at the communion rail in front of the Sacred Heart of Jesus and recited another *Our Father*.

Red vigil candles, arranged neatly in an iron stand behind the rail, burned at the foot of Jesus' statue. Christ stood wearing a red and white robe fastened at the waist by a thick golden cord. His heart, bleeding and wrapped in a crown of thorns, protruded through his chest, floating outside his garments. Jesus held one hand out to grant blessings, a bloody gash in the palm—the other hand remained at his side, its dark purple gash easily visible. The statue was old and much of the paint was cracked; patches of crumbling plaster on Christ's neck resembled blisters. Gaja was kneeling in the place where it seemed His eyes were looking.

She tightened the scapular around her fingers and repeated the prayer. When she finished, she said:

> *Our Father*
> *who art*
> *in heaven hallowed*
> *be thy name thy king*
> *dom come thy*
> *will*
> *be done*
> *on Earth as will be done*
> *will? As it*
> *will what be done in*
> *what I done and give us*
> *this day our lives*
> *in how I live this way thy*
> *will be done*
> *what I done*
> *what have I done*
> *to deserve this?*

Bronza was yelling. "What have I done to deserve this? *This* treatment?"

"You want an explanation?" asked Gaja. She tried to slam the door again, but he was too strong. "Leave me alone," she said. "Just leave me alone."

"What have I done to deserve this treatment?" Bronza shouted.

"What?"

"To come home. Every night. Find you locked up behind this God damn...this God damn door?"

"What do you mean *every* night?"

"You're always locked up."

"So what? You're always somewhere else."

"Why should I sleep in an empty bed every night? I'm a man."

Gaja tried to slam the door on his fingers. "You don't come home *every* night!" She used her entire weight. "I don't know where you go! And I don't care!"

"Where I go? I *heal* people. I feed you and your son! I give you this house."

"You bastard! He's *my* son? You have no decency!"

"Open this door! I'll break it."

"No."

"Open it. Open this door. Open it!"

Gaja pushed her back against the door and the rug under her feet slid slightly. She tried to brace herself against the bed, but the struggle was tiring her. The rug finally slipped and the door swung open—her body fell to the floor. Before she could rise, Bronza's hands grabbed her by the shoulders to lift and throw her to the bed. Her head bumped against the bedpost and the lamp fell off the nightstand, shattering, the room falling dark.

Bronza's hard fingers pulled at the buttons of her night blouse and she kicked him in the stomach. She scratched and bit his arm, but he hit her in the chest and pinned her with his heavy body. Gaja closed her eyes. His face was unshaven and rough, and his exhale was humid with heat—she smelled a breath mint and heard it click against his molars. He got off her for a moment to spread her legs, to pull at the elastic of her panties, and she kneed him in the ribs, managed to kick him hard with the ball of her foot. She kicked him again, in the ribs, all the strength and anger she had left, and she freed a hand to scratch his face. He tore at her clothes and she kicked him again. He lay on top of her and tossed away a piece of her clothing. When he forced himself in, she did not stop hitting him.

Gaja opened her eyes.

Christ's statue looked at her, she at His heart—the scapular was crumpled into a ball and crushed in her fist. She felt sick and put her forehead against the communion rail, hoping the cool white marble might be pleasant, but she felt ashamed to be slumped forward in church. Standing, Gaja took a small water bottle from her handbag and put the scapular away, then drank and wiped her lips with a handkerchief. She stuffed it down into her coat pocket and crushed it tightly.

At the offering box for candles, she donated a wrinkled dollar. As she lit a thin wooden stick to spread the fire to an unlit candle, the church bells signaled a quarter after three. The priests would leave the confessionals at four.

She looked for Yuri in the church but could not see him—a quick glance into the sacristy did not reveal him either. Very few people remained in the pews, and the confessionals were free. She genuflected before crossing in front of the tabernacle and made her way to the side aisle.

The kneeler in Cruz's dark confessional was very hard...muffled whispers carried from the confessional's other side. Gaja took a rosary from her coat pocket. With the crucifix between her thumb and forefinger, she saw and felt a prayer that didn't have any words, a series of hot and parched colors below a huge sky bleached by the sun. Her dry, chapped hands in a pool of cool water full of rough, black rocks.

The door on the other side closed. Cruz slid Gaja's confession window open and the small chamber filled with pale light. She waited while Cruz made the sign of the cross. He leaned closer to her, his eyes shut and an open palm pressed tight against his mouth. Gaja hesitated, adjusting her position on the kneeler to get closer to Cruz. She whispered, "I have not told God," and stopped. "I have not told God things in the confessional." Gaja waited. "I have told things to...to God. But alone. Alone in my room. Not *told* them, really...but God knows what He needs to know. I've admitted everything to Him in my thoughts. In my room."

Cruz whispered, "You must confess your sins if your soul is to be filled with God's grace."

"I know what brings grace. I know what the church teaches."

Cruz remained silent.

Words came slowly for Gaja. "My husband. God knows my husband is godless." Her grip on the rosary relaxed. "God knows what I want to say. God gave me a daughter. He gave me a beautiful daughter. And last week he took her from me because of a terrible sin. I have never told what that sin is. Never to a priest."

"God is willing to forgive if one is willing to confess."

"Yes. But *who* should confess? My husband...he gave me a baby. We had a baby..." She waited, felt tiny beneath that bleached sky, thirsty from the parched colors. "I was full of lust in my youth. I was lustful often. Then I had his baby. I learned the nature of that child very soon, his sinful nature. My boy is godless and wicked, like his father."

A long pause followed.

"After my first child, I stopped letting my husband touch me. I promised God I would never let him touch me after *his* baby. It is his baby, *his* boy." Gaja let the rosary slide down her arm to hang at her elbow. "Then, one day, he took me. My husband took me. I fought with him; I didn't want it, to be like one of his cheap women. I kicked him. I broke his rib."

Cruz folded his hands in his lap.

"God gave me another baby. A baby girl. When I broke his rib. You understand me, father? My baby girl, she did not come from my lust. But God took her from me." A laugh burst from Gaja, metallic and hard. "Now God wants me to tell you why?"

Cruz sat perfectly still.

Gaja put away her rosary, took a drink of water from her bottle and left the confessional.

6

Yuri went to the choir balcony to pray his penance and, as Monsignor Kilba had instructed, to recite the Act of Contrition. Done with the prayers, he sat for a moment and tried to calm down, coughing into his coat to keep from attracting attention. He was careful to keep his mother from seeing him when he left the church.

Yuri walked across the parish schoolyard and hopped a low fence. He knew a shortcut through an alley leading to 16th Street. The train tracks running in the middle of the street were one of his favorite places in Cicero. Trains never ran on them—the rails had become rusty and many of the ties had rotted. People dumped trash on the tracks, often things too big to fit in garbage drums. He remembered all the afternoons he and Anya had spent collecting metal to sell to the scrap yard.

Today he hurried across the street on his way to St. Anne's cemetery. Yuri was thinking about Monsignor Kilba's words: "Don't be afraid. Baptized children never go to hell. Your sister is in heaven for sure, Yuri. It's true."

He very much wanted to believe the Monsignor but could not stop thinking about the picture of hell from his school catechism book, the hot rocks and the fire burning all the souls. Most of them were grown-ups, but many of them were children, and he remembered their faces, how sorry they were. He knew, walking along the cyclone fence by the L tracks, that Monsignor Kilba might have only been trying to cheer him up: "Yuri, you won't die in your sleep tonight or any night. That's nonsense. If your mother said that, she's speaking from sadness and anger, and anger is making her confused. Just go say your prayers and be good. You are forgiven and you've no reason to be afraid."

Yuri entered the cemetery through the archway under the red brick tower and found his sister's grave. The gravestone had not been placed there yet, but a temporary cross, two interlocking varnished boards, their ends beveled and rounded, had been knocked into the ground. For a moment, he stood unsure of why he was there. He read the engraving on a small board:

Anna Dilienka
October 11, 1968
December 4, 1975

Yuri chose his thoughts carefully because he believed Anya's soul could hear him when he thought about her. He remembered how he and Anya would jokingly walk backwards in the snow so that their footprints would "trick everyone." They often spent time at Mayna's Pizza—most of the money they collected at the scrap metal yard was for pizza and Italian ice. Yuri tried as hard as he could, but could not avoid remembering how they had found loose railroad spikes one afternoon. Anya had said they were too good to sell—they just looked so neat. Yuri had wanted to paint them silver and turn them into rocket ships. But then mama found the spikes.

When he tried to think of other pleasant things he and Anya had done together, questions came. What would happen if Yuri went to hell? Maybe if he went down to hell, he wouldn't be allowed to see Anya anyway, and that would be his punishment. What if he died, went to heaven, and God punished him for thinking only of himself, for going to confession so that he would be forgiven when his sister wasn't? What if selfishly wanting heaven was a reason to deserve hell?

Yuri sat in the snow. He removed his winter gloves and put them in his coat pocket. Yuri always wore a second set of gloves underneath them, made of loose leather with their fingers cut off at the ends. He told people they protected his hands from a skin allergy—the gloves had become such a normal part of him that neither he nor anyone else thought twice about them.

He found a dead flower stem and used it to poke the snow's surface. All the questions about selfishness, desire, his fear of punishment, Monsignor Kilba's assurances—all of it seemed to be circling him. When he had already poked many holes in the snow, an idea came.

Yuri made a snowball as perfectly round as he could, testing it on the cleaned sidewalk to be sure it rolled nicely. Happy with it, he took the ball to Anya's cross. The top of the cross—well sanded and smooth wood—was shaped like an arch. Yuri put the snowball right up at the highest point. When he let go, the ball would roll. If it rolled to the right, he would commit a sin before going to sleep, but if it rolled to the left, he wouldn't do anything else that day and remain forgiven, absolved by Monsignor Kilba after confession, eligible for heaven if he died that night.

Yuri looked around. The cemetery was empty, only rows of gray, blue and brown gravestones, leafless trees, and footprints in the snow. He held the snowball with only one finger, checking to see if it was balanced, then thought about saying a prayer, but didn't know what side of the cross to pray for. Finally, he closed his eyes and let the snowball go. He heard it hit the ground.

The snowball had fallen directly forward. It lay broken in a soup tin Yuri had used to make a flowerpot for Anya's gravesite at the time of the funeral.

7

Listening to confessions always made Monsignor Kilba hungry. He changed out of his vestments and sat at the kitchen table to nibble on the smoked fish still left there. The large bits were too oily, the small ones too dry, so he wrapped the fish and tucked it all the way in the back of the fridge. Looking through the food, he chose some of the leftover cabbage soup a neighborhood woman had made for the priests. Kilba also took some bread, butter and Lithuanian cheese.

Cruz came in while Kilba was heating the soup at the stove. "Will you make some for me?" He wasn't changed yet.

"There's plenty," said Kilba.

"I'm hungry. I'd fry my chicken livers, but I'm too tired."

"That's disgusting."

"I'll go and change."

By the time Cruz came back, Kilba had finished heating the soup and had set the table. He didn't wait for Cruz before dipping a chunk of black bread into the broth to make it softer for his dentures.

"How is it?" Cruz asked and sat down.

The Monsignor ate in small mouthfuls but appeared greedy with the food. "Very good."

Cruz tasted it. "That woman makes pretty good soup."

"Not as good as Lars' wife used to make. She used to make the best borscht."

"Yes." Cruz wanted to eat but sat quiet for a moment. "Monsignor, would you listen to my confession before I eat, before I ask a question? Do you mind?"

"I'd like to confess as well."

"Alright. You want to go first?" Cruz broke off a piece of the bread and sliced some cheese.

"You go first."

"You sure?"

"All right," said Kilba. "I'll go first." He wiped his mouth. "Bless me, Father. I'm a quality sinner, well ripened and seasoned. It's been a week since I last reported my filthy deeds. Isn't that true?"

Cruz nodded. He dipped the bread.

"Very well. This week's filthy deeds include paging through pictures of naked women, quite young, I don't know if they were married or not. I confess to having fantasies about Lars' daughter...doesn't happen so often, but, you know...the mind is a very soft instrument. I also, believe it or not, told a calling salesman exactly what he could do with his such-and-such merchandise. A blatant use of the Lord's name in vain, also with a good surge of pride. What else? Yes...I broke a promise to my niece in Racine and did not visit her on Wednesday." Monsignor Kilba rubbed his fingers together. "You know what, Father Cruz, I also took the batteries out of your tape recorder and put them into mine."

"Yes, I was wondering about that."

"Are you angry?"

"No." Cruz spread butter over his bread.

"Well, then scratch that. Of course, we know about last night's nonsense with Lars. I drank and ate like a glutton and enjoyed it but for penance felt sick all day today."

"Is that all?"

Kilba paused. "No..." He tapped his forefingers together and sat up straight in his chair. "It isn't, actually. There's something else. I'm afraid it's quite serious."

Cruz stopped eating and set his utensils down. "What do you mean?" He was beginning to get a feel for Kilba's manners— the Monsignor's tone and posture convinced Cruz he was being sincere.

"During confession today, I heard something that alarmed me, to be honest. And I'm not certain I'm doing God's work by not telling anyone about it. I wanted to ask you. Have you ever broken the silence of the confessional?"

"Never. No! Not ever in my life."

"I never have either. But...I'm very concerned about someone. I believe something terrible is happening to someone very close to me." Kilba paused. "I'm 75 and I have heard many sins in my life. But I never had someone ask me for help in the confessional."

"You cannot, Monsignor! You're already telling me too much."

"I am not."

"You didn't do anything today, did you?" Cruz became very agitated.

"What's the matter with you? Calm down, for Pete's..." Kilba drank some water.

"Well...it's strange...I wanted to confess as well. About something similar. Not *exactly* similar, you understand. But something happened in confession..."

"I bless you. You have sinned. Tell me."

Cruz spoke hurriedly: "Apart from this week's lying and getting very angry at people...apart from that. I was furious with Lars for playing the organ today and I told him he had no self-respect. I let him leave the church with no coat."

"Lars is fine. Tell me what happened in confession."

"I don't know which part I should tell." He rubbed a butter knife on a napkin. "A woman came to confess. I know her. I have seen her many times since I began here at St. Anthony's. She comes to the parish breakfasts. I...I'm not sure what to say. I didn't...I recognized her voice and the confession was unorthodox."

"What?"

"It wasn't about anything she did. It was about what *happened* to her. I...imagined it happening. I imagined what she was saying." Cruz put the butter knife down and stared Kilba in the eyes. "I became rather fixated on the thoughts. I had a fantasy."

"Cruz," said Monsignor Kilba. "Cruz, how old are you again?"

"I'm thirty-one."

"Cruz, a fantasy is normal."

"It *isn't* normal."

"Yes, you'll repeat yourself...you're *supposed to be a priest*. This idealism of yours..."

"I'm not an idealist. That's not what I mean. I'm talking about the kinds of thoughts. They weren't thoughts about what's common."

"What? What uncommon sins can one hear?" asked Kilba.

"Look. I just want to confess that I envisioned myself hurting—forcing a woman."

Kilba understood what Cruz was saying and stared at him intently. The Monsignor remained quiet for a while before whispering, "I see."

"It never..."

"Don't...say anymore," said Kilba, gently placing an open hand on the table. "You've confessed it. Don't go any further." The men sat quietly and Kilba finally said, "We should absolve the sins."

Cruz nodded and the men made signs of the cross over each other while mumbling the Rite of Absolution. "What penance shall we give?" asked Kilba.

"I think we should fast."

"How long?"

"Two days," suggested Cruz. "Starting midnight."

"Done."

8

When Lars had finally sobered up, he put on dry socks and his warm wool cap, and went out for a bus ride and walk around Cicero. Jorgenson walked a lot, especially in the latest hours when the streets were empty and the church bells didn't sound anymore. It was always those damn church bells, first that childishly playful melody at the top of the hour, and then that melancholy toll of a bell bigger than a Volkswagen, gray as a warship. It hung there from some rotting piece of wood that would one day break, and the bell would crash through the tower's ceiling, smash the trap door where that stupid rope dangled, destroy the spiral staircase and the marble floor below, maybe killing a little nun or one of the church ushers. Or Father Cruz. He'd be right beneath and the bell would dong him into the marble.

Lars was standing in front of the church, the tower rising higher than the leafless elms and oaks along 50th Avenue. Even against the night sky, the copper at the top shimmered, and the black wood and brown bricks had softened from shadows. No single person was out, and Lars peered over the rectory's dark windows, not even a small light or candle in neighboring houses, the corner store, or the convent in the churchyard. Even the bright white bricks of Roosevelt Elementary, the public school across from St. Anthony's, had grayed, and the whole building sagged, tired of time. The gate to the playground—it was just a large asphalt parking lot where kids could play tag or baseball—had been left wide open. Lars went inside just to look at the school again.

He had once worked there as music teacher and bandleader. It had been four years ago, only a few weeks after Victoria's death, when he had been fired for screaming at the band and unbuttoning his shirt during a rehearsal. Lars had called his pupils a bunch of septic tanks; he had screamed at a percussionist, his tie flailing from his left hand. "No rhythm. It's a disgrace. Play a real instrument, piano, like a civilized person, like a human being. Your brain's a bass drum. You can't play your own brain." Lars could no longer remember if he had been drunk while screaming or if he had started in on the kids like that because he wasn't drunk. It didn't matter because he would never work there again.

He remembered conducting the band during all those school concerts and recitals. One time, Alina had played piano with the school orchestra. Her feet could barely reach the pedals, but she managed somehow, and the orchestra held its own. Lars could feel, even before the applause, how the audience and all the people in Cicero were pleased with his work, impressed with his daughter.

She was talking now. "I'm sorry. I didn't know."

It's okay, Alina. You're doing fine.

"So, what should I do?"

Nothing...you're fine. Don't talk. Just keep playing.

"I didn't think. I went to get some hot soup. It was just a few minutes."

Was that Alina? No...it must have been Victoria's voice. She was out in the audience, right in the first row, sitting with the tape recorder as always. But when the music ended and the audience stood to applaud, Victoria wasn't there. He searched back stage for her, among all the moms who came to congratulate their children. Maybe she had gone to the Corner Billiard Club to wait for him because crowds always made her nervous.

He remembered where she was. She was at home, writing in her journal, right by the window in their front room, a small chamber speckled with shadows and light falling through the leaves of a tall and broad oak. Now Lars saw himself sitting in the kitchen and watching her quietly. Even though she loved writing in the book and did it almost every day, he often knew the Russian words she wrote were sad. She couldn't tell Lars what made her sad—by telling him, she would transform her private sadness into their mutual pain, and Victoria understood Lars' inability to deal with pain. It was why he rarely spoke to her while she wrote, but also why he loved to listen to the sound of her fountain pen against the thick paper.

Lars was at the bus stop waiting for the 12th Street bus. Even though he had his good wool cap, he had lost his coat in the church, and now the temperature was dropping. But even with his chest growing cold, standing on the corner of the block and looking down the street for the bus, he could still hear the sound of Victoria's pen against paper.

It was getting cold very fast. When Lars realized he was naked, he felt the cold in his teeth and down in his nuts. All the lights blinked out and everything was pitch black—something wet and big was on his belly. He tried to touch his gut but couldn't lift his hands or turn them at the wrists. Struggling, he realized he could not move his body at all—he couldn't turn his head or bend at the waist.

Someone was touching him. It was a man with large hands. Another person was moving around somewhere close to him but Lars couldn't move or see. He tried to ask, "Who are you?" but only air rose from his throat. He heard a whisper: "You'll be okay. You'll be fine."

Bronza? Bullshit, Bronza couldn't be out. The cold hands, Lars wanted them to stop and he wanted Bronza to get rid of the heavy thing on his gut. It was some huge weight pinning him.

A siren was approaching. It was coming and Victoria was no doubt getting ready for bed. She wore earplugs while sleeping—perhaps she couldn't hear. Lars had to tell her. The siren was coming. This one screamed straight through his skin—he wanted to cover his ears as much as he wanted to find the sound and kill it. His hands were now able to move and he searched for it in the darkness in front of his face.

It stopped. There was nothing but cold for a moment but then many voices. You're the doctor? He's got a hundred and six. Okay, hold the stretcher. Can you move his bed? Careful now, ready? There's plenty of ice.

"Can I ride too?" Alina? Girl, you have to get your mother. You have to go tell her that the siren stopped. She's in the dark. She's all by herself in the dark.

Lars tried to get up, but a warm palm touched him on the chest. "Lie back," Alina said. "Don't get up."

What are you doing here? I told you. Go to the house. She's plugged her ears.

"You're going to be all right."

"Where's Victoria?" said Lars.

"Lars, don't worry. It's me. Bronza."

"It's cold."

"You have a fever."

"Fuck you. My coat."

"I have all your things, dad," said Alina, taking his hand. "I'm right here with you."

"I'll follow you guys in my car," said Bronza.

Lars mumbled something, but the only words Alina could make out were "coat" and "ear plugs." She kept repeating that he would be okay and pressed his hand and forearm tightly as the medics rolled him out to the ambulance. Occasionally, Lars pressed back, but Alina could not tell if it was from pain or fear or if he was trying to ask her something. He sometimes seemed missing from his face, did not react to the lights the medics flashed in his eyes or the needles they stuck in his skin.

In the hospital, they kept Lars in an ice bath for a while. At one moment Lars awoke and shouted, "What the hell are you doing to me?" Alina thought he would come to, but he soon passed out again.

They put him to bed and wrapped him in a thick blanket, fitting a warm, white cap around his head and ears. Alina was allowed to sit near him and keep her hand on his shoulder or forehead. She whispered, "I'm here. You're not alone," but could not bear to look at his blank expression. The medical staff spoke amongst themselves, too far away for Alina to hear. She came over and asked them, trying to angle the question at Bronza, "What's going to happen now?"

"We have to wait a bit, Alina. His temperature is down, which is good. It looks like he'll be okay. But we have to wait."

The trauma surgeon said, "You really should have called an ambulance, miss."

Tears burst out of Alina. She had not felt them coming on.

"Alina," Bronza said gently. "If you don't find him, this doesn't have a happy ending. He's lucky you found him."

"Great...great, thank you," she said. "But that's not what I mean. I mean, what's going to *happen*?"

The members of the medical staff exchanged glances.

"Forget it," she said, lightly waving a hand at them. "A happy ending? As if this is over."

"Alina..." Bronza approached her. "Please relax."

"He's impossible. I'm so tired of it all."

"Shh." He took her lightly by the shoulders. "Come on." Bronza tried to hold her, but she turned away and went to sit by herself.

9

Yuri had come home from the cemetery. As mama had taught him, he hung his coat in the closet by the front door and put his wet boots in the bathtub. His winter gloves were wet, so he put them on the radiator—he took off his sweater, folded it neatly and left it on a low shelf in the closet of his room. After double-checking to be certain all his clothing had been put away properly, he went to Anya's room to close the heavy wooden door and sit on her bed. The soup tin from the cemetery, still full of frozen dirt, was in his lap. He held it, still wearing the thin leather gloves.

Yuri listened to Kolya, Anya's parakeet, chirp and hop about. Each time the yellow bird batted his wings, seed pattered against newspaper lining the bottom of his cage, sometimes onto the room's hardwood.

Kolya's birdcage, shaped like a dome, hung right next to the room's tall narrow windows, three separated by thick wooden frames. Very little light remained in the late evening. The sun had just set and the sky was pale gray and exhausted. A light breeze swayed the branch of an evergreen to scratch the glass.

Yuri thought of how the snowball had fallen forward. He wondered what Monsignor Kilba would have to say if Yuri told him about this wager. Kilba had taught that everything was God's will—everything happens because God wishes for it. Sometimes people don't understand what God wants, but God doesn't always want people to understand Him. Sometimes He wanted people to be confused so they'd search further for answers and think more deeply about their problems. Yuri knew he was experiencing a time when God wanted him to be confused. But he was very tired and thinking was difficult. It was easier to listen to the evergreen branch scratch against the glass.

The room's door opened hard and bumped against the rubber stopper. "Yuri!" His mother startled him and he sat up. Mama asked where he was—"*Kur tu?*"—and said she'd been calling him from the kitchen, "*Iš virtuvės tavę šaukiu.*"

He apologized, "*Atsiprašau.*" He always spoke Lithuanian with mama. He let go of the tin and it rolled to the side.

"Why do I have to look around the house for you?" She saw the tin. "Is *that* what you're doing? Is that what you're doing again?"

"I'm sorry. No no. I'm not doing it." Yuri righted the tin because some of the dirt was getting loose. "No. It's from the cemetery. You can see."

"What were you thinking about?"

"Nothing."

"Do you understand me or not?"

Yuri stood to face his mother with his hands in his pockets. He did not understand her.

"I'll say it again. I bought dinner at the deli. It's time for dinner. Not for tin cans. For dinner!"

Yuri nodded.

Gaja went to the bed to pat down the blanket, ruffled in a way she didn't like. It was also slightly wet. "I can't believe you! You were sitting in the snow with your good clothes!" Before Yuri could think of an explanation, she took the tin, went next door to his room, and searched through his drawers. Yuri followed her and watched from the doorway. Gaja found his drawers either full of clothing or completely empty like they should have been. "Do you have any of those train nails? Are you hiding rusty nails again?" She lifted his blanket to look under the bed. "I *never* had to call Anya two times. Never. Do you know that?"

"I couldn't hear you because the door was closed. You were so quiet."

She stood up. "*Because.* With you, it's always *because*. Why were you in her room?"

Yuri stood still.

"And with a closed door. What were you thinking about?"

"Nothing."

"It's time for dinner."

She stepped past and left him in the doorway. He heard the tin clink against the bottom of the kitchen trashcan, and then mama went to the bathroom where she ran water in the sink. Yuri changed out of his church clothes to an old green shirt and gray corduroys. He stood by the bathroom door and waited for mama to come out so he could wash his hands before dinner.

Gaja appeared holding a vial of holy water. "Come in here. And take off your gloves."

"No."

"I'm going to wash your hands."

"I don't want to. I can do it myself."

"You can't." Gaja gripped her son tightly by the forearm and he pulled away, but she held onto his sleeve. Yuri knelt down and rolled into a ball, his forehead against the floor and his hands tightly tucked under his chin and against his chest. "Give me your hands!" Gaja tried to pull his arms out from under him. "Listen to me. Listen to me!" She struggled, rocking his body back and forth, but he would not unlock his arms. She wet two fingers and tried to stick them into Yuri's rolled up fist. Gaja could only touch the leather gloves; he had tucked his fingers underneath his shirt collar.

She stood and shut the vial, tightening the cap even after it would not turn anymore. "You can't lie on the floor forever." Gaja stepped over him to the bathroom and put the vial in the medicine cabinet.

Where had she left her pack of cigarettes? It was on the kitchen windowsill: only six cigarettes left, no matches in the tiny box. Gaja had to get Blue Tips from the pantry. When she lit a match, she heard Yuri close and lock the bathroom door— something in there broke and shattered. Gaja only sat at the kitchen table and smoked.

She unpacked all the bags she had brought from the deli and bakery. Poppy cake was Yuri's favorite and he would definitely want some, but Gaja knew he would not come out of the bathroom even if she called to him about it. She only warmed up the cabbage rolls, the mushrooms and dill potatoes and put Yuri's dinner on a plate. Gaja ate alone and had some poppy cake for desert. Next to Yuri's dinner, she left two slices of cake on a saucer.

It was still early in the evening and she had plenty of housework but felt no energy to start it. The house had a second bathroom and Gaja ran a bath—she lit candles, poured bath oil into the running water and brought her cigarettes and ashtray. The water was very hot and she first knelt in the tub to get used to the temperature. She wet her neck, shoulders and face and could finally sit in the hot water.

Lying back, she heard Yuri scampering around the basement. Gaja couldn't be bothered with him—what was he doing down there—she couldn't be bothered. She moved her hand down to rest between her legs and kept it there. With the other hand, she rubbed the sponge over her skin, squeezed it to pour water over her head. It ran over her eyes and lips and over the lobes of her ears. Gaja pressed her free hand against herself, then relaxed. For the first time that day, she wondered where her husband might have been.

Something fell in the basement and Gaja quickly pulled her hand away. Nervous, she sat up straight, poured shampoo onto her head and briskly lathered her hair, unsure exactly why she felt anxious now. She rinsed off and dried her hands to have a cigarette while the gray water emptied down the drain.

In the kitchen, she brewed a batch of concentrated chamomile tea sweetened with buckwheat honey. Gaja almost never drank alcohol but needed to sleep well tonight, so she spiked the pot with three shots of Amaretto. The Lithuanian radio program always played classical music at night and she listened to Tchaikovsky while drinking the tea in her room. After two cups, her hair had dried well enough and she could finally set her head carefully onto the pillows, the pillowcases washed and ironed earlier that day.

The booze was working. Gaja's body sank into the mattress and she relaxed, the down comforter's cotton duvet cover soft against her skin. She expected Bronza to come home any moment and, her mind cloudy, could not tell if she was remembering the jangling sound of his keys or only anticipating them. Strangely, Gaja missed him, but not as a person or a body. She lay in bed missing the period of her life when she used to see Bronza from the distance and wonder about him, imagine how it would be to speak to him.

It was why she hated alcohol. If she wanted to sleep, she had to drink more than a few shots of Amaretto because sips of booze only made Gaja nostalgic. She hated daydreaming of her childhood but now was recalling the house where she grew up with her uncle Benny, the only parent she had ever had. Gaja was cleaning up his beer bottles in the narrow front room and she heard the sound of his power saw in the backyard. Gaja's memory reached all the way back to her first day of school.

Now Gaja was moments from sleep. She wanted to see herself in the past, a young woman, feminine and strikingly beautiful, but instead she was holding her Uncle Benny's callused hand. He was taking her to school for the first time and telling her that the day would be over before she knew it. And he'd come around to pick her up.

When she awoke early the next morning, sunlight was falling over her bed through a translucent green curtain. It was not half past six, plenty of time to get ready for church. She put on her moccasins and robe and turned off the radio program that had been playing while she slept.

The kitchen was also full of bright sun and harsh, long shadows. On the table, right next to Yuri's dinner—untouched save for the eaten poppy cake—lay three large and rusty but virtually straight railroad spikes. A note had been placed near them, Yuri's handwriting: *Kunigui pasakiau.* I told the priest.

Passage: Immediately Following Gaja's First Day at St. Anthony's School, September 5, 1949

The children and teachers were speaking, but their language didn't mean anything. Gaja found the sounds of their words bulky, like bricks falling from crumbling walls. Only the loud driving school bell made any sense. Uncle Benny had told her, "*Išleis tavę,*" they'll let you out, "*kai bus skambutis,*" at the bell.

Many children, most of them much taller than Gaja, headed out the school in two single-file queues. Gaja heard children shouting and laughing in the churchyard, but the corridor was still quiet enough to hear everyone's slow footsteps. A nun stood at the door with her arms crossed—she nodded as each passing child whispered something. Gaja stepped past the nun and said "*Iki.*" This was a farewell; it meant *until,* short for *until we see each other*. The nun ignored her.

In the large and noisy crowd outside St. Anthony's School, Gaja could only see skirts and shoes, lunch sacks, knees. Her uncle was supposed to be there and she called, "*Dėde, dėde.*" The crowd kept pushing and a fat lady bumped into her, then gently laid a hand on her head and muttered something.

Gaja found a place next to the wall where she could stand apart from people. She cupped her hands around her mouth and shouted for her uncle.

A man squatted in front of her. She didn't know him. He had big eyes and a thin face—his pointy chin and ears had him resemble a big elf. All of his clothes, including a hat, were black and stiff, and he wore a priest's collar. Gaja understood his speech even though he pronounced Lithuanian words strangely. "Your hair with green ribbon," he said. "You must be Gaja."

She nodded, pressing elbows into the wall.

"Your uncle Benny sends me to take you away. I'm Father Kilba."

Gaja didn't shake his hand.

"You're supposed to come. I takes you to her uncle."

"Where is he?"

"He's over by work."

"But he said he would come get me."

"Yes. True. But he worked hard and he asks me to get you. You don't like it?"

Although the things he said sounded foolish, Father Kilba had a very calm and gentle voice. And the kids around her were so loud, the fat lady shouting over them. She took Kilba's hand.

They walked across the churchyard. Her hand was small enough to hold onto Father Kilba's finger—his skin was so much softer and warmer than her uncle's, and he wore a thin, smooth ring. As they walked, Gaja took a close look at his face and finally recognized him. "I know you," she said. "You give long speeches in church."

"Yes." Father Kilba laughed. "Yes, I do."

"I've seen you before."

"Very good."

They walked through a door and up a narrow stairwell that smelled of cedar. A second door opened up to a kitchen where her uncle was sitting at a table. His hand was wrapped in a thick, bloody bandage, only the tips of his fingers showing. "It's okay," he said. "I hurt myself a little bit."

Gaja stood at a distance. "How?"

"I was fixing a broken window here in Father Kilba's house. It's only a cut. But I think I'll have to go to the doctor."

"To the doctor?"

"I'll only be gone a short time. Come here," he patted his knee. "Come sit on my knee."

Gaja approached reluctantly. When she was close enough, uncle Benny scooped her up with his free hand. She looked at the bandage and was about to touch it before pulling her finger away. The bandage was dark with blood.

"It doesn't hurt," said Benny. "I'll go to the doctor, and when I come back I'll be healed!"

Gaja pressed her hands between her knees.

"I'm sorry I didn't get you from school," uncle said. "Did you get frightened?"

She nodded.

"No, no," said Father Kilba. "She stands boldly."

"Father Kilba's my good friend," her uncle said. "Do you remember? I told you I work for a priest. This is the priest." Gaja waved to Kilba without looking at him. Benny continued: "You'll stay in the rectory while I go to the doctor? I'll be gone just a short time."

"Stay?"

"You can play a game here or maybe you can go to the park. A very short time."

She sighed.

"You're a good girl." Benny lifted her from his knee, kissed her cheek and gently rubbed her shoulder. At the archway, another priest was waiting. Benny waved to Gaja and the priest followed him out of the kitchen to the rectory's front door.

"So," said Father Kilba, clasping his hands together. "Are you hungry?"

Gaja shook her head.

"Her uncle Benny says she like cutlets. I have one. Would you like it?"

"No, thank you," she whispered.

"No? Maybe we'd eat a duck."

"I want to eat when my uncle comes back."

"Want?" asked Kilba. He let her look around the kitchen, but felt he had to fill the silence. "Maybe we can walk on the park? Did you see, they built new things on the park? We can go if it's fun."

"Maybe," said Gaja.

"Are we going?"

Gaja crossed her arms and looked intently at the ceiling. "I have enough coins for ice cream."

They went to the soda fountain at LaVergne's drug store on 14th and shared a fudge sundae. Kilba led Gaja around the store to see if she wanted a little present and she chose a bottle of soap bubbles.

On the way to the park, Gaja held Kilba's finger.

Large groups of children were swinging and running around. Kilba assumed Gaja would want to join them. She took no interest but led him to the bench under the oak tree, and they sat facing the field house. While blowing bubbles, they spoke about what a strange and terrible place school was.

Kilba took her to the swings and pushed her so high that she shrieked from joy and laughed on the way down. The wind blew one of the green ribbons from her hair. She got off the swing only when other children grew impatient for their turns and started whining.

"I have to rest on the bench," she said, a bit out of breath. Gaja sat right next to Kilba, her thigh against his.

She was watching a young couple laughing near the big swings. It was a man with blond hair and thin, very long arms—his girlfriend walked with a cane. Gaja heard the man call her Victoria. She hobbled so awkwardly that Gaja thought she was in pain, but once on the swing the girl flew effortlessly, sweeping quickly through the air in a long powerful arc that scared her boyfriend. He kept telling her things, repeating her name, "Victoria. Vic. Victoria."

Gaja pointed at them. "I want to go high like her," she said.

"No no," said Kilba. "Those swings are for elderly."

Gaja watched Victoria fly through the air. When she finally stopped swinging, the man handed her the cane and she wobbled across the playground, coming closer to Gaja and Kilba.

"It's time to left," said Kilba, but Gaja didn't want to. She was sure the girl would get on the swing again and fly even higher, her long braid flailing behind. Father Kilba had already stood from the bench. "It's time."

They saw uncle Benny come into the park through the gate. He waved to them with his bandaged hand, clean and white. Benny scooped Gaja up. "So...I came to the right place," he said. "Everybody's here."

"Hey, Ben." The blond man came over to Uncle Benny and gripped his forearm to greet him. They jabbered together in that terrible language—Gaja could only understand the blond man's name, Lars. Benny put Gaja down to show Lars the bandage and explain how he had been hurt.

Victoria was sitting by herself, cheeks flushed, her green eyes radiant in the sun. She had a long feminine neck, beautiful black earrings, and kept brushing away a wasp that buzzed near her face. Gaja wanted Victoria to go to the swings again. She imagined that swinging high could cure that painful limp stuck in her body. It could go away; she only needed to swing and it would disappear. Gaja imagined Victoria pulling back on the chains, flying higher than the top of the fence. All on her own, without anyone to push her.

Spring, 1962

1

Victoria Jorgenson was drawing ink into her pen from an inkwell. She wrote most often with an antique fountain pen some relative had owned years ago in Russia, and she wrote daily, sometimes for more than an hour.

Victoria opened to a new page in her journal.

Last night, for the first time in my life, I actually tried to count sheep. I hugged a pillow and imagined sheep with long ears and spiral horns, pink sheep shaved of their wool, a newborn lamb, a black sheep. It jolted me to imagine them being led to slaughter. My point...counting sheep doesn't make me drowsy. It's better to count beach stones. Or the needles of a Christmas tree.

She accidentally hit the inkwell with her elbow and the small bottle was about to tip over, but she reacted quickly and grabbed it.

Alina has to play her recital next month. She doesn't seem nervous, although some things are different about the girl now. At breakfast she plays invisible keys on the table, and yesterday, while lacing her shoes, she was humming that little piece by Debussy, the one for children. Today she asked if I'd finished sewing the bow onto her dress and she stared me down with long, disappointed eyes when she saw the bow on my desk. She's asleep...I just finished sewing a few minutes ago. She'll find the dress hanging by the door in the morning.

Victoria adjusted the lamp. She watched the ink drying into the fibers of the paper—shiny, silvery wet letters. Her head hurt a little, right behind her ears, and she let her hair down to feel a release of tension.

I am imagining ink has spilled onto the rug. I pour salt all over it to try to suck it out, but I know it will always be stained. It's late, early April. Spring, but it's still cold…the mellow boom of the furnace kicks in from time to time, and the radiators knock. Lars is in his den.

He's supposed to be composing, but I know he's wired on coffee and only staring at a blank sheet of paper, biting down on a pencil. He hasn't played a single note all night long and I know his mind is utterly blank. His agitation is filling the entire house, steam whistling through the cracks in the walls and window frames. I can feel the stress in my wrists and knees, in my head. Ink spilled all over the rug, covered in salt.

My frustration becomes anger, but then I calm to pity him, which frustrates me. We've just had our eleventh anniversary and I'm finally wondering why he needs to compose. (That was a difficult sentence to write.) It's an obsession. He sees that it leads him nowhere, but the disease and curse of music can't leave him alone.

Just last Monday, yet another "old friend" from music school, the director of some small symphony, sent him a letter.

"However, I'm sorry to say that your composition will not fit into our planned program."

Lars tore it up. He made a pot of revolting tar coffee, gulped it down in less than a half-hour, and sat staring at a page, biting the pencil.

Victoria heard her husband rustling papers quietly. He soon came out to fill his coffee cup and wash his face with near-scalding water at the kitchen sink. It always amazed Victoria that he could do all these things without making much noise. Whenever she used the sink, the faucet wailed and whined. But the whole house whispered when Lars dealt with it.

He asks me how I can be so calm all the time. The little one cannot see that I'm not calm. It was like the time he asked me, when we had only known each other for a few days, are you crippled? From birth? Yes, crippled from birth. Can't you see?

It's calming to accept that I didn't have the talent to sing, or the body to be on stage. Now I realize I had probably accepted these things when we were at the conservatory together. If he could accept that he's a teacher in a grammar school, an organist in a church, and a father to an eight-year-old girl, it would calm him as well. But he's cursed and sick with music. Crippled from birth.

Victoria drank the rest of her tea before finishing her entry for the evening.

Do I envy him for it? I don't think you can love someone without wanting, at least a little, to be him. That's why at the end of any concert we might hear, inspirational music, I'm just as naïve as Lars. I'm just as unable to accept essential truths. I didn't marry him because he was talented and everyone loved him. I married him because he was talented and everyone hated him. What did you want? I suppose, you naïve little girl, that you wanted exactly what you've got, but now you're too proud to feel pity.

She blew on the wet ink and let it dry before closing the journal. Victoria put all her things away, capping the inkwell and leaving her pen in a small wooden box.

Lars finally played a few notes from his den. His touch was so quiet and gentle...in only a few gestures, he was able to create a bright and warm atmosphere. And he wasn't playing anything at all—Lars' notes searched for other notes and they stumbled, a blind man feeling around a new space with his hands. He gained confidence, playing with less restraint. One passage, a pause, then another. Lars seemed to have constructed something. Now, a different key. Victoria sat at her desk and listened to every detail.

2

Gaja rubbed the haze out of her eyes. She had been suffering from insomnia, and in the dim bedroom she had just enough light to see the hands and numbers of her clock: a quarter to five in the morning.

The thought of getting to work left her feeling like a lump of lead. She'd soon have to deal with the difficult keys of the rectory's black typewriter. The hot chrome of the coffee urn, the smell of burnt coffee grounds. The telephone's steely ring over the mass of children playing outside her window. Uncle Benny making noise in another of the rectory's rooms, drilling a hole, hammering nails. A neighborhood woman, she came unannounced, she needed a baptism, she wanted to arrange a wedding—she demanded, insisted on a day that was unavailable. A man needed to see one of the priests very urgently, his hands in his pockets, his body hanging there in front of Gaja's desk.

She needed to eat. Gaja dragged her feet to the kitchen and prepared breakfast, mashing a few boiled eggs into mayonnaise, cutting a slice of day-old pumpernickel brick, and she sat by the window.

Uncle Benny had been out drinking at the Corner Billiard Club the previous night. His snoring was always very loud when he got drunk. Their house was small, only four rooms, but the walls were built thick and sounds did not carry well—even so, she could hear him from the kitchen. Gaja sipped her steaming coffee and imagined how loud he would be if she opened his bedroom door. Pinching his nose for five seconds would stop the snoring, at least for a quarter hour, but his room probably smelled like the bar: stale beer and the bodies of grown, unwashed men.

Finished with breakfast, she dressed and smoked one of her uncle's stronger cigarettes.

He had a comfortable reading chair in the front room where she rarely got a chance to sit. Gaja liked the chair but couldn't stand the room. Her uncle had built virtually everything in it: the coffee table, the sofa, the end tables and the bookcases. The entire house was full of his knick knacks, vases and decorative clay bowls—the walls throughout the house were paneled in thin, interlocking wooden panels he had cut in his garage, which was more or less a carpenter's shop. Gaja liked the paneling because of its warm tone, but her uncle's furniture was hard and uncomfortable. Only his reading chair, inherited from a dead friend, had smooth, dark leather and cushions that embraced her.

Besides furniture and house wares, Benny made various kinds of folk art, most often from driftwood collected in Michigan. There was one piece entirely of grayish white sticks sanded smooth by beach winds; they were arranged to form a kind of sun, a crude and small octagon with radiating rays.

The Lithuanian mask on the far wall, a demon called *Velnias,* always tempted Gaja's attention—she wished she could resist but usually glanced its way when sitting in Benny's chair. Why were his empty eyes and mouth, single nostril and grotesque features so fascinating? It was like Benny was tricking her to look at demons.

She was not finished with her cigarette but put it out and went to get her coat. Before leaving, she prayed, as she often did, for God to forgive her uncle all his strange and evil thoughts.

The overcast April morning was cool, foggy and somewhat humid. The scent in the air anticipated rain. The street lamps were still on—their glowing amber ovals did not cast any light but appeared to float freely in the fog among thin branches. Gaja's block was unusually still, nobody out walking to the L station or bus stops. Farther down, the Heating Oil and Coal Company, which on most mornings had delivery trucks purring and people bustling about, remained empty of even a single customer. A man tacked something to the wall in the dimly lit office.

Gaja walked past St. Anthony's parish and reached 14th Street when she heard the tower chimes signal six o'clock. Only a few businesses were open so early: the lights were on at Carry's Bakery, and Sherwin's Fruit Market was taking deliveries. She could smell the fresh bread and cakes and wanted to sit down for more coffee.

The bakery's door was locked. Gaja saw Mrs. Carry swaying her big hips back and forth as she carried a tray of rolls—she hurried to stack them in a little basket. Gaja wanted to shout, "Don't rush!" but she also wanted to say, "At least open the door." She only leaned back against the front glass and faced the street.

In the fog, a figure slowly waddled toward her from Laramie Avenue. Gaja stared at him and soon recognized Lars' peculiar gait—he did not set his feet down in front of him but whipped them out at his sides. An empty canvas shopping bag dangled from his hand. Although he was short and on the stockier side, he was lanky, arms too long for the rest of his body, almost as long as his unbuttoned overcoat, the ends of its belt flaying about.

He raised his eyebrows when he saw Gaja. Lars pulled at the door, loudly banging it around several times. He checked his watch, briskly rubbed his nape and pulled at the door again. "Hey hey, crew. Morning morning."

"They know they're late, Mr. Jorgenson."

"Late," said Lars. He leaned next to Gaja to also face the street. "Late and late. Sure...been the same ever since old man Carry died." He pointed at her. "Gaja, you're too young to know, but that man was a wizard." Lars started laughing and Gaja wondered if there was ever a time when he wasn't hyper. "Good man, Carry. It was really something around here in those days."

Lars babbled on, but Gaja wasn't very interested in him. She thought he was a fool, one of her uncle's drinking buddies, a hypocrite who would never go to church if not for an organ and the group of choir singers he ordered around. "Old man Carry owned that bar and sometimes I played piano..." She had lost track of what he was saying, focusing instead on his face and unwashed hair. His slender nose had turned red from the cool morning air, and eczema or some mild rash had broken out on his chin. A hair in one of his nostrils needed to be plucked. "Gaja," he said, his beady eyes now stuck on her. "Hello? You don't feel like answering me?"

"I'm sorry. Oh?"

"You daydreamin'?"

"A little…"

"Sure, sure." Lars did not appear offended. "Try this." He stood up on his tiptoes while taking a deep breath and bent his knees slightly when gently exhaling *ahh.*

"I'm sorry," said Gaja. "What were you saying?"

"Saying? Nothing. Small talk. Just asked why you're out so early. Benny sent you for bread so early?"

"My uncle? No."

"No? I'm glad I'm not the only early bird."

"I'm just on my way to work."

"Work! Honestly? Kilba, slave driver! You answer his phone on Saturdays? I thought you were just the weekday girl. Since when?"

Gaja's shoulders sank. "It's Saturday?"

Lars raised his blond eyebrows and stuck out his chin. He tilted his head slightly. "I think so."

3

Sitting at the edge of her bed, Victoria used a corner of a sheet to wipe fingerprints from her glasses. She looked over the six canes kept in a cylinder by her bedside and thought about which one she would choose for the day.

All her canes were wooden except for one, made of ivory and some metal—it looked like wrought iron, but she wasn't sure. Victoria never used the ivory cane to help her walk; it was expensive, decorative and already had a small crack. That cane, like her fountain pen, was among her few possessions left over from the time before her parents had been displaced from Russia, one of the few objects Victoria had not given away or sold after their deaths. She would have hung the cane on a wall, but Lars wouldn't let her.

The canes she used most often were very simple: a straight mahogany shaft with a pointy metal end, a varnished and sanded branch of oak, cherry carved to look like a braid of hair, and a common dime-store hook of pine. Depending on what she wore, the canes complemented certain outfits perfectly.

With every new year of her marriage, she used one last cane less and less. Lars had given it to her just days after she had accepted his proposal. The black cane had a polished marble handle. A thin ring of mother of pearl, set into the cane's wood, divided it in half. It was endearing to know that Lars had found such a tacky thing beautiful. Victoria had said it was unique and would have to be saved for special occasions. She took it to places like the theater or cinema where it was dark and where people she knew were unlikely to show up.

She remembered, putting on her glasses, how often Lars used to take her to the theater. On one night early in their marriage, Alina not yet born, they went to see an embarrassingly bad production of *Romeo and Juliet*. After the play, Lars and Victoria got slaphappy drunk in their front room and mocked scenes from the performance, hooking arms to drink cognac, falling away from each other in swoons. "Don't forget that moon," said Lars. He cut a crescent out from a newspaper and Victoria laughed when he licked it to stick to a window. They continued mocking the actors' exaggerated movements and drank shots the whole time.

Victoria kissed him with a mouthful of cognac and he drank it down. They fondled each other, pulled at clothes and buttons. She tickled Lars when he tried to kiss her with another mouthful of booze, and he squirmed away, the liquor dripping down both their chins, all over their clothing. When he looked for something to wipe his face, Victoria hiked up her skirt, took off her underwear and tossed it onto his head. She lay back on the sofa, bringing her knees up to her belly. "Enough games, Jorgenson. Enough kissing games."

He wiped his face with the underwear and flung it away. "Oh...straightforward? No bullshit." Lars lifted his shirt over his head and the cuffs, still buttoned, got stuck at his wrists. Victoria laughed again, her hands on her belly, her knees falling to the side. "Minor detail," said Lars, struggling with the shirt. He finally got it off, tossed it onto a chair and wrestled with his belt and trousers. They fell to his ankles and Lars stepped out of them, stumbling. Victoria pointed at him, "Oh..."

"What...no salute?" he grabbed and held his dick. Victoria tried but couldn't keep from giggling—it had never happened to Lars before. "I had one this morning..."

"Sorry...I'm not laughing. I'm not."

He lifted the bottle from the table and put a hand on his hip, doing his best to be nonchalant. "Ladies and gentlemen." He drank. "Due to unforeseen circumstances, this evening's show is...yes, drive home safely."

"Oh, come on!" Victoria sat up and patted the sofa. "Lars, it's okay. Who cares? Come here."

He looked over the coffee table, his hand on his chin. "No no. Enough games. Enough." Lars set the bottle down and picked up various things: a fountain pen, two letter openers, a slender statuette of a ballerina. He returned to the bottle, which still had some cognac at the bottom. Lars thought about drinking it off but instead looked for a place to pour it. With his other hand, he lifted an intriguing candlestick holder.

"That's stupid," Victoria said. "Find something else." She lay back again.

Lars lost his perplexed look when he saw the black cane leaning against a nearby bookshelf. He hastily stepped over a footstool to take it, but hesitated when he approached Victoria. He held it with two hands and looked down at her. "What?" she asked.

"I..." He shrugged with one shoulder, shifting his weight from leg to leg. "I mean...would you?"

"Would *you*?"

"I'm..." He knelt down by the sofa. "Just with the handle."

"Do it."

Lars grew boyish and nervous in a way Victoria had not seen since well before their marriage. He moved her closer to the sofa's edge, and she rested the sole of one foot against his shoulder—his arm trembled slightly, but his body was warm. Lars handled the cane carefully, apparently thinking it might hurt her. It did not feel particularly good for Victoria, but she loved his expression, a mix of stiff unease and innocent curiosity. Lars was easiest to love when he was youthful and most youthful when he discovered new ways to feel safe with her. In time, he relaxed and was soon able to look her in the eye. Lars and Victoria peered intensely into one another. When she least expected it, feeling entirely settled and calm, Lars pulled the handle out, lightly set the cane on the floor and showed her. "Turns out the cane job inspired a salute." He got on top to fuck.

Victoria had not remembered that night in a long time. Still in her bedroom, she wiped her glasses again even though they were perfectly clean. She slid the black cane out of the bedside cylinder and pressed her weight against it to stand.

Walking did not cause her any pain, although her hobble was extreme through the morning's earliest steps. She stepped carefully to the kitchen and set the table for breakfast, cutting salami and smoked cheese. The kettle whistled. Victoria made a pot of strong black tea and drank two cups before Lars returned with bread. He came up from the deep stairwell and brought in the smell of fresh rolls. "Alina up yet?" he whispered.

"Not a stir."

"Sorry it took so long." Lars hung his coat on a chair. "They opened late." He placed the Kaiser rolls, a custard bismark for Alina, and a loaf of rye into a large wooden bowl. The rolls, his favorite, were still warm. He broke one in half, the crust crisp, and slapped a piece of salami onto it, wiping his fingers on his trousers. "Guess who I ran into."

"Who?"

"From the past. One of my former pupils."

"Who?"

"Guess."

"Lars." Victoria hated this sort of thing. "Who was it?"

"Gaja Laputis."

"Oh?"

"Call me a lunatic. But I realized something. Tell me if this is something good to realize." Lars brushed crumbs around his plate with a pinky. He bit the sandwich and talked while chewing. "Do you know? You are married to a guy who..." he swallowed. "I have been a teacher long enough...and now there are former pupils old enough to create new pupils. I'm on that verge. Isn't she around eighteen right now or something like that? In a few years, I might have a second generation of pupils."

Victoria smiled at him. "Was this a sudden realization?"

"Well, sudden. Not one of these, boom, right here in the bakery." Lars poured tea. "I was wandering around, and my gears were turning." He slurped when he drank.

"Lars, how many times do I have to ask you not to slurp?"

"It tastes better."

"Tastes," she mumbled and nibbled on a piece of cheese. "Did you come to bed at all last night?"

"No," Lars snorted quietly. "Last night. Composing. I got some ideas. I don't know how I feel about them. They're...eh." Lars perked up. "Hey!" He pointed to the black cane. "Why do you have that one out?"

"Oh. I don't know. I felt like it."

"No way." Lars stood and reached for it over the corner of the table. "You can't take that one out."

She held it away. "Why not?"

"No way." He grabbed it. "We're just...for breakfast at home? Pick another one."

Victoria held onto the cane firmly. "Lars. Let go of it."

"Vic, come on."

"Jorgenson!"

"Okay. Fine." He let go. "I'll go put on a good suit." He turned to go to their bedroom. Alina, still in her pajamas, blocked his path in the archway leading out of the kitchen. She rubbed the side of her head with a closed fist. "It smells like the bakery in here," she said.

4

Monsignor Kilba was surprised to find he had no appointments that Saturday. He looked over the appointment book again. Lent was a very busy time for the parish, and Gaja rarely made mistakes when handling the appointments. Kilba trusted his schedule contained only afternoon confessions.

As much as Kilba longed for free time, he never knew what to do once it came around. His study was full of unread, half-finished books and old records he had not listened to in years. Letters needed to be returned and some of them were important. But maybe he should just take a nice walk.

He really did need to tidy up. Kilba's fig tree had dropped round yellow leaves all over the blue rug. His desk was cluttered with old teacups, newspapers, church pamphlets, bent paperclips, a broken shoelace, a scotch snifter. Benny Laputis had given Kilba several small figurines as presents. A snoozing fisherman lay at the base of the desk lamp and a barefoot boy with a straw hat mischievously packed a pipe on the windowsill. A sack of unread and overdue library books was next to this fisherman. But Kilba only sat at the window and cleaned his nails with a letter opener.

The knock on his door was gentle and slow, so faint that Kilba thought it might have been down the hall. The person knocked again. "Come in. Yes. I'm here. Open."

The door creaked a little. Benny stuck his head into Kilba's study.

"Oh, it's you," said Kilba.

Benny whispered, "You are busy?"

"I'm writing my own funeral sermon."

"I can come in?"

The monsignor gestured to the chair in front of his desk with an open palm.

Benny hung his heavy jacket, the pockets weighed down by many sets of keys, on a rack. His movements were always slow and careful, and he gripped things very tightly when he handled them. His hands looked big on his small, stocky body and his skin was quite dark for a man born in the Baltic States. Even though he had shaved, his face looked rough, the lines in his forehead deep. Benny's eyes, bright amber under thin eyebrows, were always striking. His crown had been bald for many years, but he did not like to expose it and was rarely seen without his dark blue cap. It was against Catholic custom for men to have their heads covered indoors, especially in a rectory, but Kilba tolerated it.

Although Kilba had been Benny's boss and friend for fourteen years, the Monsignor felt like he depended on Benny more than Benny depended on him. Like most parishioners, he was a World War II refugee, a displaced person. He had fled Lithuania and had arrived in Cicero, drawn by the large community of Lithuanians established after the first World War. Except for Gaja, an infant during the war, Benny's entire family had been killed or deported to Siberia before he could leave Europe. On one hand, Kilba felt sorry for Benny and sometimes pitied him. But Kilba, born in the States to 19th-century Lithuanian immigrants, did not know war. Benny's life experience was so much more grand, so much more complicated and terrible than anything Kilba had ever seen, that he often felt naïve and foolish about pitying him.

"You need some tea or something?" Kilba asked. "Seltzer?"

Benny sat. He shrugged and shook his head, lethargic.

"Are you all right? You look hung over."

"Hung over?" Benny asked. "Maybe, little. Having funny morning."

"Funny? You just need something hot to drink."

"I feel decent." Benny wrapped his fist in a calloused hand.

"Well, let me get you something."

Benny didn't want anything, but Kilba left the study, his steps slowly fading down the hall.

Benny heard kids playing in the churchyard, and a boy's stick sometimes made contact with a ball. The birds were out and a light breeze puffed out Kilba's translucent white curtain and lifted the corner of a newspaper on his desk. Benny's pain returned, a knotted sharpness behind the ribcage—it felt like a growing nest of knives. The pain was worse than it had been the previous night. It surged and he put his hand to his ribs but took it away when he heard Kilba returning.

The Monsignor was holding a teapot wrapped in a dishtowel. Two cups dangled from his ring finger. "All right. Sorry about that." Kilba sat down, a bit out of breath. "Cup for you."

"Later, maybe."

"Good." Kilba poured only for himself. "So...what's going on, Benny?"

"Monsignor," Benny said. "You saw maybe Gaja this morning?"

"In this place? No." Kilba scratched the inside of his ear. "Why?"

"This morning. Very early. Gaja went to some place."

"Really? And she didn't tell you where?" There was playful but sensitive sarcasm to Kilba's words. Gaja rarely told anyone where she was going.

"I have idea where. Small idea," said Benny. "Have to ask you question."

"Please."

Benny cracked a knuckle by pinching it between his thumb and ring finger. "You are talking to her very much lately?"

"You mean...you mean discussing, what? Her personal problems?"

"Personal."

Kilba smiled. "Well...what do you think?"

"No. I not meaning regular conversations, Monsignor." Benny pulled the chair closer to Kilba's desk. "I mean about another thing. About confession." He paused, pressing a hand to his ribs. "Sometimes to you she comes in confession?"

"Now wait a second." The question surprised Kilba. "First of all, no. But even if she did, I wouldn't be telling you anything about it."

"She doesn't come?"

"I know she goes but always to the other priests." Kilba's fingers interlocked and he set his hands in his lap. "Ben, she

137

doesn't want me to know. I haven't heard one of her confessions since she was in school."

"Monsignor." He paused for a moment, his eyes softening. "I had a strong dream in the night."

"Really?" Kilba never knew what to make of Benny's fascination with his own dreams. Benny was very superstitious about them, but Kilba could never find any logic or system behind his interpretations. Still, the Monsignor was one of the few people who would listen to Benny describe them. "What was it?"

"The war. We were running. Going on bridge over river."

Kilba listened.

"I saw my sister. Gaja's mother. It was one kind of dream where all of things happens all together." Benny lightly waved his hands around. "We were running, but she was talking to me. And I could understand. My sister was saying, *Tell her*. Almost begging..." Benny now pressed his hands together, shook them and shut his eyes tightly. "I am worried for my Gaja, that's all, and I want to know. If you know something and don't tell it me, I want to know."

"I can assure you."

"I think..." Benny seemed to withdraw—his gaze dropped to the floor and he pressed his knees together, pushing his hands hard against his abdomen. He took a few short and quick breaths. "Sorry."

"Hey...you okay?" Kilba's voice was gentle. "Did you eat something bad? What's the matter?"

"You know. It's catching me."

"It? What's *it*?" Kilba scanned Benny's hardened face. "What's catching you Benny?"

"Everything." He spoke slowly. "Time. War. Work. I'm sorry, Monsignor." He sighed lightly and eased up. "This morning, I wanted nothing, just to wake up and work in garage. Have beer, listen radio. But you know about it. It comes for all men. Time when you know."

Kilba leaned onto the desk with his elbows. "Know what?"

"Know. What you think? I not healthy. I not have very much more time."

"*Benny*." Kilba hated this kind of talk. "You're on about nonsense. You have no way of knowing. Go see a doctor. You're as strong and stubborn as a mule. Believe it."

"Monsignor." Benny stared into him so thoroughly that Kilba had to lean back. "*You* believe it. I know how I feel. I didn't come for sermon. I have important thing to say."

The Monsignor nodded. "Yes, please."

Benny placed a loose fist on Kilba's desk. "I need for you to make promise."

"That's a dangerous word."

"No. Is very serious, Monsignor. I must need your promise."

"Are you telling me you want to confess something?"

"Eh..." Benny forced a laugh. "So typical. Say word *confession,* then you can make it promise. But without *confession,* promise impossible, yes?" Benny smirked. "In dark chamber, you are hearing strangers' secrets, never tell anyone. Oh, sure! *Confession.*" Kilba had never seen Benny as agitated—the little man shut his eyes tightly and a hand fell against his knee. "I tell you my confession." He got up from the chair.

"Wait, don't leave! What, you're leaving?"

Benny was searching through the pockets of the jacket. It took only a moment to find what he needed. He returned to the desk and lightly set down a small leather book. "Look in."

Kilba found an old photograph, yellowed and creased, of a handsome young man. He had pronounced cheekbones, a high and smooth brow, his expression austere and rather noble; even from the small snapshot, Kilba sensed the man's charisma and strength. He was dressed in a formal military uniform and had been decorated, a cluster of medals on his left breast. Kilba did not know much about uniforms but could tell the man had been a distinguished, high-ranking officer. Small, scripted letters read *Arvydas Laputis, Lietuvos Vandens Kelių Ministras*: Lithuanian Minister of Waterways. "This my father," said Benny. He rubbed his lips with an open palm. "Powerful man. Rich man. Owned land."

"Your father was in government." Kilba set the photo down. "I didn't know."

"Well, I never tell you. Nobody knows. Monsignor, I never tell Gaja nothing. About war, about family. About him. About *my* father." A single, fast tear rolled over Benny's cheekbone and, leaving a thin streak on his face, fell onto the cuff of his shirt. "Nothing."

Kilba slowly nodded and leaned back into his chair, crossing his arms.

"I know what Gaja says to you," Benny continued. "She tells you pray for me. Because I am sinner. Because I don't go to the mass, because I eat smoked bacon on Friday, work on Sunday. For me, maybe you pray. What you pray, I don't know. If you pray what she says, you are praying wrong prayers."

Kilba only listened.

"Sometimes, you are praying for her?" Benny asked.

Kilba nodded, shrugging lightly.

"Also probably those prayers, they for wrong things. I will tell you. This morning. Very early. Gaja goes to be in bed with boy. What you think about it?"

Kilba hesitated. "Benny...if she has a lover...that means. She's not married and that's not the best thing in the church's eyes. But Gaja is a good person. The church's eyes are not necessarily God's."

"Blind," said Benny. "Your church. Not wrong for Gaja to be with boy. Not wrong. What wrong is how she thinks...she feels she must hide. Hide him from me. From you. From everyone."

"You could be right," said Kilba.

"Together...this our fault together. Your church teaches wrong to be with boy. And I am teaching everything is silent. Quiet. Hide everything. And now I'm having strong dream about my sister. Very strong dream. And this pain, right here," he held his ribs, "on my side. For long time. I cannot hide anymore. I must tell. And you must forgive me."

"Forgive you?"

"I am not Gaja's uncle."

Kilba listened.

"I mean...yes, true, I am uncle. But I am also brother. Half-brother. Gaja's mother is my sister, young sister. And my father..." He pointed to the photograph. "Also, he is Gaja's father."

Kilba leaned toward him.

Benny spoke quickly: "It is true. I know this very certain. Gaja's mother my youngest sister." He slowed down. "She was sixteen and...it happened...it was happening many times. I know. But we all hide. Everybody quiet, look away, pretend, lie. Nobody say or do nothing." Again, a breeze ruffled Monsignor Kilba's curtain. "Except me. I do something."

"You?"

"Before war, I believed in God. I believed strong. God is good. I pray to Him. Pray so hard, maybe every night. To kill him. Dear God, kill father, kill him now. Please. Like that I never prayed again. Never since and never before. At night, for hours, in dark room, in stable, in orchard. I promised, God, if you kill him, I will never be with woman. I will live without woman if you kill him. And, you know what happens?" Benny laughed through his nose. "Yes...of course. Yes. He dies. Very soon." Benny now seemed perfectly calm. "A horse kicks him in head. My father's best, most favorite horse. Violent crushing. It happens in front my eyes." He pointed at his forehead, paused and almost smiled. "I am like you. Just like you, Monsignor. And I am also like Gaja. We all pray wrong prayer."

"I don't understand."

"I only pray for father to die. I didn't think about all possibility, of big picture. He is dead for eight months, but then Gaja is born. 1944. I never imagine this part. Or next part because they find my sister, Gaja's mother, later on. They find her dead in river. And then...what?" He waved a hand. "You know story. The Soviets come. And my whole family. Everyone." He coughed into a fist. "Only me and Gaja live. That's all."

They shared the silence together. One of the other priests walked down the hall and closed a door. Benny said, "She was always asking many question. Rarely about mother. Mostly about father. So many question. Even so recently."

"What does she think?" asked Kilba.

"She? Nothing. I tell many lies. She believes all photos lost in war."

Kilba interrupted him. "Benny...if you're asking me advice, I don't know what to say. If you feel you've sinned, perhaps...perhaps your suffering has been your penance. I can't tell you that you need to be forgiven for anything."

"But, Monsignor, I must need that you promise me."

"What can I possibly do?"

"Promise me, in future, you will watch over Gaja. Even if she is not trusting you and you don't know her confessions. You still watch over."

"Benny...I honestly believe, with all my heart, that you'll be around for many more years."

"Good. Believe it. But promise me...promise if she has child...if she ever has child, that you watch over." Benny reached out and tightly grabbed Kilba by the wrist. "And do something if troubles there. Any troubles."

Kilba managed to hold back a sigh.

"I must need it," said Benny.

"Benny."

He pressed Kilba's wrist, the tight grip driving down to the bones. "Please."

Kilba looked Benny in the eye and nodded. "I promise. I do, Benny. I promise."

5

Bronza Dilienko, 39 or 40 years old, was living in the Karavan Motel. He was sitting on his bed and eating sprats from a tin, using crusty bread to sop up the fish oil. Occasionally, he took bites from a raw cucumber and wiped his mouth with one of the motel's white towels.

The motel, while affordable, was not run down. The walls had been freshly painted, the carpets and furniture relatively new. It was day, but Bronza liked keeping the drapes drawn—his window faced Cicero Avenue, nothing to see but passing cars, rumbling trucks and the dirty, bleak machine shop across the street. And the drapes' pattern of little white butterflies, while tasteless, calmed him.

His morning had been busy. He had known for weeks that the job at the Cicero Family Clinic would be his, but that morning it had become official. He was looking to buy a house within walking distance of the clinic, and had littered his floor, the bed and the top of the little dresser with every possible real estate advertisement, pamphlets from agencies. Quite a few people were selling houses in Cicero, and Dilienko could afford virtually any one of them.

Finished with his meal, he got ready for another walk, just to check out another part of the neighborhood and to have a look at some of the houses. Bronza had been in Cicero long enough to know that most of the good houses were south of 16th. The trees lining the streets tended to be tall and leafy, and people took good care of their properties.

He walked for many blocks and soon came to a park. A sign on the small gate read, *Welcome to Park Holme. Please put litter in its place.* A field house stood in the south end, right next to a public swimming pool, a few asphalt tennis courts and a playground with swings, slides and a sandbox. Off center from the large lawn grew a broad old oak tree. Dilienko sat at the bench underneath to rest before heading back to the Karavan.

Something hit him in the head. He guessed an acorn had fallen from the tree. Soon another green acorn bounced off the bench and one more landed in front of his shoes. He heard a girl's voice quietly sing, "Catch a falling star and put it in your pocket," and an acorn hit him on the shoulder. When Bronza looked up into the tree, children laughed.

He got up and calmly said, "Who's up there?" Two pairs of little legs dangled from a thick branch. A boy sang, "Save it for a rainy day," and an acorn hit Bronza right in the eyebrow.

The shot's accuracy surprised him and his hand shot up from sheer reflex. He doubled forward, got down on his knees, and pressed his forehead into the grass, rocking back and forth. "My eye!" he said, "my eye," the ground muffling his voice.

"You're in trouble now, Reikel," said Alina.

"No way. You says to do it."

"Not me."

"It ain't me, 'cause you started it, 'Lina. All this is your idea."

"You threw it. You hit him."

Reikel hurried down to the lawn. When he finally stood next to the man, Alina following close behind, he had no idea what to do. He knelt down next to Bronza and asked, "You okay, Mister?"

"I can't see."

"You bleedin'?"

Alina came by. "He's really sorry. He didn't mean it."

"No," said Reikel, "I ain't meant no harm."

"I can't see."

Reikel was completely pale. He stood from the ground and shoved his hands deep in his pockets, twisting his toes into the grass as he backed away from the man. He wanted to say he was sorry again—he wanted the man to stand up and show how badly the eye was hurt, but Reikel knew he'd be afraid to look. He turned and ran from the park, shuffling between parked cars and disappearing into someone's gangway where he cut through a yard and into an alley.

Alina had never seen him run quite so fast. Reikel was long gone when the man knelt up and put his hands on his knees. His face was clean of blood and both his eyes were open. A few loose blades of grass had stuck to his forehead and cheeks. "Are you okay?" Alina asked.

"It's a miracle," he said. "My eye grew back."

"We're sorry."

Bronza got up from the ground to sit again on the bench. He crossed his legs and looked through his pockets for cigarettes. "Your little friend frightens easily."

"You scared him on purpose."

"His name's Reikel," said Bronza. The cigarettes were inside his sport jacket. Two remained in the pack. "Right?"

Alina nodded.

"And you." Bronza had to find his matches. "You're Alina?"

Alina nodded again, slower this time.

Bronza held out his hand. "My name's Dilienko," he said. "Dr. Yuri Dilienko. But if you want to be my friend, you have to call me Bronza."

Alina did not want to be his friend. She shook his hand only to be polite. "Hello."

"Can I ask you another question?" Bronza was sure he had brought the matches along, and they must have been in one pocket or another.

Alina stood still. "Okay."

He asked her, "У тебя доме говорят по-русски?"—if she spoke Russian at home.

"No," she replied.

"No?" Bronza stared at her skeptically. "But you understood me." He waited. "Your name's Alina."

"So."

"Is your father from Russia?"

"Yes," she lied. She did not know why.

"Do you know what part of Russia he's from, Alina?"

She shook her head.

"Hmm. What's your last name?"

She shrugged.

"You don't have to be afraid of me, Alina." By this point, he had gone through all of his pockets several times. "You can tell me." He gave up searching and hid the cigarette in his fist. "You can."

They said nothing to each other. Alina spotted the book of matches lying in the grass. All she wanted was to find Reikel.

"I'm new here," said Bronza. "I've never been in this park before. I used to know a lot of Russians. A long time ago—in another place. I'm an immigrant, probably like your father, but I'm not Russian. I'm Ukrainian. Do you know where Ukraine is?"

Alina shrugged.

"It doesn't matter." He brushed a hand through his hair. "I get along well with Russian people. Perhaps you'll tell your father you met me. Tell him you met Bronza in the park."

Alina nodded. At that moment, St. Anthony's church bells chimed their little song. "The bells," she said. "I'm late! Have to go home because I'll be in trouble."

"You need to go find Reikel," said Bronza. "He ran that way."

"Okay, bye." Alina hurried in Reikel's direction but stopped after only a few steps. She stepped over to where the matches were lying in the grass and gave them to Bronza. "Yes!" he said. "Exactly what I was looking for." He struck one on the book, and Alina left Park Holme.

6

Benny sat in his reading chair wearing only a sleeveless, loose undershirt and thin, beige trousers. His belt was unbuckled and he was resting his feet on a little footstool. Smoke rose from a cigarette in the ashtray on his leg. An empty beer bottle was stuffed between his thigh and the chair's armrest.

Gaja told him again, in Lithuanian: "*Nemeluoju tau!*" that she wasn't lying. She pressed a fist between the sofa cushions.

"*Kodėl tu bijei prisipažint?*"

"I don't have a boyfriend," she pleaded. "If I had one, I'd admit it. I'm telling you."

"Gaja, don't raise your voice, please." In Lithuanian, even after a few beers, Benny was articulate and spoke clearly, as would a radio announcer. "I'll be willing to believe you, naturally, if you tell me where you go when I'm away. And now you've started doing it early in the mornings."

She repeated, for the last time, that she had made a mistake and dressed for work. The wrinkled, dark red skirt was on her lap to prove it. Jorgenson had seen her, and uncle Benny could call him if he wanted, or he could ask him next time they met in the bar.

"All right," Benny continued. "Just for the sake of it, let's say you're capable of such a mistake. Actually, let's ignore what happened this morning. Where do you go all those other times? Where do you go when I'm in the bar?"

"I walk around. Nowhere. Just here. Just nowhere."

"You wander the streets?"

"More or less."

Benny laughed, smoke leaving his mouth like exhaust from a pipe. He pressed the cigarette out and went to the kitchen. She heard him open another bottle and toss the empty into a bin. Gaja wanted to say, "You drink too much. You should worry about yourself," but sat quietly, hoped he'd go to his room to watch television.

He spoke from the kitchen. "It's not that I care where you're going. We both know what's possible to do in this neighborhood. But why can't you tell me? What are you afraid of?"

"I walk."

"Sure. Of course." Her uncle appeared in the archway, the newly opened beer against his belly. "There's not a minute of your day that isn't planned to the second. You even take an iron to your socks. If you could, you'd catch the dust before it landed on your things. Your nails are perfectly filed." Benny came closer to her. "Gaja, before you think, you think about thinking. But, naturally, you're also the kind of person who will wander around the streets for no reason?" He headed toward his room. "Good night." Before he closed the door, he said, in English: "Go for walk."

Gaja put a knuckle to her forehead and closed her eyes. She pinched the bridge of her nose and sighed. Why was he constantly accusing her of things? All at once, she felt urges to laugh and to shout, to kick things around the room, but also to fall back onto the sofa and sleep. Gaja only paced around the little house and decided, finally, to have a quiet, very hot bath.

She smoked three cigarettes in the tub and remained in the water until it grew cold and gray. When she dried herself, it angered her to find Benny had wiped his dirty face in her freshly washed towel.

She was tired but too angry for bed. A glass of red wine or brandy, some sweet liqueur was tempting, but Gaja didn't want to be like him, drinking to fall asleep. Cups of chamomile tea, games of solitaire, chapters from a book she was reading, quiet music over her radio, and simple memories of her few high school boyfriends passed the time. Yet the minutes dragged and Gaja soon found herself in the trap of insomnia, lying on her back, her eyes so tired they stung while her mind drove fast and loud.

She kept a small trunk in the corner of her room where she locked all her most secret things. Gaja took the key from its hiding place in an old box of matches.

Among childhood toys, small dolls and wooden horses, school yearbooks and unused picture frames lay an old and battered music box. Gaja held it in her lap. She was surprised—it was easy to hold the box again, and she was now eager to open it. The tiny brass music machine was broken and silent. Only a few items lay inside: four letters and a keychain attached to a leather elm leaf. Cursive letters had been burned into the leaf, one side reading *Hobie Day Parade, 1959* and the other *Gaja Laputis & Stan Lemke.*

She flipped through the letters and found the last one he had sent:

November 18, 1961
Philadelphia

Dear Gaja,

Got your letter.

I remember what you said to me. "You're a coward. If you had any courage you'd stay or take me with you." It wasn't true. It wasn't true and you should never have said that to me. I wish you had said something different before I left Cicero because I often think about you and only remember what you said.

You're right. I know we made a whole lot of promises. You said you would write me letters and I also said I would write. We said there would be visits, but now there's all these letters about how we can't visit each other. This is Philadelphia, far from Cicero.

Gaja skipped some paragraphs.

Sometimes you just have to take a look at what you've got in front and you can't look anywhere else, because it doesn't make any sense. You can't look back. That's why this is the last letter I'll ever write. I'm writing to say good-bye. I don't know how to say it nicely and I don't know if it's possible to say good-bye nicely. I'm sorry. But that's what this letter needs to say.

The letter continued repeating itself this way for several more pages. Gaja skimmed to the part she remembered the most.

I'm babbling. God...I'm really babbling and I don't even know if I'll send this letter. If you really want me to be courageous and to tell you the truth, I'll tell you. You need help, Gaja. You need someone to take you and tell you how crazy you are. I used to be confused about you. How could such a beautiful girl be so indecent? I was afraid to tell you that. What you want is impossible. You can't have it both ways. You want me to marry you and take you away, but you don't want children. Gaja, you're lucky. Hell, we're so so so lucky that you don't already have a baby! I wanted to tell you so many times. It's luck, Gaja. That's all it is. It's not prayer or the power of God or anything like that. Just luck. Maybe you think you're more powerful or special or religious...I don't know what. But you're really just lucky, Gaja. I know you're rolling your eyes at me. It's really sad if you are.

Gaja put the letters back to the music box, returned it to the trunk, locked it, placed the blankets back on top, turned off her light and lay down. She lay awake most of the night, Stan's sentences a carousel in her head.

The next morning she came late to Sunday Mass. She had forgotten her missal, could not concentrate on any of the prayers and daydreamt through Kilba's sermon, perking up briefly only when Lars played the organ and the choir sang. She knelt and stood when the congregation did, but Gaja was only thinking of Stan.

Freshman year, high school. His locker was next to hers and Gaja often left the building with him after the final bell. She had kissed a few boys before kissing Stan, but Gaja was Stan's first kiss. A collision of cold noses, a tremble in his lips: she loved remembering it. When it was finished, Stan wouldn't look at her. He hugged her, she knew, his chin on her shoulder, just to keep from looking.

When she opened her blouse for him the first time, she had to take his hand and put it on her breast. When they lay together naked in the dark of his mother's empty house, the nightlight off, the curtain drawn, she had to move Stan's hands to discover her body, press his finger inside her. Whenever they found themselves learning something new, Stan would say, "Gaja, we don't have to do *that*."

She and Stan were at his stepmother Amanda's house. The woman was making them a meal in the kitchen and they were up in the attic. Gaja kept kissing him and he said, "Geez! She's down there. It's almost dinner time." Gaja felt his hard dick on her thigh. When she touched it through his pants, Stan said, "Stop it," and moved over to the corner where the ceiling met the floor at an angle. He sat down and crossed his legs.

The attic had only one small window. The sun was setting and the dusty light was sharp and yellow. Without hesitating, Gaja quickly unbuttoned her blouse and let it fall from her arms. "Don't..." Soon her bra and skirt fell to the rug and Gaja stood in the warm air and light wearing only her shoes. "Please put it back on," Stan said. He tried to keep his eyes at her feet. Amanda was moving around downstairs—they heard her open and close cupboards and drawers. Gaja sat on Stan's lap. She said, "She'll never imagine this."

An unexpected chord rose from Lars' pipe organ. Someone touched Gaja's shoulder, whispered "Excuse me" and brushed past her. It was time for communion; people were lining up, heading for the rails. Gaja felt the need to cover herself and she closed her shawl around her neck. "Excuse me," another person said, brushing up against her.

Gaja went into the aisle but did not receive communion. After mass, a priest always came out to sit in one of the confessionals and she went to confess her thoughts of Stan. For penance, he gave her two decades of the rosary and she prayed while kneeling at the statue of the Virgin Mary; finished with her penance, she continued the rosary on the walk home, concentrating on the words. She finished in her room, able to hear Benny's power tools out in the garage.

Gaja changed to ride the L to downtown Chicago and shop for shoes. She returned home in the evening famished. Gaja heated up a chicken thigh and a potato and grated a carrot into a bowl, then poured herself hot tea. Turning toward the table, she found a two-foot tall wooden dwarf standing there and pointing at her.

Gaja shrieked a short burst but immediately laughed. Benny's carved dwarf had a long beard that split over his round belly. Eyes bulged out of a face marked with warts. He was sitting on a stone and had large feet, the big toes about the same size as his nose. One of the legs had been set in a cast.

Gaja moved the heavy dwarf next to her uncle's reading chair. She found a whole series of figurines on the coffee table: a maid milking an invisible cow, a blindfolded man tied to a post, an elf with a slingshot and a bandaged eye. Gaja did not want them on the coffee table but would move them later. She ate in the kitchen.

She was smoking when Benny came in through the back door. His face was sweaty, some sawdust in his hair. He walked past her with his hand pressed against his ribs. It was as though she were invisible and Gaja ignored him as well. He took a beer and withdrew to his room. She dressed to go outside, making no attempt to keep quiet.

Whenever she left the house late at night, she only ever went to one place, mere steps down the block. Benny's small house was on 49th Court, in the middle of the block between 18th and 19th Streets. Gaja went to the corner of 19th.

It was a large bungalow, one of the largest in Cicero. For over two years, a *For Sale by owner* sign had been standing on the lawn, the telephone number from out of state. The owner, whoever that person was, did not live in the house—as far as Gaja knew, no one lived there. Hired workers occasionally came around to trim hedges, cut the grass and sweep the sidewalks. Now and again people would come to have a look at it, but no one who could afford the expensive house wanted to live on 19th Street and 49th Court in Cicero, Illinois.

The front stairs were built of flat stones. Because the plot of land was on the corner, the house had only one gangway and the entire south façade faced 19th, most of it blocked by large cedar trees and evergreens. The house had two stone chimneys, two fireplaces and a roof of green clay shingles. All of the windows— stained glass with all sorts of ornaments—had hardwood frames and beautiful stone sills.

Gaja always entered the garden through the gangway; that gate made the least amount of noise. The yard was completely enclosed by tall evergreens and, once she was inside, no one passing by on the sidewalk could see her. She'd follow a path of flat, round stepping stones that formed a gentle "S" and led to the garden's center where a wooden swing faced a birdbath and a small empty grotto.

Gaja sat on the swing and let her eyes adjust to the darkness. A car passed, the trees breaking the beams into a mosaic of shadows and patches of light that panned quickly across the yard. She lit a cigarette and gently rocked on the swing.

She was crying but also laughing, wiping her eyes with her wrist. The laughter took over, but only briefly—she lightly kicked some fallen evergreen needles onto the stepping stones. The swing was big enough for her to lie down and she could keep it moving by reaching the ground with her foot. Even though she felt a chill—Gaja had not dressed warmly enough—she stayed in the yard.

7

After school, in Lars' classroom, Alina had finished that day's piano lesson with her dad. Whenever she played well, her reward was to play a few songs on the church organ. Alina and Lars cut through the playground next to Roosevelt Elementary and crossed 50th Avenue.

Alina barely ever went inside the church. She had only been to mass a handful of times and then only for big celebrations, when her dad had composed a special piece of music. She liked St. Anthony's more when it was empty and when sunlight fell through the stained glass. When all the electric light was on, she couldn't help but look at the huge crucified Jesus behind the altar, the brightest spotlight on him, his side cut and all his bones showing. The crucifix always made her feel that something was horribly wrong.

When they came to the top of the spiral staircase, a familiar man was up in the choir. He wore a blue cap and a black jacket with patches on the elbows—his trousers were baggy and dirty, splattered with different colors of paint. He was removing little wooden statues from a pillowcase and lining them up on the organ.

"Benny!" said Lars. "What's all this?" When the man turned to show his face, Alina remembered he had once fixed their shower.

"You," said Benny. "You need organ?"

"I might need more than that." Lars looked at the figurines—too high for Alina to see—and turned to her. "Alina. Can you wait outside for me?"

"Why?"

"Go on and wait outside and I'll be right down."

"Can I go get something in the store?"

Lars bit the inside of his mouth. "Okay...yeah." He gave her some coins. "All right. Wait for me outside the store. Or go back to the classroom and wait there."

Alina scampered down the short and narrow corridor leading to the staircase. She stomped on some of the stairs to make it sound like she had gone down but then sat to eavesdrop. "You're sloshed," said Lars.

"I don't care."

"I'll tell you. You can't be leaving this stuff around. What is this, guy on a horse? Dancing devils? You think this is funny or something?"

"Don't take from here."

"You're sloshed buckets." Feet shuffled and something fell. "Give me that."

"Lars!"

"Gimme the bag." More shuffling. "Let me! Put it in there."

"You not understand. For me is important."

"I don't need this crap on my organ, Benny."

Alina could feel her dad holding back anger, a pressure cooker full of red paint. It was best for her to get out of there, but the stairs would creak for sure. The men were arguing, "So what! Organ not your organ but church organ."

"Cut the crap. There's no reason for this."

Alina went to the store.

The line of kids waiting to get candy was so long that the last one was standing outside. She wasn't patient enough to wait, so she sat on St. Anthony's stairs and hoped her dad would come soon. Her chance to play the organ was probably gone.

Now she saw a man off to her right walking toward the church from less than a block away. It was Dr. Dilienko from the park. He was carrying a small black bag and moving briskly. Alina did not wait for him to see her but hurried into the church.

She had not told anyone about him, but he was difficult to forget, especially his voice and the way he had looked at her, like he had known who she was for a long time. Alina believed he knew that she had lied to him, and that he deeply wanted to catch her in the lie. She watched the street through a window and hoped he wasn't coming to church. Dr. Dilienko passed by to take a left down 50th Ave.

Her dad and Benny were coming down the stairs together, a mix of footsteps and shouting. Dad was actually running down the stairs. "Don't you ever say that to me!" He had the pillowcase of wooden statues in his hand. "You DP. Never speak that way!" Lars may not have noticed that Alina was there as he paced about the vestibule.

Benny appeared, visibly shaken, his cap missing. He reached for the pillowcase, but Lars held it away from him. "Return them me now! Now!" Alina backed away from the men.

"Your crap?"

"Give me!"

"Fine." Lars opened one of the doors and tossed the pillowcase out onto the church's front stairs. "There's your crap."

"It change nothing," spat Benny. "You shit. Always will be shit."

Lars held an invisible telephone to his ear. "Hello, Benny? Yes, my toilet, very broken! Come quickly."

Benny waved both his hands at Lars in a single downward motion. "Fake! Musician? Nothing. You talk, but you nothing and know it!" He pointed a hand in the direction of Roosevelt Elementary. "Why school teacher? Why? You know why! Because shit!"

"Be happy my kid's here..."

"What?" Benny spread his arms. "You what? You nothing!" He poked Lars' chest. "People laughs from you. All Cicero laughs from you."

One of the vestibule's doors opened and Monsignor Kilba appeared. "What's the matter here? I can hear it from my kitchen."

"Yes." Benny pointed at Lars. "Tell him, Monsignor. Tell him truth."

"Get a grip." Kilba placed a gentle palm flat on Benny's chest. "Calm down."

"Lemme show you," said Lars. He left the church to bring the pillowcase back and dug around through the figurines. "Here's what he's leaving on the organ for me to find." Lars finally pulled something out and, blocking it from Alina's view, showed it to Kilba. Alina saw the Monsignor's eyes soften in disappointment. "Benny," he whispered. "What's this all about?"

Benny grabbed his pillowcase, took the figurine from Lars and hid it. "Both of you," he said. "You are pretending you not know. And you know it." He brushed the crown of his head with an open palm and looked around the floor as if he had lost something. Alina was standing near a table where pamphlets had been stacked. Benny approached. He told her, "Bye," pressing the pillowcase against his chest. He left the church.

8

On the last weekend in April, Bronza Dilienko was able to move into his new house. He had no furniture and slept on wool blankets folded together and covered with cotton sheets. The house had no fuses, and for the first few days Bronza lit his way with an oil lamp he had found in the basement among old trunks, rusty tools and dusty bottles.

He felt there was something romantic about no electricity, visualizing himself as a great landowner from an old book, and didn't rush to replace the fuses.

He often had the feeling that someone was in the house with him. The feeling must have been a natural response to living in a new house. Bronza did not believe in ghosts, but the awareness persisted, especially at night. On some days he went through all of the house's seven rooms, the closets, basement and attic in search of something he hoped to hell he wouldn't find.

After a week in the house the feeling went away. He had almost forgotten it when he first saw the glowing ember of someone smoking a cigarette in his yard. It did not frighten him. He stood at the back window and watched the glow form tracer arcs. Bronza could hear the subtle creak of the swing.

Whoever it was came often—usually between 11:00 p.m. and 1:00 a.m.—but left little trace, not even cigarette butts. Bronza checked for the visitor each night, standing in the dark and narrow back room. Sometimes Bronza felt the presence even later at night. One time he was sure the visitor had come and felt disappointed to find the yard empty.

Dilienko finally decided to wait outside for the visitor. He only wanted to see who it was. The visitor came down the gangway while Bronza sat in a corner where he was well hidden but still able to see. It was a girl. There were plenty of things to trip over, a birdbath, a bizarre grotto, a few thin stumps, but she knew the backyard well. When she lit her cigarette lighter, Bronza saw Gaja's face for the first time, her smooth skin and large eyes.

She could not have been older than twenty...probably younger. Her beauty was so striking, so inexplicable, that he thought he must have deeply wanted her to be beautiful simply because she was a strange girl in his yard. When it was dark again, Bronza sat stone stiff, only ten yards away, and controlled his breathing, pinching his nose when he wanted to cough. She soon lit another smoke and he stared at her eagerly, hoping he might memorize her face in that brief moment of firelight.

When she stood to leave he followed her. His back hurt from sitting still on the lawn and his ass was wet and cold. Bronza was careful and kept his distance—he only needed to know where she lived. After walking just down the block, she went into a small brick house with a large front window and sturdy concrete stairs. Bronza smoked one cigarette in the street and then went up to the porch where a folding chair leaned against a little table. A book of matches lay in an empty ashtray. On a sanded and lacquered piece of wood hanging below the mailbox, he found the names *Benny and Gaja Laputis*. He recognized the surname as Lithuanian, knew the "j" was pronounced like a "y". Without giving it another thought, Bronza rang the doorbell.

Benny's head appeared in the diamond shaped window in the door. "Hello?"

"Hi." Bronza waved gently. "Hi. Is Gaja home?"

Benny's wet and exhausted eyes widened. They scrutinized Bronza—Benny seemed as fascinated by him as he was skeptical, perhaps annoyed with the late visit. The door opened, and Bronza saw Benny was in his shorts. He said, "Come," his voice dry. Bronza entered the small front room, oddly cold, reeking from years of cigarette smoke. Benny turned on a table lamp and pointed to a sofa. "Sit," he said. "You need beer?"

"Sure."

As Benny busied himself in the kitchen, Bronza took a good look at the artwork on the walls: the demon, the octagon shaped sun, the idiotic dwarf next to the reading chair, and the fifteen or twenty figurines scattered all over the coffee table and floor, some of them fallen to their sides. A pillowcase next to him had been filled with more figures, but Benny returned before Bronza had a chance to look at them. "Thanks." Bronza took the beer.

"Glad to meet." Benny sat in his chair. "You are welcome here."

"Glad to meet you, too," said Bronza. "Where's Gaja?"

"Eh," he waved his hand. "Maybe bath. Maybe sleep." Bronza realized Benny was very drunk, and he did not look well. His skin was pale and he spoke with an unnatural lethargy. Movement seemed to cause him discomfort. Bronza was also struck by his bright amber, almost feminine eyes. They could have been the eyes of a calculating madman, staring intently into Bronza with the paranoid desire to know everything about him, or they could have been the eyes of a fool who'd point at a shoe and say *shoe*. Dilienko did not feel welcome but now had no idea how to leave. "Maybe," said Benny, "Gaja's in kitchen."

"Right. You just came from the kitchen."

"Tell me your name."

"Dilienko. Bronza."

"Here you are welcome, Dilienko. Bronza." Benny lifted his bottle, and Bronza returned the gesture. "Dilienko, Bronza," said Benny. "You know, she is lying me about you."

"What's she say?"

"She saying she does not—" He pressed his side, strain in his face. "She says you not exist."

Bronza was quiet.

"Why?" asked Benny. "Why she is embarrassed about you?"

"You know what she's like."

"Yes." Benny drank the beer and wiped his mouth with the back of his hand. He burped silently into a fist. "Know what she is saying now to me?"

"What?"

"I'm *invisible*." Benny leaned back into the chair, rocking his head to glare at the ceiling. "I ask question, *Gaja, you are coming? Gaja, you are eating?* and she say, *No...I'm invisible.* Like this. She speaks also to you like this?"

"No."

"Wait. In few years, if you are together. Yes, because she like my sister." Benny tapped a finger to his temple. "Right here. In head. Many complexes."

Bronza's head bobbed around.

"But she beautiful," Benny said.

Bronza nodded.

"And you Catholic?" Benny asked.

"Me?" Bronza looked Benny over very carefully. "No."

Benny's face lit up, and he smiled briefly, lifting his beer. "Good. Good." Benny drank the bottle down in a few gulps and stood from the chair, stumbling slightly when he stepped over to the sofa. He picked up the pillowcase and dug around. "I thinking have one for you." He soon found a figurine and handed it over.

It was a crucifix. The figure of Christ had been sculpted separate from the cross and Benny had nailed it down with fine nails. The cross was more like a "T," two rough and interlocking posts. Bronza was struck by the graphic detail of the bones and strained joints and how heavily the body, especially the head, hung. "This is God," said Benny. "God the Son. God the Father did this to His Son." Benny rubbed his face. "But, you know what church's teachings?"

"I don't," Bronza lied.

"Church's teachings very simple. God the Father and God the Son, they are same. You know, is like one plus one equals one. Smarter mathematics. They say it mystery, but I tell you what it means. I tell this Gaja many times, because what it means? It means suicide. God killed Himself." Benny took the pillowcase into the kitchen. He brought Bronza another beer. "She will come soon," he said, disappearing for a third time. "Just wait." Bronza heard the back door of the house open and close gently.

The small house was quiet. Bronza wanted to leave before Benny returned, but he also wished to communicate with Gaja in some way. He looked around the front room and finally found a pad by the telephone. Bronza was searching for a pen when the doorbell rang. He saw a blond man standing on the porch and opened the door. "Hi."

Lars looked past Bronza into the house. "Hi. I'm sorry," he whispered. "Know it's late. I'm a friend of Benny's. A family friend."

"Oh, you want to come in?"

"Yeah. Thanks." Lars stepped past Bronza and went into the front room where he picked up the unopened bottle of beer from the table. He set it back down. "I'm sorry. My name's Lars," he said. "Lars Jorgenson. And you?"

"I'm Dilienko. Call me Bronza."

"Sure. Bronza. You're one of Gaja's friends or something?"

Bronza stood quiet.

"Is Benny around?"

"Yes."

Lars stood calm, but Bronza could sense his discomfort. Their silence started to feel awkward, and Lars broke it by knocking on Benny's bedroom door. He pushed it open. "Not there," he said. "In the can?" Lars only approached the bathroom door. "You know," he said, "I went to the billiard club to wait for him. Thought maybe he'd come by there. Then came here. I know it's late. But he usually stays up."

"We were talking. He went out the back door."

"Back door?" asked Lars. "Does Gaja know where?"

"She's sleeping."

"Right, right. Back door? Maybe out in the garage studio?"

"Maybe."

Lars went out the front door. On the porch he saw a book of matches and took it. While walking, he lit matches and tossed them, one by one, onto the sidewalk. He went down the gangway into Benny's backyard, a square of grass—white sheets hung on a clothesline strung from the house to the garage. A dim light shone through a frosted window. Lars went up to the door and put the matches in his pocket.

"Benny?" Lars had never been in Benny's garage. "Hey, you in there?" His eyes finally adjusted to the dark, and he noticed the pillowcase of figurines hanging on a hook next to the door. Lars took the knob, turned it and the door opened, its hinges creaking. He stepped inside to see Benny's body hanging by its neck from a rope tied to the garage rafters.

9

Monsignor Kilba wanted no part of any party. Again and again, virtually each time Kilba spoke to him, Lars said: "Monsignor, you have to meet Dilienko. I've told him all about you. One of these weekends or something, I'll arrange it." But Kilba did not want to meet anyone. In the weeks following Benny's funeral—he had to arrange the whole thing himself—he tried to avoid Lars as best he could. The rectory's other priests passed Kilba in the halls and sat with him at dinner, but he spoke little at the table. He barely ever left the rectory, and took only the most essential telephone calls. Besides some young women interviewing to fill Gaja's position, Kilba saw very few people.

The Monsignor spent his afternoons and evenings praying in his study. He reread Jesus' parables, especially those of the mustard seed and the lost lamb. Kilba often read the account of how Jesus kept high priests from stoning Mary Magdalene, and almost each night he returned to the Bible's suicides: King Saul and his armor-bearer, Ahithophel, King Zimri, Judas Iscariot and Samson. He thought the most about Judas and Samson, because Jesus knew Judas and must have forgiven him, and because God had given Samson strength to kill himself along with hundreds of others. He looked for wisdom in the book of Proverbs and used the Bible in ways he never had before, flipping to random pages, hoping some haphazard passage would answer the question he felt within him even though it had no words Kilba knew.

Sleep crept up on him each night. He awoke most mornings with the reading light still on and the Bible or another book flat on his chest. He told himself each day, "Today I'll do something. I'll get out to the bakery or the park. Drive out to see my niece." But he would soon sit down in a chair and feel absurd lethargy, again remember and feel himself standing before the congregation at Benny's funeral.

The only ones attending were a few of the convent's nuns and several teachers from St. Anthony's school. Most of the others were total strangers, scruffy misfits Kilba had never seen before. They were scattered throughout the church and sat alone: bartenders, a fat woman in a pink shirt and blue eye shadow, thin unshaven men, a bald fellow who did not know when to stand or kneel and rustled the wrappers of hard candies at the quietest moments. Gaja was not there.

Victoria and Alina joined Lars in the choir—he played brand new, inspired music composed the day following Benny's death. How did Lars know to compose such precise and confident music, sorrowful but warm and simple, utterly free of anger or doubt? Compared to him, Kilba felt so self-conscious that he did not know, even while reading from the Gospel, what he would preach in the next minute.

He closed the missal and folded his hands. Occasional coughs broke the church's stillness, and parishioners looked off to different directions, some down at their shoes, others at the covered casket, but Kilba had never before felt a congregation as eager for his words. Did they want an explanation from him? "There are those of us here," he said, "among us and out in the community who believe there can be no forgiveness for our friend, Benediktas Laputis. Because he chose to take his own life, we believe God won't forgive him." He pulled at the missal's ribbon. "I don't know," he said. "I cannot tell you what God will do. And I don't wish to. I can only remind us that God, the God I know, He is a merciful God. Merciful, loving and just. I can only remind us of this."

Now, in the days following the funeral, he could not keep recalling that funeral mass. He had work to finish. Yet it wouldn't leave him. Signing checks in his study, Kilba felt a headache developing at his temples. And now someone was at his door. Kilba felt a surge of anger when the door opened. It was Lars. "Hey," he whispered. "Knew you'd be in here."

"Lars, go ahead, let yourself in." Kilba stirred his tea with a pen.

"No, Monsignor. I...sorry." Lars gripped the backrest of the chair facing Kilba's desk.

"What is it, Lars?"

"You can't. I mean. Okay. I'm sorry I came in like that."

"No you're not."

Jorgenson sat on the edge of the chair, his forearms on his knees. "I came to see you."

"A master at pointing out the obvious."

"Why are you being like this?"

"You're here to tell me about the party, right?" Kilba checked his watch.

Lars sighed. "Okay," he whispered. "I didn't come over to trouble you. But actually, you know, you're taking it all wrong. It's not a *party*. What, you think it's *blow your brain out*? Let's all be chums and celebrate? It's just a gathering, sit around, be with people." He paused and looked intently at Kilba, his eyes soft. "Most everyone's feeling...like this. Like you feel. And also, Victoria—"

"A *gathering*, Lars!" Kilba interrupted. "I've heard it now, bless me St. Peter if I've lost count...yes, to be with people! And we are all very interested in this, this Ukrainian doctor. But Lars...have you lost count? How many times should I say it? I am not," he poked his palm with the pen, "in the mood."

Lars crossed his arms. "I'm not here to tell you what to do. Just came to tell you, if you'd give me a chance, that Victoria's dug up where Gaja's been hiding out all these weeks. Gaja's not run away anywhere."

Kilba tapped his pen against a knuckle.

"She's been at his house," said Lars.

"His?"

"At Bronza's house. Just some of the time, I guess. Now, don't look at me like that. I don't know anything more. If you ask me, it's a good thing. If you'd meet him, you'd agree. Please come. You don't have to sit here all closed up. Give yourself a break." Lars let himself out but made intent eye contact with Kilba before closing the door.

For about a day Kilba could pretend he'd stay home from the party, although he knew it was impossible. He spent a few hours praying before leaving for the "gathering" at Bronza's house, the final Saturday of May.

Benny's house was on the way, and Monsignor Kilba stopped briefly to look at it. The front lawn had not been mowed, and the place felt almost foreign, stranger than a stranger's home. Once in front of Dilienko's bungalow, Kilba also stood to look at it, but really to sense how he was feeling before going in. Numb? He soon caught himself admiring the home's stone stairs and stained glass.

A sign on the front door read, *Enter in back,* so Kilba followed the path of stepping-stones through the shady garden behind evergreens. Alina and Reikel were swinging on the wooden swing. The girl immediately shouted, "Monsignor!" Kilba smiled and waved to the children.

Another sign: *Doorbell's broken—door's open.* A wooden staircase led to a square kitchen of dark cupboards, its lamp a tiny chandelier with electric candles. The smell of fresh paint lingered. Kilba was struck by the hardwood floor, planks arranged so that darker tones in the grain formed islands in a tan sea. He continued to the front of the house where he heard laughter and Lars' dominating voice.

Kilba entered the room and the organist erupted, "Oh, well, hey!" Lars raised a snifter. "You made it!" He was seated on a pianist's bench between an upright piano and a large oval coffee table covered with plates of cheese, cold meats and fruit. Other than the folding chair Victoria sat on, the room, like the house, had no other furniture. Other guests sat on cushions: Reikel's parents, a doctor Kilba recognized, the Cicero Family Clinic's receptionist, a nurse, and then the tall man who must have been Dilienko. They all had their jovial and lubed up greetings.

Dilienko introduced himself, and his clammy hand gripped Kilba's fingertips.

"I'm Monsignor Kilba. A pleasure."

Dilienko smiled. "They told me you weren't coming, but I didn't believe them. I've a chair for you in the other room." He disappeared briefly and the guests stared at Kilba, a few of them smiling from drink, Lars whistling some odd song, his cheeks flushed. Bronza finally appeared, pushing a chair on a small rug so that the floor wouldn't scratch.

Kilba immediately recognized it was Benny's reading chair. He wanted to ask about it...or what, refuse to sit in it...accuse Bronza of having the chair? The guests stared and smiled at him.

Kilba only said, "Thank you," and sat. Dilienko asked, "What'll you drink?"

"Drink…"

"Lars says you're a scotch and cognac man."

"Try his scotch, Monsignor," said Lars.

Kilba nodded. "Thank you. With water."

"You don't want water in this stuff," said Lars, pointing at it.

"No? Then…whichever way."

Dilienko soon handed the scotch, neat, over to Kilba. When Bronza sat, Lars continued a story he'd been telling. Kilba had heard him tell it countless times, about how his grandfather, living then in Minnesota, was running moonshine somewhere in the woods.

"Yeah yeah. So then my grandfather, right, he's got his glass and he's waiting for the first drop. The best one, the first drop. Tear of a naughty angel, he used to call it. Amazing stuff. So waiting…waiting. And then, right there in the bushes, they can hear rustling…something, it's over there in the bushes. Granddad tells the intruder he's armed. *I gotta rifle. Who's there?* Again. *Who's there?* Still no answer. So, what can he do, right, he gets the old gun out. Pants are full, right. God damn, it's quiet as all hell, crickets holding their breath. Grandpa hears another rustle. And bam, a warning shot! And *moo!* Shot his neighbor's cow dead!"

The party laughed. Kilba's laughter, although mild, was sincere.

He finally tasted the scotch, the smoothest he had ever tried. It was so easy to drink that Kilba finished the snifter quickly. Bronza filled it again.

Reikel's parents, visibly drunk, were the first to leave—they took both Reikel and Alina with them. Kilba remained in Benny's chair, relaxed from the scotch, while the people said their good-byes and fetched jackets. Lars started playing a pleasant improvisation on the piano. With all the noise, voices and movement around him, Kilba's attention stayed consistently on Bronza. Their eye contact was occasional but striking—Dilienko knew how many questions Kilba had. Yet, there was no threat, no game. You'll have your explanations soon. Relax.

The women took to Bronza. Victoria was cool about her admiration, but the nurse and receptionist, seated at both his sides, battled for his attention. The more they drank, the closer to him they inched. The nurse never actually touched Bronza, but the receptionist took every opportunity to touch his shoulder or wrist while speaking. At one point, when Dilienko was telling Lars to play something they could all sing, she even had her head on his shoulder. "Yeah, sing!" she blared.

Lars was drinking like it was the eve of Prohibition, both beer and scotch. He played highlights from *Carmen*. His singing started out with promise but was soon way off—Victoria tried to save the song, and her formal training showed. Bronza sang along, his voice a decent baritone, although he sang from the throat. They were ruining the arias, humming and singing vowels because they didn't know the words, laughing and making faces but enjoying the kind of fun that the receptionist, nurse and doctor could not. With *Carmen* exhausted, Lars changed to the famous "Figaro" aria from *The Barber of Seville*. In the middle of it, the receptionist stood, yawning, to get her things. The music broke entirely when she made a fuss, asked Bronza to call her a cab, and Dilienko had to leave the room.

Some general commotion followed, people getting up and wandering around. Kilba found the bottle and poured himself another.

"It's nice, isn't it?" said Lars, touching Kilba's shoulder.

"I'm enjoying myself."

"No, the scotch."

"Oh. Smooth." He smiled. "Just perfect."

"He's got all kinds in the basement. Damn ass gold mine. And look at the color." Lars held the bottle up to the light. "The copper of pennies." He uncorked it, clinked Kilba's glass with the bottleneck—"To the passage of time"—and drank two good gulps. Kilba sipped his. The Monsignor was about to speak when Lars turned and hugged him tightly, patting him on a shoulder blade so that his drink almost spilled. "We're here," said Lars. "Here. I'm glad you're here. It's all in front of us."

"Lars..."

"Lemme play you something." He grabbed a bottle of beer from a bucket and—ice water dripping from his hand—almost fell over the table. Victoria spoke, "Lars, could you? Will you get it over with and break something?"

"Monsignor, okay, I'll play this. You tell me what the music makes you see."

Kilba returned to Benny's chair. "I'm listening." The first mellow notes...Lars was playing soft and bright music, sad in a tiny place, as if a gumdrop of sorrow had fallen among the dolls and stuffed animals collected in a delighted girl's toy chest. Victoria whispered, "Don't think too hard about it, Monsignor."

"Make sure you listen," said Lars.

Kilba found himself staring at Victoria's profile. She was looking at Lars, twirling a cane Kilba had never seen before—black with a marble handle—in a ring shaped by her forefinger and thumb. Kilba whispered to her, "What am I supposed to see?"

Victoria waved her hand. "He's drunk."

Lars was finished before Kilba knew it, the last chord sustained by the pedal. "Well," he said. "What do you think?"

"It's pretty," said Kilba. "Lyrical."

"What images?"

"Not sure." Kilba drank and rubbed his knee lightly. "I think. It's rather an old man. Sitting on his front stairs, white wooden house. As they do in New England."

Victoria laughed out loud, tilting her head back and lightly pressing her hand into her breast. The cane fell to the floor and Kilba picked it up. "What's funny?"

"That's totally wrong," said Lars.

"Oh?"

"Thanks," Victoria took the cane, still sniggering.

"It's called *Woman at the Window*," said Lars.

"It's supposed to be about me," she said.

"An old man?" asked Lars.

Kilba felt he should explain himself: "Certainly, it could be about a woman. Not old...I'll say, yes a beautiful—What the hell, Lars! What is this anyway?"

Dilienko came into the room carrying bottles of scotch and wine. "Okay, I convinced the doctor to drive them *both* home. How about that? If we hear the taxi honk, should just ignore it."

"Call and cancel," said Kilba.

"Eh, forget it." He put the bottles down and clapped his hands once. "All right. Monsignor, some more for you? Good, you're full. Victoria, some wine?" She handed him her glass. "Nobody's eating the cheese. It's good cheese. Lars, you want to lie on your back and I'll put a funnel in your mouth? Or you need it right in your vein?"

Bronza was expecting an answer from Lars, but Jorgenson was only staring intensely at Kilba. The Monsignor spoke up, "Cat got your tongue?"

"That...that chair," Lars said. "Yeah. You're sitting in it. I know that *chair*." Kilba did not react. "Bronza, fuckin' Benny's old chair." Lars drank beer through the side of his mouth. "What do you got it for?"

Bronza sat on a cushion. "I've been hiding it." He lit a cigarette. "Gaja's been wanting me to throw it out along with other things from over there. But it's too comfortable a chair. So I've had it in the other room."

"Can I ask you," said Kilba. "Mr. Dilienko..."

"Bronza."

"Bronza. Where...where is Gaja?"

Bronza shrugged. "One of several places, probably. But most likely across the street. In her house."

"Wait a minute," said Lars. "You sit in it? In a dead man's chair?"

"Why not?" asked Bronza.

"Because it's fucking weird," said Lars. "A dead man's chair." He put the beer down. "What if he's still sitting in it?"

"Sitting?" asked Kilba.

"Yeah yeah. I'm saying, what if you're sitting in it and you don't even know that Benny's sitting in it right there. And you're...you're on top of him." He stood. "Hold that thought. Nature calls." Lars left the room.

"But, Bronza," Kilba continued. "You've seen her. She's been avoiding me. At great effort, it seems."

"Yes."

"If I went over there, what would she do?"

"Do?" Bronza exhaled smoke over his knees. "I can't say."

"She'll come around," said Victoria. "Time. It'll take time."

"I can't say what she'd do," Bronza continued. "I think she'd ignore you, Monsignor. Or ask you to leave. She might not even answer the door."

"Do you know why?"

Bronza nodded. "She thinks you're a hypocrite."

"A what?"

Dilienko said, "I'm sure you know what she thinks."

"I don't."

"Monsignor. I'm not Catholic. I'm not even religious. But if you asked me, I'd be on your side. She thinks her uncle should not have had a funeral. She doesn't even think he should be buried in a Catholic cemetery."

Kilba leaned back.

"That's stupid," said Victoria.

"It's what she believes," said Bronza.

They were quiet. Bronza exhaled up into the ceiling lamp, a convex square of frosted glass. The taxi honked, but no one moved. Dilienko spoke: "She wondered. She knows Benny went to see you shortly before he did it. She wondered if he went to confession."

"Where did Lars go?" asked Victoria and looked to the other room.

"To confession? In my study, you mean?"

"Just a few days before it happened," said Bronza.

"Lars..." she called him.

"Benny came to see me," said Kilba. "Yes. We had a strange conversation."

"What did he tell you?" Bronza asked.

"Lars." Victoria continued looking through the adjacent room and down the corridor. "Excuse me, gentlemen," she said. She pressed her weight against the cane and slowly waddled to the other end of the house.

"That's not something I can share with you, I'm afraid," said Kilba.

"It's a secret?"

"I can't tell you."

"Monsignor, you can."

"I'm afraid I can't."

"You can."

"Mr. Dilienko—"

"I've asked you..."

"Bronza." Kilba took a deep breath. "Please don't make me repeat myself."

"Fine...You say you can't tell me. Are you trying to say—"

"I'm trying to say that Benny came to me in confidence. Perhaps I'm also trying to say that what he told me is none of your business." Kilba set an empty snifter on the table.

Bronza filled it again. "My business? Did he tell you, for example, that Gaja is involved with a man?"

Kilba took his glass.

"And did Benny tell you that he killed his father? That he rode a horse over him and trampled him to death?"

Kilba was silent.

"You see...I know something. I might even know more about Benny than you do."

"You're a conceited man, Mr. Dilienko."

"I'm also free. Free to say whatever I want to whomever I want. I don't have to listen to people's evil and bottle it all up, carry their bundles of guilt around with me. And I'm not the one who's keeping Gaja from knowing what was troubling her uncle before he died. I'm not the one who's refusing to relieve her of questions. Release her of a burden."

"Release?" Kilba asked. "I've not had a chance to speak to her. Not one! I came here only because I thought she'd be here."

They were quiet and Bronza extinguished his cigarette. "Know what I think? You came here because you knew she *wouldn't* be here. You could say you tried to find her, yet again, when you were safe knowing you'd find nothing. You're avoiding her just as much as she's avoiding you, but you're placing the blame on her."

"I came here looking for answers."

"Answers," said Bronza. "But you're the one who has them, Monsignor." He stuffed a bit of ham into his mouth. "I'm not convinced by these traditions. There is no 'silence' to your church's confessional. We all know what priests claim to hide. This is a town of displaced persons. Like me. In every silent old man...in barroom drunks...there's killing. Identity protection, wife swapping. Infants left on roadsides. Men shot in the back. Women raped. People buried alive. How many of these Lithuanians ended up holding rifles in the Nazi army? And the Italians in your parish? That little boy, Reikel's parents, Lars' neighbors, aren't they Germans?" He lit a cigarette. "They've all come to you and told you unspeakable sorrows. Things that, to you, conveniently remain stories. You can 'forgive' them or act as intercessor. But you can't even tell a girl who's lost her only relative, in the name of the god damn Catholic church, why her uncle hanged himself."

172

Kilba was now sitting on the pianist's bench. "Do you love her, Mr. Dilienko?"

"What?"

"The girl you're staging such a brilliant attack on me to defend?"

"That's none of your business."

"Not yet."

Bronza laughed.

"It's a straightforward question," said Kilba. "What's so hard to answer?"

"You're the one being evasive."

"Am I?" Kilba leaned forward. "Her uncle carried her here through the very hell you've described. All on his own. A girl who wasn't even his. It's hard for me to think of someone who's done more for any single person than Benny did for Gaja. And it wasn't me who kept her in the dark, my friend. It was Benny."

"Please..."

"Those you love...Gaja, for example. Are there things your love would keep you from telling her?" Kilba asked. "Is there anything about yourself you'd want to hide, keep secret because you know it would be more painful than the pain of knowing nothing at all?"

"Fuck it." Bronza stood up. He now seemed rather dazed, eyes wet and big, and his brow beaded with sweat. "Come with me."

"Where?"

"Just come. I'm tired of bullshitting."

Bronza's stepped out of the room with almost anxious haste. He was already down the hall by the time Kilba stood from the bench. When the Monsignor met up with him, he was standing at his bedroom doorway. "Look at that," he said, pointing. Lars and Victoria were in bed together, Lars on his back, snoring quietly—Victoria had her arm thrown across his chest. "They're comfortable," said Bronza and moved further, through the kitchen and down the wooden stairway. He fought with the back door to the basement. "There aren't any lights down here," he said in the dark. He lit an oil lamp left on a small table and found a room Kilba estimated to be below the kitchen. The linoleum tiles were sticky under their shoes and there was a smell of rust. Bronza set the lamp down and looked for something in a corner.

The brick walls had been painted either yellow or white, hard to tell from the haze of the lamp. Various wooden trunks rested against the walls, some larger than others. When Kilba turned around, a shrill buzzed over his back and neck. Bronza had perhaps fifty of Benny's little figurines stacked up on shelves. "I need a key," Dilienko said. He found it in a small box and opened one of the trunks, full of even more figurines.

"Why do you have all this?" asked Kilba.

He brushed his forehead. "Look at these. All of them. Again and again. Look at this." Bronza handed Kilba the photograph of Benny's father, the same one he had already seen. "And here." Bronza picked up a figurine of a man riding a horse over another man. "Look at the faces. The rider. And the guy below. There are so many like this one. It's *him* riding the horse. It's Benny. Look at the detail in the face, do you see? That's why, Monsignor. He couldn't live with it anymore. Patricide."

"But you can't know. These are just figurines. Expressions. They might be of feelings. Maybe of something imagined. You *can't know* from this."

"But *look* at them, Monsignor."

The men were quiet. Kilba looked through the figurines, erotic ones of couples making love—Kilba was familiar with many of the dwarves, elves and little devils, but many were brand new. The ones Bronza had put on the shelves all showed, one way or another, a man being trampled by a horse. Bronza finally whispered, "I didn't want to get into an argument with you, Monsignor. I wanted to talk to you about something very different."

"Well, you failed."

"I don't believe in God."

Kilba sat on one of the closed trunks. The mellow lamplight was throwing a soft shadow of Bronza's profile onto a wall across the room. He appeared exhausted but also nervous. Although he moved little, he seemed restless, unaware of what to do with himself. Bronza lit yet another cigarette and blew the smoke towards the lamp where a plume of heat rose through the cloud. "Tell me. Do you really believe?"

Kilba nodded.

"God is good. All that stuff?"

"Sometimes it gets difficult to believe. But I always come out believing."

"Yeah...yeah. Sometimes it gets difficult not to believe. But I don't ever come out believing."

"Bronza..."

"Shh. Listen. Do you ever want to cut the crap? Cut to the chase?"

"What do you mean?"

"I mean...on one hand...there's Gaja. I can just look at her. Be near her. I say, 'I think...this is why you're alive.' Because there's beauty. Beautiful people who make you feel beautiful."

"I think."

"But she believes all this hocus pocus. All this if and only if...if this, then that. Like God's setting rules for some kid's game." His eyes were shiny black in the lamplight. "Angels and devils. It's like a cartoon with good guys and bad guys. For Benny it was dwarves, but for her it's flaming swords. Fireballs falling from the sky. She's so afraid...so so afraid of burning in hell. But she can't control it."

"Control?"

"You talk about love. If two people make love, to her, it brings hellfire. But it doesn't stop her. It's stronger than she is. And she...I have no other word. It doesn't stop her."

Kilba leaned back against the wall.

"Is she right? Is it forbidden to enjoy your bodies...why else stick around here? I love the things that make you know you're alive. When you're with someone...and feeling pleasure." He took a strong drag from the cigarette. "Pleasure that lasts even for a fleeting moment. Who's right? Don't you ever want to know?"

"Know?"

"For certain," he closed his eyes. "To know. Like Benny." He brushed a hand through his hair. "It's all there is. It's certain. Every heartbeat takes you one pump closer. Everything else, even loving a woman...it's temporary. A job. A drink." His body swayed. "To cut to the chase. To get there. To cut the crap and to know. Sometimes." He adjusted the height of the lamp flame. "I want to know what happens next. Who's right? I want it more than anything sometimes. Don't you?"

"I feel," Kilba whispered, "it's important to be mindful of our conceit."

Bronza took a step one way, then another. He turned to the figurines on the shelves and back to Kilba. His shadow loomed over the entire room. The ember of his cigarette glowed and he exhaled through his nose. "Bronza, what's the matter with you?" Dilienko took the cigarette out of his mouth and, in a single motion, pressed the live ember into the flat and hard palm of his hand.

Passage: The Piano Delivery, February 24, 1968

When Yuri was five years old, each Saturday morning he and papachka made breakfast for mama. Yuri toasted bread and cracked eggs into the pan. When he set the table with the Saturday dishes, he secretly placed the raspberry jam slightly closer to his own plate. Papachka's coffee was perking and it was Yuri's job to shut the machine off and take cream from the fridge.

The table wasn't quite ready, but mama came out of her room. She hurried to the toilet and managed to close the door, but Yuri could hear her throwing up. Papachka shook his head slightly, "Мамы плохо. Ее живот болит немного."

"Почему?"

"Не знаю."

When mama came out, she had washed her hands and mouth and Yuri could smell her lilac scented soap. While sprinkling pepper over her egg, she said everything looked so good. As always, she broke the yolk and the lava spread everywhere, carrying bits of pepper. She did try to eat but grimaced and told papa, "I can't," pushing the small plate to the side. "No appetite."

Yuri always felt it was his fault mama was sick. When she went away from the table to listen to the radio in her room, Yuri couldn't eat anymore but forced down the food, almost as fast as papachka, then he helped clean the table, throwing away mama's egg.

Papachka went to her room, something he almost never did. They were whispering and it was hard for Yuri to hear, but he understood what the word *pregnant* meant. It left him sensing his own body, his stomach stuffed with breakfast, but he felt little, distant from his parents. Still, Yuri felt the courage to draw closer to the door. Papachka asked, "What are you going to do about it?"

"What'll I do?"

"For instance. What's your plan?"

Mama asked, "What do you think?"

"I have no idea what to think."

"Well, don't think. It's not in your hands, anyway."

Now Yuri was close enough to smell their cigarette smoke and hear mama's exhale. She said, "Are you going to call someone *this* time? Let them know?"

"You're that way about it, right?" Papa waited a while. "I don't know if it's a good idea, Gaja. Another one? Like this? Not like this."

"Why? Wasn't your idea? You didn't have this in mind? Wasn't what you had wanted?"

"Everything's always on my shoulders? My fault, right?"

"Told you it's not in your hands even vaguely."

Papachka's dark silhouette rose in the beaded glass window, and Yuri trotted away quickly, his socks quiet against the floor. He sat on the floor in his room. Papa sat alone in the front of the house for a long time before he finally spoke, projecting his heavy voice, "Lars knows I'm having the new piano delivered. Will probably be over to look at it."

Mama had gone to the kitchen. "Couldn't resist telling him? Can never resist. But you want everyone else to resist."

"He'll probably be here," papa said on the way to the den, "in a few hours." Yuri recognized the Bach papa played on his small record player. The piano music sounded like a bird pecking seeds. He felt like he and papa were listening to the music together even though he was in another room. But Yuri was also ignoring the music just as mama was doing in the kitchen.

The delivery truck came early and Yuri watched the broad-shouldered, bellied men setting it up. When they were finished, the piano stood shiny black, a strange dark mirror. Papa told him, "You're going to learn how to play. Mr. Jorgenson will teach you," but Yuri didn't completely believe him. He did want to play the piano just because it was so beautiful. But the instrument was also a stranger in the house, bigger than Yuri's bed.

Papachka opened it up and called mama to see it. She only said, "I have to get ready for confessions," and her heels clicked against the hardwood.

When Lars came to look at the piano, his face turned red. "Oh, the comforts of home. Here's comfort." He sat at the bench. "Do you mind? Just a few notes." Lars didn't wait for papa's response but played a flowing melody, lifting his right hand up almost to his chin in between phrases. His movements matched the music perfectly. Even mama came to listen, although she sat further from everyone.

"Bravo," said Lars, still playing. "Now that's sound." At the end of the passage, he closed his eyes, rocking his head back and forth and smirking. Finished, Lars rubbed his mustache and, looking right at Yuri, said, "Just what the doctor ordered." Jorgenson stood and approached papachka, gripping his shoulder. "This calls for a celebration."

"Yes," said Gaja. "There are plenty of reasons."

"Pardon?" said Lars.

She sat at the piano herself. "There's an announcement to make."

"Oh?"

"I'm expecting," she said, lifting one shoulder. Mama looked at Yuri. "This one here," she pointed, "is going to be a brother."

Lars' mouth was open. "You're kidding? Well, you keep filling the house," he said. "You keep pickin' 'em out in the cabbage patch. Ha! Who'd you tell? D'you tell someone?"

Yuri was watching papachka. He shook his head, said, "No. You're the first," and smiled. It was a real smile, full of something like happiness, but Yuri understood that papa had been defeated.

The adults kept talking together, Lars making all his exclamations, but Yuri's imagination had wandered off so that the adult conversation had become a hush of noise. He was wondering how it would feel to have a creature growing in his stomach. He knew that's where babies grew, but he didn't want strange doctors to operate on mama or touch her in any way.

Yuri had gone to his room to continue the daydream. When he came out, Lars and mama were gone and papa was down in the basement, Yuri knew, because the kitchen door had been left open. He hated when papa went down there—sometimes he sat by himself in the dark for hours. Yuri always wanted to go make him come upstairs but was afraid of the basement.

When papa finally did come back, he went straight to the small bathroom by the kitchen. From the doorway, Yuri watched him pour peroxide over a wound in his hand. He asked what was wrong, "Что случилось?"

Bronza answered, as always, in Russian: "It's a burn."

Yuri could see the little circle in his palm bubbling with foam. "How did you burn yourself?"

"By accident," said Bronza. "It was by accident."

Advent, 1975 (continued)

1

An overcast early morning sky in winter. Alina parked her blue Datsun across the street from St. Anthony's parish and used her dad's keys to enter the church. The sound of her boots against the floor disturbed not a peaceful stillness but an overarching and imposing silence. Because of the dark morning, the flames of candles on the communion rails and at the feet of statues burned especially bright, yet offered no impression of warmth in the massive church.

Alina was tired. She had spent the night in the hospital and, although Bronza had been able to finagle her a bed, had slept little. The shock of her father's illness and near death was gradually leaving her, but the more Alina calmed, the heavier her body felt, especially now that she was climbing the tower's spiral staircase. On the choir, she set her handbag down on the organ and spread out her coat to lie on a pew.

So much of the church's plaster was crumbling, especially around windows and in the arches. A century of dust had collected on the black chains of the hanging lamps. The rising organ pipes, dirty brass tubes, needed polish.

No one had asked her to replace Lars at Sunday Mass—Alina had not even told Kilba that her dad was sick. As she got up from the pew to sort through the notes kept on the choir's messy shelves, she didn't know how to explain it to the Monsignor. Why hadn't she called yesterday? When she sat at the organ and turned it on to hear the muffled knock and deep buzz from somewhere behind the back wall, Alina felt she wouldn't want to play. Her fingers and feet touched the organ's foreign but familiar controls and she held a subtle C-chord. She pulled off her silver ring to lighten her left hand. Alina adjusted the mirror meant to see the altar behind her.

Lars always chose the hymns and compositions for each mass. The little white numbers he hung on a black board near the altar corresponded to hymns in misalettes. Alina wanted to play the easiest hymns, "Amazing Grace" and "How Great Thou Art," but it was Advent and she had to find Christmas hymns. The 7:30 mass was in Lithuanian and Alina had no idea what the titles meant. But dad kept detailed notes with dates to keep from repeating music. She decided to play his order from the previous week.

Practicing, she made mistakes, especially on the pedals, but it took less than two hymns for her hands to feel at home on the keys. The experience was soon nostalgic. Alina played "That's Amore" by ear, screwing up a few parts, but the organ sounded good.

Someone was coming up the stairs. Perhaps the music was a bit loud, so she pulled back on the volume pedal, switching to one of the Lithuanian hymns. She changed the organ's tone to sound more solemn and kept her eyes on the notes.

A priest entered the choir through the narrow passage from the stairs. Alina had never met him but knew his name was Father Cruz. He waved to her and she stopped playing. "Hello," said Alina.

"Good morning. I'm sorry," he said. "I didn't mean to disturb. I thought you were Lars."

"I'm Alina."

"I've heard of you. It's great to finally meet." He stepped right up to the organ and shook her hand.

Cruz had a youthful glow that Alina could not remember seeing in a priest. She yawned, "Pleased to meet you," covering her mouth. "Sorry."

"And your father? Where is he?"

Alina shook her head. "I..."

"What's the matter?"

"Last night was pretty crazy."

"Oh?"

Alina thought she heard something from the back of the choir. She stood to see over the organ. "Did you...hear that?"

"Hear what?"

"Over there." She pointed to the back pew. "Am I hearing things? There's something."

"No, I don't think so."

"Really. I'm certain I heard it." She got out from behind the organ and took cautious steps to the back pew. Halfway between the organ and the choir's back wall, Alina was sure she'd find nothing and would look like an idiot. But the small human figure, wrapped in a long, gray wool coat, startled her.

She recognized Yuri before she realized he was wrapped in her father's coat. The lapel was covering his mouth and he coughed again, soon sensing Alina's presence. Yuri sat right up. "I'm not sleeping," he said, obviously disoriented. "I'm not."

2

Bronza Dilienko was smoking on the sidewalk outside the emergency room's entrance. The wind tossed snow flurries around—stronger gusts blew the thinnest powder off the small drifts and over his shoes. The clouds had broken in places and he thought the sun might come out, but a thin cloud, almost a mist, veiled it.

When his feet grew cold he went to check on Lars. The curtains drawn, the room was dark. Lars was asleep, his head turned away from the windows, and Bronza pulled the curtain open. The sun had now broken through. Brilliant winter light shone off the chrome fixtures, giving Dilienko, who had not slept all night, a jolt of energy.

He turned on the radio and listened to the news. Alina had left several magazines, one about jewelry and another about travel, next to tissues. He read in the sunlight, hoping to get his second wind. But Bronza soon curled up in the room's other bed, its sheets and pillow lightly scented from Alina's perfume.

Bronza could have easily slept into the afternoon, but Lars woke him within the hour. He called "Bronza!" many times. "Hey. Wake up."

Dilienko rolled over. "Morning, maestro," he said. "Welcome to," he yawned, "room 611."

"I'm in the hospital," Lars murmured.

"Most definitely."

"Under my ass. A piss can."

Bronza smiled. "Easier to change than diapers, Lars."

"Who? Put me here?"

"Me."

"My head hurts," Lars said. "And thirsty." He took time to feel his whole body. "Right knee, it throbs. Feel my heartbeat in it."

"That means your heart's beating. You smashed the knee someplace."

"Smashed?" said Lars, trying to get up. Bronza gently pushed him back down. "Yeah sore," said Lars. "Muscles sore." He lay quietly. "What...ah? Diagnosis?"

"Diagno*ses*. A case of extreme dehydration. You had pneumonia, still have pneumonia, but you were drinking and on the verge of alcohol poisoning. A valiant effort. Victoria found you."

"What?"

"Of course, *Alina*," he corrected himself. "Alina found you. She thought you were drunk, but your brain was slowly cooking in a fever. Feel any damage?"

"I've been here long?"

"Less than 24 hours."

"Today's what day?"

"Sunday."

"Does Kilba know?"

"Lars." Bronza sighed. "If he doesn't, he'll know later. Who cares?" Bronza pulled up the chair. "If something feels shitty, I want to know immediately. Otherwise, rest."

Jorgenson took a deep breath and touched the IV in his vein. He reached down for his knee and tapped it. "Please. The piss can. I don't need it." Bronza took the bedpan to the toilet. Lars continued, "I remember...drinking with Kilba. God, was he sloshed. And then that Cruz yelled at me. You met him yet?"

"No."

Lars rubbed his cheek. "It's all I remember. Yeah...I took the bus or something. I remember Cruz was yelling at me. Guy's got something against me."

"I don't know anything about it," said Bronza.

Lars shut his eyes tightly and pressed his head deep in the pillow. He touched his temple and whispered, "Dammit dammit. Do you know? Dammit." His set his palms flat on his belly. "My *birthday*. It was my birthday. Alina was probably coming."

"Happy birthday, Lars," said Bronza.

"Feathers and tar. Hanged, drawn, quartered." Lars took a cup of water from Bronza. He said, "You know, Kilba's senile," and drank carefully. Then he lay back and turned to face the sunlight. "Senile. Only explanation. Old man should fire me, you know. Maybe I'm already fired and I don't even remember."

Bronza poured more water into the cup and put it within Lars' easy reach. Jorgenson's wet and pale eyes trembled, but he soon closed them, sleeping instantly. Dilienko sat for a while, looking over Lars' expression, at once calm yet pained.

He couldn't believe he had slipped that way, to say Victoria instead of Alina.

3

Alina played the final procession of the last mass with confident, precise fingers—the eight members of the church choir were responding well, pleased with her leadership. As the parishioners bottlenecked at the back and side doors, she pressed down even further on the volume pedal and played freely, virtually improvising within the final passages. Her morning was finally over, the church growing empty, choir members already packing their things and looking for their coats, but Alina clung to the music.

She took her father's coat and walked out into the loud buzz of voices in St. Anthony's yard. A few people again thanked her for coming and invited her for high balls, but Alina only smiled. She excused herself and went to the rectory.

Yuri was sitting alone in the rectory's kitchen. "Hey," she whispered. He raised one of his gloved hands. "You're still here?" Alina folded her father's coat over the back of a chair. She sat by the window, pressing and turning the silver ring on her finger, her nervous habit. She asked, "You hungry?"

He nodded. "But I don't want to go to the Parish Breakfast."

"I know. Me neither." Alina squatted to see what Kilba had in the fridge. "Raw chicken livers."

"Real ones?"

"Gross, right? What else? Sour dills...some kind of soup...this weird, disgusting fish." She moved things around. "How about something simple? How about eggs?"

Alina fried four. She ate her portion in a hurry, hungrier than she had realized, and then she toasted an extra slice of bread. Yuri had covered his eggs with pepper and broke the yolks to watch the lava ooze out, carrying bits of pepper with it. He nibbled. Alina could sense his grief even though he showed only subtle hints, a soft glow in the eyes, and careful movements while setting down utensils. His question surprised her. "Where did you get that ring?"

"The ring. My ring?"

He nodded. "I never saw one like that."

Alina put her hand flat on the table. "Well. I made it."

Now the ring seemed different, prettier, more elegant and feminine.

"You don't know what I do, Yuri? It's my job. I make things for women. Sometimes for myself. Want to look at it?"

"Sure." He wiped his hands and held the ring gently with the very tips of his fingers. To see better, he took the ring to the window where sunlight fell through the tiny emerald. "You made this," he said. "But how do you make it?" He set it down on the sill and looked at it closely, curved rays of silver strands radiating from the gem. After a moment, he brought it back to the table and admired the ring while eating. He said, "I think lots of times people forget. Everyone forgets that people make things. Everything gets made by somebody."

"Maybe you would like to come see the shop?"

He seemed to withdraw.

"The owner would say okay. We'd make a date. It would be fun."

"It's too far away," said Yuri.

"It's in Chicago. You can take the L."

Yuri broke the other egg yolk. "When?"

"Whenever. Later on, during your school vacation. The day after Christmas or something."

Yuri thought about it only briefly. "Mom won't let me," he rattled.

"I'll talk to your dad. They'll let you go."

"No way, Alina. I'm going to be in big trouble for running away last night. I'd have to sneak away again. And then I'd get in even bigger trouble."

"I can talk to your dad. He can persuade your mom."

192

"He can't." Yuri toyed with his food. "He can't persuade her." Alina could sense him weakening, feelings rushing up. Looking down at his plate, he showered his remaining breakfast in pepper, set his fork gently on a napkin and stood from the table to go to the bathroom.

4

Monsignor Kilba hated fasting. At the Parish Breakfast, the Monsignor did his duty and thanked the cooks, said Grace but then very politely excused himself. People complained and delayed him, trying to draw him to conversations, but he managed to get away.

On his way out, he passed a table covered with Napoleon torte, black forest cake, and cabbage and mushroom pies baked by parish ladies. Rolled Eastern European style pancakes with various fruit syrups, jams, honey and crushed walnuts. The tiny pumpernickel, cucumber and cream cheese sandwiches, then the canned blueberries next to sour cream, and the oatmeal with raisins, brown sugar, hazelnuts and butter. In the churchyard, he passed the kitchen's exhaust fan and caught a whiff of the bacon frying on the griddle. Kilba could see the little strips, wrinkled and perfectly brown. He could have eaten a half-dozen set on top of cucumber sandwiches.

He and Cruz had agreed to fast two days. Why did he agree to it? Kilba took a moment to realize what time it was, calculated the hours, came up with the number 36. Thirty-six hours of fasting remained.

Alina was still in the kitchen with Yuri. She was doing dishes. The young woman's sudden but smooth movements, the way she rubbed her forehead with the back of her hand...it was all Victoria, a resemblance that always struck Kilba so that he hesitated. "Alina," he said. "You don't have to wash dishes."

"Monsignor." She looked up. "Breakfast over? So soon? Well...but look, there's only a cup and a knife left."

"Leave it."

"Sure?"

"Of course."

Kilba approached the table where Yuri sat quietly. He was holding Alina's silver ring and examining it carefully, turning it to make the light shine through the emerald at different angles. Alina wiped her hands with a dishrag. "I'm going to have to get going," she said.

Yuri nodded. Kilba said, "That's fine. Alina, thank you."

"Thanks," said Yuri. "You make good eggs."

"It's all I know how to make." She took her father's winter clothes. "Eggs and rings."

"Here," Yuri said, handing it back.

She sat next to him. "So...you okay?"

He nodded.

"Don't forget our date, okay. I'll call your dad and he'll let you go for sure. I promise. The day after Christmas."

"I won't forget."

"Good." She kissed his forehead and he blushed. Alina turned to Kilba, said, "Thanks for everything," shook his hand and headed to the archway. "Maybe I'll see you at the hospital later."

"In a few hours," said Kilba. "Maybe less."

With Alina gone, Yuri's mood changed and he slumped in his chair. His head didn't hang, but he avoided eye contact with Kilba and sat on one of his hands. The Monsignor poured himself a cup of water and sat at the table. "So," he said. "Here we are."

"I think I have to go home soon," Yuri muttered. Kilba was looking at him sternly. "Did you tell my mom I'm here?"

"I didn't see your mother. She didn't come to either of my masses. I don't know where she is."

"Maybe she went to Father Cruz's mass."

"I don't think he's seen her either. I can't be sure your mother knows where you are."

"So, you didn't tell her?" He seemed relieved.

"No. But, you know, I'm not crazy about this. How'd she feel if she knew I agreed to hide you? I'll have to bring you home at some point." He sipped the water. "We'll have to tell her something."

"What?"

"It's what we need to talk about. You understand that we need to talk, don't you?"

Yuri scratched his wrist. "But we don't have to. We can just go home now. And I'll tell her..."

"Yuri. I'll have to tell her that you came to my house."

The boy shrugged.

"Look," said Kilba. "I want to be on your side. To do that, I need to know what's going on."

Yuri thought about it.

"You have to tell me what all this 'secret' business is all about. Because I don't understand a word of it, what you told me in the confessional yesterday. Frankly, I'm completely disoriented. I'm sure Father Cruz doesn't understand any of it either, even if he remembers it."

"But I can't."

"Here's what I've got, Yuri. You told me your sister died because she told a secret. Now you've told it, apparently, to Father Cruz. And you said you were going to die, too, as a result."

He nodded.

"Well? Here we are. You just had a real breakfast, and you made a real date with a lovely young lady. You're not dead."

"No."

"So, someone's lying to you. Blaming Anya for her own death. It isn't true, Yuri."

"Yes," Yuri said. "But," he shook his head. "Nothing."

"Please continue."

"I think," said Yuri, "maybe it's wrong."

"What's wrong?"

"What I told."

Kilba had to control his impatience. He set cool, stern eyes on the boy.

"It takes a really long time to tell the whole story," said Yuri.

"We have all afternoon."

Despite his unease, Yuri seemed pragmatic, thinking meticulously. "It's really hard to understand the secret," he said. "Because there's a difference between you and Father Cruz. To Father Cruz, it's just a confession, just a boy talking. But, to you, you will try to understand. And you will think about it for a long time. But you can't understand. And you'll get so angry."

"When do I ever get angry?"

"When I flushed paint down the toilet."

"That was different." He drank water. "Let's not remind ourselves of that."

"But, you can't tell my mother. Or papachka. But especially mama, you can't tell her."

"I promise not to tell anyone."

Yuri took a subtle breath and put his hands flat on the table. The color slowly faded from his cheeks. "The secret has lots of parts to it," he said. "Some of them are together and some of them are not together. I only told Father Cruz the most important parts. But there are more parts. But three parts are the most important. The first part is statues. These wooden statues. So many of them."

"Go on."

"Yes. And the second part is railroad spikes."

"Railroad?"

"Yeah. I found them on the tracks. And the last part is," Yuri raised his hands, "my gloves. Because I wear these gloves."

"Your skin allergy?"

"Papachka tells everyone about an allergy. People believe because he's a doctor. And I tell people. But it's not true. I don't have a skin allergy."

"No?"

"No."

Kilba finished his water.

"I remember when it was second grade, because Sister Aquinata was my teacher. I got in trouble that day and I had to kneel in the corner. I was talking in class. Mama got so angry and she made me clean out the basement. I had to go down there all alone, take all this garbage and put it in the alley."

"All right."

"I found this key in papachka's room one time. It was an old, really big metal key. I found it when I was dressing up with his shoes...it was hidden there, in a shoe. I kept the key because it just looked so neat and old. Then that day when I was cleaning out all this garbage from the basement, I understood something about it. That key was exactly big enough for these big, these really huge wooden trunks down there. They are so heavy. And they were always locked. But that key, it worked. I opened one of the trunks, and inside there I found all these statues, wooden ones. They're only about this big." He showed with his hands.

Kilba poured himself another cup of water.

"When I found them, I was so ashamed. I knew it was wrong—I knew I wasn't supposed to see them. They were all really bad. I closed the trunk right away and didn't look at them again for a long time. But I thought about them all the time. Sometimes they scared me, but other times I felt sorry for them. And another time I wondered what it would be like to make them. I thought about that so much. So many times. That's what I thought about the most. I don't know why. I wanted to make my own statue even though I didn't even know how.

"So I went downstairs one time when mama was swinging on the swing and smoking. And I took some statues, one of a horse and another of this little funny devil. He's from old Lithuanian stories, and he always loses at cards against farmers, and that's how farmers get their daughters back from him. I took those statues and I hid them in my shoes. I looked at them at night when nobody knew. After a while, it became easy to look at them, but I was still ashamed sometimes. But not so much.

"Then, mama found them. She got so angry. She gave me the belt and she made me wash my hands with holy water."

Kilba crossed his arms.

"She washed them. Because, all those statues, the devil made them. Those statues come from the devil and I understood why it was so hard to look at them. But the devil gets easier and easier and soon he becomes normal. You said that one time."

"Go on."

"So, that's the first part of the secret. I really like those statues and I think about them. Mama knows. She took away my paper and my pencils because I used to draw statues.

"One time, later, papachka and mama got into a big fight about it. Mama wanted to throw all of them out with the trunks, but papachka wouldn't let her. He hid them somewhere. They're not in the house. Anyway, I can't look at them anymore."

"What's the second part of the secret?" asked Kilba.

"Railroad spikes. That happened later. When the statues were all gone, I started thinking about making things from other stuff. From paper and gluing together pieces of broken glass or just anything I could find, sticks or wood chips. But then one time

I found these rusty but really good railroad spikes. Anya found them with me. We hid them in her room because mama never searched her stuff, just sometimes, though usually never. I wanted to paint them silver. But mama found them. And she knew they weren't Anya's. She knew the devil was making me find *nails*. She called them *nails*. I don't think she knows where they really come from."

"Did she get angry?" asked Kilba.

"So much." Yuri slowed down. His eyes were wet and he suddenly seemed nervous, pushing back on his chair and rubbing an eyebrow. "She got so angry."

"Did she punish you?"

Yuri nodded.

"How?"

"She..." He froze, pale, distant. "She punished me."

Kilba whispered, asking gently, "Yuri, what's wrong with your hands?"

"I can't say."

"Please tell me."

"I can't tell anyone."

"Yuri," Kilba spoke quietly. "I want you to trust me."

"She already knows," whispered Yuri. "She knows I told it. Because I left her a note."

"Yuri," Kilba was firm but warm. "I want you to show me your hands."

Yuri shook his head slowly.

"Please."

The boy put his hands on the table, palms up and invited Kilba to take the gloves off himself. Now Kilba hesitated—he had not expected this. But he did it. He unbuttoned the gloves, slipping them off. Yuri's hands looked completely normal, a bit too white, as if they'd been soaked in a bath, but then Kilba noticed the scars. Three on one hand and two, one very large, on the other. "Yuri? These?" he asked. "From cigarettes?"

The boy nodded.

"Your mother? It's not your mother. Are you telling me the truth?"

He nodded.

"Your father does this to you."

"No." said Yuri. "It's mama."

5

Gaja didn't know where else to look for Yuri. St. Anne's Cemetery, Park Holme, Carry's, Sherwin's, LaVergne's, the National grocery store—she had even gone to Vin's for the first time in over ten years. Yuri didn't like the confectioner on 22nd Street very much, but Gaja went there, forgetting the little shop didn't work on Sundays. The library, just a few blocks from the confectioner, would stay open until one o'clock, but Yuri's favorite chair, between a drinking fountain and a spider plant, was empty. Walking away from 22nd, Gaja heard the L and wondered about the unlikely possibility that Yuri had taken it downtown. The previous night had been very cold and he'd be smart enough to find shelter in a familiar place. Gaja did briefly think he'd gone to church or the parish breakfast, but St. Anthony's was the last place she wanted to find him.

Walking in the direction of 49th Court, Gaja saw she was almost home. She didn't want to go there, but where could she go? She'd feel a bad mother for giving up the search, though continuing was useless. Her feet were numb.

She quietly checked each room in the house, then the basement and attic. With the house empty, Gaja felt mild joy, almost like the freedom a child feels without guardians, a feeling that soaked her heart in guilt. She slipped into moccasins and a clean sweater and sat down on her bed with a pack of strong cigarettes and a cup of piping hot tea. The parakeet chattered from the other room, his birdseed occasionally dropping against the hardwood.

Smoking, she felt at once impatient and anxious. The time she had to herself would be brief—she intuitively sensed someone about to return. And now she wanted to look at something.

Her music box, the one that held Stan Lemke's letters, was hidden in a locked trunk. Gaja took the key from the hiding place and opened it. She looked at Lemke's things with total indifference, his letter and the stupid keychain, but she had hidden another note in the box, a small folded square of yellow paper, its corners soft and dirty. Bronza had written *For Gaja* there.

The note was thirteen years old. The reality astounded her: she had been eighteen—a child, really—when Bronza had written it. Gaja admired the masculine handwriting, the angled "G" and long reaching "j." To a secret part of her, the handwriting was even more attractive now after all this time. Her fingers handled the note gently and she set it in her lap.

The bungalow's *For Sale* sign. The large bungalow...*that* house, the one with her garden—no matter how different it seemed, it was the same house where she was now living.

One day in her youth, she had gone outside to find someone had taken the sign away. She had refused to believe it had been sold. Nothing had changed about the house. The garden was exactly as it had always been: dark, secluded and private. And nobody ever turned on any lights in any windows. Nobody came through the front door or out to ask what she was doing in the yard. It was still her garden, and she could still hide there.

Gaja finally saw Bronza in broad daylight. He was on the bungalow's front stairs, inspecting something small held in his hand. When Gaja came closer, careful not to seem curious, she realized he was trying to repair a broken cigarette. He finally tossed it away, found a fresh one and was presently walking directly toward Gaja, his strides long and hasty.

He was tall and broad-shouldered, with prominent but well-proportioned cheekbones. He wore an expensive jacket and slacks—the Italian leather shoes were not bought in any of Cicero's shops. As he walked past, searching through all his pockets for matches, Gaja could sense him thinking deeply about something. He did not notice having passed her in the street. As he hurried away, his back to her, Gaja watched him, the precise heel-toe placement of his feet, a hand constantly rising to rub his forehead. He turned at the next street and was gone.

Gaja often found herself imagining him. What would their first conversation be—that they would talk was inevitable. She often wanted to follow him; really, Gaja wanted him to discover her when no one was around. She imagined touching him, unclipping the large watch from his wrist and gently resting her hand on his forearm.

Sitting on his swing one night, she finally saw his oil lamp, his dimly illumined figure like an apparition deep in the home's darkness. Seeing him did not keep her from coming back to the garden. She would smoke and watch the light of Bronza's lamp fade and flicker as he moved in the back of the house. Especially on nights when the house was completely dark, she had blithe fantasies about being watched.

On one very quiet night, the sky moonless, not the slightest breeze in the air, the fantasy became a sensation. Mild at first, its intensity rose. Gaja did not only feel that someone was watching, but that the person was near, perhaps right behind her, looking down on the back of her head. He was about to put a hand on her shoulder, fingers on her naked neck, squeeze without letting go. She knew it was her imagination, of course, but it was intense. A man was breathing in the darkness not more than ten yards to her right.

She lit another cigarette, blinding herself for a moment. Gaja exhaled, listening deeply, and she heard it. Subtle, warm and restrained breathing. She stood and tried to keep her steps from appearing eager, her shoes from sounding too loudly against the gangway's cement. She went straight home, afraid to look back, certain at moments that someone was only two steps behind.

Uncle Benny was drunk in his reading chair. Gaja went to her bedroom without washing up. When the doorbell rang, she had been under the covers and in her pajamas. Benny let someone in.

She could not make out who it was or what they were saying, only that they were talking. But the late night visitor was not one of her uncle's drinking friends. His voice resonated, its timbre strong even when he tried to whisper. In the quiet breaks when neither of them spoke, Gaja wondered if she should feign thirst, go to the kitchen for water.

She heard the back door close. Gaja sensed someone walking around, but it could have been her mind again playing tricks. *Just go out there, you stupid girl. Look at whichever drinking buddy has come to visit, say hi and go back to bed. You'll see it's some fool.*

The doorbell rang a second time. Gaja heard footsteps, the baritone timbre, and now a second man was talking. Lars. His voice destroyed any sense of mystery or exhilaration, but when she found the gumption to come out, everybody was already gone. Only cigarette smoke lingered in the lamplight.

She whispered "*Dėde*," but Benny wasn't in bed. When she sat in his chair, Gaja saw the note among her uncle's figurines on the coffee table: a folded up square of yellow paper from the writing tablet by the phone.

For Gaja.

She unfolded the note.

Isn't it strange? If I invited you to come to my garden, if I told you you're free to come and go as you please, stay as long as you like, leave your cigarette butts in one of those old flowerpots, you'd probably stop coming. I had to follow you here to your home and sit with your grandfather for a few minutes to realize that was the case: there's nothing I can tell you or write here that will make you feel comfortable. Please know I did not come to chase you away and, at any rate, I'm glad you like the garden. I'm glad you're so careful not to disturb it. I invite you to come when the sun is out.

Bronza Dilienko

Gaja read the note several times. The words did not move her in any way—she was neither confused nor impressed by them. She brought a glass of water and read the note, whispering its words.

She was ready to put it back in the music box and lock it away when she heard her husband stomping his feet on the welcome mat outside the front door. Gaja returned everything to the hiding place and finished her cigarette. When she came out of her room, she felt the hint of cold air Bronza's body had brought in. "You home?" she called and soon found him in his den.

Gaja admired him from the doorway, his eyes hollow and tired from work, hands chalky white and folded, resting against his unshaven chin. He had not removed his coat or hat. She sat on a footstool near a bookshelf, closer to him. His whisper surprised her. "Have you found out?"

She waited a moment. "What?"

"Had to take Jorgenson to emergency. Yesterday."

"Emergency?" She shook her head slowly. "And? He's sick?"

Bronza nodded, staring straight ahead. "But he'll be fine."

"It took all night?" She leaned back against the shelf. "And most of the afternoon?"

Bronza sighed, rubbing his face and eyes. He tapped a pencil against a notebook and tossed it to the side. In the quiet, they were barely able to hear Kolya's sounds carry from Anya's room. Wind blew through the cedars outside the window and a powder of ice crystals tinkled lightly against the glass. Bronza went over to Gaja and kissed the side of her head, just above her ear. His nose and cheeks were still cold. When he left the room, Gaja repeated, "It took all night?" but Bronza only mumbled in the hallway.

He saw the leftover food on the kitchen table, the cabbage rolls in small puddles of cold juice. Bronza picked up one of Yuri's three railroad spikes. He could not imagine why they were on the table. Then he saw the note scribbled in Lithuanian. "Gaja," he said. "Gaja...what's all this? Yuri's written this. What's this note read?"

She hit herself lightly in the forehead with a half closed fist. How could she have left Yuri's scene in the kitchen? Now she remembered the boy wasn't even home.

"Gaja."

Bronza was neither angry nor confused by what he saw and only called his wife from sheer reflex. She appeared in the archway.

She pressed hands against her belly, and her vivid blue eyes stared intensely at the table. It seemed she might burst into tears or scream at Bronza, accuse him of something or try to hit him, and he prepared himself for one of her outbursts. Gaja's lips parted, but then she pressed them together. "Shh," she said. Her fingers pinched the top button of her sweater and she began to undress, catching Bronza completely off-guard. When she exposed her shoulders and bra, Bronza covered her. "Gaja. Please!"

"It can be different," she said. "I can change. You told me so. I believe it. You're right."

"Gaja?"

"Shh." She put a hand over his mouth. "I *can*. I really can. We can be like it was before. Like in the beginning."

"Just sit down. You're shaking."

"I'm thinking only about change. But you'll have to help me."

"I'll put this stuff away. I'll make some tea. Here, take my cigarettes." Bronza stashed the railroad spikes and note on top of a shelf in his den. As he searched through his drawer for an extra pack of cigarettes and box of matches, he heard someone knock on the door. Gaja called from the kitchen, "Someone's here." Bronza saw Monsignor Kilba in the diamond shaped window, his face calm as always. Yuri was beside him. Bronza said, "Hey," and let them in. "Yuri. Well. Monsignor, you've driven him home?"

Kilba nodded. "We had a little chat after church together. I'm sorry I didn't call. I hope I didn't keep you worried."

"No. No, not worried. Not really," said Bronza. Yuri slipped past his father. "But...yes, thank you, Monsignor. I hope it wasn't any trouble."

"No trouble," said Kilba. "Of course, at some point...we'll have to. I'm certain you understand we'll have to talk."

"Talk? Yes, yes. Anytime you think so, just come over." Bronza tucked his hands in his pockets. "But right now's actually not the best time."

"Of course." Kilba cleared his throat. "I'm on my way to visit Lars. How is he?"

"Better than expected."

"Well," Kilba pressed Bronza's forearm. "God willing, he'll be well soon. I'm off. Perhaps I'll see you there. Till then, good-bye."

"Okay. Bye, yes."

Bronza watched Kilba step down their front stairs. Then he approached Gaja, standing at the door to Yuri's room. The lock had been removed from the boy's door, but Gaja was not going to barge in. She tapped lightly and whispered, "Please let me see you." Bronza took her lightly by the wrist and brought her to the front room. "Where was he?" he asked.

Gaja shrugged.

"What happened?"

"Shh," she said.

"What *happened*?"

"No no," she said, and put her hand on his forehead, then held his neck in both hands. "Please. Never again." Her touches surprised him—they almost felt foreign, but their warmth and intimacy also calmed him, let him sense how badly he needed to rest. They inched towards each other, and he reached out for her cheek as her hands fell to his shoulders, to his shoulder blades, then down to the small of his back. Gaja and Bronza held each other, tightly for a moment, but then swayed, gentle and quiet.

6

Lars' constitution amazed the hospital staff. After two days he showed only mild signs of sickness. Lars could walk around, tell bad jokes to the nurses: "You might have a good oncologist, but what you really need to hire around here is a gastronomist," and he'd wander to parts of the hospital where they didn't want him, leaving the back of his gown open without any inhibition. They soon let him go.

Alina drove him home. She had cleaned and completely reorganized his garage. Lars found all his papers arranged in marked folders and stacked neatly on the shelves. She had made his bed with brand new sheets, pillows and a pricey down comforter. The fridge was stocked with his favorite foods: head cheese and vinegar, pickled herring, red onions, limburger, pumpernickel brick, jars of Kosher dills, and two smoked mackerel. She had removed the Wisconsin shine and his few bottles of bourbon, a half-case of leftover beer from one of the cupboards. Lars never asked about any of the booze.

More than anything, he wanted to sit at the piano. When Alina left, he played scales just to limber up, and his fingers glided over the keys. Then he improvised so that several hours had passed before he knew it. Lars heard Reikel—the guy still lived across the street with his parents—talking to someone in the alley. Normally, he'd go out for a chat, but Lars just kept at the piano.

The next day he didn't talk to anyone. His tenants, a Mexican named Franklin and a young Croatian couple, came around to pay their rent, but he just shouted to them to slide it under the door. Going out to the winter cold raised a heavy, clogged feeling in his lungs, but Lars bore it to take a short walk to the corner store. When he returned with sweet rolls and sat to try to compose, lethargy weighed him down. Lars didn't even bother brewing any coffee, and he didn't bite any pencils. Nothing would come of this lethargy and there was no use fighting, so he went to sleep.

He was cutting red onions and toasting bread late the next morning when the telephone rang. It was Bronza. "What are you doing?"

"Cutting an onion," said Lars.

"Your appetite's okay? How's the health?"

"Comes and goes."

"Hold on a second." Lars heard Bronza talking to the clinic's receptionist. "Sorry about that. Hands full. But I had to remind you. Didn't know if you remembered, I actually forgot about it myself, but Yuri's supposed to have a lesson today."

"The lesson?" Lars felt a jolt of joy.

"He reminded me about it this morning," said Bronza. "Asked if you're too sick to do it."

"No, no. As a matter of fact, no." Lars sat on his bed. "Slipped my mind, too. Still, I'm well enough. Have him come around."

Yuri had been Lars' private student for five years. The boy had poor rhythm, very little ability to distinguish pitch, only vague music memory, and Lars knew he rarely practiced. The gloves interfered, and his hands never learned proper form. Normally Lars would have discontinued such lessons, admitting the waste of time and money, but he loved Yuri's company. He went out to the Polish deli for a sack of chocolate prunes and the boy's favorite bacon buns.

Yuri arrived bundled up, a long scarf tied over his nose. He appeared cheerful and said, "Hi, Mr. Jorgenson," voice muffled.

After peeling the layers, Yuri sat not at the pianist's bench but on the teacher's stool close to Lars' desk. He took one of the fresh buns, broke it in half and picked the bits of meat out. Lars unwrapped a chocolate prune and stuffed it into his mouth. "How are you?" he asked, chewing.

"It's different in here now," Yuri said.

"Alina cleaned up. Everyone's nice to you when you almost die of pneumonia."

"Are you still so sick?"

"Not *so* sick," said Lars. "We should have a good lesson."

With Yuri in his home, Lars' played piano with a sense of reason and meaning. He improvised, a painful and isolated little footpath through a shady forest, and Yuri listened attentively to every single note. He watched Lars, amazed that his fingers always knew where the sharps and flats were...how did his body change from a lanky, awkward rag doll to a delicate dancer with flowing arms and a straight back? Yuri had always believed, even when he was younger, that Lars was actually two people: one guy played piano and the other guy didn't.

He kept on playing. The music was a pair of hands and a piece of wood. Yuri also saw a tool...he didn't know what it was called, but it carved the wood, gouging into it to form the shape of a person. As the music continued, the dark yellow and cobalt of a late winter evening sky, Yuri saw the shape coming together, a man with thin arms and legs, profound bones, twisted and crooked knees. He was hungry but also strong, so real that he could come alive, sit down to eat bacon buns with them in the garage.

Lars held a final, fading chord. When he lifted his hand from the keys, he reached for a prune and held it hidden in his fist. "There," he said. "I'm sorry if it was sad. Was that too sad?"

Yuri shook his head.

"I wanted to play something happy. A chipper little squirrel. But it didn't really come out that way."

"It was a little piece of wood. Two hands were making a statue out of it."

"I can see it." Lars slowly unwrapped the prune and picked off all the chocolate. He pinched the prune, mushing it into a little ball and chewing it slowly. "For me, it was like a path. There's only enough room on that path for one person. And nobody ever goes there, anyway. So it's a good place."

Yuri was wiping his greasy fingers. "Mr. Jorgenson," he said timidly. "Can I show you something?"

"On piano?" Lars was surprised. "You want to play?"

"I have something in my coat. I brought it. I was going to hide it someplace...I didn't really know where. But maybe you want to see it."

"What is it?"

He removed a small bundle from his coat and placed it lightly on Lars' desk, something wrapped in a handkerchief. Yuri said, "You should look."

When Lars saw the crucifix—undeniably sculpted by Benny Laputis—he felt cold pebbles sink between his lungs. The figure of Christ had been sculpted separate from the cross and Benny had nailed it down with fine nails. The cross was more like a "T," two rough and interlocking posts. Lars was struck by the graphic detail of the bones and strained joints and how heavily the body, especially the head, hung. He did not know that Benny had given this crucifix to Bronza only minutes before his death, but seeing the thing transported him, instantly and vividly, to the white sheets hanging in Benny's back yard and the pillowcase of figurines by the door. "Yuri," he whispered, leaving the figurine on the table. "Why do you have this?"

"I found it in the basement. And I was hiding it in my room."

"Why are you showing me?"

"I wanted to know what you think about it."

"What I think?" Lars pressed a knuckle into his mustache. "You need to tell me what you know about this."

"It's a statue. Mama said it's really bad. But Kilba said it's not true."

"Really bad? And Monsignor Kilba?" Lars nodded, wrapping the figurine back in the handkerchief and pushing it closer to the desk's center. "Do you know who made that crucifix?"

"They're papachka's. He said they were in the house when he bought it."

"Right."

"There are lots of statues like this. Some of them are really funny. But others are terrible. Some of them are naked people. Men and women, together sometimes. Papa took them away and hid them all somewhere, but I still have a couple. I have this one. What do you think of it?"

Lars really didn't understand what the boy wanted to know. Yuri asked him, "Do you think it's wrong to make statues like this? Do you think it's a sin?"

"Sin. Um...no." Lars chuckled. "No. I don't. But you don't want to ask me about sin, kiddo. I don't really think about stuff that way."

"What do you think about it?"

Lars sighed out slowly. "Let me. Let me show you." Because of Alina's rearrangements, it took him a moment to find the folder he wanted. "I'll show you." He set some notes on the piano and clapped his hands.

Yuri noticed a name written on the notes, *Benny Laputis*. It was the music Lars had composed for Benny's funeral, and he played all four short pieces for the Processions, Offering and Communion of a Catholic Funeral Mass.

Yuri saw a winter evening full of gray birds, a dark red moon low in the sky. He could feel the cold of the winter as well as the warmth of the red, and he understood that something terrible had happened that hurt many people. In the same space, something was vibrating and powerfully alive—Yuri kept seeing a gray bird beating its wings and flying fast right over the snow in Park Holme, a relentless bird that could swoop and cut with the greatest energy. All four pieces of music, they were different from one another, but each contained the bird, the cold air and the red moon.

The music stopped at the most unexpected moment. Lars was getting himself a glass of water.

Yuri took the little bundle and put it back in his coat. When Lars sat at the piano again, he and Yuri felt like they understood each other's feelings completely, and Yuri thought he had learned something important, the kind of lesson filled with true feelings and images but no words.

He told Lars, "I used to be really scared of that statue. But I always wanted to look at it. And I would think about it. Sometimes, I would draw pictures of it and then tear them up."

Lars nodded. "I haven't played that music for thirteen years." He drank from the little glass. Round beads of water were stuck in his mustache. Lars said, "It seems like yesterday. Like I did it thirteen minutes ago."

Yuri understood. "When you were sick, I saw Alina in church. She said she's going to show me where she makes rings. And papachka said I could go."

"I'm glad," said Lars. He shelved the notes, noticing Alina had put all the photo albums together on one shelf. For a moment, Lars imagined he'd show Yuri a picture of Benny Laputis, tell him the whole story.

Playing that music had energized him, and now he wanted Yuri to leave; he had an idea for a brand new piece of music and felt like he could compose it in one night. They spoke for a short time about Alina's job, but soon the lesson was over. As usual, Yuri left the garage without playing a single note and Lars didn't give him anything to practice at home.

Yuri always felt at peace after Lars' lesson. The feeling persisted as he walked to the bus stop and got his fare ready.

Standing among the bundled-up people in the bus shelter, he could not stop thinking about the gray bird and the open snowy field. Seeing his reflection in the Plexiglas, Yuri realized something about himself for the first time.

He had always known he was Yuri, one person, different from all the other people around him. But after hearing Lars play that music, he understood, strangely and completely, that he would *always* be himself. He would never become someone else and no one else would ever become him...only Yuri would ever know what it was like to be him, to like the things he liked and to imagine the things he imagined. Maybe it was a dumb thing to learn, something obvious, but Yuri didn't feel stupid. He knew he had understood something definitely true.

For the rest of the day, he thought about the name *Benny Laputis.* It was a funny name...in Lithuanian, laputis meant *Little Leaf,* and he had never met anyone with the name. But something about it still seemed familiar. He knew for sure that no one had ever mentioned it, but Yuri thought he had seen that name somewhere before. Written down. Not at home but someplace in Cicero. A place he had recently been. He couldn't remember where but was sure he'd find it again someday.

7

Even though Monsignor Kilba had finished fasting, Father Cruz continued. Whenever it was time to eat, he'd take food to his study where he'd wrap it in foil and hide it in a small sack. Later—on his way to the bakery or a deli for "lunch"—he'd give the food away to beggars on 14th or Laramie.

Besides daily Communion, Cruz never took more than one glass of water per hour and he prayed the entire rosary at least once per day. Before sleep, he'd kneel at the foot of his bed and speak Acts of Contrition until the repetition entranced him, wiping his thoughts clean so that he sensed a coal black vastness that left him feeling pure.

Gaja came to church every single morning to hear his 8:00 mass. She always sat in the same place, off to the left by a pillar, almost directly in front of the podium where Cruz read the Gospels and gave his sermons. She never seemed to be listening to him; her eyes wandered about the church, often up to the murals on the ceiling. When she waited to receive Communion, Cruz was always aware of how many people stood between her and him.

Interestingly, the longer he fasted, the more Gaja's confession—or admission...what was it...a revelation of being violated—haunted him, and he'd imagine forcing himself on her just as he thought about giving her refuge, a place to rest and retreat from everyone. Cruz could be by himself in his study or walking through the churchyard, and Gaja would whisper, *I broke his rib.* He was polishing his shoes one morning when he imagined it, a sharp sudden pain, but Cruz also saw himself wrapping her up in a blanket and letting her sleep in his bed, safely locked in his room.

Gaja came back to confession each week. She told him she was a terrible mother, that she had done nothing when her son had run away from home. She had tried to undress in front of her husband. Cruz absolved her sins and told her to pray an Our Father ten times at the Sacred Heart. When he came out of the confessional, he saw her kneeling in prayer at the statue.

Cruz had no idea who her son was. He didn't know the boy who had muttered some nonsense confession about statues and railroad spikes—a confession Cruz had virtually ignored and all but forgotten—was the same boy who had snuck into church during evening mass and then spent the night on the choir bundled up in Lars' coat. Cruz didn't really care that she had a son. One night—his fasting hunger no longer uncomfortable and now simply a constant sensation—he tried to imagine what her husband may have looked like. He saw a young man, a lawyer who wore expensive ties and made money in a downtown skyscraper. He was a braggart and a fool, nothing more than a heartless, soulless body.

Father Cruz had still not eaten on Christmas Eve. Before Midnight Mass, he and Kilba were vesting with a bishop. Cruz silently prayed the vesting prayer to himself when he put on his alb, a long white robe, *Make me white, O Lord, and cleanse my heart; that being made white in the Blood of the Lamb I may deserve an eternal reward.* When he crossed the stole over his heart, Cruz prayed, "*Restore to me, O Lord, the state of immortality which I lost through the sin of my first parents and, although unworthy to approach Thy Sacred Mysteries, may I deserve nevertheless eternal joy.*"

Monsignor Kilba, already vested, asked him, "So, when are you going to quit the fast?"

"I'm sorry?"

"The fast, Cruz. Just curious."

Cruz had thought he was keeping it hidden perfectly. "I'll have Christmas dinner tomorrow."

"Anything on your mind?"

Cruz lifted the final vestment over his head. "I just felt it called for more. That's all."

The church was packed with people spilling into the aisles, entire families in the vestibule and side alcoves. Kilba blasted every light the church had, and Lars had brought in extra musicians, a flutist with a trumpet player and violinist to join the choir. Parishioners had come well dressed, men in suits and women in long coats. Old women in the aisles knelt right on the marble when it came time to consecrate the Host. It was Cruz's first Christmas at the parish and he was impressed with the mass, more so with the parishioners themselves.

He saw Gaja had taken a place towards the middle, deeper in the church than she normally sat. Yuri was next to her, but the connection between them meant very little to him. Father Cruz realized what Gaja was going through—she was celebrating the birth of the Christ child only weeks after her own daughter had choked in her sleep. Her eyes radiated vividly amid the black, dark green and red coats, and she had wrapped an elegant scarf around her neck, tastefully matched to her hat. For a short moment, the whole congregation had become a sea of colors and vague shapes swirling around her.

When she stood to receive Communion, Cruz hoped she would come to him, but Gaja got in line to receive from the bishop. Her body swayed when she moved along the center aisle. Lars accompanied a mezzo-soprano who sang *Oh Night, Divine*, the bright church filled with soaring high notes. It was finally Gaja's turn to receive and the bishop held the body of Christ out in front of her. She said, "Amen" and Cruz watched the bishop's fingers place the small white wafer on her tongue.

8

Running late, Alina tossed away clutter on her dresser to find the car keys. She drove fast, weaving through traffic, rolling through stop signs and honking at a delivery van for stopping at a yellow signal. On the expressways, she flew well over the speed limit, darting in and out of lanes and tailgating people.

She knew the trip to pick up Yuri might end up a waste of time. Gaja had given him permission to "go downtown" for the day, but you never knew with her—the woman could change her mind at any moment, drop one of her lame excuses. *You know, he's just not feeling well.* Or, *Alina, please forgive me...I forgot that he's got an appointment at the dentist's. It's impossible to cancel, and I suppose I should have called you.*

The woman was too stupid to come up with decent bullshit. She thought the whole world was her fool, and Alina wanted one day to just walk right up and tell her off. *You're nothing more than a wound-up snob and huge fake.* Nobody had ever told her off. People either pitied her or thought she was beautiful.

But Gaja Dilienko wasn't beautiful. She had money for makeup and clothes, but her taste was ordinary and prudish: long skirts and stupid blouses buttoned up to the neck. Now she was getting crow's feet around her eyes and lips, and her teeth were stained from cigarettes and tea. Gaja looked down on everyone, and no one, nothing was ever good enough for her—the Dilienkos were so much better than the Jorgensons. Even if her uncle Benny hanged himself and her daughter had choked, why the hell should Alina pity her?

She double-parked in front of Yuri's house. He was waiting for her on the stairs and scolded her in the car. "You're ten minutes late."

Gaja was standing in the doorway, a bit pale, shivering without a coat. "I don't want to keep you," she shouted. "But about money. His father gave him thirty dollars." Gaja held more money out so that Alina could see it. "Is that enough?"

"I'm not sure," said Alina. "Maybe a few bucks more, just in case."

Gaja sighed and came to the car, handed over the bills. "Please don't let him eat too much junk food."

"I don't eat junk food."

"And he'll be home before dinner?"

"Yes," said Alina. "He'll be on time."

They drove out of Cicero. Yuri had never really seen Alina so impatient. She held onto the steering wheel tightly and glanced at all her mirrors, frantic when she ended up behind a slow car. He knew it was best to let her feel grumpy, because a small thing would soon make her happy. She eventually asked, "What did you get for Christmas?"

"Some stuff. Shoes."

"Shoes?"

"I always get shoes. Every year I get new shoes. Brown or black ones for school."

"That's boring. Why do you get shoes?"

"Because my feet grow every year."

"Was your Christmas nice?"

Yuri was playing with the glove compartment. He opened it and took out a wrinkled and worn interstate map. When he realized it was too big to unfold, he put it away and sat still but then opened the glove again.

"No answer?"

"Mama and papachka think I don't know what they were doing. But I know about it already. I know what it is."

"What were they doing?"

"They were screwing."

Alina laughed to herself. "Oh, really?" She glanced at him, but he was looking out the window. "And you know about it?"

"We went to have dinner over at that other doctor's house. This weird doctor who doesn't have a wife or kids, just a big dog and four cats. And a fish that eats worms. He's from the clinic."

"I know him."

"Mama and papa drank a lot of cognac. And they came home and told me I had to go to bed. But I know mama let papachka come to her room. She thinks I don't know about it, but that's where papachka went."

"Big deal, Yuri. Your parents wanted to be together. Sometimes the kids just have to go play in their rooms."

"They want to replace Anya," he said.

Alina was quiet.

"There was a present for Anya under the tree. It's what mama wants the most, I think. A new baby girl."

Alina didn't ask any more questions.

Yuri only looked at the passing sights, the peaks of the tallest skyscrapers hidden in the bellies of low clouds, and the men in orange hats working on the sides of the road.

Soon, Alina was driving through a part of Chicago Yuri had never seen. The brick houses, mostly red or brown, had black iron fences around very small front lawns. The neighborhood was dirtier and rougher than Cicero, damaged cars parked on the streets and homeless guys huddled up together in the cold, but Yuri thought the houses were prettier. The whole place seemed very alive, many people walking around in front of busy shops and restaurants. The L rumbled loud on a rusty bridge and vibrated the whole car.

They parked in front of Alina's house, across the street from a park shaped in a triangle. "You live here," said Yuri.

"We have to go over there. The shop's just a short walk."

The shop, right on Shiller and Hoyne, was on the ground floor of a corner house. A small sign in the front window read *Anderssen's*. Underneath hung a handwritten sign, *Post-Christmas Sale, This Week Only*. "Here we are," she said. "And we're not so late at all."

Chimes sounded when they pushed the door open. The store was completely different from any of the places where mama shopped. The small front room smelled of burnt-out candles, and steam hissed from a hidden radiator. Some of the paint was cracking, and old roughed-up chairs and shelves might have been found in an alley. Pale light bulbs dangled from black extension cords over glass cases full of rings, bracelets, necklaces and earrings, most of them brown or gray. Black candleholders and table lamps stood on wooden pedestals. The shop also sold picture frames, and they all showed the same black and white photograph of a smiling African woman with hoop earrings. A girl with a crew cut was reading a book behind an old cash register. She only lifted her eyes from the page to greet Alina.

Yuri stood in the middle of the floor. He asked Alina, "What did you make?"

"In this case over here." She showed him. "I've finally learned enough to have my own case. All these are mine. The design, everything."

Yuri noticed a difference between Alina's rings and the shop's other stuff. Lots of the stuff was bulky and the color of rust, but Alina used smooth, shiny metal and all her gems were blue or green, the rings much thinner. "You'll get a better chance to look at them later," she said. "Right now we have to go back here. Downstairs. It's where we make everything."

He followed her down a narrow corridor with a low ceiling. Alina pushed hard on a door with her hip and Yuri followed her down a steep wooden stairwell, a haze of fluorescent light down below. In the cramped brick basement, a large, very dusty exhaust fan hummed over the entire room.

The tall, balding guy with the huge beard was Mr. Jan Anderssen. He wore yellow goggles and sat at a worktable cluttered with tools. A large black vice held a metal rod for him and he waved the blue flame of a torch over the glowing end. "Hey," Alina said. "Good morning."

Jan looked up. He checked his watch and extinguished the torch. Very slowly, he lifted his goggles onto his forehead and came over to shake Yuri's hand. "Good morning to you, sir."

Jan Anderssen's right hand was missing a pinky and part of the ring finger. But his grip was very strong, the skin hard, dry and prickly, as if full of slivers.

Jan crossed his arms and leaned back against the worktable to brush his beard. His eyes had looked into Yuri so intensely that Yuri feared it might insult Jan if he looked away. "Alina told me all about you. I'm glad your mom let you out."

Yuri said, "It's really different down here."

"Different? In what way?"

Yuri didn't want to say the place looked like a mechanic's shop. "I imagined something different."

Jan nodded. "Good. Look around. Make yourself at home." He went back to his workspace, lowered his yellow goggles and lit his torch. "Ask questions and hang out. But don't touch anything without me or Alina to help you."

Yuri watched them work through the morning. The tools fascinated him. The exhaust fan was really for the small forge resting on a slab of concrete. They didn't use it that morning and only heated their material with torches.

Yuri loved how metal became soft when it was hot. Jan twisted and bent handles for sliding doors, sometimes beating them hard with a hammer. When finished, the handles resembled archers' bows, only without strings. He worked quickly, etching designs onto them, and answered Yuri's questions with short sentences. Before the morning was over, he had finished six handles, leaving them to cool on a block.

Alina worked much slower, touching up a sharp copper brooch. It was a long, sharpened and very elegant raindrop—she etched a complicated symbol on its side and then set it with a pin. She worked with her hair pulled back, a bandana wrapped around her forehead and safety glasses over her eyes, intense and patient.

A white, green-eyed cat tiptoed around the worktable, occasionally hopping off to lick herself on the basement's bottom stair. Yuri liked that her name was Shadow. She often came right up and rubbed her head on his forearms or sniffed him, reaching up to his shoulder with her front paws.

Whenever Shadow came close to Jan, Yuri could pretend to look at her when he was actually staring at the injured hand. The ring finger was a stub, virtually useless, but Jan's agile hand held tools tightly. It must have been terribly painful to lose a finger— under the worktable, Yuri pinched his pinky with the edges of his fingernails and imagined how it would feel all the way down through his bone.

When Alina left the basement for a moment, Jan's monotone question surprised Yuri. "Want me to tell you?"

Yuri shook his head. "No." He stuttered briefly, his attention on Shadow.

The corner of Jan's mouth rose high into his cheekbone and wrinkled the side of his face. "I'll tell you." He held up the hand, palm toward himself. "It's one of the most important things that ever happened to me." He took a pair of tongs. "When I was a kid. Right around your age. My neighbor, right down the street from here, actually, he had a dog named Lou." Jan worked while speaking. "The neighbor was an old man, kinda deaf, yelled at us kids all the time. Lou was old also, but he was big, a tough old sled dog always chained to this apple tree. The backyard was pretty big, with this rotting wood fence. Me and all the neighborhood kids, you know, we'd tease Lou. Get him all riled. Throw rocks. Stand where he couldn't get us. Put food where he couldn't reach it. Sling shots sometimes. Even firecrackers."

"Why?"

Jan looked up briefly, the goggles covering his eyes. "We were being mean." He lit his torch and heated a thin black tube. "I didn't want to hurt Lou. Maybe none of the other kids did either. I actually felt sorry for the bag of bones. It was hard to admit it to my friends. I never hurt Lou when I was alone. Not once. But when the other kids were around, I sometimes threw a rock before anyone else. Would stand just past the length of the chain and spit on him while he barked."

Now Jan put his hand flat on the table. "Lou finally busted loose of his chains one day."

"He bit you?"

"Went right for me. Chased me, caught me easily. And he bit me all over the place, got my hand and clamped down, yanking like a psycho. He only let me go when another neighbor grabbed him by the chain and pulled. I ran away and hid. My grandmother found me later, but then it was too late for the doctor to fix anything." Jan extinguished the torch, lifted his goggles, and his intense gaze settled deep into Yuri. "Lost one and a half fingers. Dislocated wrist and elbow. Got some nerve damage. Half of my hand, I can't even feel anymore."

Yuri was sure it would hurt much more than a cigarette burn.

"They killed Lou, of course. What they do to a dog, they poison him, call it putting him asleep." Jan told the story without any shame or fear. When he was finished, he kept on working, and Yuri imagined Lou's wet, hot mouth and the strong thrashing of his neck. The whole time, Jan's soft blue flame flowed over a little tube, its end glowing bright orange, the mix of colors intensely beautiful.

At lunchtime, Alina took Yuri to her apartment for sandwiches. The small one-bedroom overlooked the triangular park, now full of students, old men and moms with kids. Alina's place smelled like a girl, but it was also messy, her dirty jeans draped over a chair's backrest, and socks and newspapers all over the floor. Abstract metal sculptures hung on the walls beside many small paintings of color blobs. She called out from the kitchen, "What kinda sandwich you want?"

"Don't care." Yuri sat on the couch, a bench covered with blue, yellow and purple cushions, all different sizes. "Just without mustard."

Alina took a phone call, annoyed when she answered, sighing while cutting bread, but then she perked up. "Hey, Reikel."

While she kept busy in the kitchen, Yuri got up to have a closer look at some of the art. He stood by the beaten metal triangles, hung so they floated a half-inch off the wall. They formed an erratic pattern, and his head spun when he tried to follow all the intersecting lines. The color blobs—one blue and green, another yellow and a dripping bloody red—reminded him of the music papachka listened to, Ravel and Sibelius, when he closed himself up in his den. Down the short hallway, Yuri found a photograph of a nude woman kneeling and leaning forward, her arms outstretched, head down, the dark hair spread over the floor in the shape of a fan.

Alina's bedroom was cluttered with girl's things...hairbrushes, curlers and cotton balls spilling from a paper bag. She had hung Mrs. Jorgenson's five canes in the middle of one wall, nailed up at angles above a tidy bookshelf. When Yuri looked over the shelf, he realized most of the books were Russian. Papachka had some of these in his den, Братья Карамазовы, Машенька, Мертвые души, Евгений Онегин, Война и мир, books papachka said would be easier to understand when Yuri got a bit older. He touched some of their old, cracked spines.

The black books at the bottom of the shelf, over thirty of them, didn't have any titles at all. Curious, Yuri slipped one out of its place and sat on the floor to peek inside. He found the most beautiful, flowing handwriting, much like papachka's, only easier to read, the letters larger and more graceful. All of it was in Russian:

Lars is having trouble (slight trouble, but trouble all the same) with the paradox. He had nothing, not a single worthwhile idea for composition when things were peaceful, when his life offered him simplicity: bread at the bakery, students in a classroom and piano recitals. But then it came time to bury Laputis and music welled from him. Why at that moment? So quickly, instantly. Last night he asked me, Why does it take something like Benny? What might it take in the future?

"Yuri? Where are you?" He shut the book quickly and scrambled to return it to the shelf. "Hey, what are you doing?" She yanked the journal away from him. "You can't read that! Not these!"

He left the room quietly and went to sit on the bench with the cushions.

"Take something from someone's shelf like that?" Alina put the journal back exactly where it belonged. "This isn't yours." She closed her bedroom door with force, and he saw her face, more upset than she had ever been with him. Alina brought the sandwiches over to the table and sat alone for a moment, sipping from a glass of cranberry juice. She relaxed after some time and said, "I'm sorry," but Yuri felt her anger. "Those are my mom's. You're not supposed to read them."

"I thought they were just books."

"They're not."

They sat with the distance of the entire room between them. The longer Alina remained quiet, the more Yuri could drift away and wonder about the name *Benny Laputis*. A dull mix of excitement and frustration formed knots in his belly. He felt like searching, lifting boxes, looking through drawers. And in that moment Yuri remembered where he had seen the name before.

It had been in the cemetery, on a gravesite right next to Anya's. He thought that remembering would help him understand something, erase all of his questions. But now Yuri was more curious than he had been before.

Alina's silence endured and he felt more and more alone. The gray bird from Lars' music darted and swooped over the snowy field, and the low red moon was glowing hot. Jan's tight hand held the tongs, and the blue flame glided over the metal tube, at once gentle and intense. Lou's chain kept pulling and jerking against the apple tree until it finally broke and the dog ran off, the chain dragging behind him. Yuri was looking into the color blobs when Alina finally asked, "How much of it do you understand?"

He sat up straight.

"Could you *read* it? Did you understand what she wrote in there?"

Yuri nodded.

"I can't," she said. "I can't read Russian."

"Papachka teaches me. We read together."

"When I was little, mama and I used to speak. But I hated speaking it. Forgot most of it. She used to read Russian by herself all the time, and she wrote almost every day. But she never taught me."

"The alphabet?" Yuri whispered.

"I've never even read a regular Russian book."

Yuri crept into the words carefully. "Ты," he whispered, to ask if she spoke Russian. "Ты... говориш по-русски, да??"

"Немного," Alina replied, her accent heavy. "I can understand a lot when people talk. But to read or to say it myself, barely anything."

Yuri had come near his food to sip some of his juice, bite down on the wedge of a pickle. "Why didn't you like to speak it?"

"It was just so boring. So hard and so old." She shrugged. "But mama also gave up. She didn't care if I learned, really. Maybe that was part of it. Russian was her place to hide from everything. She was really private. When I got older, I don't think she wanted me to learn."

"Do you want to learn?"

"I'd have to." Alina toyed with the food on her plate. "I really have to."

"It's not that hard," he said. "If you already know some."

"I don't know very much at all."

"If you really wanted, Alina." She finally looked at him and he could be sure all her anger had passed. "I could teach you."

9

Monsignor Kilba was at the Dilienkos' front door while Gaja was kneeling on pillows in front of Bronza and he was leaning back against the piano. He was just about to finish when she stopped and looked up at him, her eyes wide. Kilba knocked on the glass of their front door. Bronza's shirt and pants were still in the kitchen. He had thrown Gaja's dress into a corner by the dining table...she scrambled into it and realized the hem of the sleeve was torn slightly and one of the buttons had popped off.

"I didn't expect him so soon," she whispered.

Bronza yelled "One second" from his room. He wiped himself with an undershirt, grabbed any sweater and a pair of jeans. Gaja was already at the front door when Dilienko took his shirt and pants from the kitchen and rushed to throw them into the den.

Gaja let Kilba in. "I'm going to make tea," she said.

Monsignor Kilba took a seat at a small round table by the window. Bronza came out of his den to greet and sit with the Monsignor. "Sorry if I'm caught unaware." He lit a cigarette. "I thought you were Alina bringing Yuri home. Gaja didn't tell me you were coming."

"I did too," she called from the kitchen.

"Actually, no. You didn't."

"You both seem flustered," Kilba said. "Really, if this is a bad time."

"No no no," Bronza laughed. "No no. It's fine. Would you like a drink?"

Kilba took his scotch neat and the men sat alone while Gaja prepared tea. She returned having changed to a new dress, brown and simple. The three of them chatted for a while, commenting about the new tea, Lars' sickness, and how Bronza had yet to meet Father Cruz. But Kilba soon brought things to the point. "I actually have some very wonderful news."

"About what?" Bronza asked.

"A friend of mine, he's also a priest. We attended seminary together, a very good man. He happens to be the rector at St. Quentin's. If you don't know, that's a high school in Chicago, over by North Michigan Avenue. A rather selective place, mind you, Jesuits. I'll be honest, it's mostly the kids of snobs who go there." He blew on his tea. "But the rector also does a lot of recruiting from the grammar schools in the archdiocese."

"What's this leading to?" asked Bronza.

"My friend recently called me," Kilba lied. The Monsignor had called St. Quentin's on his own. "I took the liberty of getting Yuri's grades from our parish school. And it turns out that he's an ideal student for St. Quentin's. His grades are, while not the best in math, rather impressive everywhere else."

"I don't understand why you're bringing this up."

"Because, Bronza, it's a terrific boarding school. He'd be living there. Yes, it's pricey. But you're a capable provider. And," Kilba raised a finger modestly, "it seems Yuri qualifies for a substantial scholarship."

Gaja drank her tea.

"A handsome scholarship."

"Monsignor," said Bronza. "What kind of priests?"

"We're Jesuits. Didn't I say that?"

"Jesuits?" He extinguished his cigarette. Two shafts of smoke fell from his nose. "I'm sorry. But, no. I'm very sorry." He glanced at Gaja. "You didn't tell me about any of this."

"She didn't know about it," Kilba said. "I wanted to come and let you both know, in person, face to face, with Alina entertaining the boy so as not to trouble him while you listen to the wonderful news. It's wonderful news. Yuri's qualified for one of the best college preparatory academies in the archdiocese. And, to have him live there, where he can focus on rigorous studies, it's only slightly more than the tuition you pay at our parish school. Given the scholarship, of course."

"Out of the question. It's the other side of the city. When he finishes the parish school here," said Bronza, "I want him to go to a secular school. And I know about these boarding schools, what kind of lunatics attend them. Gaja, we agreed, no more Catholic schools."

Gaja said, "I'm not sure about anything."

Kilba set his glass of scotch down. "There is an alternative." He glanced at Gaja, but she wouldn't look at him. "We could, for example, arrange to have him see an allergist. We could bring one to the school, primarily one that specializes in skin allergies, and have him check all the kids. Yuri included."

Bronza crossed his legs. He took his pack of smokes from the table and lit up again.

"A secular allergist," Kilba emphasized. "Of course."

Bronza tried to find Gaja's eyes, but she was hiding from them both.

Kilba continued, "I'm sure you'll agree. That would be too much trouble and effort. The arrangement that's been made seems perfectly comfortable and suitable for everyone. Affordable, a good school, good teachers. A safe, healthy environment. I should tell you, as a matter of fact, that I attended a boarding school, right around when I was Yuri's age. And look at me. I have my vices, sure," he pointed to his glass. "But I didn't turn out all that bad in the end."

Passage: A Free Friday, April 27, 1979

Yuri finished the last Chemistry problem. He double-checked his math, revising a few of the harder problems, but finally handed in the test. With ten minutes to spare before the end of the period, he sketched the façade visible outside the window.

St. Quentin's Seminary North was an old building, gothic and gray, built around a tight courtyard of arches, balconies and rising spires. Virtually all the classrooms faced the yard, while others faced a beautiful street of old limestone houses. Yuri now sketched some of those houses from memory and had almost finished one when the test period ended. The whole room sighed out, and the boys' tense bodies slackened.

It was the end of the school day on a Friday. Most of the boys hurried to their rooms—the school had organized several outings that afternoon, including a trip to the cinema and one to the White Sox game, but Yuri wasn't going to any of those. He changed out of his uniform into the school's "work clothes," black cotton trousers and a St. Quentin's t-shirt. He crossed the courtyard to attend his seventh period Art class in the "attic."

The "attic" was a long wooden room with huge rafters and slanted walls, a small window high in the A-frame. On the sunny afternoon, a powerful shaft of light cut in through the window, so vibrant Yuri felt it accentuated the room's smell of dust. The place smelled dry, a mix of sawdust, plaster, paint and clay.

Father Lucent was already sitting at his teacher's desk in the corner. He was a weird priest with a thin, bony body, age spots on the top of his long, bald head, and a pinch of skin that dangled below his chin. One of his original paintings hung behind his desk:

a desperate Lot bargaining with wicked men and offering them two of his daughters, the girls obedient and lowly, the wicked men dressed in animal skins. The painting was like Lucent himself: calm and serious but also mischievous.

He was only strict about the subjects his students chose: they had to come from the Bible or classical mythology. Besides that, he really didn't care if the sketches were voluptuous or violent. Yuri had figured out early that he could sculpt any pin-up girl, call her *Danae* and Lucent would love it.

For this project Yuri had chosen Judas Iscariot. Yuri had sketched him lying on the ground already cut down from the sycamore, his neck elongated and bent, face lifeless but sorrowful. Of course, only Yuri knew it was Benny's face.

Alina had told him the whole story, and Monsignor Kilba had given him a photo. Yuri saw an enormous amount of himself in his great-uncle Benny, and he believed he understood the feelings of loneliness and confusion expressed by his wooden figurines.

He still had a long way to go before finishing the sculpture. Faces were so much easier to draw than to shape. Yuri's hands really could not create what he saw in his mind and he'd often grow frustrated. When he struggled, Father Lucent helped him follow the sketch, to allow the face to rise *out* of the clay instead of being shaped *into* it. Although the piece did begin to resemble what he had sketched, Yuri felt like he had accomplished little when the period was over. He cleaned up his workspace and covered it for the night.

With so many boys gone, the dormitory halls loomed long; occasionally, distant footsteps echoed from unknown directions. Yuri changed and took dinner in the cafeteria. Then he waited for Alina in the school's front lobby where he signed himself out.

Students were allowed to leave the school grounds with a guardian two weekends out of the month, and Bronza had arranged to let Alina take Yuri away from St. Quentin's. She always drove him straight to Jan's shop where they worked after the store had closed. Jan taught Yuri about molds, the properties of different metals, and he let him try using the tools.

Jan had been making daggers for a rich man who wanted to decorate his office with them. Modern and sleek, they were powerfully violent, but Yuri also sensed something sexual in the weapons. He didn't talk about it because he believed he was the only one who had this sense.

At her apartment, Alina and Yuri had their Russian lesson. She had been surprised, initially, by how much she remembered from childhood. Alina only needed to revive, then build the language. She read from Russian books every evening and gave Yuri lists of words she couldn't find in dictionaries. He helped her stress, pronounce them, decline and conjugate them properly. She had learned so much that she started bringing words he didn't know—they described old things, farming tools or clothing, accessories to suits and dresses.

Alina showed him the book she had just read. "I got this Russian translation of *Huck Finn*," she said. "I know the original really well." She showed him the long list of words. "It's weird. The Russian book's half as long. And the male nudie show—that part's gone."

"Nobody's ever naked in Russian books."

"But this *isn't* a Russian book. They just changed it."

"It's weird, I guess."

Alina put the book to the side.

"You don't think you're ready to try your mom's stuff?" he asked.

Alina went over to the refrigerator. "Not yet."

"Why?"

She was crouching down in front of the mostly empty fridge. "Not yet," she said.

They went to eat at the Busy Bee, a Polish deli under the L tracks. Whenever Yuri sat with Alina, he felt there was something he was supposed to tell or ask even though he didn't know what that was. It always seemed like they both knew something but didn't talk about it. And the conversations in Russian about Jan's knives, Reikel's stupid inheritance of his dad's meat store, Alina's wish to sell more jewelry, her dream to get out of Wicker Park, happened only so they wouldn't have to talk about *it*.

Alina showered before sleep and Yuri made his bed on the sofa. He tossed a sheet over the cushions, tucking it around them, then took the blanket down from the top shelf in a closet. He had drunk a lot of water and ginger ale and really had to pee, but Alina was taking forever. When she came out of the bathroom in her thick robe, letting out the scents of shampoo and moisture, Alina said "G'night," and closed herself in her bedroom.

She always left a night lamp in the bathroom, and its timid glow fell soft through the short but dark hallway, brightest in the shiny wet footprints Alina's feet had left on the hardwood. He stopped to look at them, symmetric outlines, each one with only four toes. They were small, smaller than Alina's white tennis shoes. After he finished in the bathroom, he came out to see some of the toes had already dried. The footprints really looked like a kid had left them, someone even younger than Yuri, younger than sixteen.

Episode: Summer, 1999

When Lita came in from the pouring rain, she left her sandals by the door and stepped barefoot across Yuri's room, leaving a narrow track of small footprints. Yuri had arranged skylines of candles on his shelves and the small coffee table. Lita took tamales out of a soaked paper bag and put them on plates. "They didn't have *pollo*," she said. "*Solo con carne y queso.*"

"*Gracias*," he said.

The homemade chessboard was already set up. Yuri had woven pieces from paper clips, and he had spray painted one set black. Lita complained, "Not black," when she sat down to play. "I'm not playing with black."

"But I always get black," said Yuri.

"They make me lose all the time."

Yuri turned the board around. She gave him his plate of tamales and a small plastic dish of salsa with tortilla chips. Unwrapping the husks, he noticed her short trail of footprints cutting straight across the floor. Yuri said, "You can move, Alina."

He didn't catch himself, didn't hear he'd mixed up the names. Lita watched him eat the chips and salsa, waiting for him to wake up to what he'd said. When she looked at the board, flustered, she had no plan and just moved a knight out into the field. Yuri moved a pawn to open up a lane for his queen.

Lita placed a finger on one of her pawns but then drew it back. She should tell him, "You just called me Alina." Would it embarrass him, make him withdraw? She didn't want him to space out, as he did so often, siting in a corner sketching candles or a ladle. But she couldn't ignore this. Maybe she should go to the shelf where he kept Alina's picture tucked away in a book. Lita knew exactly where it was.

He almost never spoke about her. Lita could actually count how often she had heard her name.

He had told her all about his past, stories triggered by odd objects. A bread roll. The smell of whiskey. A leather glove trampled in the dirt. Yuri would start talking about Monsignor Kilba or his sister, Anya, patches of a cut-up story, usually quite disorienting, now about Uncle Benny, then about his parents, again about Lars and Victoria, sometimes from one point of his childhood, then—without a segue—another, even to periods of time from before he was born. He'd break off in the middle of stories and leave wide-open holes, spaces Lita knew he didn't understand or couldn't remember.

Alina was a hole like this for him. One time Lita had asked him, "What about Alina," and Yuri had only shrugged. "She's still alive somewhere," he had said before withdrawing into silence and sketches.

Lita admitted Alina was prettier. Her fresh green eyes shone vibrant against her soft, clean complexion. She only touched up her lids with liner, didn't need lipstick or blush for her pink cheeks. Her nose was an odd button tagged to her face, but her hair flowed blond and shiny. What Lita envied most of all was that Alina pulsed with an amazing sense of self in the photograph. She knew something about Yuri no one else did. Lita wanted to take this secret and keep it all to herself.

"It's your move," he said. "Lita..."

"I'm thinking."

"You're spacing out."

"I am not." She moved another pawn.

"You're putting yourself in check. Look at it. Don't you see?"

"Where?"

"Right here." He showed her the queen's path. "Right there."

Lita put the pawn back and played her other knight. Yuri sighed, "Do you even want to play?"

"Yeah."

"Then what's this thing with the knights?"

"I have a plan."

"Yeah," he muttered. His hands were flat beside the chessboard.

She watched his eyelids twitch as he thought about the game. Then Lita did it. She felt a wave of nervousness, but it didn't matter. She set her hand on Yuri's. It surprised him and he looked up, but only at her forehead and down at her chin, her shoulders. Lita kept her hand there for a moment and turned his palm up. Gently, she pressed the tips of his fingers and brushed the palm.

Yuri was trembling when she came over to kiss him. He had always imagined this moment. It would be under a street lamp or at some lonely bus stop where he had plenty of time to prepare, plan it out. He could be a cool and relaxed man about it. But now Yuri felt tremors in his hands, and his stomach tightened; he felt himself a high school kid who didn't know his own body, a clown about to topple from stilts.

She got him to lie back, slid her hands behind his shivering neck and massaged his nape, straddling his belly. When she kissed his eyelids, licking the corners of his mouth with the tip of her tongue, a tense column of air escaped his lungs, and it was a relief when she unzipped his pants and grabbed him gently, then tightly.

Lita made sure the door was locked before she undressed. She thought she could take her clothes off slowly, but she'd begun shivering, her hands and feet cold, the candlelight now brighter than it had been. Yuri rolled his clothes up and threw them against a wall. The softness of their smooth bodies pressing together excited and stunned them.

Now that he knew it was definite, their togetherness real, his hands touched her everywhere. Yuri kissed everything, her dry elbows, the salty sweat under her breast, her chin and temples, belly button, thighs, pubic hair, the bones of her ankles and the arches of her feet. She rose and pushed him down and pinned him back, her hands tight around his wrists. Lita let her long hair hang down over her head, and she brushed his chest, throat and face with its light, feathery ends. She let him kiss and pinch her nipples, and squirmed away ticklish when he squeezed her ribcage. Yuri reached down to guide himself inside her and Lita helped him.

Finished, Lita and Yuri lay curled in a heap. They found new yet curiously familiar laughter. Pulling a blanket over themselves, they napped together very briefly.

Outside it was raining harder. Lita went to the window wrapped in Yuri's sheet. The light of the gray evening fell through the brown and green glass in a restrained, gentle melody so that she hesitated before swinging the window open to smoke grass. Yuri crawled over to smoke, sitting right next to her on the floor. Lita whispered, "Let's go somewhere."

"Where?"

"I don't know." She scooted closer to him. "Let's take the train."

"How far?"

Lita packed her hitter again. "I mean the L. What train did you mean?"

"Forget trains," said Yuri. "We could hitchhike."

"Or we could get a motorcycle."

"I can't drive—"

"I'll *drive* it," she said. "I'll totally drive it. For the whole summer. We'd go, you know, who cares where we go? Who cares how far?" She took another hit.

"I always wanted to go to Santa Fe."

"Where's it at?"

"New Mexico. In high school, I thought I'd go to art school in Santa Fe. I got accepted out there."

"You told me," she said. "I remember. That would've been sweet."

"A trip out that way now wouldn't mean anything."

"Who cares what it means." She stood to dress and Yuri watched her battle into the jeans. Slipping into her blouse, she said, "Let's take the L someplace." She came over and kissed him softly on the mouth. "We can go over by your old high school. Wander by the Water Tower. Maybe go down to the lake."

Passage: A Surprise Visit, April 11, 1981

On a Saturday afternoon, Yuri was cleaning the desktops in Father Malloy's Geography class. He also had to mop the floors and clean the windows.

It was his punishment for writing on a desk: *If I had 50 minutes left to live, I would spend them here because they'd last forever.* "If you're so witty and clever," Father Malloy had said, "why didn't you disguise your handwriting?"

Yuri had taken his punishment without protest. He washed the tables, dumping a few splashes of dirty ammonia water into the potted plants Malloy kept on bookshelves.

The priest had a whole section about the American Southwest, and Yuri dried his hands to page through a book about Santa Fe. He flipped through the spectacular photos of purple and red deserts, plateaus, sunsets and the modest but beautiful Spanish-style homes.

Brother Leonard lumbered into the room. He was gray and fat with pinkish hands and small gold spectacles, their arms stretched wide by his big head. He cleared his throat in the doorway. Yuri put the book away.

"There's someone here to see you." Leonard's wiry gray eyebrows floated up. Yuri never received any visitors besides Kilba and Alina. "I think it's your old man," said Leonard. "He's waiting for you in the dorm lobby."

Bronza was sitting on a wooden bench by the telephones. With his long coat folded over his lap, he looked neither upset nor happy. Yuri greeted him, "Здравствуйте, папа. You're waiting a long time?"

"Forgot to bring a book to read."

"I was busy in the other building."

"That fat priest said you're punished today." Bronza smiled. "For writing on desks."

Yuri nodded. Awkward silence lingered. Yuri asked, "Why'd you come? Is something wrong?"

"Can we go up to your room?"

Yuri signed his father in, and they went up the old iron staircase to Yuri's floor. His roommate was gone. Bronza tossed his coat over the back of a chair and leaned against the windowsill to stare into the school's courtyard. Yuri sat on the lower bunk. He asked, "Why have you come?"

"I wish I had more time to be here." Bronza turned around. He seemed oddly pleased about something. "Ran into Alina the other day. She told me the news."

"What news?"

"You got accepted to New Mexico or someplace, right?"

Yuri didn't respond immediately. "She told you?"

"Well, she thought I knew. So did Father Cruz. He congratulated me in the bakery." Bronza pulled out a chair. "Why didn't you tell me?"

Yuri said nothing.

"What kind of a school is it?"

Yuri fidgeted, sliding his hands under his thighs. "I made a decision," he said.

"What kind of a school is it? What will you study?"

"Look. You won't know what it is."

"Yuri." Bronza brought the chair closer and sat, leaning forward. "Why so defensive? You don't have to be afraid to tell me. You don't have to worry about what we're going to do. You should know it, without you at home, your mother's been...I know you don't know anything about it. It'll be hard for you to believe me. But she's better. She's a lot calmer. It's all very different now."

They were quiet.

Bronza asked, "What are you studying?"

"It's the Santa Fe Academy of Visual Art."

Bronza nodded. "She was hoping you'd stay closer to home. But—"

He interrupted, "Why do you always take her side?"

"Her side?" Bronza leaned back. "What side? I'm not. Don't accuse me." He stood and went to lean back against the sill. "I'm very happy for you. For your mother, an art school that's far away won't be the best news. But we can work on it. She'll support you."

Yuri wrapped a hand around a fist.

Bronza stared him down. "What's all this crassness? This attitude? Is that what these Catholics teach you here?" After a moment, Bronza asked, "What did you have to do to get in?"

"Fill out an application. Show them a portfolio."

"Do you have this portfolio?"

"You don't want to see it."

"I really want to see it."

Yuri pointed to a large, flat leather case tucked between his bed and desk. Bronza looked through the photos of clay and metal sculptures. Most were complete abstractions, although he found a few portraits, one dark silhouette of a thin woman, her skin rough. The only sculpture that struck him was titled *Jan*, a battered hand with two missing fingers, the bones exposed and the flesh torn.

"That's not everything I've ever made," said Yuri. "It's what I thought was the best."

"Didn't you think there were any good art schools in this area?"

"No."

"But did you look at them?"

"I've made a decision."

Bronza closed the portfolio and put it away. "But Santa Fe is far and it'll cost a lot of money."

"I'm going."

"Maybe we could explore all the options. Look at price and distance."

"I didn't ask you for money."

"What's gotten into you? What's the matter?"

Yuri stared into a wall.

Bronza said, "I'm sure it's not a cheap school. I'm just assuming."

"Papa, I don't want your money. I'm going. Myself. I'm doing it myself."

Now Bronza smirked. "Oh, really? Can you tell me how much this school costs?"

"To the penny," Yuri lied. "I've already taken care of most of it. I'm going to get a scholarship and I'll take a loan and I'll go. I've looked into it. I've already applied for the scholarships."

"Yuri, I'll pay for school."

"No you won't."

Bronza leaned forward. "Yuri, if you want to know the truth. Mama doesn't even know about this. She doesn't know I'm here."

"Well, call her and tell her."

Bronza got angry. "What are you talking about?"

"Call her and tell her everything. It doesn't matter. It changes nothing. She can't do anything."

"Yuri. Calm yourself."

"I'm not fucking afraid of you!"

Bronza took a moment to settle himself. "Please." He mellowed his voice. "It's time for things to be better. And if you'd calm down and listen you'd understand what I'm trying to say. I'm on your side. I've always been on your side."

Yuri laughed falsely, his eyes wet. Bronza felt the rage in them, adult-like and new, but the pain was a child's. Or perhaps it was the other way around? Bronza didn't know and, in the cumbersome silence between them, he did not have any room to think. "I'm very much on your side."

Yuri forced laughter. "What's my phone number?"

"Excuse me?"

"Or my favorite book." He lay back in the bunk. "My favorite color. What kind of chicks do I fuck?"

Bronza stood instantly, stepping to the door, unable to appear stoic. "I had no idea you were like this," he said. Silence dragged. "You're extraordinarily proud. And self-absorbed. Extraordinarily." He left, closing the door gently.

Yuri lay in bed for a long time, the anger sharp and hot in him, before he realized he had to finish washing the desks. He went back to the other building, passing the reception, empty for some reason, and the narrow phone booths by the front door. Yuri slipped into one and called Alina.

Autumn, 1981

1

Alina was driving home from her new job. After Jan's store had closed down, she found work at an Old Town jeweler. She never made anything original and only did repairs, resizing rings, fixing clasps on necklaces and replacing wristbands of watches. The bossy owner treated her badly, and she always felt the wish to rush home after work. But today she was too burned out to hurry and just guided her Datsun about without weaving through traffic. Parked a block from her place, she sat in the car for a moment, leaned back and almost fell asleep.

Her apartment was a mess. Clean clothes were gnarled up in a laundry basket where she rummaged to find a comfortable pair of sweats. Dust had accumulated on her bookshelves and dresser. Her mother's old canes, still hanging on the wall, hadn't been wiped down in ages. She wanted to dust them, but the sink was full of dirty dishes. The trash in the kitchen was piling up. The floor really needed to be mopped and there was bad milk in the fridge.

She heated up leftover Chinese, pouring chicken stock into the rice to soften it. A cup of tea and a few pieces of chocolate boosted her mood. She left everything in the apartment as it was and sat down in her reading chair to continue with her mother's journals.

Alina still kept a dictionary nearby but used it sparingly. Most of the time she found her mother's Russian flowing quite naturally for her. As easy as it had become to read, and as much as Alina wanted to know what mama would say next, she read with nervousness and caution, aware—even as her mother detailed so much trivia from her life, what she would wear, how much it had rained—that every page and passing volume brought her closer to an unknown, frightening space. Something loomed in the journals, and Alina wasn't sure if she'd be better off discovering it.

In the place where she was now reading, Alina was still years from being born. Her parents' third anniversary was approaching and mama wondered about dad's plans, painstakingly detailing the trivia of possibilities. He surprised her with tickets to *Romeo and Juliet*.

Mama wrote several boring paragraphs about the theater and clothing. The entry ended with an odd list of actors' names.

Mama had waited two whole days to make her next entry. It was unusually difficult to read and Alina actually had to use the dictionary now.

In one word, an eventful night.

The play was a nightmare. I thought Lars was going to cheer when the young lovers killed themselves under a purple cardboard moon. Tone deaf violinists poured cherry syrup all over the audience and we left with it dripping from our ears.

I laughed at him. I don't think it matters now...it barely mattered then, because we набухались.

Alina looked but couldn't find that word in a dictionary.

Properly, an entire bottle of cognac by ourselves. We giggled and spat all over each other, kissing with mouthfuls of booze; here came the lecherous moment we both wanted more than any theater tickets.

I laughed at him. It happened rather naturally, and I still find it funny in a guilty, sad way, although the longer it sits with me and the more I remember it (how I remember anything at all is a miracle), the more the humor seems to fade.

I threw my underwear on his head. He was so drunk that he couldn't get out of his clothes and almost stumbled over the table...he forgot to unbutton his cuffs before taking off his shirt, a bit of his own theater, I'm sure. Lars stood in the middle of the room without (to use his words) a salute. I stared at his soft thing like I had seen it for the first time. In a way, I suppose I had. I think I might have even pointed.

Alina was used to mama writing about sex. She did it very often. Even so, Alina always paused and set the journal to the side.

She would do absurd things like make sure the window blinds were pulled all the way down.

Lars picked through the room for a surrogate. The bottle of cognac, a statuette of a ballerina, the very fountain pen I'm using right now, and a candle holder. He finally saw the black cane and hopped over, excited by the notion, but then withdrew, unsure of himself, probably unsure of me. I let him use the handle.

Our roles reversed. It was now as if he was finally seeing me with all the lights on. With a new toy, he'd found a new way to play, but he was so sweet and careful, afraid it might hurt me. I was already used to the discomfort and the handle had already warmed when he set the cane down. Watching had sobered and aroused him so that he didn't need it anymore.

Alina imagined her parents lying together in their hazy, bluish room, resting beside each other. It was true that her mother had once been a young woman. A real one, not a photograph or the story of a young woman. Alina began thinking that all mothers were two separate people, or that motherhood was a kind of disguise, while the whole of a mother's womanhood was a carefully kept secret.

Setting the journal down, Alina went to her bedroom to look at the black cane with the marble handle. It was really there, now a dusty memento on the wall. Alina felt the dreamy, story-like space of time behind her, as the empty, unknown space of the future frightened her. With her body tired but mind strangely relaxed, Alina understood, for the first time in twenty-seven years of life, that childhood was finished and would never return. Just an eye blink ago, she was holding the cane for mama so she could take money from her purse and pay for Alina's dress. Now Alina was wiping the canes down with a dry cloth and arranging them to be sure they hung nicely.

2

Yuri finished cutting the last beef shoulder into steaks and packed them away. He unplugged the band saw to clean it, brushing bone dust and bits of meat onto the floor, then spraying the stainless steel down with pink cleaning solution. He scrubbed the machine and mopped the back room. The last customers had probably already left the shop, but Yuri peeked into the front just to be sure. Reikel had locked the shop's door and was counting money at the register. Yuri tossed his stained apron into a bin and washed his hands. He said, "Done back here."

Reikel glanced over a shoulder. "Cleaned up?"

"Steaks packed for that order tomorrow."

"Good good." Reikel had Yuri's paycheck ready and slid it to him along the counter. Yuri stuffed the envelope in his back pocket.

After a month of working at 14th Street Meats, Yuri had learned to know these awkward moments when Reikel had something to ask. He'd stutter: "I mean, ah, yeah. Hey, Yurs. I got somethin' special I need to tell you about."

"What, Reik?"

"I'm wonderin'. It's a big shindig this Sunday over at the Lutheran church. Wonder if there's chance you'll come in Saturday. Maybe help out. Pay you time'n half."

"I can't do it."

"Maybe just a couple hours."

"Not weekends, Reik. We agreed."

With his thumbs as hooks, Reikel hung his arms from the straps of his apron. "But you got nothin' to do. And it's money, right?"

"No, Reikel." Yuri grew impatient. "I'm working on Saturday."

"But this is real work. And time'n half."

"I sculpt on Saturdays."

Reikel smirked. "Just a couple of hours away from it? Why losin' a chance like this for cash? Almost free cash?"

"Free cash, Reik?"

"Almost free, t'be fair. Almost." He wiped his mouth with a wide-open palm to make a moist, subtle sucking sound that disgusted Yuri. "Take a couple hours' break?"

Yuri hopped over the counter. "I'll be in tomorrow. On time."

"What's that tone, Yurs? How come I can never ask? What's the big deal?"

"I'll see you tomorrow." Yuri closed the door behind him and walked to the bus stop.

Real work.

Reikel said it on purpose to get under his skin and he hated it. Recently, he had found himself hating quite a few things. These old women walking to his bus station with pull carts, the Mexican girls riding with boyfriends named Javier and Manuel, the construction workers with bellies and dirty jeans. Why didn't any of these people think a butcher was a stupid thing to be? Why was it acceptable to cut animals up in a secret back room but foolish to shape metal into art?

Yuri got off at Austin and walked to Lars' property. He was renting there, living in the same apartment where Alina had grown up and where Lars had refused to live after Victoria's death.

Jan Anderssen had bought him a pipe for his eighteenth birthday. After eating, Yuri always smoked cheap tobacco while looking over sketches at his kitchen table. The sketches always made him impatient to go down to the basement and begin.

Yuri had acquired castaway torches, tools, an anvil and other old items Jan and Alina didn't need anymore. He also got a load of sculpting metal: copper and iron sheets, rods, a few steel plates and a small bronze cube. Almost everything Yuri had ever sculpted—mostly trinkets and chess pieces but also a few busts—

was down in the basement, arranged on water-warped shelves. He privately called the shelves his "gallery," although he would never have said this to anyone.

When he looked at his recent works—a few birds, a tired woman's profile—all he saw were errors. One of the birds was off balance and couldn't stand. The welding jobs were crappy, the etching terrible. He needed better ideas, not just birds and faces.

Santa Fe had not given him a scholarship. Yuri didn't qualify for any federal grants and was allowed only small loans, but he had discovered a cheaper school, Southern Illinois University in Carbondale. They had a metals department, but while loans could cover tuition, he'd have to wait another year to apply. The idea of applying energized him whenever he thought of it, and the promise of leaving Cicero helped him sculpt even after the most exhausting days in the meat shop.

He strapped the goggles to his head and cracked the basement's small window for some air, lighting his torch. Yuri sat at his worktable, just an old door thrown onto workhorses. From one of the nearby shelves, he took down the piece he wanted to work on, a small sculpture titled *Self-Portrait*. It was very simple, two square mirrors, one shattered, the other painted opaque. They faced each other, set into a copper sheet, the whole thing supported by a piece of sanded wood.

Working, Yuri could not hear Lars knocking on the door. Lars took a liberty and let himself in to Yuri's basement.

Lars never really did like his basement, its spider webs and centipedes, a musty smell from the times it had flooded. And Yuri worked so diligently that Lars could feel a bit guilty—he had plenty of free time but never composed for more than a few hours each week. Standing right behind Yuri, Lars knew the boy had no idea he was there and now didn't want to disturb him.

Lars looked over the sculptures on the shelves, seeing many for the first time. They were really rather juvenile, embarrassingly loaded up with teen angst. One was a woman's portrait sculpted from the surface of a flattened chrome shovel, and Lars believed this was Gaja. Yuri had somehow etched and melted the spade's face, patches of the metal discolored to form a disfigured but legible face. Her eyes, unnaturally large and crooked, were dripping out of their sockets and onto the cheeks. She also wore a crown of thorns, so many sharp and pointy ends of medical scissors. A chaotic mesh made her hair, the warped and curled wires of a cyclone fence. Lars wanted to tell Yuri, "Here's why it's immature. You're inflicting pain on your subject instead of evoking it in the viewer." Yet Lars had to admit that the piece was holding his attention and curiosity so intensely that he almost forgot why he had come down to the basement.

"Lars," said Yuri, turning around. "You're so quiet. I didn't hear you come in."

"No," said Lars, startled. "Yeah. Just let myself in. Got a message for you." He stuffed his hands into the back pockets of his corduroys. "Reikel called just now. Seems upset. Wants you to call him."

"Why?"

"He's worried or something. You got into an argument or something? Says he didn't mean to piss you off." Lars glanced briefly over Yuri's sculptures one more time. "You want to use my phone?"

"I'll talk to him tomorrow."

"Yeah," said Lars. "But another thing also. Since I'm here, just wondering. You'll pay your rent this week?"

"I'm late? Shit." Yuri touched all his pockets. "I know all about it, I was thinking the other day. I got off the bus and forgot to go to the bank."

"Yuri, pay whenever."

"No. I got paid today." Yuri produced the check. "It's right here. The bank's closed. But that's okay. Maybe just sign it over to you? Take the rent out. Give me change later?"

Lars took the check. "Sounds good." He looked at it. "Sure, I can cash this."

Yuri followed Lars out to the garage and sat near the piano to sign his paycheck over. Lars was counting money out of the vitamin bottles and handed him a wad. "Wait, it's too much," said Yuri. He showed Lars the bills. "You didn't take out enough."

"No, I double checked," said Lars.

"But my rent's seventy five—"

"Forget it. You save your money, kid."

Yuri looked at the cash.

"Some day, you'll think, and you'll remember all the people who gave you shit. But God dammit, Lars wasn't one of 'em."

3

Insomnia.

Bronza wandered around the house ever unable to settle in any one space for very long. He would tinker in the kitchen or read old books in his den. He was smoking large amounts of cigarettes and sometimes a violent cough tore through him, so strong that he felt consistent strain in his chest from pulled muscles.

He often drank through the nights, slowly sipping cheaper scotch mixed with lukewarm water, or he'd spike chamomile or valerian tea. If it ever made him drowsy, it was only for an hour or two, and he'd wake on a sofa or in his chair. Bronza even went to work slightly drunk a few times.

He was looking over their large bed, Gaja sleeping in the middle, and wanted so much to lie down next to her and crash. But he wouldn't crash. He'd lie wired alive, constant pressure in his head, and the questions...*what the hell am I doing? What am I doing here? How did I get here?*

He wondered if Gaja was healthy. She could seem perfectly happy while polishing glasses in the kitchen or walking with him around town. They had started going to films in the city, but she always found something immoral about them. He hated the word. *Immoral.* It could follow him around, keep him awake. Everything was immoral. You couldn't live. Life was immoral.

He didn't like sex with her anymore. Bronza was always worried she'd break down into some hysteria, weighed into the earth by some Catholic idea. He couldn't sleep with her but rarely refused when she came to him. He'd stare at her, like a man watching a film, and wonder what she was enjoying, waiting for the moment when she'd push him away and curl up in the corner of the mattress. Sometimes she'd lie in bed afterwards, relaxed and content, and fall asleep. But in the mornings Bronza could feel guilt and negativity covering her like a cloak and rising out like steam from a pot.

Who the hell was she, actually? Gaja didn't seem to be aging. It drove him crazy that she grew more beautiful every year, more feminine, a fresh and living glow to her skin. Her moments of happiness...*what was she happy about*...they drove him insane. She'd chop celery in the kitchen, smile at him when he came back from the clinic. At the strangest times—at three in the morning when his insomnia had him reading two-day-old newspapers— she'd come to him. *At those times, she manages, somehow, to make me feel guilty.* "I miss you," she'd say. "Don't you miss me?"

Now it was already Saturday afternoon. Bronza was reading in his den...he really wanted to read Shakespeare because it reminded him of being a young student. Gaja was getting dressed to go to confession. She always did it with seriousness, her heels hard and direct against the wood, and her neck straight and stiff. When he stepped past her on the way to the kitchen, she looked away as if ashamed. When she left the house, Bronza waited exactly one minute before stepping out to the sidewalk to watch her walking down 49th Court, on her way to tell Cruz every detail of their marriage.

Bronza flipped to a random page of Shakespeare's complete works. He did this often, mockingly, because there was nothing particular he wanted to read. Or maybe he really did want to read *Hamlet*, Act III, Scene I, the famous soliloquy. The heartache and the thousand natural shocks, the undiscover'd country from whose bourn no traveler returns. Bronza took the volume to bed and read until a patch of sleep choked his awareness away.

He awoke with the book tucked under his arm, his hand grown numb. Gaja had not returned. Unable to find anything to do, he put on a pressed shirt and new pants and left to visit some patients in the hospital.

One Mexican woman—young, only thirty-two—was dying of ovarian cancer. Bronza had pulled strings to keep her in the hospital because the family could not care for her at home. When he came to her room, her father—an ancient man with deep wrinkles in his dark skin—and her seventeen-year-old son were standing bedside. Father Cruz was performing Extreme Unction, the blessing of the dying. Dilienko stood to the side solemnly while Cruz anointed the woman with oil.

He hated watching priests deal with the dying. It was even worse when the patients actually died; the priests always reassured everyone—their authority absurd, almost obscene—that the dead were actually alive. It infuriated Bronza to watch Cruz make the sign of the cross over the body. With the rite finished, the four of them sat in the cumbersome silence that always accompanies the dying, a silence that priests loved.

Bronza imagined nudging the priest, "Come on. Why don't you heal her sickness? If you had the faith of a mustard seed." He wondered if the woman had ever come to Cruz's confession and what she might have told him. Because Cruz was there, Bronza perverted memories of her topless on his examination table, imagined groping and pinching her. Without Cruz he would have only been thinking of the disease gaining on her, poisoning her blood—he'd wonder how it was to feel life leaving you, and he'd wish she could talk, tell him everything.

Bronza and Cruz ended up leaving the hospital together. The priest had taken a taxi, so Dilienko offered him a ride to the rectory. "Thank you," said Cruz. "I'd appreciate a ride, yes."

Driving out of the parking lot, Bronza asked him, "Didn't you have confessions today?"

"Certain things take precedence."

"Like the dead?"

"The dying. She's dying."

"She's good as dead," said Bronza. "She's got 48 hours, tops."

"Yes," said Cruz. "Yes."

Bronza stopped at a red light. He pressed his car lighter. "Did you hear Gaja today?"

"Hear?"

"She went to confession today. Right around one o'clock. She goes to you."

"Quite a few people come. I may have. I don't recall."

"But you know it's her, when she's there. You know it's her when she's talking."

The lighter clicked out, but Bronza left it. Cruz said, "Are you going to take that?"

"Father Cruz. You know it's her."

"There are occasions when I recognize voices. I'd be a fool to lie to you about it. But I can't say I remember hearing her come today. Today, I don't remember."

"You know...you and I. We probably know a lot together." Bronza pushed in the lighter one more time. He was tailgating a motorcycle and it made Cruz uneasy. "She's probably told you she's had her tubes tied. That's a pretty big sin, isn't it?"

Cruz was quiet.

"So, she's told you about it, right? I'm wondering what kind of penance you'd give for something like that. She won't tell me about it, even if I ask."

"I'm not at liberty."

"Forget liberty. Just, say, theoretically, if a married woman has her tubes tied, what sort of penance do you give?"

"It's a vulgar thing to ask, doctor. It's your wife."

"So you do know. You do."

Cruz could not hide his embarrassment. Dilienko pestered him a few more times, but Cruz sat silent, disgusted with him. They soon arrived at the rectory. Bronza said one last time, "We can talk about it. It's not like you'll tell me anything I don't know myself. Your vow of secrecy is safe with me."

"Thank you for the ride, doctor."

Cruz was walking across the churchyard and Bronza called out to him from the Buick's open window, "You know, your penance doesn't really work. It really hasn't changed her very much." Cruz turned around and waved to him before disappearing through a side door.

Bronza was now furious. He wanted to hammer the car's engine straight down 50th Avenue. He wanted to get stumbling drunk in some shit shack dive full of truckers and cops, then drive to the highway. He saw himself crashing the car into the brick wall of a factory, straight through a bus shelter, a death nest of twisted, wrangled metal and glass. Driving down 50th, he gripped the steering wheel tightly and imagined jacking it violently into an oncoming taxi.

At dinner that evening, Gaja was cheery and pleasant, talking about plans to make autumn's first borscht later that week.

She even poured a glass of wine and invited Bronza to come sit in the yard with her. Bronza went and listened about her hope to fix the garden up before winter, perhaps get the fence painted. Next spring she wanted to try planting some flowers. "Gardening's a healthy hobby," she said. "I'm sure it's not difficult. And we'd have some color back here."

"I'd really like it if you took care of the garden," he said.

She soon prepared for bed, and he tried to sleep next to her but couldn't. Careful not to wake her, he went down to the basement to smoke in the dark.

Dim light from the amber street lamps fell through the small window by the ceiling. Bronza's eyes adjusted and he could see the chests and trunks—now empty of Benny's figurines—the shelves where some of the pieces of wood had once stood, and the ragged table in the corner where he had piled things he liked. The old wine bottles that had come with the house and a pair of outdated hi-fi speakers. Boxes of Anya and Yuri's old clothes. School books and the parakeet's old birdcage.

Bronza finally let himself cry. Even though Gaja could never hear him through the floorboards, he still pressed a handkerchief tightly over his nose and mouth.

Bronza knew what he wanted more than anything in the world.

Thinking about it carefully, he compared it to the heaven and everlasting life all of Cruz's followers wanted. By comparison, Bronza's desire was only a modest miracle, one that, if performed right, no one would even notice.

Dearest Lord, it's the perfect time for You to make something happen. You don't have to rise from the dead, calm any storms. Roman soldiers haven't cut my ear off and I'm not a leper—don't need myself cured. I haven't run out of wine at my wedding. But if You're in the mood for miracles, I just need You to wind the clock backwards. Wind it back about ten years and let me take over. None of these fools would know what happened, and I could handle the rest.

But You won't come around.

I could sow a holy garden, nothing but mustard seeds for acres, pack enough mustard for a factory of hungry Ukrainian drunks. You still wouldn't come around.

I'm not asking You to show Your face. You know, I could walk out into the middle of the mustard orchard with Benny's rope, if You wanted. Judas Iscariot's rope. All your little lambs, desperate for You, could bear witness.

Just keep believing, Doubting Thomas. Stick your finger in my wounds.

Happy are those who do not see.

Of course they are, happy to sleep, perchance to dream. Be all my sins remembered. I hear You coming. Withdraw, My Lord.

A shadow moving over the room startled Bronza: someone's leg by the small window near the ceiling. Bronza thought it was the neighbor walking down the gangway, but the shadow grew. Someone's silhouette leaned down, placed both hands on the window and pushed it forward. The window swung freely—Bronza never had any reason to lock it, but now someone was breaking in. He put out his cigarette and sat without a stir.

The intruder entered feet first, belly and chest towards the wall. He kept his movements slow and subtle. Bronza only needed a second to recognize Yuri from the way he brushed his hands through his hair. Yuri squatted by the window and waited an awfully long time before finally lighting a small flashlight. He started looking through stuff on the table.

Bronza struck a match and Yuri jumped, disoriented for a moment, taking one step toward the window and another to the table. "What?" he asked. "It's you. You're down here."

"What are you doing?" Bronza asked.

"Nothing."

"What are you looking for?" The flame glowed brighter, neared his fingers and Bronza dropped it to die on the floor.

Yuri said, "I came to get something." He turned his flashlight toward the ceiling. "What are you doing?"

"Smoking."

"Get in a fight with mama? Or did you burn yourself? By accident."

"What did you come to get?"

"Kolya's birdcage, just the birdcage."

"Why?"

"To make something."

Bronza rubbed his knuckles with a hard thumb. "I thought—thought you don't need anything from us." He heard himself saying what he was about to and wished to say something different, but it came right out: "You're all on your own. Independent. Working for a butcher and paying for Jorgenson's scotch."

"No," said Yuri. "I'm not doing any of that."

"Take the cage. And get out. Before your mother hears and wakes up."

Kolya's cage barely fit through the window, and it banged around on the sidewalk when Yuri tossed it. He grabbed the windowsill and struggled to pull himself up. Bronza came over. He let Yuri use his hand as a step to get out of the house.

4

Early on a Friday morning, Lars gathered the loose papers of his most recent composition and carried the awkward bundle to the alley garbage drum. Lars dumped the papers and went back for charcoal fluid and a broomstick to pack the composition down to the drum's bottom. He lit the bastard up and, crossing his arms, stared into the flames. For effect, he squirted some more fluid and the fumes dirtied his garage wall.

He watched the sheets burn until the glowing outline of the last flake of ash, bending and curling to a restrained rhythm, died and left nothing but gray dust and smoke. Rainwater had collected in an old can and Lars poured it into the drum.

In the garage, he washed his face and hands vigorously with the hottest water, drying himself with a coarse flax towel. Lars made a pot of strong, very hot coffee and sat at his desk biting a pencil to stare at a blank page. He finished half the pot before marking a meaningless D sharp in the bass clef. Lars played it loud with his forefinger, repeating it again and again. "A moron," he said. "Shit shit shit shit shit."

He was hearing every instrument sounding at once. Vibraphones and banjos, timpani and bagpipes, a highly distorted electric guitar. Lars started improvising at the piano, the music barreling forward at manic speed, notes on top of notes, chords of noise choking one another.

In the next instant, Lars stood from the piano and found the small metal box where he kept the many keys to his house. He never went through his tenants' rooms when they weren't around, but Lars had something to settle. Yuri's stupid and juvenile sculpture with the crown of thorns had imprinted itself in his head and he couldn't get it out.

The sculpture had now been fitted to a stand; a broomstick fit neatly into the spade's neck. Yuri had placed it in the far corner, away from the shelves, perhaps to decorate the studio.

Lars must have been thinking about this sculpture because it had surprised him. Perhaps he was only fascinated because Alina had been one of Yuri's teachers. That's right! This was actually Alina's product, which made it Lars' product-of-sorts. It was her work, and she had taught him a lot. But that aside, the sculpture still should not have been interesting. Lars was supposed to see a novice effort.

Was this even a sculpture? A crown from the ends of medical scissors? All this self-absorbed "pain," this loony wish to torture your mother?

Lars took the thing to his garage.

5

The autumn wasn't even cold yet, but Gaja didn't care. She was going to make the first batch of Lithuanian borscht. She worked all morning, boiling bones and grating beets so that the dark purple juice showed all the wrinkles and lines in her hands. Gaja added dried boletus mushrooms and a secret hint of dill to the stock.

When the soup was finished, she wanted to taste a bowl before Bronza came home. She found her old soup ladle missing from the cylinder on the counter. She looked through the kitchen's drawers and cupboards. Gaja searched again, opening drawers used to keep shopping bags, rubber bands and seldom used tools, but the ladle was gone. Irritated, she stood by the sink to smoke, dropping ash onto the beet peels.

The first thing to disappear from the house had been her little metal comb. Such a good comb, handy and well made. Later, certain forks and knives had vanished. They were easy to lose or misplace, especially when Bronza ate in the garden. But they'd be in the lawn...or somewhere. A cheap, insignificant silver ring was gone from the large jewelry box on her dresser. It was exactly the cheapest one, and she almost never wore it. Then a shovel had gone from the garage. Now a ladle.

Gaja had known all along that Yuri was taking these things, although she kept pretending that they had only been misplaced. Now, with the crushed cigarette butt wet in the sink's food scraps, it angered her to know he was snooping around the house, probably on Sundays when she was in church, maybe on Saturdays when she was confessing and Bronza was out. Her mild anger, aimed primarily at herself, embarrassed her. Yuri was trying to communicate, get under her skin, because he knew how much she hated when something happened without her knowing. Now something had to be done about it. Gaja understood it was time.

Gaja dressed for 14th Street, decent shoes and a bit of makeup. While walking under the tall elms, trees patient with the autumn's first yellow and orange, she believed she could convince Yuri to leave Lars' house and come back to the bungalow. She even believed he would listen to her, that all he wanted was to hear her ask for him to come home. Gaja's courage remained strong at 16th Street; turning down 14th, she was still determined to face Yuri and let him know. He didn't have to live with a lowlife and act like a thief. She heard herself telling him, "I'm sorry, Yuri. I'm very very sorry." But when she saw the meat shop's sign hanging over the street, swaying lightly in the wind, her courage turned to nerves. She went over to the Cicero Family Clinic.

When they let her in, Gaja wandered down the clinic's back corridors where she had not been in years. Bronza took her to the little room where he liked to smoke and listen to the radio. "Why are you here?" he asked. What's the matter?"

"I decided."

"What? Now what, what?" He knew no matter what he said she wouldn't listen to him. "Gaja, sit down here."

"Yuri's taking things. A ladle. He took a ladle. And other things."

"Calm down. What are you talking about?"

"First the shovel and...didn't I tell you about the shovel? And my ring, and now a ladle. He's stealing from me."

"Gaja, here." He gave her a chair. "Tell me exactly what's the matter."

She did not sit. "Bronza...don't pretend. Are you helping him? And you won't tell me?"

"We can talk about this when I come home."

"He took a ring and a ladle."

"Gaja," he sighed. "A ladle. So what if he took it? It's a damn spoon."

"So, you *are* helping him." Gaja knew it was absurd to be angry but couldn't help it. "I knew you were helping him. You've known all along but kept it from me. Behind my back, out of spite."

"I've kept nothing."

"You're a liar."

Bronza held out a cigarette for her. "I caught Yuri snooping around the basement one night."

She left the room and hurried from the clinic, courageous again. Gaja did not think twice about going in or slowing down, smoking outside, rethinking what she was doing. Yuri was simply going to listen to her once and for all. She pulled Reikel's heavy door open and the little cowbell announced her entrance.

Monsignor Kilba was standing at the counter, a few white paper packages wrapped in front of him. Reikel was slicing cold cuts and chattering, "Oh, that stuff's best Virginia Ham ever." Gaja said, quietly and without looking either man in the eye, "I want to see Yuri."

"Gaja?" said Kilba.

"Hello, Mrs. D," said Reikel. "Yuri? Yeah, he's in back."

"I want to see him right now. Monsignor Kilba, excuse me for interrupting. Reikel, please ask him to come out."

"Gaja, what's the matter?" asked Kilba.

"Reikel," she insisted, "right now, please." Reikel shut down the circular blade, but the stainless doors swung open and Yuri appeared without being called, his apron and yellow baseball cap stained with red smears. "Hi, mama." His voice was calm. "What do you need?"

She was holding tightly to the strap of her handbag. Everyone just stared at her. Gaja spoke as gently as she could, "I want you to change out of those clothes and come with me. Right now. I've come all this way."

"Why?" Yuri did not seem affected by her at all, although Monsignor Kilba could sense his furious agitation. "I have to work."

"We close in coupla hours, Mrs. Dilienko," said Reikel. "Just not even two."

"Yuri. Please. Now."

"Why?"

Kilba intervened: "Gaja, please. Let's go outside."

"I insist," she raised her voice. "I insist you come home. And change out of those clothes, Yuri. Now, Monsignor, don't you tell me." She took a step towards Kilba. "Neither you nor anyone else will accuse me. Do you know what he's been doing?" She pointed at Yuri with a quick elbow. "Want to know?"

"I'm sure they'd like to, mama," Yuri said. "Tell them."

"Stealing shovels and ladles from me. As if I'm supposed to pretend I've misplaced them."

"Well—" Kilba's cheeks filled with air. "I'm sure there's an explanation."

"What else have you taken? What haven't I found? More rings? Jewels? Money?"

"No. Just metal."

"Just?"

Reikel stood with his arms hung from his apron straps, his head moving from person to person. Kilba had approached Gaja and seemed to be trying to decide how to touch her, perhaps on the shoulder, on the forearm? Yuri leaned on the counter. Gaja repeated, "I want you to leave this place."

"What will you do?" asked Yuri.

"I insist."

"Yurs," said Reikel. "Yeah, I can finish up here."

"Forget it, Reik," said Yuri. "She's not serious."

"I am very serious. You thought I wouldn't do anything. Monsignor Kilba, he's doing it while I'm in church."

"Yuri," said Kilba. "Let's go outside together."

"Why, Monsignor? We've got nowhere to go," Yuri said. "And nothing to say."

"Do you see, Monsignor?" asked Gaja. "He'll speak this way. And without consequences."

"Consequences?" asked Yuri, now showing a touch of irritation, his eyes pained. He faked laughter poorly, false in a way he had never been before Kilba. "There are no consequences," he said, staring at her. "I can tell everyone. School counselors. Monsignor Kilba over here. Priests at St. Quentin's. I can write it on a wall and nobody will do a thing." Yuri backed away from the counter. "I can tell Reikel. And nothing will happen."

"Yuri, please," said Kilba.

Gaja stood frozen.

"Here, Reikel," said Yuri. "Let me show you."

Reikel was only wishing for these people to leave his store. Yuri was now showing him the palm of his hand. "I told you about these scars, remember, when you asked. Said they were from a skin allergy, remember?"

Reikel shrugged.

Yuri rubbed his palm. "All that's bullshit." He brought his hand closer to the fluorescent light falling from a glass case. "They're from burns. Mama used to burn me when I was little."

6

From the window of Carry's Bakery, Father Cruz could see Gaja wandering along 14th Street. He rarely saw her outside of church; when he did, it was always from a distance and when she didn't know he was watching. She was walking briskly, and he was remembering—surprising, how a memory like this could just arise on its own—the scent of perfume she always left in her wake. Floral.

Ever since the conversation in Bronza's car, Cruz had been having problems controlling his mind and memories. He forced himself to concentrate on prayers—intense, quick repetitions of Hail Mary. He tried to empty his mind of all images of Gaja, feel nothing but the grace of God, His eternal promise, His ability to forgive any sin.

She was walking down 14th. Her small feet, short steps. The silhouette of her figure against the orange light of dusk.

Once, weeks ago, he had seen her stepping onto a bus, and Cruz imagined holding out a hand to help her. Gaja always wore tasteful and chaste outfits to church, the kind all women should wear.

The delicate lightness of her hands when she reached out for bread at the parish breakfast.

Again, the fragrance of her signature perfume...Cruz often knew she was in the confessional before hearing her utter a word. Now, whenever he heard her voice from behind the screen, he could anticipate her sins.

Cruz wandered back to the rectory and prayed decades of the rosary. In his bedroom, he read from the Epistles of St. Paul.

The sermon Cruz wanted to write poured out of him, exactly on the topic of forgiveness. Soon, it had gotten very late.

Cruz always knelt and prayed intensely before sleep—so many people asked for his prayers, especially from the town's growing Mexican community. When he lay back in bed, Cruz kept praying, now for himself, for strength and purity of mind. But as he became drowsy, the prayers gradually lost energy and images floated to the surface, some fading out as others sharpened. Cruz was soon a wayside observer with no chance to control anything.

Of course he knew Gaja's tubes had been tied. It was shortly after the death of Anya, her daughter. Cruz imagined Bronza performing the surgery, cutting his wife with a scalpel.

Gaja knew well enough, but Cruz had to tell her often, sometimes week to week...knowing her husband after this operation was a mortal sin. If she did it on Holy Days of Obligation, during Advent and Lent, on Sundays, the sin was dangerously heightened. It angered Cruz whenever she took her husband in the mouth or allowed him to take her in his. Gaja could not control her thoughts, had many fantasies and occasionally pleased herself. Cruz could assign her ten or more Acts of Contrition for penance, and he'd tell her it was very important to pray at the communion rail. He told her to abstain, to pray the rosary, and asked each week if she had performed her penance.

But Cruz didn't have time to deal only with her. Other parishioners needed him, sick old men and the woman dying of ovarian cancer. He had so much to do when he looked at his agenda...a child to baptize...tomorrow's mass. Cruz stood at the podium, telling the parishioners, "Your every moment of every day must be spent preparing for the Lord." But the idiots didn't prepare themselves. They didn't realize how close judgment was. The hypocrites wanted sanctity and forgiveness, but how did they behave?

Now he had to marry two of them. The girl, a done-up doll, the center of attention, was barely nineteen. Cruz could already see her lies. She was more interested in her wedding dress and limousine than in marriage, but she and her boy recited their vows, meaningless words, and then they kissed in front of everyone. They left the church and other hypocrites threw rice all over them.

Cruz found himself alone in the dark sacristy. He hung his vestments in the wooden wardrobe and slowly packed his small bag, returning a vial of holy water and oil, the small missal, the green stole he wore around his neck when saying Mass. Cruz took the bag, his hat and coat and went out into the street to walk.

He had only ever seen Gaja's bungalow from outside and across the street. When he dreamt about it or imagined its interior, it was identical to the house where he had grown up. Gaja smiled at him as he sat at the kitchen table where she had set his dinner of soup and chicken stewed in tomatoes. They ate together quietly. Afterwards, Cruz helped Gaja wash the dishes. She told him, "I think I'm sick."

"I think so," Cruz said.

"But you'll have a lot of work to do?"

"There's time. And I remembered all my things."

Gaja went to the other room and lay down on an examination table. Cruz washed his hands and put the dishrag away. Except for her face and belly, her body was now covered by squares of light blue cloth. Cruz first rubbed her belly with alcohol and then went to his bag. He found surgical scissors and hooks but no scalpels. One must be here somewhere among these instruments. A scalpel. Cruz must have lost it.

7

On her way to Sunday Mass, Gaja paused to look over the house where she had grown up. Although Gaja lived only a block away, she rarely walked past her old house. It seemed a place where time had stopped and nothing ever changed. She knew an obese woman who dressed in t-shirts lived there now, but still imagined, if she went inside, she'd find a young version of herself in the small bedroom down the hall from the kitchen.

The house should have been demolished. Wandering towards 16th, she thought it could easily be razed. Workers could break it up with one of those swinging balls and then some special machine could crush all the bricks to dust. Gaja imagined two powerful metal rollers breaking and crushing a conveyor belt of bricks. They scattered dust, a large cloud blowing down the street.

She was carrying Bronza's old leather bag, the one he used to bring to house calls. Her knuckles ached from its weight.

People were walking solemnly to church. Men were buying newspapers from the guy outside the corner store, and others were coming out with sacks of bacon buns and sweets. Most of them looked at Gaja but remained politely indifferent to her. She was amazed with people. Now that word was out and all these fools knew her to the core, her worst and most private actions, she could feel how Cicero judged and thoroughly hated her, but in the street these people barely looked her way. Magdalene herself could have walked among these people, and they would loathe her privately but show no sign.

The church bells were calling them to mass. The men buying papers would come in late, rustle around and bother everyone. Gaja could have hurled stones at them. She went to the Roosevelt Elementary playground to wait for all of them to disappear.

Thoughts and strands of memories swayed and slashed about her mind. She was thinking about the obese woman and the sound of the doorbell in the house, the doorbell Gaja had known as a child. Two flat and muffled tones. Gaja wanted to go to the rectory but could not be sure if Kilba's mass had started. She did not want him to open the door. Was it half-past ten...had the chimes already sounded?

In the next moment, she couldn't remember why she was outside. Gaja felt the need to cover herself, her neck with the lapels of her wool jacket, tighten it around her body. She was sweating underneath the wool. Why had she dressed in such a warm jacket on the mild day? Gaja could not remember deciding. She could not remember leaving her house.

Lars' organ music sounded from the church and the choir sang. Kilba's mass had begun. She could go see the priest and slowly wandered out into 50th Avenue, eyeing the rectory's door, a one-way mirror. Now that the organ was silent, she didn't know if she had only imagined the music. What would she do if Kilba answered at the rectory?

Gaja stepped closer to the church and listened very carefully for Kilba's amplified voice. A car with a bad muffler passed. The playground gate clanged when the wind closed it. The obese woman was coughing into her forearm. The doorbell at home. Benny's sandpaper against wood. An electric saw cut through a hunk of driftwood in the garage and Benny was throwing out empty beer bottles. Lars' organ music, sustained and familiar. "Yuri." Yes...that was Kilba's voice. "Let's go outside together."

Gaja rang the rectory's bell, looked herself over in the tall mirror that was the rectory's front door. Her '50s style sunglasses covered her eyes, and she had wrapped her head in a blue scarf. Bronza's old handbag for house calls dangled from her arm. Yes...the items inside, she had to show them to a priest as soon as possible.

Father Cruz opened. He was holding a metal watering can with a narrow spout. "Gaja?" He frowned at her from curiosity, setting the can on a windowsill. "Good morning. Did you need something?"

"I've come to talk," she whispered.

"I'm sorry?"

"To talk. I've come to talk."

"Before mass?" He briefly leaned out the door and then, as if he had only now realized how rude he had been, said "Come in."

Without waiting, Gaja went up the stairs to his study. He had no choice but to follow. While Cruz had been perfectly relaxed and collected before her arrival, he now felt he had drunk too much coffee. Her slender figure rose up the stairs and she was waiting by his study's door.

She held her sunglasses firmly by their frames, unsure if she should take them off, but finally folded and slipped them into her jacket pocket. Cruz had never seen her without eye makeup and her eyes looked swollen, possibly tired, but still large and radiant blue.

"The door's open," he said. Gaja only dropped her eyes to the doorknob. Cruz reached past her, pushed the door open and followed her into the study. She did not take off her jacket but sat before his desk, leaving the leather bag on the floor.

Cruz stood behind his desk. With slow movements, he briefly rearranged some papers. "I'm sorry about how it looks in here," he said. His desk was dusted, polished and tidy, although a few pencils had been left out of their cylinder and a spiral notebook lay open under the reading lamp, thin pencil shavings on the paper. Cruz put the pencils away, brushed the shavings into a wastebasket and closed the notebook. "Wasn't expecting anyone just yet."

Gaja nodded slightly.

"Has something?" He adjusted the blinds to let through a bit more light. "Something's happened?"

"By now." She folded her hands. "You know, by now, what's been happening."

"By now?"

She nodded.

Kilba hadn't told him anything that had happened at Reikel's shop. "I'm afraid I don't."

"Are you mocking me, Father? I've just come from the street. Are you going to smile?"

"I?"

"You never smile. If you don't want me to talk about it, fine. But don't make me tell you the whole story. I'm not here for that. And don't force me into it. That's not why I've come."

Cruz sat at his desk. He was wishing she'd take off her jacket, hang it on the rack, then he falsely hoped she'd leave, let him finish watering the plants. "Please explain why you've come."

She stuttered, "I didn't. I didn't. That's it, I forgot." Now she bit inside her cheek. "I didn't come to confession yesterday."

"Oh?"

"I didn't come to confession yesterday."

"Gaja, if you'd like to confess, we could do it after mass."

"I'm never going to confession again. You know I've never really gone to confession anyway. I don't even know what I was doing."

"Never again?" asked Cruz. "And why not?"

She stared into the window blind. "It's not like I've ever confessed anything." Gaja's fingers intertwined, white from pressure. "Not anything."

Cruz wanted to encourage her somehow but instead uttered, "Beautiful." Impossible. How could he have said this? Still, he remained stoic and touched his chest lightly with a fist. "In the soul. You really...always...I sense it constantly. You always want to do the right, the beautiful thing."

Gaja said, "You're one of them."

"Who?"

"You think you know me. It isn't true, first of all. You all think it's true, but it isn't."

"Gaja." He sighed lightly. "You have this idea. I've realized this about you. You think people go about their days thinking about you. They don't. Relieve yourself of that. If you don't mind me being frank, I'll say, living that way is a bit self-absorbed."

"It isn't true, first of all," she said. "I never laid hands on Yuri. Never."

"I believe you." His mind was afire with images of her, memories of her confessions, and his dream about the scalpel and scissors. He saw himself getting up from the chair, grabbing her by the shoulders and forcing her from his study, shouting at her down the hall, "Get out and get your life in order!" His fingers pressed into her shoulders and he was pushing her out the door so that she almost fell, but he also brought her body to his and held her tightly. "I believe you."

"Before I broke my husband's rib—I don't want to repeat it—but before Anya was born. I never laid hands on anyone. I've told you. I was trying to live properly. Before my little girl was born, my husband and I kept separate rooms." She tightened the lapels around her neck. "But he started cheating on me. Now don't yell at me. The woman's dead now, the one he was with. When he was cheating."

"I hadn't known." Cruz shook his head. "No, I hadn't known your husband was cheating."

"And now my son. He's living in that woman's house. And Yuri's spreading lies. But don't yell at me."

"I won't." Cruz turned to crack the window, let in some air. "Why would I yell?"

"I never laid hands. Now, don't yell at me. I asked you!"

"Gaja..."

"Stop it!" She stood from her chair and, angry, picked up the leather bag. "Stop yelling! What do I look like? If you want to be like your father, I'll make you like him."

"Shh. Please." Cruz was scared she might throw the bag.

"You see what you've done? You see what you've made me do! Fine. Well, if you need it. Fine. I don't care. It's all in here." She tossed the bag on his desk, knocking the pencils all over the floor, and immediately backed toward the door. "In there. Understand everything—it's there. None of it's true, what they're lying and what Yuri's lying. If you knew him like I know him. Deceptive and ill." She stumbled out and Cruz heard her feet stomping down the stairs.

He did not move for quite some time. His heart was beating, and the leather bag seemed the most foreign object he had ever seen. He first picked up all his pencils. When he took the leather bag he found it surprisingly heavy.

It held three somewhat rusty railroad spikes. The bag also contained a graphically erotic wooden figurine of a man and a young girl. Its vulgarity was shameful, a piece entirely devoid of love or passion, and Cruz would not look at it. At the bottom of the bag lay two pieces of paper, one yellow and the other white. Cruz unfolded the yellow one, a very old and brittle note, to read:

Isn't it strange? If I invited you to come to my garden, if I told you you're free to come and go as you please, stay as long as you like, leave your cigarette butts in one of those old flowerpots, you'd probably stop coming. I had to follow you here to your home and sit with your grandfather for a few minutes to realize that was the case: there's nothing I can tell you or write here that will make you feel comfortable. Please know I did not come to chase you away and, at any rate, I'm glad you like the garden. I'm glad you're so careful not to disturb it. I invite you to come when the sun is out.

Bronza Dilienko

Cruz didn't know what to make of it. Perhaps the other note held a clue. He unfolded the crisp paper:

Monsignor Kilba,

Please help me! If driven to it, I am very angry and I am very scared. Stop me before I don't know what I will do if I am driven to it.

Gaja

8

Lars was alive.

For the first time since Victoria's death, he had real energy, the kind that used to overtake him when he had been younger. It might have been the most important energy of his life, because Lars believed he was composing the composition he had been born to compose. He simply called it *The Fugue*. It flowed through him like no music ever had, clean and direct, vibrant; at times it seemed the piece was writing itself with Lars a bystander only watching in amazement.

The Fugue was a pair of voices. Lars considered them portraits of Alina and Victoria. They played simultaneously, Alina in the left hand with Victoria in the right. He had been thinking of his wife and daughter in two ways: they were individual people, Alina deep and terse, Victoria high and mature, but they shared each other's traits and together made up his home. Often both Alina and Victoria created extraordinary clarity together...other times only one of them did...but occasionally their voices dissipated and *The Fugue* let all comfort go.

Lars finished the composition in only eight days. One part of him felt as though he had completed something for the first time, but another part, the largest and most sincere part, felt like he was standing at the beginning of something.

At the moment he knew it was done, he did not want to scream or dance in celebration, drink with anyone or make any announcements. He wished for someone—for Yuri—to experience the music along with him. But Yuri wasn't around. Lars went to a corner diner where he ate hot soup and a slice of blueberry pie. He sat in a booth away from people.

A few days later he went to church when it was completely empty and played *The Fugue* quietly on the organ. The piece sounded brilliant through the instrument, Lars playing out of sheer joy.

He came to the first moment when *The Fugue* let safety and clarity go. The music receded into painful confusion, mixed up and illogical time, a structure that seemed to move both forwards and backwards at once. The chaos felt improvised but drove forward with such authority that it seemed chaos might last forever, with no way out.

Monsignor Kilba was listening in the choir's stairwell. This is pure madness, he thought, but so beautiful, and Lars is playing it so honestly. He climbed the stairs to the choir and sat in one of the pews, completely absorbed by the demented sound. Soon it began to change. The Monsignor realized the music wasn't demented at all—it was now returning to a simple and clean shape. But some evil fought to keep beauty from collecting itself, a battle was taking place between hope and despair. Now the Monsignor sensed it would happen—the music was going to culminate and Kilba would understand something.

It stopped. The organ left only a hollow echo reverberating through the church. "Damn," Jorgenson whispered.

"What? Lars!" Kilba stood up.

Lars was only mildly startled. "Monsignor?"

"Lars! But you've stopped. What for? This music," he stuttered, "It was heading to that nostalgic space you were playing just minutes ago. How can you stop just like that? Just in the middle like that?"

"Dammit," said Lars, his fingers still on the keys. "I lost it. I can't remember how it goes." He played a few passages again.

"Not that part! I don't want to hear that anymore. It was heading in a completely different direction."

Jorgenson scratched his mustache and rubbed the back of his neck. "I can't remember how it modulates." His entire body seemed glued to the organ, but his wet eyes darted about and he was biting the exposed tip of his tongue so hard that it hurt Kilba to look. In an abrupt movement, Lars shut off the organ and stood to organize his papers. "I'm sorry. I can't remember it right now. Sorry."

The Monsignor sat on one of the closer pews. Lars carried on with his papers, sliding them into appropriate folders. Every snap of a rubber band and shuffle resonated through the church so that Kilba felt the distance between the choir and the altar, the church's ceiling and floor, and how small he was in the building. He asked Lars, "Do you remember—"

Lars interrupted, "I'm sorry. I won't remember. I'm not going to try thinking about it right now."

"Listen to me." Kilba spoke slowly. "Do you remember that time? Benny came up here with his pillowcase, all those carvings in a pillowcase. He was leaving them around and you wanted to thrash him."

"What the hell're you reminding me that for?" His eyes finally met Kilba's to see his intense facial expression and slumped body. The Monsignor was not carrying any of his normal relaxed warmth, and Lars had never seen him as frail...he seemed incredibly old, the flesh hanging off his cheekbones. "Monsignor," said Lars. "Hey. You day dreamin'?"

"You remember it?"

"Monsignor. You okay?" Lars took a few steps towards Kilba but stopped before getting too close. "You sick? Are you out of it?"

"He was here with all those very graphic carvings."

Lars shrugged. "What are you bringing it up for?"

"Do you remember why they made you so upset?"

"His little statues?" Lars fidgeted. "They were perverted. A guy and some little girl. I didn't need them around here. And Alina was with me. She was in grammar school."

"But, Lars, don't you remember? You showed me one. Particularly *one*. When I came out to settle the argument. You showed it to me and you said *Look, monsignor. Look what he's leaving around.* Do you remember it?"

"That was a long time ago," he said. "Benny's gone. I'd rather not, to be honest."

Kilba's gentle eyes narrowed for a moment. "Yes," he whispered. "And I don't, either, really." He brushed his chin with the knuckle of a thumb. "I know the whole story. I know why Benny carved those things, even the carvings of horses. Trampling, kicking a man. But I never wanted to know. Still, today, I don't want to know."

"Monsignor. *What's* the matter?"

Would you tell her? If you knew the reason he carved all those things? Could it make anything worse?

The Monsignor only stood from the pew. "I'm sorry, Lars." He seemed to gather himself, his movements a bit crisper. "I'm just a little tired. A long, long day. And that...that music you were playing was something really great. It caught my attention. But, I'll have to..." He looked around. "I didn't bring anything up here, did I?"

Lars tucked his folders into a duffel bag. "Monsignor, you're carrying around too much." He swung the bag up over his shoulder and flashed half a smile. "You have to let some out. Maybe I should get you a drum or something."

"I'd love a drum, actually."

Kilba followed Lars down the stairs and, saying bye, went to his study. The black leather bag Cruz had given him was there on Kilba's desk—Cruz had said little about it, only that Gaja had come around briefly, agitated, and had left the bag in the rectory. The Monsignor had read the note, *Stop me before I don't know what I will do if I am driven to it* but had done nothing for an entire week. A week? For the last eighteen years, Kilba had done nothing.

Now he took the bag and drove to the Dilienkos' house.

The Monsignor entered through the garden. He thought he heard the swing creaking but saw no one. The back door had been left open a crack and Kilba placed his hand on the wood, a bit unsure. He pushed it open and gently asked, "Anyone home?" his voice unwieldy in the quiet.

Odors of cigarette smoke and fried food lingered in the kitchen. A greasy pan had been left in the sink, pools of fat floating atop mucky water. The warmth of the little chandelier, its electric candles burning, only accentuated the kitchen's ragged abandonment, its floor unswept and old magazines on the counter beside used dishrags. Kilba sensed someone was home and uttered, "Hello?" but the corridors and rooms loomed before him. He took off his hat and jacket and wandered into the beautiful front room where he found Gaja quietly sitting by the window, apparently dressed to go out. She was smoking and looking into the street.

Kilba felt futility and embarrassing pity for her. She very naturally drew so much of his attention that Kilba only noticed Father Cruz in the next moment, as if by accident. Cruz was standing at a nearby table, packing away the green stole he wore while administering sacraments. "Father Cruz," he said. "I didn't know."

"I brought the Eucharist." His inability to hide nervousness struck Kilba—Cruz tried to seem patient while taking his things to leave, but his haste was obvious. "I was already on my way." By the coat rack, Cruz raised a hand to them both and said, "I have another appointment."

With him gone, a new stillness filled the house, familiar discomfort. Kilba found a place to sit by the piano, about five yards from Gaja, a round table before him. The only time Gaja moved was to inhale smoke; she'd blow it in a delicate stream that crashed and disappeared into the translucent curtains. "I've come to your place," said Kilba.

"Are you going to take me somewhere?"

"I don't think there's anywhere for you to go."

"Why did you come, then?" She finally looked up, her eyes accusing Kilba of something he had not done and searching for a feeling he didn't have.

"You wrote in a message. Stop me before I et cetera, et cetera." Gaja extinguished her cigarette and crossed her arms so that Kilba thought she might pout like a child. "I'm embarrassed it took me this long. But I'm wondering what is it you might do? Are you going to hurt someone?"

"That was a week ago. I'm better now, thank you."

Gaja angered Kilba, an unexpected feeling. "You don't seem better."

"Well, Yuri's stopped talking around town." She put her pack of cigarettes in her lap. "Thankfully."

"What difference does it make?" asked Kilba. "The boy's right. Ears are deaf. We're all dumb."

Gaja seemed trapped in a daydream and unable to hear him. It angered Kilba further. He sat right beside her, holding Benny's figurine, the one she had left for him in the leather bag; it was still wrapped in the flax cloth. Kilba set the bundle near her ashtray. "You wanted me to see this?"

"Did you bring the nails back too?"

"The spikes? You wanted me to bring them?"

"You saw them, didn't you?"

"Gaja!" He raised his voice. "Yes. I saw them. Yes! And I saw this!" He unwrapped the figurine. "So what? And now what should I, blame someone? Must I suddenly understand something? Feel shock, guilt, compassion?"

"You understand a lot."

"What do I understand?"

"You understand everything everyone tells you," she babbled, struggling for words. "Everyone tells everyone else. All kinds of things. But I don't know anything."

"Gaja." Kilba almost laughed. "I don't know why you're bringing this piece of wood to my rectory, but if it's for pity, know I can't pity you anymore. No diversions, no spikes found on abandoned tracks. No stupid piece of wood."

"That's where it all started," Gaja said, nodding her head to the table. She took a cigarette. "That's how it all started."

"Well, it's finished," said Kilba. He took Gaja's matches with the bundled figurine and stood.

"Where are you going?" she asked.

Kilba squatted by the fireplace. He placed the figurine on an old charred log. Gaja quietly uttered something behind him, but he paid no attention. An oil lamp stood on the mantelpiece, and Kilba used the oil to douse the flax cloth and light it on fire. When he was sure the fire was good and hot, he let it burn and kept the flames fed until the figurine was nothing but a red coal.

9

Yuri was cutting frozen beef into T-bone steaks at the band saw. He pushed lightly as the thin saw drove steadily through the bone, releasing ultra-fine dust that smelled moist and cold.

The worst was the sound, at times high pitched, other times muffled. Yuri could feel the powerful vibrations in his shoulders. He had taught himself to like the repeated movements and the idea that the pain was already finished, the cows or bulls dead long before his hands touched them.

Yuri was sweating. The back room was cool, a slight breeze from the pull of an exhaust fan, but his brow was wet. He felt tingles in other parts of his body, behind his knees, between his shoulder blades, and a powerful force gummed up his insides, making it hard to swallow the pasty film in his mouth.

Nobody knew.

Yuri cut the bones and the high-pitched whine repeated, repeated, but nobody knew.

A powerful force in his center, like a glass sphere packed with the molten heat of a red sun, wanted to charge up his throat.

At the end of the workday, Reikel smiled to Yuri as he left, said, "See ya Monday." On the way to the bus stop, Yuri threw up his lunch...popcorn, salami and apple juice. This was the third time he had thrown up, the onset of nausea unexpected, gone as soon as he had vomited, since he had shown Reikel his hands. Nobody ever saw Yuri vomit.

Cicero had become a ghost town surrounding him. Hundreds of sparrows were chattering in a small yellowing elm.

Their bickering and chirping grew so loud and overwhelming that Yuri stood entranced until a woman exited a nearby car.

On 12th Street, he saw his bus lumber away without him, so he went to a diner to rinse his mouth in the bathroom and wipe his face and chin to be sure he was clean.

Once home, he couldn't sculpt. Every idea and sketch seemed pointless and stupid. He was always hungry, although nothing tasted good and no drink quenched his thirst or wet his constantly dry mouth. The hardest place to be in all of Cicero was home. While he sat in his kitchen, it felt as though parts of him were gradually disappearing. If it had not been for the occasional sounds of Lars' piano, that new composition—Yuri would listen for the music on purpose, the window of his back porch wide open— he would not have been able to stay in the apartment. Whenever the music ended, Yuri felt extreme nervousness, a shifting fuzziness in his periphery, and that powerful glass sphere inside him.

Everything required hands. At Reikel's, his hands seemed to do what he asked them, but at home they refused to obey. *Everything* required hands. Warming up a plate of leftover macaroni and cheese. Washing himself, his entire body...before he could wash his body he'd have to wash his hands. Flipping through the sketches on the table seemed such a chore. When Lars used his hands, music came so easily, like air through a wide open door. Yuri could tell that Lars never thought about borrowing hands or finding new ones, and he didn't have nightmares that his hands were left wrapped up in aluminum foil at the bottom of a paper bag.

Yuri swept out his studio and moved sculptures around. He lit his torch and stared into the blue flame so long that it became a glowing plastic cone. He felt hollow hunger and went up to boil rice and beans. Eating, he grew scared that he had left the torch burning and rushed down. It lay right where he had left it, extinguished on his worktable, still warm in the gray light.

The arrangement of the sculptures on his shelves agitated him, and he moved a few around, taking the broom to sweep out the corner. Yuri realized for the first time that the sculpture of his mother's head had been moved. The one from the spade, it had been moved slightly to the left. But how? Yuri could not remember touching it—he was certain he had never moved it. He didn't like the sculpture, thought it was ugly and dumb, that crown of medical scissors poorly soldered. Sometimes he wanted to cover it with a sheet or turn it to face the wall but had never bothered. Now it had definitely been moved to the left.

Yuri felt a subtle tremble of nervousness. His memory was going. He was losing his ability to recall life.

The glass sphere swelled inside him, rising up into his throat, pushing pressure behind his eyes. Furious, he cut the portrait from the wooden stand and beat it with his sharpest hammer. When his wrist started to hurt, he ignited his torch and heated the spade until a small circle glowed hot. Yuri poked it through. He wrapped the thing up in foil and threw to the back alley.

Upstairs, he ate his food, now cold. When he lay back on his thin mattress, he slept instantly, falling right into nightmares about missing hands, torches that would not ignite, memories that had been lost, sculptures that moved on their own.

Whenever he awoke, he had trouble knowing what day it was. He found busses running on the Saturday schedule. Weekends were the worst because he had so much time to sculpt but found plenty of excuses, shopping for things he didn't need— paper clips and deodorant—always walking to the largest stores on 22nd with the biggest crowds. Among these people, nobody knew. Sometimes Yuri walked out on the yellow lines in the middle of 12th Street's busiest traffic and felt completely invisible.

When he next came to work, Reikel showed him a load of pork that needed to be trimmed for a large order. Yuri went and found a clean apron and sharpened a knife. He had barely started working when a spark of yellow light, a small but overwhelming flower-shaped flash, blinked in his left periphery. The hallucination was short, but terrible nervousness followed, a sudden sinking feeling and numbness. He put the knife down to look around the back room and felt he had to hold onto the table or lose his balance.

The buzz of the exhaust fan and the meat cooler. People yapping in the alley. The smooth, cool tiles and stainless steel. For a second, Yuri thought he heard someone calling his name. He thought he'd be sick, but the feeling passed. Everything in front of him: the meat and the machines, the tables, the drain on the floor and the many organized knives. The whole thing was now pointless. Completely, irrefutably meaningless. He didn't even bother taking his hat or sweatshirt and left out the shop's back door.

Yuri rode the L into Chicago. He removed his apron and baseball cap to leave on an empty seat before getting off at Damen, Wicker Park, and he walked to Alina's place. It was still early and she was at work, all the way in Old Town. He was embarrassed to be standing by her front door and wanted to leave.

She must have seen him through the window. Yuri heard her walking down the stairs to answer the door. She was clicking the knobs and bolts. The door opened, wood scraping against wood. "Yuri..." she whispered, a bit surprised.

"I ditched Reikel's."

"Are you in trouble?"

Yuri seemed to nod, but he also shrugged and shook his head.

Alina let him in and followed him up the stairs, told him to sit in her reading chair near the window.

Yuri saw her force a smile. Alina's greasy hair had not been washed in days. Her apartment was messier than normal, clothes and papers all around, and she did not have a single light on. She asked him, "What's the matter?"

"I'm fucked."

Alina didn't react one way or another. She stirred a cup of cold tea. "I'm glad you came here. I've been thinking about you."

"I'm fucked, Alina."

"You're exhausted." She touched his forearm. Her hand was inexplicably soft and warm, so easily extended out to him, and Yuri felt different immediately, safer than he had felt in weeks. A few tears escaped and fell onto his jeans and Yuri did not understand why Alina showed no surprise. He was so happy she wasn't asking questions—Alina only pressed his arm tightly with her warm hand. She finally whispered, "I finished them."

He thought she was talking about an order of jewelry.

She pointed to the coffee table. "A few days ago." Yuri saw an unwashed glass cup where an old wrinkled tea bag had been smashed to the bottom. But then he saw one of Victoria's journals lying next to a small notebook. "That's the last one," she said. "I just finished yesterday. In the afternoon. A lot of late nights, with a lot of sleepless pauses. But it felt like I couldn't stop."

The feeling of meaninglessness that had developed in Reikel's shop now retreated. "I have to tell you something, Alina. You'll have to help me."

She nodded.

"Since I was a kid."

Alina sat down on the floor in front of him. She put her hands on his knees and it seemed she already knew what he was going to say. It almost made speaking pointless and Yuri just turned one of his palms to her. "I know," she said, touching his palm with two warm fingers.

"You?"

Alina took him by the wrists and pulled him down from the reading chair to sit on the floor with her. She hugged him, pressing his face into her neck, and felt his body sobbing, although Yuri didn't make a sound. Time passed this way. When she kissed him above the ear, some final lock broke and he could weep and howl. It left through his whole face, the front of Alina's t-shirt soaked and stained.

"How do you know?"

"From my mom."

"But, what did she know?"

"From your dad," said Alina. "He told her what was going on."

Passage: The Evening following Victoria Jorgenson's First Day at Work, February 19, 1968

Spilled tea into the office typewriter. Had set the cup on the machine. Trying to feed a form between the rollers, answer a phone, turn to give the other woman a stapler, remember the question the man on the phone had asked—he was some pink-faced Pole at the reception's window—when my elbow hit the cup and the whole thing poured into the typewriter's open throat. I looked inside to see the teabag lay on the little levers that clap letters through the ribbon, flattened like a body bag thrown from a roof. The other woman (I can't remember her name) had the sense to unplug the machine before I stuck my fingers inside.

Bronza and the optometrist had a good laugh while rivulets of tea carried particles of dried ink and greasy dust onto my skirt. They traded fraternity jokes, bad ironies, masculine ho-hum. Maggie (her name has returned) helped me clean the floor, but I don't think she'll help me retype all the forms I ruined, all the now illegible records.

She has a brick for a brain. The woman knows almost nothing of my relationship with Bronza, that I can speak to him in a language she'd never understand, but she's already keeping track of my eyes.

—Are you looking at the doctor?

Later in the day, just before my shift ended, she told me there is nothing wrong with enjoying my work. The foolish woman winked. Didn't she know that winks are supposed to be subtle? Private and stealthy?

Bronza bought me pie and tea at the bakery. It is fascinating to see the roles he plays...the doctor with patient, *doctor with clinic staff, doctor walking around while patients wait, and doctor off duty. At the bakery, he was Bronza with cigarettes. We seemed to agree that Maggie and everyone else at the clinic are stupid. I wondered, then, what their stupidity made us. He said, —Something else.*

What?

—We are stupid too. But we're intelligent about our stupidity.

This is what we speak about in Russian when no one can understand us. It was what my parents used to do in New York...the topic never got boring. Look at these pridurki Americans and look at this durak here and that durak there. With Bronza today I did the exact same thing, and had forgotten how much I loathed it.

I realize, of course, why I have taken the job at the clinic. It's not because Alina is in high school, Lars is locked away with his musical curse, and I sit around bored. It is because, each day at 12:30 when my shift ends, Bronza and I will go to the bakery. We'll feel better about ourselves by pointing out just how many fools surround us.

Bad irony. Look in the mirror and wink at yourself, Victoria. Subtle. Keep it subtle.

Spring, 1971

1

Lars didn't care about any stupid mirror. Victoria asked again if he had seen it, and he looked under a newspaper in the kitchen, a dishrag next to the fruit basket. "Not the slightest clue," he said. "I don't even know what you're talking about."

"Well, I just bought it."

"I've never seen it."

"It's small, silver. Fits right in the palm. Clasps nicely." Victoria followed Lars into their bedroom. He took a sport coat and tossed one of his very plain ties over the shoulder. "I haven't seen it in this room," he said. "Guarantee that."

"Что тут происходит?" she said. She was pressing a fist into her hip. "It's supposed to be right here in this purse." Victoria had hung it on the doorknob. "Such a nice mirror." She looked over the mess on her dresser.

Lars left her to fuss and went to the front room to sit by the phone and tie his necktie. After a few minutes, Alina came out wearing a tasteful beige dress. "What are you guys yelling about?" she asked.

"She's lost something. Mirror."

Her dad kept tying and untying his tie until he crumpled it up and left it in a ball on the couch. She stepped over to put on the radio, but Lars stopped her. "No. Not now. I don't want to hear any of it."

"Why not?"

"What kind of teeny crap you want to play?"

"Jesus." Alina stared him through, annoyed. "Just wanted to see what's on."

"Well, don't." He had taken the tie again, and she watched him loop and tighten it around his neck, a bit crooked under the collar. Then he pulled his socks up and leaned back. In time, his expression softened. "Sorry," he whispered. "Sorry, Alina. You can put the music on."

She went to sit by herself in the kitchen.

2

Yuri and Anya were sitting on the floor of her room and drawing with crayons and colored pencils. Anya was very excited. On an extra large sheet of paper—so big she could kneel on it—she drew with vigorous strokes and repetitive lines. She was only three and her lines did not form anything, really, but she insisted her drawing was a chicken.

Yuri was trying to sketch Kolya's birdcage. He had learned in school to draw with very short strokes and to shade with the edge of the pencil tip. His picture did not come out very well, so he tried to draw a horse from memory. Sometimes it was easier, freer, than looking at something. When he struggled drawing the horse's legs, he wished he could look at the wooden horse he had stuffed in an old sock to hide behind Anya's dresser.

He decided to teach Anya how to draw a turkey—he called it a chicken—by making an outline of his hand. When Anya tried to do it herself, she wrapped her tiny fist around the pencil and pressed hard against the paper, ripping through and marking the floor.

Anya knew this was bad and looked up at Yuri. Mama was working in the kitchen. She probably wouldn't find the markings until much later, but Yuri didn't want to risk it and had to clean up right away. If he went for a rag and cleaner, mama would ask him what was dirty and demand to see. He went for a glass of water and thought he'd clean Anya's markings with a sock or napkins from the wastepaper basket.

In the kitchen, mama was nervous and busy. From the archway, Yuri could feel the heat from the oven and the pots on the stove. She moved in short bursts, mostly from the table to the oven, but then to the sink, and again to the table where her cigarette smoldered in an ashtray. Yuri could smell the spring air coming up the back stairs. Papachka had left the back door open and was probably getting seltzer from the garage. Yuri chose to get water from the bathroom, but then mama asked him why he was standing there. "*Ko tu ten stovi?*"

She was very angry. He knew it was probably something about papachka. Gaja asked him again, "*Nu, ko?*"

"*Noriu vandens atsigert.*"

"Water?" asked Gaja. "You want *me* to get it for you?"

"I'll get it myself."

"Hurry up."

Yuri wasn't sure what to do.

"Now. Get it now."

In the kitchen, he felt the immense energy of her nervousness, but also her confusion and hurt. Using a small footstool, he took a cup from the clean dishes—she kept telling him to hurry as the cup filled. Yuri climbed down, careful not to spill any water, but she told him to drink it in the kitchen. "*Gerk čia.* Put that cup back. I don't want to clean up after you."

"But I wanted to drink it while drawing."

"Did you hear what I said? The guests are coming. You want me to clean the whole house again?"

"But Anya wanted some water—" Yuri couldn't finish. Mama slapped the cup from his hand, hurting his wrist, and the ceramic shattered on the floor. He hurried off to his room while mama shouted, "You clean this floor. You clean it now," but Yuri had locked himself in. "You're leaving this for me?"

She was banging on his door and pulling at the knob. The door rattled in its frame. "Come out now. Come out and wipe that water." The knob was turned all the way to its side and mama was twisting it with all her strength. Then it gave way. Yuri heard mama's footsteps on the hardwood and immediately put his ear up to listen.

"*Kas čia dabar?*" She was in Anya's room. He was sure, even though the markings on the floor were small, that she would see them and yell at Anya terribly, maybe even make her stand in the corner. She shouted, "You're here drawing. Always you're drawing. And what kind of pictures? Enough! Enough!" Anya started crying. "These pencils. You've got nothing better to do?" Yuri heard paper rustle and something fell in the garbage. "What are these pictures?"

Anya kept crying but Yuri knew she wasn't really scared. He had learned that Anya understood how mama's anger and words were always pointed at Yuri, even if he was in the other room.

His sister suddenly shrieked out. "Come with me. Your brother can't clean it, then you'll clean it."

Yuri heard Anya's protest. Objects banged around in the kitchen. "Pick up the pieces," mama said. This was very different...mama usually favored Anya and punished her lightly, if at all. Yuri imagined Anya picking up bits of ceramic with her little fingers. He hoped papachka would come home. When Anya shrieked out again, Yuri unlocked his door and went to the kitchen. Gaja had her by the hand and was pointing to the floor. "All these, your brother's pieces."

"Mama, please," said Yuri. He had never seen her this angry. Her face had transformed into a stranger's. She seemed thin and tall, strands of hair wiry around her head, all her features pointy, like a tree without any leaves. "I'll clean up," said Yuri.

"Do you see what you've done?"

Yuri stepped toward her, Anya still whimpering. When he was close enough for mama to reach him, she grabbed Yuri by the wrist, pulling him toward herself. Anya walked though the wet floor and tracked tiny footprints into the front room where she turned around to stare at her brother, a hand on top of her head. Mama twisted Yuri's wrist backwards and pulled him even closer to the table.

It was how it happened the first time—Yuri didn't even know what caused the unexpected, stinging and hot pain to press fiery sharp through his palm, immediately through his whole body, down to the soles of his feet and behind his eyes. He howled, his voice low, and fought to get away. She let him, and he pressed his hand against his stomach, his eyes closed, but then looked up at Anya who was pulling her braid, her eyes wide and warm with surprise. Mama whispered, "You see?"

Time froze to a block of glass. Yuri felt sudden, unfamiliar cold over his skin, colder now that mama opened the oven to check something. When he saw Anya raise one hand and say, "Papachka," he only wanted to hide.

"What the hell's gone on here?" Bronza asked, speaking English, a paper bag rustling. Yuri turned to look at him and Gaja left for her bedroom where she closed and locked the door. Yuri scampered to the front room to sit under the piano. "What's happened?" asked papachka and Anya pointed at Yuri to say, "*Bo bo,*" her toddler's word for *hurt*.

"*Bo bo*?" asked Bronza. After some pestering and pleading, Yuri finally showed papachka the wound.

Bronza treated it with ointment and a white bandage. Yuri did not grimace from the stinging ointment but sat stiff, wanting only to close himself away. Bronza's kiss on his forehead felt cold and meaningless, just disgustingly wet.

3

Lars, Victoria and Alina were waiting by the Dilienkos' front door. Bronza had barely let them in before excusing himself. "Lars, pour the girls drinks. I've got to clean up a spill." Lars helped himself to scotch and opened a bottle of wine for Victoria and Alina; going on seventeen, she was allowed wine or champagne in company. The whole family sat in the front room.

Bronza came back and took a glass from the buffet. "What's spilled?" asked Lars.

"Just some water."

"Where's the old lady?"

"She'll be out in a moment."

Gaja appeared smiling and greeting everyone. She wore a red dress—the shade more appropriate, Victoria and Alina felt, for autumn than spring—and a grayish-white apron. "Victoria, you look great," she said and kissed her cheek. "That brooch is so elegant. And Alina...you're blossoming to a young woman." She kissed Alina but only shook the ends of Lars' fingers. "I'll bring out some ham and things in a moment. I'm almost ready. Just a few more things in the kitchen."

Lars noticed that Bronza's one knee was slightly wet. He wanted to say "Doc's got water on the knee," but this dimwitted pun was too dimwitted. Smalltalk began and he listened in the beginning. In one good gulp, he shot whiskey down the back of his throat, then poured himself another. Lars sat at the piano. "Oh, please," said Victoria. "You're so grumpy today. I don't think you should play right now."

"Why not?" asked Alina.

"Sure, play something," said Bronza. "Go ahead, Lars."

"I don't want to play." Lars was honest. "Vic's right. Not right now." He lightly touched the piano's black finish. "Hey," he said, turning to them and grimacing. "You smell that?"

"Smell what?" asked Alina. Victoria and Bronza sniffed. "Smell what, dad?"

"In the oven," he said. He knew they could all smell the burning food. "Maybe turn the oven off?"

Bronza laughed. "Did you start drinking early today?"

"I know you guys smell it too."

Little Anya trotted in from some other room. She called out to Victoria, *Tsiotsi Toria,* and came to sit on her lap. The girl noticed Victoria's cane, the braid of wood, and said, "Касичка ," giggling so hard, pulling on her own braid. Victoria told her that, yes, "Да да да. У меня тоже есть касичка," she also had a braid, laughing along. Anya's contagious laughter soon spread to Alina and Bronza, but Lars only smiled.

From a sharp angle down a narrow corridor, Lars could see Yuri peering into their conversation, off on his own as always. Bronza noticed him looking Yuri's way and immediately asked him, "Hey Lars, you want to taste something new?"

"Yeah, sure. Bring it out."

"It's actually in my car."

Lars followed Bronza to the garage. The side door had been left unlocked as always and Bronza had left the keys in the Buick's ignition. He took them to unlock the trunk. Next to a large red can of gasoline and a toolbox was a case of cognac, a sack of bread and sweet rolls, and one engraved wooden box. Bronza reached for this box. "A better patient of mine," he said, turning a clasp and opening it. He lifted a bottle of cognac out of red felt. "Take a look at this."

The bottle completely bored Lars, and he showed interest poorly. "That's nice."

"You want to try a bit?"

"Here? In the garage?"

"We can take it inside. Try one over dinner."

"Sure," he shrugged. "Why not?" Lars helped him carry all the stuff into the house.

While Bronza put the case of cognac away, Lars lingered in the kitchen where Gaja was spooning food into serving dishes. He stepped up to the cluttered table. "Hey. You need some help in here?"

"No," she said, holding a burnt potato casserole. "We'll be eating in ten minutes."

"Then I'll go sit on the swing."

A drink still in his hand, Jorgenson followed the stepping-stones out to the yard's private nook. He wanted to tell Gaja she was full of dogshit. Lars hated it—you burned the casserole. The whole house smells like smoke. Just admit it.

Gaja was Lugan trash. Back in Benny's Luganland, she'd have been boiling horse livers for dinner and worshipping elms. Now the little bitch had a piano in her front room and a casserole of dogshit. A case of cognac in the trunk and a bottle in red felt. No patient gave him that shit, Lars knew; Bronza had bought that bottle himself. He always pretended people gave him expensive shit, as if they loved him so much.

In an impulse, Lars stood and headed for the back gate. He left the yard and wandered up the alley towards 12th Street, throwing the glass into someone's bushes when he had finished the scotch.

The party realized he was gone only after the table had been set. Victoria and Alina did not hide their embarrassment. "He seemed moody," said Bronza. "Maybe we should go look for him?"

"No need to look," said Victoria, sitting down. "I know where he is."

Alina took her place at the table next to Yuri. She said, "There's no point looking for him. He'll just insult you. It's better to leave him alone."

"Was something the matter?"

Victoria explained what had happened to Lars the previous day. A man who had graduated from music school with him had taken a job as the director of an orchestra in a small Midwest town. Lars thought the man would agree to include some of his compositions in the year's program, but he had refused. "Why?" asked Bronza.

Victoria's shoulders straightened. Alina eyed Bronza. "Let's eat dinner," she said, her eyebrows narrow. "I'm starved."

They ate and Bronza changed the subject with a toast, "To a nice evening." Everyone said, "Yes," and drank. Then everyone complimented Gaja's food.

She would slip away to the kitchen from time to time to refill serving dishes. Gaja also took secret shots of Amaretto from a small bottle stashed in one of the cupboards. Combined with the shots of vodka Bronza poured, the booze was enough to make her neck and shoulders feel like gelatin. She tried to sit straight and spoke very little. It was easy, because Victoria and Bronza were talking only to each other.

Yuri sat quietly the whole time, his hand under the table. The adults kept making toasts, one to Lars, another to good friends, a third to the children, one more to Gaja for the good food, and a longer, both sentimental and funny toast to Lithuanians and Russians and Ukrainians and missing Scandinavians. The adults were soon happily drunk and could laugh about anything. Yuri felt it easy to hide, to feel invisible in their drunkenness.

The party wound down after Anya grew cranky. Bronza put her to bed and Alina took the chance to call friends. At his window, Yuri stood to watch her while she waited outside for someone to pick her up. A car full of young people soon drove her away.

Victoria sat with Gaja after they had tidied up. She had never seen Gaja drunk like this—she was sweetening chilled vodka with cherry syrup and sipping it from a shot glass that resembled a giant thimble. Gaja slurred her words and could barely keep her balance on the way to the bathroom. When Bronza came back from Anya's room, Victoria asked him why she was drinking. "Почему она напивается?" Bronza shrugged, tapping his temple twice with a forefinger.

Gaja came back with water dripping from her hands. She moved everyone over to the front room. In a quiet, hazy moment, Gaja stared at Victoria intently, her drunken eyes deep inside the shadows of their sockets. She asked, "Lars? He'sn't, 'sint home now?"

"He's most likely at a bar. Sometimes he goes to Kilba's. But I doubt it tonight."

Gaja nodded, pulling the dress down tight over her knees. She pointed at Bronza and asked, "Does he? He's telling you 'bout me?"

"Gaja," Bronza said. "You're really drunk."

"*You're*," she said. "You. Is you'n. You did it."

"Could you stop? Please."

"'Toria. You tell me. He's telling you 'bout me?"

"No," said Victoria. "He isn't. Maybe you should lie down, Gaja."

She tried to speak again, but her body swayed forward slightly. A hand rose to her mouth and the other reached for air as she looked for a place to hold her balance. Bronza tried to help her but only managed to lead her to the dinner table where she threw up in a salad bowl. Yuri came out to look, but Victoria took him to his room. "Your mother's sick. Just sick."

Gaja was still mumbling to Bronza. "You did it. You're drunk. Telling 'bout me."

Bronza cleaned her up in the bathtub, wiping her face and washing her soiled sleeve. He left her in bed on her stomach, a bucket on the floor and glass of water on the nightstand.

He and Victoria waited for her taxi on the bungalow's front stairs. A gentle breeze blew through the cool and quiet night. A few people were out walking dogs or sitting on balconies and porches. In the west, far down where 19th Street ended, the sky was still glowing navy blue behind silhouettes of blockhouses with chimneys and antennas. Bronza lit a cigarette and spoke Russian. "Could you tell what she was doing? Drinking Amaretto in the kitchen?"

"Wasn't paying attention."

From one of the flowerpots on the stairs, Bronza picked a white flower petal and crushed it between his fingers, rolling it into a tiny, moist ball. "She's accusing me of having affairs."

"With whom?"

"Just affairs. Says I smell like perfume whenever I come back from house calls."

Victoria looked up the street.

"Would you stay with her?"

She leaned hard against her cane. "That's not my business."

"But would you?"

"It's a bad question. You're drunk. I don't know."

"You wouldn't. Nobody would."

"It's tactless. I don't want you asking me."

"I'm not practicing tact." Bronza pulled a fallen twig out of the flowerpot. "You won't understand why I did it," he said, snapping the twig in half. "But I stole your mirror."

It took Victoria a moment to realize what he was talking about. "Mirror. My new one?"

He managed to frown and smirk at the same time. "Now you know what I'm like, Victoria. I really want you to know what I'm like. And what's happening to me."

"You're arrogant. It's not clever." She was feeling her body's weight against the bad hip, aware, now, of just how much alcohol she had drunk. "You went through my bag. When? At work."

"You want it back?"

"I don't want anything from you." She sat on the second stair from the bottom. "Where is it?"

"I have it."

She pressed the point of her cane into the soft grass. "I know what you're like, Bronza. You're a terrified little kid. It's why you married a girl." She laid the cane across her knees. "It's why."

"Is it?"

"I'm bored." She struggled to stand up and he tried to help her, but Victoria pulled her arm away. Then the taxi pulled up.

4

Victoria would not write a word in her journal for the next several days. She would sit and stare at the page, draw ink into her pen, but for the first time in years she wondered what it would mean if someone found these journals and could read them. Sitting now on a Sunday evening, she penned the word обыкновенный; it meant *ordinary* or *common*. Looking at it, she pressed the tip of her pen into the thick paper and let the ink bleed into a large black bruise.

At the clinic, she avoided Bronza for several days, dealing with him only when necessary, leaving before he could ask her to lunch. Monsignor Kilba came to have his heart checked and ended up chatting with both Bronza and Victoria, but they said little to each other after he left. When he did finally ask her the next day if she wanted lunch, Victoria lied to him. "Lars has people from the church choir coming over. I have to get back. But thanks."

For a second, she wrote later that day, *I almost believed people from the choir were coming over.*

I look through my bag each afternoon before leaving the clinic. I always feel he's returned the mirror. While I'm in the reception. He's put the mirror back. I'm surprised he hasn't done it.

That's not true.

I'm not surprised at all. It's what I hate and admire about him, that he's surprising and predictable. He's scared and courageous and filthy and sterile. He'd demand you use a sterile needle to draw his ill blood.

I can avoid the idea of his hands in my bag. The purse dangles from a hook and his hands pick through my keys and makeup, my folded scarf, coin purse and used tissue paper. I can even avoid the idea of him searching through for that mirror, unable to find it, desperate now that steps echo in the hall. I'm about to open the door. I've caught him rummaging.

I'll also imagine I don't know he took the mirror. He hasn't told me. Bronza is silent, alone in a sunlit room. Linden trees outside the window, their scent in a breeze.

That's nostalgia.

The mirror rests open on his desk. Does he look at himself while I sit, a great distance between us, and express wonder and regret—how could I think I've misplaced my mirror? Where could it be? Does he instead reflect sunlight with it, signal for help? Do I recognize the tiny but brilliant flash shining out from a great distance?

He goes to smoke in that back room at least once every half-hour. My jacket, even the inside of my bag will often smell of his cigarettes. At home, I open the bag to take out my lipstick and the inside smells like that room, like the inside of his polluted lungs.

Victoria drew more ink.

I can imagine him snooping around our flat in the dark. His hands reach into the drawers of my desk and his fingers pick through my jewels and necklaces, brooches and pins. Throughout the flat, fingerprints on kitchen knives, books rearranged on shelves. A candleholder that had been on the coffee table moves to my desk. He steals ink, writes a quiet word in my journal.

I can't imagine what quiet word he would choose.

At night, last night, it'll happen again when I lie down. It's already happening as I scribble right now. In the quiet, he sneaks into the room—his feet know which floorboards creak and which are silent—and he lays two warm hands on my naked hips. I open my eyes, but his body's absent. He's invisible but I can only feel him touching me. Lars snores away, notes bubbling up in his mind like gas in a flute of champagne.

Victoria reread what she had written and felt the urge to tear out the page. But she never did that and left it as it was. She had not finished writing—further ideas and words clawed at her, but she closed the journal and put on the kettle. Later that evening, she wrote one last thing:

I'll finally face him with it, tomorrow.

Bronza showed his face at work as easily as ever, smiling to patients and taking care of them in turn, sociable as always. But when 12:30 came and the clinic took its break, he closed himself in the back room.

Victoria had to get her purse and jacket. When she came in, he was smoking by the window, looking out into the alley. She said, "You're having a break."

He didn't move.

"Hey," she whispered, taking down her jacket. "Hello?"

"I heard you," he said, monotone, glancing at her reflection in the window. "Are you going for lunch?"

"No." One of the fluorescent tubes in the ceiling was flickering. "No. I just came to tell you—"

"It doesn't matter," he interrupted. "I'm not going to lunch either. It's payday, right?"

"So what."

"Places get packed when these people all get their money. The whole street gets paid on the same day. The same hour, probably."

"It does get packed. You're right." Victoria pressed her cane into the floor. "Listen," she said, "I want you to give it back."

Bronza's posture straightened. The tube above them had started buzzing. He extinguished his cigarette, crushed the filter with extra, unnecessary force, and dumped the ashtray into the alley.

She raised the handbag to her shoulder and pressed her weight against the cane to step closer to him but stopped before reaching the middle of the tight room. It felt too small for them.

"You don't have to give it back today," she said. "Or soon. But it isn't yours."

"I'll give it back," he said. "I'm glad you want it back." Bronza lightly tapped the nails of his thumbs together and she could hear it. "It's a funny mistake to make."

"What mistake?"

"I thought telling you would correct it."

"What do you mean?"

He rubbed the back of his head.

"Bronza, I feel sorry for you." She backed closer to the door. "Maybe you need help of some kind. But I don't know how to help you. Maybe you need to open up to someone. But I can't force you to do that."

"Let's forget I took the mirror, for now. Let's go for lunch."

"For tea only. I've no appetite."

He came to the coat rack and took his jacket; it seemed to lift itself onto his shoulders. Closer to her, his tall body now shortened the room's space even more. When he moved toward her...Victoria felt it...he was approaching her and not the door. He reached out for the knob, but then turned to face her, gentle and soft.

The first moment of their kiss was not uncomfortable—it seemed inevitable and natural. But the entire room had constricted and now Victoria had no space. His chest flattened against her breasts and she was pushed up to the wall behind her. His fingers, scented from the clinic's antiseptic soap, briefly and lightly touched her cheek. Victoria shook her head away and he stepped back, only a few inches.

Victoria felt a fool, shocked that he'd try it, repelled that she had given in. She slapped him hard across the face. He took it and stood still as if he had expected the blow. She hit him harder, the ball of her hand against his jawbone so that her wrist stung, and this time it hurt him. With her cane, she pushed him back towards the other wall, but he was already moving on his own. Bronza took his place on the chair beside the back window. He did not watch Victoria leave.

5

Lars was tweezing longer whiskers from his mustache and burning them in a candle. The heat ate them up quickly, leaving the faint but distinct odor of burnt human hair. His pencil was in his mouth, but he didn't bite it. Sometimes he brought the whiskers to the flame with his fingers to feel them singed. The tiny hairs seemed alive, scrambling to escape the flame, curdling and bubbling where the heat was the highest, liquefying slightly before turning to charred dust.

The papers, folders and crumpled napkins on the desk had been shoved to the side, forming a landscape of paper hills with the candle towering in the lowlands. He did not have a single idea for a new composition. All he heard in his head was a humid wind blowing through an empty white room.

What could be taking Victoria? It was already 4:00. He was getting hungry and took a few pieces of herring and a cold boiled potato to his den. Lars made sure to leave room in his stomach so that he could sit and eat with her when she came home. Her keys finally sounded in the stairwell and the door thumped when she pushed it open with her shoulder.

Lars stayed in the den and played a few empty passages on the piano to make it seem like he had been working. He soon came out, expecting to see her at the kitchen table. He glanced through the archway to her desk in the front room. "Vic?" She had bought some limes, left in a yellow bowl on the counter. Lars squeezed a whole lime into a glass of seltzer and drank the refreshing cold and tangy water quickly. "Vic? You in the can?" He made one more glass, this time squeezing the lime extra hard to get out every drop of juice as he chewed on a bit of rind.

She had bought a few magazines. Lars took the copy of *Time* to read in the front room. He found Victoria sitting in the corner by the bookshelf on her writing stool. She was topless, her back straight and legs crossed under a long and loose green skirt, hands cupped on one knee. Her hair was down almost to her shoulders, loosely combed and a bit shaggy. Lars couldn't tell if the powerful red lipstick was new or from so long ago that he couldn't remember. Its color pulled the green from her eyes with force that tingled Lars' skin and left him feeling boyish.

Victoria said, "I'm not wearing underwear."

"Um."

"Yes...You're saying?"

"Alina." He pointed to the door. "It's any minute'll come home."

"She's not coming home today."

Lars' hands trembled subtly when he put the magazine on the coffee table. He stuffed his hands in his back pockets. "Not today?"

"She's out with friends."

"No, no." He rubbed his mustache and sat down on the recliner. "What's gotten into you? What's this?"

She hiked up her skirt and spread her legs slightly. "I'm not wearing anything. You see?" Lars leaned forward, a quirky, uncertain smile on his face. He was sure that any moment now, if he reached out for her, a bunch of idiots with accordions and party hats would storm out from the closets. But he touched her knee, the inside of her thigh lightly and she grabbed him by the hair gently so that he'd lean towards her. "Vic? What?"

She whispered, "Shut up," and smiled, setting his hand on her breast. It was softer than he remembered—Lars hadn't touched her naked body in over a year—but her breast was beautifully round, feminine and heavy. He pinched her lightly and she sighed out, reaching for the buttons of his shirt. They kissed, cautious, even curious at first, but then giving in to deep longing for each other. Victoria stood from the stool, holding him to balance herself. "Alina's really not coming home?"

"Just shut up. Just trust me."

"I can't promise. I can't promise."

She didn't plead with him anymore or whisper anything, but allowed him to set her gently on the sofa. She slipped out of the skirt and revealed her hip and its awkward bone, a great, immovable bulb, like a small eggplant tucked under her skin. Lars hadn't seen it in so long—it always looked like it hurt terribly, but he touched and kissed the hip, squeezing her breast and the back of her neck when he kissed her lips again. She said, "Stand up."

"I want to sit."

"Stand up, Lars."

He listened. She undid his belt and let his trousers fall from the weight of his wallet and keys—Lars stepped out and kicked them to the side. She was gentle with him, kissing him everywhere, and he did get bigger; Lars thought it was working for a moment. He shut his eyes, keeping his balance by holding her shoulders, and tried to concentrate, feel only her mouth and fingertips. He felt her trying to love him as best she could, but he also sensed her desperation—it was actually panic. Something had to change immediately. She did it faster and Lars tried, but he knew nothing would change. He was limp and small, his heart beating, a gorgeous, erotic shrill buzzing through his entire body, into his lungs and belly, the muscles of his thighs, the bones of his shoulders and skull. But it brought nothing. The strain became awkward and foolish. Lars mumbled, "I'll do it to you."

Her fingers pressed into his thighs and she kept moving.

"Vic..." Lars tapped her on the shoulder. "Vic—"

She stopped, exhaling, wiping her mouth and falling against the sofa's backrest. "Fuck. I'm sorry."

"It's okay." He knelt down in front of her. "It's okay. I'll—I can do it for you. We'll just lie here. There's nothing wrong with that."

"Why doesn't it work? What's wrong?"

"You tried. Hey," he took her by the wrists, then the cheeks. "Hey. You had to. Right? It's just finished, that's all."

"No it isn't."

"Hey. Look. Look at me."

"What?"

"I know. I've missed you too, Vic." The tenants downstairs were hammering something and a voice sounded just below the hardwood.

315

"You're so fatal about it," said Victoria. "Something can be done, you know. It's not finished. It's just that we need a real break. We need to get out of here."

Lars wrapped her in the dark brown blanket covering the recliner. He turned her body on the sofa so that he could sit in front and hold her. She pressed his body to herself and scratched his head. "Maybe we need to take a trip," she said.

"A trip?" He kissed her above the ear. Lars could still feel tightness in her shoulders and back.

"All these people in this town. Do you know what kind of people come to the clinic? Do you know what kind of people I deal with over there?"

"You want to go to Michigan?"

"Far, god dammit. Europe. France, or something. Scandinavia. Remember? I remember you always wanted to go. Before Alina was born, you always wanted to go to Copenhagen. We can do it," she said. "Why not? Why not *do* something for a change? I can quit the job. I can quit, you know, and we'll take off for a while. We won't tell anyone."

Lars was quiet.

"Tell me we'll go," she said, sticking her nose into his neck. "Say we'll go."

Lars said, "Sure," pressing her shoulder, then gently pushing his knuckles against her spine. "Maybe you're right. Summer. Maybe in summer."

6

Yuri's class was reviewing homework exercises. His teacher, Sister Evangelista, a bony and ancient nun with paper-white hair and horn-rimmed glasses, had not called him to the board in two days. By remaining quiet and avoiding other kids, Yuri had developed a reputation for being slow. Sister Evangelista mostly called the smart kids so they could do something like *Demonstrate to the class how to do example eleven of the multiplication exercises.*

But Yuri knew the moment was approaching. Sure enough, while he wrote *44 x 4 = 176* over and over to appear busy, Sr. Evangelista announced, "Next..." A very serious pause followed. "Yuri. Go up to the board. The class will see your solution for example nine."

Yuri's right hand immediately formed a small fist. The burn on his palm had turned into a crescent shaped wound, red in the middle. It only hurt when he stretched his skin. It had been secreting a clear, thick juice and Yuri kept a loose bandage to absorb it. At first kids had asked him about the bandage, but soon everyone had lost interest.

Now it was different. Forty-eight eyes peered at him as he stood in front of the class. He believed even Mick Rheinhart, scratching his nose in the back, and Sonia Cervantez, peeling a purple crayon, even these two could see he had tightened his fist. They could feel how strongly he wished to tuck it into his pocket.

Sister Evangelista spoke. "Yuri. Pick up the chalk. We would like to see your solution to example nine."

He had forgotten the example. What was the problem? Sofie Krakowski had her book open and Yuri nonchalantly glanced there to find number nine. "You will not look at anyone else's solution, young man," said the nun. "Pick up the chalk and keep your eyes on the board."

Example nine was *24 x 2*, a simple problem. Yuri's fingers mishandled the chalk and it shattered on the floor. He bent down to pick it up, but the chalk had shattered into dust and shards, and now he remembered Anya. She was picking up sharp pieces of broken ceramic in the kitchen while Yuri was hiding in his room. "Sorry, sister," he said. Some of the kids giggled quietly and he stood up straight, unsure what to do.

"Yuri," said the nun. Her bony finger pointed to the cabinet in the corner. "Take the dustpan and hand broom. Clean up the chalk. Do it quickly and then give us your solution to the example."

He did everything Sister Evangelista said. Some of the kids in the front kicked bits of chalk out from under their desks so that Yuri could sweep them.

At the board, he wrote in his neat and straight handwriting, *24 x 4*. After working out the problem, he came up with the answer *96*. Yuri turned to face the nun, confident his answer was correct, his body warm for some reason and the wound in his hand hurting a little. A few of his classmates exchanged glances and giggled. The nun stared at him with very tight lips. "No," she said. "You are wasting the time of the entire class." Yuri looked at the problem, but was so nervous that he couldn't tell what he had done wrong. Sister Evangelista asked, "Are you looking to show off?"

"No, Sister."

"Then why would you solve an example different from the one you've been assigned?"

Yuri set the chalk on the ledge and held his hands behind his back. "I'm sorry, sister. I don't remember how to solve example nine."

She pointed out the door with one sweeping motion. "Go to the Sacred Heart of Jesus. You will pray there until I bring you a writing assignment."

Out in the school's quiet and cool corridor, Yuri actually felt relieved. Someone had opened a window and he could smell fresh pizza baking in the corner store. In front of the massive window at the hall's far end stood the statue of the Sacred Heart of

Jesus, His one hand lifted to grant blessings and the other at His side. Yuri knelt by the statue and folded his hands.

He knew he was supposed to be looking at Christ's wounds. All pupils sent to the Sacred Heart had to realize Christ's sacrifice and imagine how difficult it would be to die on the cross—that way, they could understand how blessed they really were. But Yuri could never think about what he was supposed to. He always thought the wrong things at the wrong times.

He remembered Sr. Evangelista's lesson. "You may think," she had said, "that your thoughts are invisible, but they are very clear to God. Jesus, God the Father, the Holy Spirit and all the angels, the saints and the Virgin Mary...even all the people who have died since Adam and Eve...they all hear very clearly what you're thinking. And when you're thinking what Lucifer wants you to think—when you give in to his temptations and your thoughts become wicked, they become even louder to Jesus, to God the Father, the Holy Ghost, all the angels, saints and especially to Our Blessed Virgin. All of heaven hears a wicked thought, and a wicked thought is already a very serious sin. Therefore, you will think only clean thoughts and concentrate on what your teachers and parents show you. Nothing more."

7

Anya always listened to some music to help her sleep. Bronza had set the record player in the corner of her room to play Mozart softly, barely audible. He shut her blinds and left the door cracked.

Yuri was still doing math and spelling homework, trying to finish the extra problems Sr. Evangelista had assigned. He could barely think after his long day and his hand was tired from writing out the punishment 200 times *I will do what I am assigned and pay close attention to my work,* but Yuri carried on and finished everything.

Papachka checked his math. Sometimes Bronza pushed him one or two lessons further, especially in reading and math, but tonight he saw how tired the boy was and only helped him find mistakes, understand how to fix them.

Each night before bed, Yuri got to hear a story, usually a chapter from a longer book. Bronza and Gaja used to alternate— one night he would read in Russian, the next she'd read from a tome of Lithuanian fables. But since she had burned his hand, only Bronza had been reading. Yuri used to pay close attention to the stories. Now his eyes were distant and Bronza could tell he barely listened and mostly stared at the movements of shadows and branches outside the window until he'd give in to sleep.

In the dark and quiet house, Bronza poured a few fingers of expensive scotch. A second glass of scotch didn't help him get drowsy. He wandered around the dark in his socks but then put on shoes to go out to the garden.

The night was chilly, with gusts blowing through the tops of the trees, but in the garden– protected by the house, garage and evergreens–only the shadows moved. He sat on the swing, exactly where Gaja used to sit, and smoked.

Bronza rubbed the jaw where Victoria had hit him. If anyone had noticed the slight swelling, they hadn't cared. The jaw hurt when he touched it and he had a nice tender area on the bone. Bronza pressed it and, to his surprise, his eyes watered.

Victoria's mouth was larger than Gaja's, and she didn't smoke. Her breath was so clean that the kiss left him tasting his own bad stink of tobacco and coffee. He could still smell her...fresh water and a hint of baby powder. Swinging in his yard, Bronza felt completely alone, the only man awake in a town of people who were tired of him.

He imagined all of Chicago and Cicero's lights had blacked out, their orange glow instantly extinguished from the sky. He could get into his car and glide through the darkness, appear in a place where no one knew him. A town out in the mountains. Take a new name.

The telephone was ringing in the house. He did not get up all that quickly to go answer but still knocked over the coffee can full of rainwater and cigarette butts. By the time he got inside, Gaja, groggy, had already answered. She handed him the receiver, whispering, "Here."

8

Victoria was jabbing Lars gently in his ribs with the cane's handle. "Wake up. Alina's got an earache." His mouth twitched, but he lay motionless, eyelids wrinkled and thick. Victoria clicked off the light and left him alone.

Her pen had dried out. Drawing ink from the well, she could not shake her jumpiness and trickled three black drops onto the page and desk, staining her thumb when cleaning up. She tossed the fountain pen to the side and scribbled with a common ballpoint:

He's coming. On his way. No pleading with Alina, no way to explain why she should wait until morning. Wait five hours, my God, it's almost daybreak. No—she whined and whined. Spoiled. —It's getting worse, mama, it's getting worse. I finally called.

I could have faked it. Alina would have believed I'd dialed his number. Could have claimed there was no answer.

He's an idiot. The fool couldn't think of an excuse to stay home. And the way he spoke to me. I'm some patient in his waiting room, I'm another

Alina called out, "Mama. This compress's 'ready cold."

Victoria rested her forehead against a fist. "One second." Although the page was still wet with spots of ink, she closed the journal and reached for her cane. In the kitchen, she put the kettle on and sat without any light, just the blue flame of the gas burner and the dim glow from the front room's lamp.

"Make it really hot."

"I'm boiling water. He'll be here any minute, anyway."

Victoria poured the water over a clean dishrag and squeezed the nearly scalding excess out, dripping just enough cool water over the compress. She pressed it gently on the side of her daughter's head. "Does that help at all?"

Alina nodded. "When it's really hot. But it gets cold so fast."

Bronza had arrived. She had to waddle down the stairs. "Alina's in her room," she muttered. Victoria had the door swung just wide enough for him to come through, hiding most of her body behind it.

"I won't be long," he said. "I'll be in and out." He trotted ahead, radiating impatience. In the middle of the stairway, she took a rest, her hip aching. By the time she got to Alina's room, Bronza was already leaning over her ear with a long pair of tweezers. "God, there's *more*?" he asked. "Who put this cotton in here?"

"Me," said Alina.

"Ticket to the emergency room." Bronza removed a few oily clumps, leaving them on a piece of tissue paper. "You're supposed to be smarter than this, Alina."

Victoria wanted to tell him to stop criticizing. Occasionally, Bronza glanced up at her but only quickly. Sometimes he set his fingertips gently on Alina's cheek—not at all in the way he had taken Victoria's head to kiss her—but still touching her with gentle hands. "Okay." He had cleaned out her ear. "Sit up." Alina grimaced but sat. He had a tuning fork on his knee and was twisting a black attachment onto a bulky, chrome handle. "We'll see what you've got. When did this start to hurt?"

"Last night. I think."

"Alina!" The name leaped from Victoria. "You told me it started this afternoon."

"It was just a weird itch at first."

Bronza was looking inside. "And it kept getting worse?"

"I thought it would go away. Mama didn't believe me, anyway."

"I did too," said Victoria, knocking her cane against the bed.

Bronza was ignoring them, concentrating on his work. "Let's look at the other one," he said. "Any trouble keeping your balance?"

"I don't know." Alina thought about it. "No."

He finished and set his instruments down. "Well, you've got a nice, fat and purple infection there, girl. The left ear. The sooner you treat it, the better." Bronza put his things away and searched through the bag for two little bottles. "Here's this syrup. Drink two spoons of this stuff and it'll knock you out in a few minutes. You'll feel kind of hung over, really groggy when you wake up. But you'll sleep." He set down a bottle of pills. "These are for pain. Take them tomorrow after a normal meal, but *only only only* if the pain gets too intense. They slow down your heart rate." Bronza rolled some thicker, better cotton in his fingers and gently covered her ear canal. "Now don't touch that. If it falls out, get your mom. And don't stuff anything on top of it. I'll write you a prescription for drops. Someone'll have to get them in the morning."

9

Barely fifteen minutes had passed since his arrival, but he was done—Bronza had only unbuttoned his long and light coat, had not even taken off his shoes. In the front room, he sat at Victoria's desk without asking her permission and changed to Russian. "I'll write the prescription now. This one's for eardrops. Four times a day. The pharmacy will explain." He checked his watch for the precise date, whispering the numbers to himself while scribbling, leaving his signature, a wavy line. He tore the grayish-blue paper squares from the pad and said, "That's all then," holding them out to her. Victoria set them lightly on the coffee table. "If she's not better by Monday, bring her to the clinic."

"Конечно," said Victoria, "Хорошо."

He closed his bag and buttoned up. His hand had already reached for the knob when Victoria stabbed him in the back of the leg with her cane. *"Don't you dare—*leave like that." She tried to stand, but her hip hurt. "Not like that."

"There's nothing else I can do here, Victoria."

"There's plenty," she whispered.

He turned. "I didn't bring your mirror." Bronza stood lanky, like a massive wooden puppet. "I didn't think about that."

"Be quiet and sit down." He stared at her for a moment, unused to someone ordering him around. "Not at my desk," she said. "Somewhere else." Bronza found a place between two limp cushions on the sofa. Victoria moved to her desk, the pain in her body obvious. He almost asked her about it.

Silence lingered, at once familiar and foreign. Bronza fidgeted, looking for a place to put his bag. The silence persisted and she noticed the slight swelling on his jaw. Now Bronza smiled, rubbing the stubble of his beard and he was soon laughing quietly. He said, "Now what?"

"Excuse me?"

"Now what?" His cheeks had flushed and he pinched his upper lip. "That's what she said. Now what?"

She smirked at him painfully. "I don't understand a word."

"No. I know." He picked through papers and envelopes on the coffee table, checking the date on a magazine. "Gaja said it. Now, I've said it too. Haven't I?"

"I didn't expect you to babble nonsense. It's time for us to act like adults. I'm tired of guessing what the other is thinking."

"You've been filling in thoughts for me?" he asked. "I'd love to know how. What am I thinking?"

His tone baffled her. She set her cane across her knees. "Don't you have any shame?" A single, very fast tear suddenly dropped from Bronza's eye. It fell into the carpet, leaving no trace. She shook her head. "You're phony. Even now. It's every second of your day. You walk around, this great masterpiece of a personality. They couldn't pay someone...they couldn't—if people knew you. If they could see."

"Pleased to meet you."

Victoria laced her fingers. She leaned back and sighed, "Fine. *Fine.* I thought we could be normal about it, but this is boring. Just go." She waved a hand towards the door. "Get out of here."

"Go?"

"Please."

"You're kicking me out."

"I think you should go."

"Oh? Leave, *like this.* Since I've already tried an exit. But you didn't want me to leave *like that*; you want me to leave *like this*. And where do I go?" he asked. "Should I go back to my *girl*? The one I married, because I'm a terrified little kid?"

"Please."

"What stays behind then when he's gone?" The next tear seeped out slowly, as if the trail it was leaving on his cheek fought to pull the heavy drop back. "What thoughts do you give that child? I've sent him away. He's gone now. What's he thinking?"

"It's ugly," she whispered intensely. "What you're doing now is ugly."

"Do you know why you're beautiful, Victoria? Because you *never* hide your feelings. A pillar of honesty. Because when you're attracted to someone—"

"Get out."

"No no no. Just the kid." He stood. Bronza was able to keep his voice above a whisper and under control. "The terrified kid has gone. Frightened that someone might see him. You'll get what you want."

"I'll scream out loud."

"Go ahead." Bronza tossed his coat on a recliner. He sat on the floor. "Lars will come out."

"I'm going to ask you once more to leave."

"The man will follow the kid. Eventually and in time. You'll get what you want." He found the prescription he had written and stuffed it into his shirt pocket. "Maybe you can tell me. If people knew what I am, what would it matter?"

"They'd hate you."

"Do you hate me?"

"Do you want me to?"

Bronza smirked. "Let's experience it first hand. You want to know why I married the girl? I'll tell you. At least you'll know what accusation to make." He was still sitting on the floor—he had unbuttoned the cuff of one sleeve and his socks had slumped down so that she could see the hair of his legs. "All I did was buy a house," he said and pointed out the window. "Walking distance from work. It's rather a nice house. The next thing I know, there's a girl coming to visit." He tore a long strip from an old newspaper. "Did you ever tell someone? Too early. That you love him?"

Victoria sat still.

"I did that once. Before I came to Cicero. It's a useless story, really. Swore to myself—the good doctor's capable of oaths— I'd never tell anyone anything like that again. Even if I meant it. You believe me, I know. I'm capable of meaning it. But I should have been able to recognize that Gaja didn't mean it."

Victoria listened.

"What difference does it make now, right?" he asked. "Gaja and I barely had time to figure out how the hell our paths had crossed. She got pregnant."

"We all know your story," said Victoria. "Are you looking for a pat on the back? You took a pregnant girl to the altar." She complimented him, "Молодец!"

"She didn't want the kid." He wiped his mouth. "I had always known it. I should have run off with Yuri someplace, left her."

"Steal a woman's baby?"

"As much mine as hers. If you'd listen to me." He inched closer to her. "She knew she was pregnant. Virtually from the first moment." Bronza buttoned his cuff. "At first, she tried to hide her morning puke. But then she started asking what doctors I knew. Where can we go to take care of it? She even asked me if I could do the operation myself. *No one can know. Not this.* Each minute...she made these demands, totally irrational, really feverish. *No one can know.*"

Victoria sat still.

"We argued," he said. "Sometimes, I thought she'd scratch my eyes out. But I wasn't going to allow it. Not my kid. Before she could run off on her own to some crackpot, I called Kilba and told him she's pregnant." Bronza looked down at his knuckles. "Yes, it *is* wonderful news, Monsignor. Though, I'm sure you understand, for her sake, we need to be married as soon as possible. Before she starts showing."

"Bronza..."

"Listen to me." He inched even closer. "Kilba called to congratulate her. That tied her hands. If she tampered in any way, I told her, I wouldn't keep any secrets. Maybe she prayed for a miscarriage. I don't know." He paused, remembering. "As long as no one knows it's her, Gaja can injure, come out smiling. That was me in her, my entire history." He pointed to his head and pressed a finger hard into his temple. "That's how Yuri was born."

Victoria set the cane down on the table.

"Gaja took her own room. She called me filthy, told me I'm the devil. Made accusations. *You have your house calls.* Every damn night she'd be locked up behind the door. But if she ever got drunk, a few times here or there, the night would end up in my bed. The next day, my house would be a nunnery again. All of it on purpose, because she's not that way."

"But what? So, you thought...kissing me?"

"I *thought*? Don't accuse me of thought."

"What then?"

"Nothing."

"Nothing?"

He started babbling: "I *used* to think. I used to." Bronza took a fistful of hair. "But I don't think anymore. Like Benny on that last night. What's one more mistake right alongside the rest of them? Funny, it's funny, right, because a kiss can be an insult. Worse than a crack in the jaw. A broken rib. I've learned Gaja was right...she really was, all along. You don't bring children to this world. Not this world. We're better off finished before we begin."

"You really believe that?"

"I didn't want to have a kid. I did it, because I needed to know."

"Bronza." She leaned toward him. "*What* the hell are you talking about? What are you hiding?"

He lay on the floor, the cushion behind his spine. "I can't remember."

"Will you?" Her forehead rested against a long finger. "Will you please make sense?"

"I'm not bullshitting. I'm trying to tell you that I can't remember. Especially my childhood." He crossed his arms and stared at the ceiling. "No memory. It's not even black or empty...it's just not there. Zero."

Victoria sighed.

"Just listen. If you want." The color had gone from his face and chin, but his eyes were wide and red. "I get dreams. Sometimes they can creep up in broad daylight. If I'm stirring coffee or holding a damn tongue depressor in some guy's mouth. They're nightmares, really, though I often crave them when they're gone. I wish to see them again, maybe to understand them fully. I actually believe they're memories."

"Tell me."

"In the most vivid, where I stand a chance to understand, I'm maybe three or four years old. In some countryside—I don't know if I live there." He stood to sit on the coffee table. "I'm little, on this bench and my feet are dangling. I see this old man next to me, and he's got a dog. Now please listen. It's a rich and vivid scene, a hot and muggy day. I can smell the dog. I know this man, I know him like you'd know your most intimate. But now I don't know how, who he is. It's Europe somewhere, but who knows the place? A place I can feel, but I don't see it, really. Just a black trail winding off, and then a dog. She's an old bitch with a wrinkled face, and she's tired, thin, these shoulders...these shoulder blades. A face full of flies. When she turns her head, she looks right into me like she knows. She lies down on her side, slowly, gracefully somehow, and she breathes. Once, once more, and then her life sinks right out of her. Sinks into the dirt of the trail. The man just nods, slowly, a hard fist at his forehead.

"Now, please don't ask anything. No. Please wait. Occasionally...in another part, it's dark. Wartime. I hear these voices all around me. Always a man and a woman. They're afraid. I have no idea what time of day, if my eyes are closed or what. But I know we have to leave, we're desperate to leave. And we have to hide. I'm older now, but I can't tell how much. I know I have to hide. It's panic...a loose, impossible panic and fear. When it starts, it never ends. There's no start to it. No finish. No middle. No sensible order."

Victoria spoke cautiously. "Isn't there anything pleasant?"

"No no, yeah. Yeah." He shook his head and wiped an eye with his sleeve. "It's true. Not all of it's like that. I sometimes also see a lake. I'm swimming." His arms did the breaststroke. "The surface of the water is covered with cottonwood seeds. Lake's surrounded by low bushes, willows, the branches hanging into the water. The water is still and cool. I swim, stroke after stroke, so happy about it, the happiness deep inside, like I've been rewarded, allowed to go to the lake where I've wanted to go for days. These green, beautiful stones on the bottom. And cottonwood seeds." He sat on the floor again. "Maybe it's not really a memory. Because I have a powerful imagination."

"When do things get clear?"

"It's like I appeared on planet earth, wide awake, with the cleanest head. Something out of nothing. 1941. I know the date because I have a newspaper. I'm with two women, two sisters...they're in their sixties. They're my foster parents, Liuba and Nadia Dilienko—from Kiev—they eventually brought me to America. I can see the lines in the corners of their eyes, the veins in *Tsiotsi* Liuba's hand. We're in an old car on the way to northern Germany. It's damn hot again. A boy next to me has a cabbage on his lap. You can smell the exhaust. People sweating in old clothes. These beautiful German fields and small farmhouses."

"You had foster parents?"

"Please, listen." He stood. "You have to listen." Bronza presently seemed electric, as if it might shock Victoria to touch him. "I don't remember meeting them. Just, only two women. From Kiev. And, later, an old man, their relative, but he had a heart attack. They were hardly used to speaking any Ukrainian. But they weren't Russian. Said they found me walking down a road, and I said I was from West Ukraine. I knew my name was Yuri."

"Bronza..."

He paced around the room. "My knees were all bruised up, shoes torn to shreds. I was carrying a shovel and a small backpack full of bread and clothes. I couldn't tell them anything. I was seventeen or eighteen."

"Yuri?" she whispered.

Bronza nodded. "I essentially stopped using the name in medical school. Here or there I'd mention it to someone. Because when Liuba and Nadia eventually died—you understand, they claimed me as their son and nephew. I was Yuri only to them. I had to learn to live that way." He waited. "I only realized later, when I was in college, just how much I couldn't remember. Victoria, I speak Polish, *mówię płynnie po polsku*. But I don't know how or why, have no memory of ever learning it. I realized, to my bewilderment, how much I didn't remember about my youth when girls asked to hear about my childhood. I knew I was sick. I'd been on autopilot all those years. I actually thought about studying psychology, if you believe it. Just to figure out who I was."

"To figure out..."

"What's wrong with me," he said. "I'm sick. You *know* I'm sick, Victoria. My mind. It could be amnesia. Just simple amnesia, from shock or from trauma. But it could be something else."

She was quiet.

"I read about memory loss. Case studies. I became fixated on them. And I've spoken to professional people. In college, I came across texts about a particular condition, transient fugue. The sufferer is really nothing more than a wandering actor—a freak who gets up and travels, takes off, especially during wartime, sometimes across countries. Develops a completely different identity, assumes a new personality, new name, new posture, new gait. Loses all memory of his original self. It can last a day, only a few weeks, any amount of time. Some cases have gone decades. I became obsessed with reading about cases like these, drawn to them as if by gravity, naturally, against all logic. I read about a guy who had a fugue within a fugue."

"I doubt it," said Victoria. "I doubt this."

"Why?"

"It's probably amnesia," she said. "From the war. You're paranoid. It's paranoia."

Bronza stood very close to her. "Victoria, I might be a walking nobody. If it's amnesia, that's a blessing. Memory can't hurt an amnesiac...it can't kill what he's become. An amnesiac, if the priests are right, has a soul, will live on. But if this is all a fugue, pure fabrication, it might be better to drop dead. If I snap out, suddenly remember who I am, where I come from, I'll have no memory of this." He took out the prescription, flashed his watch. "No memory of you. Of my kids. Of anything that happened since I wandered off. A young man I'll never meet will wake up in this man's body. I'll have been his invention, one that'll disappear instantly, no afterlife." He was quiet for a while, crinkling the prescription. "I thought it might be possible," he whispered. "To see what I was like through Yuri. And to remember. Remember something from him. But I didn't," Bronza said. "I didn't."

She whispered to him very gently, "Chsh, chsh. Look at me. Calm down." She pulled him by the sleeve so he'd sit, then pressed the back of her hand against his forehead. "You're warm. You should drink water."

A great silence followed. She watched him stare at the curtains and over the things on her desk. Tears still escaped him, hard and round beads, but they didn't affect his voice or breathing—had she been blind, she wouldn't have known he was crying. Bronza said, "I want to smoke."

"You can go by the back window. On the porch."

Bronza took his cigarettes to go very quietly out the back door. Victoria followed him, passing the glass of her buffet that reflected her face. Her dirtied thumb had left ink stains on her cheek, but Bronza hadn't told her. She tried to wash it and did get some of the ink off. While she dried her hands, she heard Lars knocking on her door. "Vic?"

She let him in. He was naked under a sheet he had dragged off the bed. "Gotta piss." He squinted from the mellow light and sat on the toilet with the sheet still wrapped around him. "Alina's sick," she said.

"Mm." He nodded. "Mm."

"Bronza's here."

"No," he said. "I'm sure it's a rip-off." He wandered past her, the sheet up around his shoulders. She flushed the toilet and heard him close the bedroom door. Bronza came out a moment later. "Lars is up?"

She shook her head. "Not really."

"I think I should go." Bronza looked at her, the shadows in his face soft and round. "Can't stay all night," he said. "The sun'll be up."

Victoria waited for him by the door. He looked around to be sure he had taken everything, including his medical bag. Then he sat on the sofa and told her, "She's torturing him."

Victoria hesitated. They shared intense eye contact, Bronza's stare beautiful but fierce.

He opened up his palm. "You've seen my hand before."

Victoria had noticed the flat white scars on his palm many times. "You said they were burns." He let her look, brushing his hand with a fingertip, unsure if she understood.

"I used to do it myself. It used to make me feel...I can't explain it. Really alive. Instant relief from so much." Bronza took his hand away and hid it in his coat pocket. "Now she tells me I'm doing it to him."

Passage: Victoria Jorgenson's Final Journal
Entry, April 26, 1971

Tonight, *a foolish spring drizzle, mild but incessant. Earlier, on my way to the travel agent's, I stood waiting for the elevated train on 54th and could smell the cool water on the planks and tracks. Metal, wood, water, and under the dome of my umbrella, the delicate patter. A chill and gray canvas sky.*

The decision is made...I will put in notice tomorrow. I sound so blasé about it, but I'm finished, the devil with it, and tired of the clinic.

I keep seeing Yuri. Feel the way one does when we learn new words, once invisible, now blaring out from billboards and newspapers. Ever since Easter Mass when his face was a sad little moon, he's been everywhere. Gaja came with him to the clinic the other day. Then, today, on the way to the trains, I saw him out the bus window. So many random boys are Yuri for a half second. Every short brown haircut catches my attention until I focus and see a fat kid. A girl in a jumper. A man bending down to smoothen wet cement with a trowel.

Anyushka was with her. Braided hair and a bubble of flesh and skin. What should I write about them?

Bronza tells me something every day, and I listen.

Anya's birth.

Listened to every word like a glutton for him and imagined it happening. I should not force myself to write a description of what I imagine. I'll say this much: I am able to imagine breaking his rib as I feel my own break. I can see the act from the position of the assaulting and assaulted. This makes me better than no one.

The plane tickets are in an envelope on my shelf. As quickly as these papers will take me away from here, they will also return me. I checked. We return in late August. Right back to Cicero where nothing ever changes, no matter how much you learn.

I am abominable. Want to lie to myself and hate him. Yes. I want to hate myself and love him. Pin him down and force this confusion and fixation on him. Here, in the safety of these written words, Bronza's just large enough to fit. He fits. Or sometimes he's just large enough for pleasant pain—so deep, I feel it at the ends of my fingers, my arms outstretched above my head—I can feel it in my stomach and throat. When it's finished, we both become a wealthy girl's playthings in a dollhouse where he carries me up stairs. I'm weightless.

I see him walking half a block away, and I shoot an arrow into the base of his spine, watch him fall to his knees, keel over in agony.

We make love on trains. A train leaves on Sundays when Lars is off playing organ. For four long masses, the train rides in a great circle around a space (neither of us look out the window to see it) and returns to the station it departed. We love each other in the brightest daylight. It happens only once each time and will never happen again. Wide open windows in the daylight, a fast train on brand new tracks, sleek, elegant wagons and white sheets in the compartment. Then no one can remember a thing. Worldwide amnesia. I ink the event here into my inside world where it stays locked like a criminal incapable of ever causing anyone harm.

Outside my written word, Bronza couldn't lift anyone. He'd lift a woman to have her feel her own weight, every ounce a strain on his arms and knees. Around him I feel my weight so fully against the cane. I feel my entire weight press against this paper through the tip of this pen.

You've polluted my imagination and left me quiet in a room with plane tickets and a pen. You won't realize I'm gone.

If it is the Monsignor I'll tell about this tortured little boy, or someone in that school...if I speak in more places than one, to officers and teachers, perhaps to Alina—she'd never keep her mouth shut—the whole town will know about Yuri's wounds. In the meantime, I'll be away.

Yuri, don't think about him. Your father has amnesia. He doesn't know who you are.

After murdering him, strangling him with a chord, boiling him in a bath brewed for a witch, I have made love to your father on boats, their sails tense with wind. On a roof in a city pulsing with the restrained rhythm of distant evening traffic. On coarse tablecloths after the restaurant has closed. Amid funhouse mirrors, an abandoned carnival, grotesque masks staring at us from the walls. I've abandoned my body to him. And I hate it when he can only talk about her.

I'll talk about her. I won't leave, neither by train this Sunday nor plane on June 11th, until I know I'm not like the rest of us. If you believe in amnesia, know there's no difference between having forgotten everything and having remained silent about all you know. He's made me feel like a cousin of his, and I can see how much easier it is for him to bear himself when he confesses what he's done to her, what she's done to the boy.

So I'll whisper to little birds and let the monsters fight this out. Will tell Lars just before we return, so he knows where we're going, where we've been and what's in store when the plane touches down. He won't believe me anyway.

Who would?

Autumn, 1981 (continued)

1

A thin slice of the dimmest morning sunlight fell through a crack in the blinds. Yuri admired the hazy impression of Alina's face, her skin delicate as tissue. His naked shin rested against the side of her leg, the soft cotton of her pajamas. It was stunning to know her scent: girl's deodorant and a fresh sunny air.

Yuri put out cereal, milk and juice. With the food on the small table, and the light intensifying outside, he read the final pages of Mrs. Jorgenson's journal one last time. He looked over other entries Alina had showed him, the ones that described papa's amnesia and times Mrs. Jorgenson had tried to peek at his hands. For the last few months of her life, she wrote something about papa almost every day. The place where he kissed her and how she had hit him. Her stolen mirror. All her confusion and desire.

It didn't surprise Yuri that papachka loved Mrs. Jorgenson. "He didn't love her," Alina had said. "She was just available. She just wasn't your mother. That's all." Yuri didn't know if it was true. He knew Alina was available—such a terrible word—but he had fallen asleep right next to her, and nudged his body to rest against hers for a different reason.

They spoke very little over breakfast. They cleaned up together, put all the journals away on a shelf, and Alina said she'd drive him to Cicero.

Cars shot past her on the highway. Yuri asked, "I wonder, did I quit Reikel's shop? I walked out in the middle of work. You think that means I quit?"

"He thinks you quit."

"He probably can't stand me now," said Yuri. "Should I go back there?"

"Want to?"

"Think I'm supposed to?"

"What'll you say?"

Yuri was watching the cars speed past his window, some of them swerving in a great, tight arc to get in front of Alina. She normally got off at Austin but took the Laramie Avenue ramp this time, passing Loretto Hospital and the spray-painted concrete monoliths that held up bridges. Yuri understood where she was going. Alina parked right on 50th Avenue and 12th and they went to the bus shelter across the street.

It was where Victoria had been killed. A car flying down 50th had veered off, jumped the curb and crashed through the shelter. Most of the people inside had managed to see the car and hop to the side, but Victoria hadn't been fast enough. The driver died in the hospital and no one ever found out why he was speeding, why he veered off. Witnesses saw what was going to happen before it did, but nobody could help her.

Alina and Yuri sat in the new bus shelter. "It's a nice design," she said.

"Yeah. Aluminum."

"I like how the Plexiglas has been beaten out with a bat."

"And this burnt part here," said Yuri. "I like when the shitheads take lighters to the Plexiglas."

"That bulb of burnt plastic kind of looks like a brain."

Yuri nodded. "A bus shelter's brain."

They sat with no bus in sight, no passengers around. With the flow of traffic, a rhythm developed—they both felt it—the incessant monstrosity of time flowing forward. Trucks exhaled black diesel soot and their engines wheezed. In a jagged pothole, Yuri saw the rainbow film of gasoline floating in a gray puddle that reflected a sky deep with clouds.

2

Lars told Kilba Yuri had taken a new job at the Karavan Motel as the graveyard shift housekeeper.

The Monsignor knew things about The Karavan. It was a few doors from a strip club, the Show of Shows, rumored to be a brothel—the motel was somehow connected, famous for its one-hour room rentals and a sign that read *Truckers Welcome*.

The Monsignor needed to see Yuri but didn't want to corner him at work. He told Lars to have the boy call the rectory yet knew it was pointless—Yuri wouldn't call. Kilba didn't want to visit him at home because he feared Yuri wouldn't let him in, and the rejection would crush him. He had no choice but to visit the Karavan late in the week.

Unsavory fellows often stood around on that corner after dark. Afraid his priest's collar might attract unwanted attention, and secretly worried that someone might see him, a priest, going to a place of ill repute, Kilba put on a white shirt and tan slacks with a long coat and a small winter cap.

The motel was almost deserted, only a few cars in the parking lot. Yuri was tending the rooms on the second floor, pushing a little cart.

Yuri did not recognize Kilba as he walked up the narrow, iron stairs. When he did realize who it was, they faced each other, neither one able to understand what the other was doing there. Yuri sorted through a load of freshly washed sheets. Kilba said, "Lars told me you've changed jobs."

"I work here now."

Kilba nodded, his fingers laced at the belly. "When do you finish?"

"At six."

"In the morning?"

"Yeah." He pushed the cart closer to the wall. One pillowcase fell on the floor, but Yuri put it right back on top of the stack. "It works out. Sometimes there's nothing to do...I just sit doing laundry and read magazines. But they pay me anyway."

Kilba's eyes sharpened and he nodded again, only subtly. "Maybe...we could sit down? Inside one of these rooms."

"Only for a while. Owner's here today," Yuri lied.

They went into a tight, sparse room that smelled heavily of naphthalene. The walls had been painted olive green and the curtains were speckled with little white butterflies. Although Kilba hadn't touched anything, he immediately wanted to wash his hands. In the bathroom, someone had scribbled *Light at the start of my tunnel, 7-17-79* and drawn an arrow pointing to the light bulb. Kilba washed with icy water and realized the room had no towel or toilet paper, so he let his hands drip.

Yuri was making a bed. "These sheets are still wet," he said. "It's so stupid. The dryer's busted."

Kilba sat right on the edge of a chair. "Don't you think?" Kilba scanned the walls and stained carpet. "La Vergne's drug store is hiring."

"It's too close to Reikel's. And these hours are better, anyway. I wake up and sculpt. Then I come here. Fold sheets and read magazines."

Kilba watched him rush to finish the bed. "Could you stop making that bed for a moment?" His voice was extra calm, the way it always was when he spoke seriously. Yuri dropped the comforter on the mattress. At the right moment, the Monsignor said, "Yuri. You don't need to be working."

The boy looked away, annoyed.

"I'm getting too old to be patient." Two long fingers rested on his chin. "And I don't want to spend all night arguing in this miserable place."

"More miserable than any other?"

"Listen." Kilba shut his eyes briefly. "It's time for you to stop your stubbornness. I've given this a lot of thought. It's time to let us help you."

"Who's *us*?"

"Them, they. Whomever. It. Me—why won't you accept help?"

"Did you come here to give me money?" Yuri snapped. "I'll take it."

Kilba stood with unexpected speed and approached him, stopping only inches from Yuri's face. The skin and flesh of Kilba's cheeks hung loose over his bones, and wiry red nerves tangled themselves among the deep pores of his nose. "Excuse me? You need money?"

Yuri said nothing.

"I've come here to offer help."

"What help?" Yuri tried to back up, but Kilba had driven him to the bed's edge. "What?"

"You tell me," Kilba muttered. "You tell me. If it's money you want, I can guarantee you, that's easy. But I feel you want something else."

Yuri managed to move away from him and switched places with Kilba, sitting down on the tattered chair. He tied a shoe that had come undone and then sat straight, like an attentive student. "You don't even know who they are."

"Your parents?"

"You think you know. But you don't."

"I'm not talking about them. You want to leave Cicero? You want to go away to school?"

Yuri raised his voice. "Why'd *you* come here? What's this got to do with *you*? You've been talking to *them*?"

Kilba crossed his arms.

"You know what they want?" Yuri asked. "They only ever wanted two things...me out of the way and themselves off the hook. Mama wanted to get rid of me before I was even born."

"That's not true."

Yuri laughed painfully. "What the hell do you know?"

"Don't shout."

"Why not? Loud! Loudness, loud loud! *No moleste.* Truckers passed out next to whores!"

"Yuri..."

"Monsignor." He stood to finish making the bed. "You want to do something? I know what. You come here, tell me I don't need to work, 'cause you'll figure out how to send me away. Out of the

347

way, what, to some Catholic college? That's bullshit. You want to send someone away? You want to help me out?"

"I'm leaving."

"No, you!" Yuri leapt and grabbed the Monsignor by the coat to turn him around. The strength in his arm surprised them both. "No, you. You don't leave, Monsignor. I'll tell you first!" Yuri held Kilba fast and shouted as loud as he could, repeating again and again. "You go over there. But then you get rid of *them*." His fury rose. "You don't rid me. This time, you get rid of *them*. You get rid of *them*."

3

With the house empty early on Sunday morning, Gaja was rummaging through her drawers and closets. She wanted to wear something different and was opening spaces that had been closed for years, sorting through dresses that would never fit. She found expensive pieces of jewelry, shawls and scarves, pieces of silk, dusty shoes and old handbags. All of it was useless. She piled the junk up in corners and on the dining room table.

After mass, she'd throw all this stuff away. The jewels. Everything.

In one small box where she had packed safety pins and cheap rings, a pocket watch destroyed by water, a fountain pen with the tip broken off, Gaja happened across Victoria's silver mirror. Her chest and throat warmed when she saw it, and she scurried to pull the mirror out and hold it. It clasped nicely and fit right in the palm of her hand...the silver had tarnished only slightly. Gaja had forgotten she had hidden it so long ago. But here it was. She could open it and look at herself.

There had been a time when she could have thrown the mirror through a window or smashed it someplace, crushed it in a vice. But Gaja didn't feel that way anymore. She remembered the night she had found it, when Alina's ear had hurt, when Bronza hadn't come home for hours. Finding this mirror now calmed Gaja, and she went to church deeply satisfied.

She was sitting for Cruz's sermon. Listening to his monotone voice, she had almost finished folding all the corners of a misallette when she heard him use the word *beautiful*.

It was not just the word but the way he had said it. It came up again in his sermon. In church, she believed people were all looking at her through the corners of their eyes. Cruz held himself stoic in front of parishioners, his shoulders straight, the pale light from the podium's reading lamp softening his skin, but when he said *beautiful* one last time, Gaja remembered all the details of his study—the sharpened pencils in a cylinder, the shavings on a notebook, the squeaky leather of his chair—and she saw him touching his chest lightly with a fist, heard his voice: *In the soul. You really...always...I sense it constantly. You always want to do the right, the beautiful thing.*

She left mass without taking communion and did not go to breakfast. Gaja bought cigarettes at the corner store and wandered around town for many hours, taking breaks to smoke at bus stops, in diners and at benches.

She had wandered to 16th Street's train tracks, right in front of the Barrett Varnish Company's brick chimney. Someplace down by Central, blocks to the west, the rails converged to a sharp point. She tossed her cigarette butt, and the ember landed between a rail and the old wood tie to smolder and die. The sun was already low in the sky when Gaja headed back to St. Anthony's.

Random parishioners still lingered around the churchyard. The nun who took care of the sacristies and priests' garments left the rectory's back door wide open on her way out. Gaja tiptoed into the building.

The rectory smelled of Kilba's aging body and the sweat in his clothes. She slipped off her flats and left them by the back door, stepping around the rectory in silence. The kitchen was empty, a large ham left out on the table beside a tiny bowl of horseradish and basket of bread. The Monsignor had dozed off in the library and she could hear him breathing, see him through a crack in the door. She took great care up the stairs, placing her feet only along the edges where the wood was most solid.

Cruz was not in his study. Gaja sat in the chair across from his desk and sharpened a pencil, twisting the point against the razor's edge, letting the shavings fall all over the rug. When she had sharpened it down to the eraser, she started another, then one more, wasting several pencils by the time her hands grew tired.

Outside, cobalt twilight. She recognized Kilba's voice gently mumbling in the churchyard. For a moment, she grew scared he might find her shoes by the door. Actually...so what if he found them? What could he possibly do?

Gaja heard Cruz's steps. He walked up and down the corridor a few times before coming to the study. He stood at the doorway without saying a word—Gaja did not turn to look at him but felt his unease. "I'm sorry," he whispered, closing the door. "Gaja. You can't be here."

She did not look back at him. "I need to talk to you."

"How did you get in?"

She shrugged.

Cruz saw the shavings all over the floor, the stubs of pencils scattered over his desk. "What's this?" He spoke with restraint. "Why this mess?"

"I'm sorry about it."

He sat on his windowsill, leaning against the frame with a shoulder. "You'll have to leave. I have a lot of work to do."

"I need to talk to you."

"What's happened to you this time?"

She wiped her face with a tissue from her purse. "I remembered one thing. I just remembered, an important moment. One thing."

His neck straightened. "Fine." Kilba was still out in the courtyard, chatting with a nun. "Fine. Confess it."

Gaja set her purse on the desk and Cruz was sure she had brought another strange object. He said, "I'll absolve you, but then you'll have to leave. I'm very sorry. I don't feel comfortable like this."

"Like what?"

"Like this, without announcement. And with my pencils, I'm not pleased with this at all. Did the Monsignor let you in? He knows you're here and wouldn't tell me?"

"I said I was sorry. What else do you want?"

Cruz crossed his arms tightly. "You'll go ahead and confess it." He took his place behind the desk, made the sign of the cross, more haphazard than usual, and mumbled a rite. "Please begin," he said, "because I have work."

"You don't have any *work*."

"Pardon?"

"Don't lie to me. If you want me to leave, I'll leave. I can go how I came in. If you're uncomfortable."

Cruz sighed, lightly rubbing one eyebrow. "I'll invite you, Gaja, please. Please confess it." He collected the pencil stubs and threw them away. "Has it to do with your husband? What is it?"

Cruz knew it: she took her purse from the desk. Her eyes were at once manic and sad, yet no warmth remained in them. First she looked at herself in the little mirror, wiping carefully around the eyes with a tissue, but then Gaja clasped it shut and put it on the desk in front of him. "Do you like my mirror?"

"It's...fine. It's quite nice."

"Take it." Gaja waited, but he didn't move. "Go ahead. Look at yourself."

"Gaja, I thought you wanted to confess."

"I never said that."

With some reluctance, Cruz picked up the mirror and opened it. "Well, it's broken. I'm sorry it's broken, Gaja. But you can fix it easily, I think."

"What do you think of me?" she asked. "When I'm not around."

"What?"

"You wish I'd be out of your life," she said. "Don't you? You wish I could just get out and you'd be done with me. Listening to me each week."

"No."

"Don't lie to me."

"I have no reason to lie."

"I said don't."

"Gaja, there's no reason for this. I'm very sorry. But there's no reason. Yes, this is a very nice mirror." He set it down. "Unfortunately, it's broken, that's all."

"I don't give a damn about that mirror."

He crossed his arms again. Then he reached out and clasped the mirror shut so that it clicked. To feel her hand on his stunned him, and he realized how bright the room's lights were, that the curtain was open. "I want to be done with it," she said. "I want to be done with me, too."

"Please, Gaja." He managed to pull his hand away gently and naturally. "All this past year. Think back to where you were a year ago. You've gotten to know God better. You've been forgiven for so much, granted so much grace."

Gaja shrugged.

"Well, that's impossible. You've made such strides and...to be honest...sometimes I feel like you come in here because—" He paused. "You'll have to grow past depending on people to assure you. You always want someone to assure you. But you'll have to gain some confidence about yourself. Perhaps you treat yourself like a child."

"Myself?"

"I think so. Often. You aren't fair to yourself."

A heavy, slow laugh spilled from deep in her lungs. "You think so?"

"Yes," said Cruz. "You've been forgiven for so much."

She stood. Gaja moved the chair clear out of the way, over by the bookshelf, and told him, "Stand up."

"Pardon?"

"Pardon me. Stand up." She was suddenly flush with energy, her eyes magnetic and daytime blue. Cruz did not want to stand, but she pestered him, calling him a liar, her voice growing uncomfortably loud. They stood in the middle of the study facing each other, a pillow of distance between them. In the silence, Cruz finally understood, finally admitted what she was going to do and the brief moment he had to escape was slowly passing.

"What do you think of me when I'm gone?" she asked.

"Nothing," he said.

"I don't care if you judge me," she said. "But you think of me?"

Cruz managed the word, "Think," and pressed his tongue against his teeth. "Not like you think I do. But yes, I do think. For caring."

She took his hands and pressed them against his hips. Gaja said, "I'm glad," and allowed him to see every detail of her face, the most honest moment she had ever shared with him. Cruz saw furious red blood vessels against the tired whites of her eyes, and her pupil, an impenetrable black hole, bottomless and cold. The longer he admired her face, the more complicated it became, chapped lips, wrinkled eyelids. Cruz thought he could kiss her, but Gaja didn't allow it. She didn't want to return anyone's kiss.

She brought his fingers to the buttons of her blouse and Cruz pulled his hands away, taking a step back, a useless gesture. She smiled and gently touched his face, forehead, kissing her own two fingers lightly and touching his chin. Gaja left him standing by

353

the bookshelf and went to lock the study's door. He pulled the curtain. She guided his hands over her clothing until he had undressed her completely. In the middle of it, he whispered, "If you tell anyone..."

"Quiet," she said. "No one will ever know."

4

Alina was walking back to her apartment along Damen Avenue. She had just sold four rings to a long-time customer and was pinching the wad of cash in her jacket pocket. It wasn't very much money, just a few hundred dollars, but she hadn't sold any jewelry in a long time.

She enjoyed the colors of Indian summer, her favorite moment out of any year, a rare last ditch of warmth before rainy and gray November. A twig cracked crisp under her heel and she breathed the air deeply. Some old man had raked his leaves into a pile on his lawn and Alina looked around before winding up and kicking. Dust rose from the rustling explosion and she could smell the leaves' fine dryness.

Further down the block, Alina found a green pepper someone had dropped on the sidewalk. The shiny pepper was firm and ripe, vivid against the gray cement. Next to an old patch of tar, it seemed so out of place, so forgotten that Alina grew sad. She brushed it off to carry home.

Less than a hundred yards from her front door, she saw her dad's lanky figure—the ends of his coat belt flaying about, briefcase in hand—passing through the shadows of houses and paths of sunlight falling through gangways. Alina knew her dad didn't see her—she could have slipped into her home and ignored the doorbell, pretended to be elsewhere. But she waited for him in front of her house. As soon as he waved, she wanted to hide up at the top of a tree, a little girl whose mother was looking to punish her for lying. For a second, she felt as if mama had never died and was waiting for both of them to come home.

"You're out in the street," said Lars.

"I made a sale!" she said. "I'm on my way back."

Lars nodded and swung his briefcase easily. "Cheap payments these days." He poked his chin toward the green pepper.

She commanded him, "Hold," handing over the vegetable. Alina opened the difficult door and he followed her up to the apartment, setting his briefcase and the pepper on a pile of art magazines.

From the coat rack, Alina watched him move around like a sleepwalker, his old coat worn and dirty. He petted a plant as if it were a cat. In the kitchen he poured some water into a measuring cup just because it was at hand.

"Oh, Jesus. I have normal cups. Are you dehydrated?"

"What's that question? I'm just thirsty."

Alina said, "I've got some cider from the farmers market, bought yesterday, still so fresh."

"I just want water."

He sat in the front room, slipping off his shoes before setting his feet on the coffee table. Alina brought a mug of warm cider. His socks were stinking up her apartment.

Lars drank the whole glass down in five good gulps and wiped his mouth with the sleeve of his coat, exhaling. He passed the glass from hand to hand and knocked his knees together.

Another lunchtime conversation with Bronza. At Carry's— for some reason, it's especially true in that bakery—his eyes shimmer with so many drowned secrets, a few just below the surface, but the deepest are wrecked warships. Heavy gray steel sunk to the bottom where no light can reach. That's the Bronza who accidentally grabs the saltshaker when he wants sugar. The one who pushes a woman against a wall when he wants to pull her to himself.

"Man oh man," said Lars. "Man oh man." He shook his head and rubbed his knees, then stood for more water. "I've had it out with myself, Alina" he said, raising his voice over the faucet's high-pitched whine. "Man oh man."

His eyes are hard and opaque balls of tarnished copper. I cannot look into them for very long because I'm unable to match that impassable hardness. He looks at me, and I feel he'll find me and tear me out of myself. I want to ride a train with him and get amnesia. He'd look at me and know.

Although Lars had filled the cup with water, he spilled it out and opened the fridge. "Where's that juice?"

"The cider? In front of the milk."

He poured half a glass, drank it quickly, then filled it to the brim. Walking towards her, he said, "Man oh man. I've had it out, Alina. Had it out with myself."

"Dad, you're babbling."

He nodded, stirring the cider with a pinky.

Bronza's told me. He's made me responsible.

"You've had it out?" Alina asked. "What do you mean?"

"It's in the briefcase. Brought you a copy. One for you...you get one and Kilba gets one. Just in case my garage burns down or something. Just in case." He kicked the briefcase lightly with a heel. "This one's going to survive."

"What is it?"

His head fell backwards. "Why don't you answer your phone ever?"

"Never home...I don't know. I'm gone all the time."

"Selling rings?"

"That. And other stuff."

"Well...It's on paper." Lars slurped the cider. He leaned forward to set the cup down, take the green pepper, toss it from hand to hand. "I figured it out. Sixty-one years. Sixty-one years."

"What?"

"I finished this fugue. And now I know why I'm here. Finally. When I finished it, I felt like I'd woken up on a bright day. I know what I'm here for, Alina." He wiped the pepper with a shirttail. "My reason's in the briefcase."

"A fugue?"

"When you see it. I think you'll understand what it is."

I can pour ink all over myself. Take a bath in the blackest ink and come out dripping, nothing else covering my skin. Stand before him, admired.

"That's great, dad. You want me to look at it?"

He bit deep into the green pepper and three white seeds stuck in his mustache. "I don't know what you'll think," he said, chewing. "For the first time, I don't care what anyone thinks." Seeds fell all over the floor. "If you don't want to look at it, don't. But just hold onto it for me. For safety."

Alina opened the briefcase timidly. It contained a single score held together with a rusty paperclip that had stained the paper.

The Fugue. The music fit both organ and piano, but Alina heard it on piano, two strands of music wrapped tightly around one another. She did not have perfect pitch and heard the music with difficulty but could still feel its energy. Alina imagined playing the fugue while Yuri listened to her.

They were running away together. Yuri and Alina took turns driving the Datsun so the other could sleep while their trip never stopped. She imagined a place where the asphalt turned to gravel and the gravel turned to dirt and then the dirt turned to sand. Nearby stood a small wooden house, in a place that never knew any cold winters. With the music about to die, the final note approaching, Alina remembered her mother had written, *he stays deep in that room, his teeth deep in the flesh of a pencil.*

She returned to the top of the fugue and read it again, aware now she wasn't skilled enough to actually play the piece. Alina was humming to try to understand it better.

"Alina," Lars raised his voice. "Can you answer me!"

"No no."

"Alina—"

"Dad. Will you. Just quiet down."

"But I'm asking you!"

"I'm trying to read this..."

"You're ignoring me," he said.

"You're..." She set down the score and stood. "Will you stop dropping those seeds all over the place. Why don't you get a plate?"

"What the hell are you talking about?"

When she looked again, there was no pepper at all. Lars had wiped the table clean and picked all the seeds from the floor. "You're imagining shit," he said. "What the hell're you daydreaming?"

"I think...I'm sorry." Alina took the score again. "I'm not."

"What do you think of it?"

She sat again, slumping into her chair. "I mean, it's. Yes. It's—yeah."

"What?"

"It's total chaos. But totally under control. It's a flight." She looked at the notes. "It's amazing how those two voices are so similar to each other but totally opposite. Still, they're totally together."

"Who do you think those voices are?"

"Dad...is this even possible to play? This chaotic part? I know I can't play or even keep track. Who can play it?"

"Can you tell how one voice is old and wise and the other is so young and naïve?"

Alina put the mug down. "Not naïve. Just misunderstood. And alone, nowhere to turn. But growing up. Fast."

"What do you see? Can you tell it's people?"

"Dad. You always have some idea in your head. And when someone has something different, you get grumpy."

"What do you think your mom would say?"

"She'd say."

He's cursed and captured, stays deep in that room, his teeth deep in the flesh of a pencil.

"She'd love it a lot."

5

Late at night, two dogs started fighting in the rectory's alley—the noise shook Father Cruz. They barked and gnashed below his study, tearing at each other, their skulls knocking together. Cruz had been trying to read the Sermon on the Mount, but the sound of the dogs was so intense that he could imagine them, their white teeth and bleeding gums.

The fight ended as unexpectedly as it had started, a hollow echo sounding off some far wall, and the night was still again. He waited before reading further, sure that the dogs would start. He closed the book and prayed a few decades of the rosary while pacing slowly up and down the rectory's corridor.

Cruz was out of sleeping pills. Only a torn-apart, graying piece of cotton remained at the bottom of the white pill bottle. He threw it away and carried the wastebasket downstairs.

The smell of strong herbal tea spiked with cognac intensified as Cruz approached the kitchen. Kilba was reading a magazine in the corner, wisps of steam rising from his cup. He only muttered, "G'night, Cruz," and lifted a hand. Cruz dumped the trash and sat at the table.

Father Cruz asked, "Did you hear those dogs?"

Kilba nodded. "Rabies."

"I almost wished they'd kill each other. So irritating."

Kilba lifted a shoulder. "Irritating, yes..."

"Have you had a lot to drink?"

"Relaxed. Almost time to sleep." Kilba sipped from the hot tea and pressed his lips together to swallow. He said, "This is calming. Wish you'd try it. You're a bit agitated now, I can sense."

"I'm not agitated."

"You're agitated," said Kilba. "You're uptight and pissed, because dogs were killing each other in the alley. It's an outrage. Why can't dogs behave?" Kilba sniggered and pushed the magazine to the middle of the table. "It's a very sad thing that dogs have to kill each other in this world our Lord has made."

"Why would you make fun of me?"

"Cruz...you're all worked up. Be like me. Pick a vice of choice. I have my vice, avoid stress, and so everything is fine. And try tea this way, I'm telling you. I'll hear your confession first thing in the morning. Absolve you of the evil sin of drink and you'll be good as new." Kilba stood from the table with some difficulty, but he was still smiling when he pushed the magazine even closer to Cruz. "Great article in there, by the way."

It was one of those east coast literary magazines—the cover story was about a poet who had killed herself with sleeping pills. Kilba said, "There's humor in that article. I'm going to bed. Good night." He disappeared beyond the archway, slurping the tea somewhere near the rectory's front door.

Cruz threw the magazine away. The trash was full of food scraps, raw chicken fat and skin that would stink by morning. He tied the bag tightly and found his cap and jacket to take the trash out.

The rectory's dumpster was behind a fence that separated the alley from a pathway to the convent. He was outside before it occurred to him the dogs might still be around. But he didn't grow scared. At the chain-link fence, he looked down the narrow alley, lit by bluish-white street lamps. The dogs were gone. The alley stretched out quiet and empty in the haze of electric light.

He wandered without any haste to the convenience store on 14th. He was forty five cents short for a bottle of sleeping pills, but the Mexican at the cash register said, "Holy discount," and made a sign of the cross over the bottle, smiling. Cruz promised to bring the rest tomorrow.

He took a heavy dose of the pills and drank an extra glass of water, forcing it down into himself, cold in his stomach. Cruz went to the rectory's library. Kilba had a number of rare books, including a Latin King James Bible. Cruz took it along with a Spanish translation and sat to reread both versions of the Sermon on the Mount. Ever since his moment of weakness with Gaja, he had been reading it each night.

Christ explained adultery, particularly the desire for someone's wife—anyone who desired another man's wife committed adultery without even touching her. It actually calmed Cruz to understand that he had been an adulterer long before Gaja had come to him. Their short moment together only consummated his adultery. Even now, by reading the sermon and thinking of her, he was an adulterer. He could confess the sin tomorrow, but moments after praying his penance, he would desire her again.

It was also a sin to imagine murder. He wanted to strangle Gaja but knew it would change nothing. Even with Gaja dead, he would still be a living adulterer. On his deathbed, his final confession made, penance finished, Extreme Unction already performed, at the last moment before his light went out, he'd think of Gaja. He'd remember their short moment together and wish to see her, if even from a great distance, one last time.

A man and a woman fit together so perfectly, like pieces of a great puzzle. At the moment when it was happening, Cruz had felt no shame. But it ended so quickly. Just a few minutes, five, even less. Cruz's entire burden, all the weight he carried, the stiffness in his neck, his obsession and fear of sin—it had all left him in an instant burst of relief. His body felt heavy and light all at once, like it was floating to collapse. He wanted to sleep straight through till midday, awaken rested and calm.

When Cruz awoke in the library's reading chair, feet up on the footrest, he felt his back and neck stiff and throbbing. The rare bibles had fallen; in the middle of the night, he had somehow managed to slip off one shoe. The scent of fried potatoes and eggs wafted from the kitchen. He heard Alina and Kilba talking quietly over breakfast.

What day was today? Wednesday or Tuesday—what was the last thing he had done before bed? In the daze from the pills, he really didn't care if he had missed an appointment or forgotten someone. The potatoes smelled good and he was very hungry but ashamed to leave the library and wander to the kitchen. They would know he had passed out in a chair. His shirt and trousers were wrinkled, hair probably a mess.

Cruz heard Kilba say, "You don't have to lose admiration of your mother, Alina."

Alina was waiting to speak. "I haven't," she said. "Not totally. But. If I'm quiet about it, it makes me feel like an accomplice."

"That's not an unusual feeling."

They were quiet again. Cruz sat up straight and leaned closer to the crack in the door. When they started speaking, he crept even closer.

Kilba repeated, "But it's not really true, Alina, that you're an accomplice. Just knowing another's actions or thoughts doesn't make you an accomplice. Think of me. Keeping confessions to myself might make me a madman or fool, a man betraying his faith, a hypocrite, perhaps, but not an accomplice."

"What about dad?" she asked.

"What about him?"

"It's so difficult to think about him in all this."

"Your father's always difficult to think about."

"That's not completely true."

"Partial truth is still truth," said Kilba. "He's been through a lot, I think, already. He really has, and he's a strong man, in the end."

Again, they did not speak for a long while. Cruz heard a fork or knife tap against a plate. Alina said, "I think I know why I'm...I mean, why I *feel* like an accomplice."

"Oh?"

"Because when I think of it," said Alina. "When I know all the details and all the things mama was going through. She learned about the abuses. Just like I've learned them, too, by accident. You learn them and...you know...you just feel alone. And when the only other person who knows them...Monsignor, think about it." She cleared her throat. "Think about it. When a guy like Bronza's told you all this, opened up that way. Maybe you can't help but fall for him. When you feel sorry for someone, it can make you forget whom you really love. Who you're supposed to love."

"You could be right."

"It feels wrong, but I can *understand* why mama had this guilty thing for Bronza."

The Monsignor was quiet. He finally said, "That's not how an accomplice feels." His voice was really low and Cruz had to strain to hear him. "You're trying to understand another's point of view. You're trying to forgive. You're not an accomplice, Alina. You're the opposite. You're trying to forgive your mother."

"But I feel like I'm betraying him."

"That's guilt." Kilba sighed. "It's not your fault your mother loved Bronza, or desired him. Or obsessed or fantasized, whatever she did with him. If you can understand some small corner, why she did half of it, then you can see her point of view. Believe me. I hope you'll believe me sooner rather than later. If you can see her point of view, you can forgive her." Kilba was quiet again. "It was like that for me with Benny," he said. "When you can forgive someone, from the depth of it, you can live with anything." Kilba managed to laugh. "Of course, that's easy to say. If we are only interested in being able to live with things, I often wonder, what sort of life is that, really?"

They continued talking, Alina asking more questions, explaining more ideas, but Cruz's drug-dazed mind was wandering. Had he failed to make the connection in the past? Yes, Gaja had hinted at it. When he searched through his memory, he was sure she had hinted it. Bronza used to cheat on her, he knew that, but with Jorgenson's wife? Cruz remembered Gaja telling him once, *She's dead now, the woman he was with. The one when he was cheating.* It seemed to him that Gaja was sitting there again, before anything had happened between them, and Cruz now felt deeply ashamed. He wanted to leave the library at once, confess everything to a priest, even to Kilba.

Alina and the Monsignor were now gone, the kitchen quiet. He peeked out to be sure the corridor was clear and managed to wander up to his room while the receptionist had slipped away. Cruz washed himself and came down to eat before noon. People with business greeted him, nuns who cleaned the place, other visitors. He couldn't seem to shake the haze of the sleeping pills. Not even a cup of coffee helped.

He went to the church to sit in a back pew. Good people had come to pray in the light of the stained glass. Others lit candles and knelt at the rail, at the statues of the Virgin and the Sacred Heart. One man just sat like an island in the gray pews with his expression of deep concentration. Cruz tried to do it, to feel sincerely troubled and sorrowful about his actions, yet he could only feel fake. Everything around him was fake. The light falling on statues. Plaster pillars painted to resemble marble. He even wondered if the pews were made of real wood, the altar's candleholders of actual brass.

The sun hid behind a cloud and the church darkened. The candle flames in white, blue and red glass glowed brighter, flickering from gentle currents of air. The first quiet and subtle notes of the organ seemed natural and did not anger him. Lars was up there playing. When Jorgenson was in the middle of *The Fugue*, Cruz felt very close to him, as if he and Lars had always shared some understanding that neither of them could articulate.

He went up to the choir. Save for them, the church was now empty. Cruz sat right near the organ and listened to the music with care. It was comforting but soon drifted to its maddening chaos and Cruz's body hardened. He wanted to leave the choir, knots in his stomach and neck. At that pained moment—almost in a flash of inspiration—Cruz understood what Lars was doing. He listened to the chaos fade, calm, the composition return to a subtle and gentle fugue where it remained and pressed on. The music finished peacefully, the sounds beautiful and authentic.

Lars sat at the organ and rubbed his face. He flipped switches.

Cruz whispered, "That music." He moved timidly toward him and kept his voice low. "I hate to startle you, Lars. Excuse me. That music you've just played."

Lars was standing on the boards alongside the pedals and peeked over the organ. "Father Cruz?"

"I heard you playing and came up here to listen."

"Priests 'r us," he said. "I came just because I don't have an organ at home. Maybe you can't imagine it on piano—but this music sounds totally different on organ, and I wanted to hear it."

"It. It's very clever."

"Well, thanks. Appreciate it." Lars sat again and stared at the keys. "It's about my family."

Cruz came near the organ. "That part right in the middle," he said. "The part when it becomes just frightening to listen to. That agitation."

"Sorry...frightening? Why frightening?"

"Lars, excuse me. I hate to bring this up. And don't answer if you don't want to. But is that how it feels? Is that what you're trying to express with those sounds...how it feels? When you learn that your wife has cheated on you?"

"What?"

"Is that what you mean by those sounds?"

"Why would I mean that? No. My music is images. I see landscapes and feel people."

"Well, I'm sorry. I'm afraid I have to admit, I just learned very recently. I had never known about it and it's fresh in my mind. I didn't know you were betrayed that way. No one told me. But now it's actually helped me understand you, Lars."

Lars withdrew. "Just lay off me, okay."

"Please. I'm sorry. I didn't mean to refresh the pain. But it's in that music, isn't it? It's in there...I really could hear it. That kind of pain. And the misunderstanding." Cruz finally noticed Lars' angered expression. His voice softened. "I feel I've misinterpreted. Have I made a mistake?"

6

Yuri finished sculpting his parents' death masks in only a few short hours. They were simple pieces of thicker aluminum, the eyes gouged out of the metal, as if an unskilled hand had torn through them with a large can opener. The masks looked virtually identical—mama smaller than papa, the face rounder than it was long. In the empty spaces of their mouths and eyes, Yuri had left the corners sharp. He formed noses by buckling and scratching the metal into crude, battered shapes.

In his apartment, he hung the masks in a new room each day, sometimes moving them from wall to wall several times every hour, now a foot higher or lower. The walls were soon peppered with thin nails. Yuri didn't pull the nails out, because he'd eventually move the masks. Even now, waiting for water to boil, he wasn't sure if he wanted them hanging above the archway.

He tore a brand new package of ballpoint pens open with his teeth and neatly set them into a cracked coffee mug. Yuri packed a pipe and had a smoke while paging through the spiral notebook where he kept his notes—Mrs. Jorgenson's journals had inspired him to start keeping his own. He read some of his writing from the previous day, inking his cuticle, tracing the arch above his fingernail with thick black ink. There was one particular entry that he liked to reread.

Alina wants to see papachka staring at her through the windshield, remember it forever, push the pedal and see his face. I understand that. If I would get a car, they'd both be in the windshield and my car would be faster than Alina's, bigger, and they could see it coming from far off. Boom. They can't move, it's like something's petrified them into one space that's forever approaching them and they can't escape.

When we woke up together that morning and I was looking at Alina's face. When I was little, I used to feel weird because I thought the Virgin Mary looked pretty. In church I would look at her sometimes and think she's so pretty it's horrible to feel this. With Alina it's kind of like that.

She loves both her parents so much. Yesterday I tried to imagine it like that, love without confusion. I'm going to kill my parents. I won't care if I get away with it and I won't even try. I've already sculpted their death masks. I already know how their faces will look when it's over and nobody's thinking about it anymore. Flat aluminum, torn out, sharp.

Yuri made coffee. The caffeine worked and he felt jumpy, impatient; he blackened all of the cuticles on his left hand with oily ink. Yuri poured milk in his coffee and grounds came up to the surface in swirls.

Lars found out about Victoria and dad, don't know how, old man hasn't even come out of that garage in a couple days, maybe three, and I don't think he's leaving his place when I'm at the motel. In the garage yesterday with the door closed and locked and all that music coming out of there, but now even louder and more forward, more crashing. First time in more than a couple weeks, I hear him writing a new piece. It's not that old fugue anymore but a new one this time, he's writing these two tornadoes that are dancing together, around and around each other, destroying fucking everything in their path, but also very quiet, like there are all these lambs trapped inside trying to bust out, scared what's going to hurt them. Maybe he's finished with it. Anyway, he wouldn't let me in there to pay my rent no matter how hard I knocked on the door. Even when I said, "Hey, Lars, the rent."

Yuri took a toke from the pipe and a sip of the lukewarm coffee. He closed the notebook once, but then opened it to keep writing.

This is an important thing, because Alina was talking to me on the phone and her voice sounded dark gray, the way mopwater looks in a bucket. She said, he's found out, he's found out. I think she thinks I told him. I didn't, but I couldn't explain.

That's why she's coming over, I'm not supposed to go anywhere. She's gonna tell me off.

Do you remember, I wanted to sculpt her portrait and leave it lying around the house over here? Do you remember? That was what I wanted to do.

Yuri made himself a pitcher of lemonade from crappy powder. He moved his father's death mask to the kitchen's larger wall, but left his mother hanging above the archway. The hammer and box of nails were still in his hands when he heard the door open downstairs, steps rising to the second floor. Alina still had keys to the house. It seemed for a moment that they were living together and she was only coming home, as always, after a day of work or a round of errands. Yuri unlocked the door for her and waited by the front windows.

She had not been back in the flat since her mother's death...since the time Lars had moved out. With her winter cap pulled over her eyebrows, Alina tiptoed around the place, one hand behind her neck, the other across her belly. Yuri said, "Hi, Alina," and she smiled at him. Her second smile, forced and odd, left him self-conscious. Cautiously, she wandered to the kitchen, to the bathroom, then back to the front door where she hung her winter cap on a small hook. "Do you hate your walls?" she asked softly. "All these nails?"

"They're nothing."

She asked, "What the hell is that?" and pointed at the mask with a pinky.

"A small thing," he said. "I hammered it together." Yuri quickly took the masks down and placed them out of sight atop a bookshelf. On the way to her old bedroom, Alina said, "I can't believe these walls. Your coffee table's just particle board?" She sat by the front windows.

The soft light of the gray autumn fell on her tired profile. When she rested her elbow against the windowsill, and her cheek against the palm of her hand, she said, matter-of-fact, "He's found out."

Yuri was quiet.

"Did you hear what I said?"

"Yeah."

"My dad. Your landlord. He's found out about mama and your dad."

"I never told him." Alina wouldn't look at Yuri. "We barely talk these days. You think it's me? Do you think it's me?"

"Yuri," she sighed out. "No. I told him. It was me." She turned the chair around completely and her eyes flashed with intensity. "Cruz overheard me talking to Kilba. And the idiot thought it was common knowledge."

"Kilba knows?"

"It just got so large in me, I started to feel so sick about it." She sat down on the floor, leaning against the wall. "Cruz went and asked dad some fuckheaded question. It set him off...dad called me demanding to know...he wanted to know. So I told him. I couldn't pretend."

"How much did you say?"

"Alina, I want to know everything about your mother. Rumors going around. Rumors coming to me. How long's this been going on? You're part of this behind my back."

She had no real expression in her face, and the vibrant green had drained from her eyes, now hollow spheres of dark glass. She unbuttoned the cuff of her blouse, then buttoned it again.

Now Yuri approached her, thinking he should hold her...rub her shoulder or pet her hair?

Lars was knocking on the back door. Yuri's eyes asked Alina if he should let him in. Alina said, "Get that," and followed to the kitchen where she boiled water to occupy herself.

"Oh," said Lars. "This a disturbance?" He didn't cross the threshold right away but stood in the pale, shadowy light of the back porch. "An interruption?"

"Come in, Lars," said Yuri. "You want some tea?"

Lars put on the light, a powerful bulb that whitened everything. He didn't look any different than usual, although he hadn't bathed in a few days. "Alina," he said, apparently to greet her. "And McDilienkoson. How're you, McDilienkoson?"

"I'm okay."

"I hear you're a really great Russian teacher. *Pani mayupa ruski?* I don't *pani mayupa ruski* now. But this one," he pointed, "She's a good translator." They could smell the booze on him. "Good at translating the *pani mayu,* for a guy like me who don't *pani* no fuckin' *mayu.*"

"I'm sorry," Yuri said. "I'm really sorry."

"Cuckolds and whores," said Lars. "Not here for funny games, just to get the rent. You remember, McDilienkoson? It's rental property. You're renting property."

Yuri got the money and put it on the table. Lars picked up the limp bills, "Past due," and counted the cash twice, licking his thumb for emphasis. Satisfied, he left. "Strumpet," he said, setting his feet carefully down the back stairs. "Strumpet and Dr. Hardon. Made a pretty little nest for each other. Pretty little house on the prairie."

7

Monsignor Kilba and Father Cruz were arguing again, this time near the reception. Whenever Cruz had to do something near Kilba, he tried to mind his own business, but the Monsignor usually had something to say. This time it was about the boxes of canned food Cruz was collecting for a food drive. "All this for Cicero's haggard beggars," Kilba said. "Whatsoever you do, right? Is this what you are doing unto Him?"

Cruz looked back from the archway. "I won't allow you to mock me."

"But you'll allow yourself every liberty—"

"You're the pastor of this parish." Cruz's jaw tightened. "What happens when people learn you think the food drive's for haggard beggars?"

"They'll probably have me replaced." Kilba was peeling a banana. "And you'll make a great pastor, Cruz."

"I don't want your job. Who would?" He moved a box to the front door. "And I didn't mock anyone."

"You ruined a man's sanity. A man who's never done anything to you."

Cruz started up the stairs with empty boxes. He stopped midway and said, half turned, "I'm not the one who slept with his wife. I said nothing out of malice."

"Altruism. That you do unto Him, the least of His people."

"You're a broken record," said Cruz, his footsteps continuing upwards. "I've apologized. It was sincere. Don't take your anger out on me." He kept talking but was out of Kilba's earshot.

Left alone, Kilba immediately felt sorry for arguing—the agitation worsened his arthritis. He took two strong pain pills and sat by himself in the reception.

Night had fallen. Kilba put on a lamp. On the table were requests for prayers, but Kilba didn't bother praying for anyone. There were people for that, somewhere, he was sure.

A figure was standing at the front door. It was Lars. Kilba had been longing to see him, but now, with him just on the other side of the door, he felt the depth of his own futility and an incredible distance from the man. Kilba opened the door and whispered, "Come in." Lars waddled to the kitchen like an accomplished town drunk.

Kilba didn't bother making tea, but went for a bottle of bourbon stashed away in a cupboard above the fridge. Lars saw the bottle and took glasses—Kilba poured generously and they sat drinking at the table. Lars asked, cautiously, "How you know about her?"

"When did I learn of Victoria's affair?"

Lars motioned with his hand, as if to say *Follow me.*

"Alina came in here. She told me."

"And that's...that's true?"

"I've no reason to lie," Kilba insisted. "I was shocked. I'd tell you the truth. Especially now, now that Cruz—"

"You pissed at him? You sound pissed."

"Well, you'd have to be clueless to—"

"Clueless," Lars interrupted. "Stupid. Fuckhead, to tell the drunk organist—"

"Lars, that's not what I mean. Of course, keeping it from you—"

"You would have kept it from me." Lars pulled the cork from the bottle and set it next to lemons on a cutting board. "You'd keep it."

Lars sipped the drink. He cut one of the lemons in half to wet his finger on the watery flesh, stuttering, "I was clueless. Two, two possibilities. Clueless or, or this. Ripped." He pointed to himself. "Hit the sauce today. Since morning. Can you tell?"

"I'm truly very sorry, Lars."

"M'senior, I'm all cut up." His eyebrows narrowed. "Was blind like a dead mole." He picked whiskers. "But now, I'm right...now. Today, I'm all over this area. Hit sauce. Can you tell?"

"A little."

"That's right. Booze is losing its touch. Not much works anymore."

"Lars?"

"Since morning, enough bourbon, kill a man. But walked here from bus. Could teach fifth graders, if they'd pay me. If those fuckers'd pay me," he pointed, "I could do it right now."

Kilba clenched Lars by the wrist and the men were quiet.

"Monsignor, why'd she do it?"

Kilba lightly took his glass.

"I treated her decent. Why shit? On a man's face?"

"I think." Kilba corked the bottle. "I think people do it because." He breathed and pushed the bottle to the side. "Eighty-one years later. When it comes to this. God...I just don't know."

"Couldn't get my dick up. A lot more Wonka than Willy." Lars quartered the lemon's half. "For years and years, no salute, so you gotta take it in consideration. But lately, you know what? You know what happened? I found out she was doing him. Guess what my pee pee can do now?"

"Lars, Victoria was not doing that."

"Doughboy rose. New comp'ny for my morning toilet."

"Lars, listen to me. She was never with him. It's not true."

"Morning glory, soldier, full attention. Got up at dawn, raving mad nationalist, decorated w'medals." He squeezed lemon into his drink. "Home by myself with piano keys, questions, and these damn ass," he slapped the side of his head hard several times, "these damn ass sounds in my head." Lars took out an envelope and slid it closer to Kilba. "And a good soldier in all his glory, between my loins, Private Stumps. Stumpy, what good are you now?"

Kilba took the envelope. "What is this?"

"I heard from Alina. It's true? You're done with the parish?"

"Well." Kilba's eyes softened. "I failed to tell you. Wanted to keep it quiet. At the end of the year, yes. I'm retiring."

"Where you going?"

"To retire. Downtown. The church takes care of us."

"Downtown, good. Here, read this. That's official paperwork."

Kilba used the knife to open the envelope, addressed To St. Anthony's.

Dear St. Anthony's Parish,

I am writing this letter of resignation to tell you that I, Lars Jorgenson, am going to quit. My final day of choir and organ will be the last Sunday of December, 1981, this year. I was happy to work here for many years. I will return the keys to the church when I pick up the last check.

Sincerely,
Lars Jorgenson

Kilba set the letter on the table.

Lars had stood, his coat unbuttoned. "Got 'nother thing." From the breast pocket he pulled out a thick stack of folded paper fastened with a shiny paper clip. "This's 'portant. Keep i'safe. In case. Jus' in case."

"Lars. Thank you, very good...I'll look at this. But sit down. Why are you standing like that? You'll fall." Lars waddled into the rectory's front room. Kilba glanced over a musical score called *The Second Fugue.* He said, "You know I can't read music."

"Sure, you can," Lars called out from beyond the archway.

"What am I supposed to do with this?"

Kilba heard him mumble from the other room, his feet shuffling as he wandered the rectory.

8

Bronza was lighting his cigarette off the blue flame of the stove. He had to make some toast—Gaja wanted toast—but couldn't find the toaster. He used a set of tongs to hold a slice of bread above the blue flame. As he spread soft butter—it had been left out for days—a bit of cigarette ash fell on the food. He just bit that part off and brought the plate to Gaja.

She had come down with a virus, a temperature of 101. Bronza had told her she had 99.8, nothing to worry about, and Gaja had called him a liar. Minutes later, she asked for toast and grapefruit juice. Now she had fallen asleep, her peaceful head deep in a pillow.

Seated beside her, he ate the toast, feeling the heat she radiated. Bronza lowered the sheet from her chin so that he could kiss her naked shoulders and neck. He kissed her where her neck sloped to the collarbone. When he sat back again, Bronza imagined the blade of a guillotine falling from a great height to strike her throat.

The moment the blade hit her skin. The precise instant. Not the moment when her skin broke, but a sliver of time just prior, when the blade was still clean, her body whole and mind conscious. How would her prayer sound at that moment? "I'll cover you up," he said, finishing the bread. "The house is a bit cold, actually." Bronza handled the blankets with care. "You're turning pink."

Like you're swimming upstream.

He went to make more toast, waving it over the blue flame, and he left it on Gaja's nightstand beside a glass of grapefruit juice and a bottle of aspirin. Bronza whispered, "Sleep, it's just a fever," thinking to measure her temperature again. But he only brought a tall glass of cool water to leave beside the other items.

Bronza smoked by himself at the piano and sensed the house sprawling in every direction around him. He was convinced the bungalow had mice...crumbs and food had been left everywhere, the floor not swept for who knew how long, the sink full of greasy pans. Certainly there were mice, yet he only ever saw them in his periphery, gray whispers. Here again: in the corner of his eye he saw a gray mouse dart out from under a curtain, but it was gone so soon as he looked over, and there was nothing behind the curtain when he moved it.

His mind was playing tricks. Last night he had thought Gaja was up and walking around when he knew she wasn't, when he could feel her lying next to him.

Were guests waiting for him in far away rooms? He often thought he had to bring Victoria some wine. Many years ago, Gaja had told him, "I felt Anya in the house today." Bronza had laughed at her, taking off his tie and falling back into the chair. He was laughing that way now, wandering through the house to put on lights, even by the front stairs and the back door. Bronza flooded the house with light in preparation for a party.

In his den he turned on a tape recorder and waited for the reels to wind a few times before speaking. "Hello." He leaned back to smoke and gather thoughts. "I'm so hungry. It's almost ten or eleven, p.m. Right now, I've just put on the lights. There's no food in the house. A frozen chicken. Frozen sticks of butter. Yes, a loaf of fresh bread." The recorder hissed subtly. "You're wondering why I don't go out to buy something. Well, she's in bed with a fever, and I don't feel I should leave her alone.

"Yesterday, I could handle about nine minutes of complete silence before it came up over me, right over my shoulders and up my neck, and the side of my face turned numb. I'm sure I spoke about it. It was in this chair. Seems like every night it's taking less and less time to come." The reels ran and he tapped his fingers against a newspaper. "Yes, and I have a mousetrap in the basement and one in the kitchen. Another under the bathtub. But for five days now no trapped mice. Still, I see them. They're not just smudges of light or hair in my periphery. They run."

He shut the recorder off. Everything appeared ultra-vivid. The shine of the light through a small snifter dirty with fingerprints. The widening and narrowing grain of his desk's wood. The aftertaste of butter in the large space of his warm, dry mouth. Crushed cigarette filters in a heap of ash, some with lipstick, most without.

Bronza was recording his voice again. "Still, I've so many hours to wait. Easier when I've got my voice to hear, although I talk such bullshit. I think I really yearn for music, but I am afraid to play anything. It's another difficulty: when I put on music, I feel trapped in this room, trapped near the record player. And now she's sick. Loud music will bother her."

He reached for an empty glass and his elbow knocked over an oil lamp. The glass chimney shattered on the hardwood, some oil spilling out amid socks, old newspapers, books and record sleeves. He knew he had to clean all that mess up, but couldn't find the energy to stand from Benny's chair.

Everyone around me is getting more and more fucked up. And there are so many more people around now, more than ever before. Actually, there are fewer people around, a lot of them dead. But in my feelings people are everywhere and they are completely wrong, very confused.

It's not that I'm feeling the people who're dead. Don't accuse me. For so long, I've wanted to shake You alive and ask why You'd do this to the people. Your children, right? Why are they so...have You seen them or spoken to them? I was looking at them today, walking around town. All of them trapped in Your great web of interconnected strands. You're like the spider who creates everything for Himself to trap and devour. Why do You like trapping people?

Bronza's familiar feeling finally crept up. It starting somewhere far behind, but then raced to the bottom of his spine where it buzzed, electric and warm, to shoot up his back. He thought he'd be unable to move, but then he was looking through the records on the floor, incapable of remembering how he had left the chair not one minute before. Bronza did not read the sleeves but just put one on.

Bach's first cello suite.

He took the cassette where he had recorded his voice and was going to dunk it in water, then throw it out. Holding it tightly in his hands, he saw himself leaving the den, but also felt the remorse he'd have in future—without the tape, he'd be unable to know what he had been thinking right now. Bronza tucked the cassette tightly between volumes *S* and *T* of his encyclopedia.

On top of his highest shelf, right next to a dry, almost dead plant, Bronza had left a long and thick leather belt. He had also mounted a solid hook into his ceiling, one that looked inconspicuous enough—he had driven it right into the stud and tested it to see if it would hold. In the music, rich and full of life, Bronza found enormous courage. He turned it up, every note connected to the next in a system of meaningful perfection. Bach was amazing: mystery without confusion.

That's it. That's what I want. In that music, there's no sense that You're going to leave us without an answer. When I'm by myself in the quiet I feel You're going to leave me where I can't know anything. What comes next?

What would you like?

Bronza refused to talk to himself. He picked through the shattered oil lamp, just a few shards of delicate glass on the hardwood.

A modest miracle. All I need, he thought, is for all of it to be set straight...everything in the right place. Don't raise the dead. Don't show Your face. I refuse to talk to You.

Bronza turned up the music. It protected him and allowed his mind to focus. On what? On the notes and the progression, the crescendo, the climax. Bach was a madman. The fool sat around thinking of this shit.

He went to check on Gaja. She had not touched her water or aspirin. "Now didn't I tell you to take your aspirin?" Her forehead was still very hot. How much time had passed since he had measured? Bronza shook down the thermometer, but then he thought, No, not *me*...it's You who should measure it. That's Yours, take care of Your children, sort out this mess, all these sick and foolish. But You won't do that. You leave that to us.

The music ended. Bronza came to watch the stylus oscillating in the plastic moat between the grooves and paper circle in the record's center. He wanted to reset the thing to play from the beginning, but now the presence was so strong, so visceral and physical that he didn't dare look at the floor or over to the doorway. He was sure he'd see a body or face. Bronza sat in

Benny's chair and kept his eyes and mind on his own hands. There was another blank tape in one of his drawers and he set it in the machine, hitting *record*.

Go ahead, now, talk. That's a modest enough miracle, isn't it? Your voice? It's not even a miracle. You see what You've done? You don't exist. It's my imagination. Be clear. I'm imagining You.

The house was heavy with silence around the buzz and subtle hiss of the winding tape. Bronza remained aware of the bungalow's rooms and wings, sprawled out around, above and beneath him.

You don't exist, he repeated. It doesn't exist. You're in my mind. Just because I feel it all winding down, You creep up. And I refuse to be fooled by my own self.

I'll show you what you want if only you believe.

Believe in what?

Believe in the possible, in what's waiting for you.

I don't want to be Your fool.

No one's making a fool of you...don't fight yourself...go and look at the pictures you have of Victoria. When you worked in the clinic together. When she came over so many times.

No! I see through it—You're only tempting me.

Stop playing tricks on yourself...I'm inviting you to admit what's true.

No! She won't meet me. She's not waiting for me anywhere.

The recorder's reels were still winding.

I am my own imagination. Maybe real selves get salvation, loved ones to greet. But You and I are invented. We're meant to be forgotten. We've never been real in the first place.

The cassette tape whined and clicked. Bronza opened the recorder to find it had eaten the tape. He handled it gently yet grew terribly angry as he unwound the thin ribbon from the capstan and rollers. He finally tossed the disemboweled and useless machine to the side.

He sat with his forehead against a palm and felt warm, still thirsty, but for something other than water. Something tangy, effervescent. Bronza needed more music—and very, very loud. The highest level, a concerto grosso from Bach, or Rachmaninoff's piano, but he wasn't sure where the records had been left. He saw the pack of cigarettes and thought he'd smoke, but there wasn't a match in the house. Had he forgotten? He had to light a smoke off the blue flame in his kitchen.

9

The temperature was falling. Lars smelled particles of ice blowing in the strong wind that tunneled between houses and curled over roofs. He was walking briskly from the Roosevelt bus stop to 19th and 49th Court, his hands, numb and stiff, carrying a canvas sack.

Bronza's house was ablaze with light. Lars let himself into the backyard and checked if the side door to the garage had been left open. It was locked, as were the windows, and Lars noticed the brown Buick parked inside. He took a crowbar from the canvas sack and left it among the evergreens. At the front door, he rang the bell.

No one answered. He played an annoying cadence on the bell to stir Bronza out—Lars would break in if he had to. After eight or ten minutes, Bronza came and put his forehead to the window. "Who's it?"

"Look." Lars held up a bottle of cognac. "I've brought something a little special."

"Lars?" Bronza backed away from the glass, but then his face returned. "That's you?"

"It's freezing out here, to let you know."

Bronza let him in, mostly from curiosity. Lars hung his coat on one of the hooks and fussed with a canvas sack. "Your hair?" Bronza said, touching Lars' scalp. "You shaved your head? And your mustache."

"New look," he said. "But don't look at me. Look at the bottle."

Bronza took the cognac but could not stop gawking at him. He would never have recognized Lars without hearing his voice outside the door. Jorgenson looked like a cross between a Greek theater mask and the man in the moon, his face round and white, cheeks flushed from the cold. And he was wearing a priest's black shirt, collar and trousers, and had put on white pallbearer's gloves. Lars said, "Just have a look at that bottle. Quality stuff."

"Lars, this is..." Bronza set the bottle on the floor. He said, "This isn't good. Not tonight," but Jorgenson was already deep in the house. He looked for glasses in the buffet and said, "Your place is a sty. How did it get like this?"

"This isn't good," Dilienko muttered. "No no. Tonight, I've realized something. Just now."

"Yeah, well, we'll let ourselves relax."

Lars was removing the pile of clothes Gaja had left on the dining room table, the box of jewels and a bunch of old newspapers. He set the table with three glass tumblers and an etched bowl. "You've got ice? In the freezer?" Lars took exaggerated steps to the kitchen, and Bronza approached the buffet, leaving the cognac next to a vase. Jorgenson called out, "Hey, there's no food. Nothing to eat in the fridge." When he brought two ice trays back to the dining room, Bronza was gone. Lars cracked the ice into the bowl and shut off some lights.

He couldn't believe the state of the house. All of the plants were dying, their leaves brown and brittle. Piles of old mail had been stacked on the piano and the rugs had not been vacuumed in weeks, maybe a month. He found a full jewelry box wide open on the table and pocketed a handful of them before going to look for Bronza. Dilienko was in the master bedroom, sitting in the bed next to Gaja, a cigarette in an ashtray on his lap.

Lars brought in a chair and sat for a while, fidgeting and restless. He took Gaja's water and drank half the glass. "What's going on here?" he asked. "What's she sleeping for?"

"She's sick, Lars."

"Who isn't?"

"Shh," whispered Bronza. "Not so loud."

Outside, the wind was getting stronger. A strong gust rattled the window in its frame. Lars had never seen Bronza as tired, bags around his eyes, his shirt terribly wrinkled, the cuffs unbuttoned, tails hanging outside the pants. Bronza wasn't smoking the cigarette but watching it disintegrate, playing a finger through the rising stream of smoke. Lars spoke up, "What's wrong with her?"

"She's sick."

"What? With what?"

"Lars..." Bronza perked up, as if from a daydream. He took a strong drag, then put the smoke out. "Are you, did you come alone?"

"The hell're you talking about?"

"Was anyone with you?"

"Yeah. Jacqueline Kennedy. And St. Louis. The fourteenth."

"How long were you at the door?"

"I don't know. Who cares? We're wasting our time. You need to come with me. I've got the most special bottles. There are a few more in that package by the door." He slapped the bed. "You haven't tried it."

"Not so loud. Jesus, Lars...look it's...she's like this now. I can't be drinking."

Lars went to the front room, all of his movements hasty yet decisive. He poured four fingers of cognac into three glasses and called Bronza over. "But you haven't tried it." Bronza refused to come out.

Lars opened the piano and played *The Second Fugue*. These were violent but nuanced and subtle notes. He lost himself for a brief moment, hot and red rage behind his eyelids, and he increased the volume skillfully as he played. Bronza soon came into the front room. "What are you doing here?"

"We're drinking."

"We're not. No, so late. Look at the hour."

"What do you have to do in the morning?"

"You don't know. My tape recorder's broken. I'll have to sort it out."

"You look like shit." His hands lifted from the keys. "And why's this place such a sty?"

Bronza didn't respond. "Gentleness," he said, now standing near a window. "I can only explain, not even half of it. Maybe it's calming down."

"Let's drink to that." Lars rushed over to the table and handed Bronza a glass. "To calm gentleness." He raised his glass, but Bronza sat at the table with the cognac in his lap. He said, "I don't want this."

"Wait a second. You haven't read the bottle. Here, have a good look at it." Lars shoved it between Bronza's legs and he grabbed it, startled. "Read the label, Dick Moe. You see all that French shit on there. At one point, this bottle was in red velvet, probably on some boat."

"I don't speak French."

"Good. Let's have a little."

Bronza put the glass and bottle on the table. "You can't be here, Lars."

"Why not?"

"I don't feel right. Nothing personal...I have to do something."

"What, do what?"

"That tape recorder's broken...And Gaja's sick."

"You need to heal your wife?"

"She's running a pretty good fever."

"I'm so sorry." Lars put a hand flat on his bald head. "What is it? Do you need some time to yourself?"

"I might." Bronza reached for his cigarettes. "Maybe." A small box of matches—it must have been under the pile of clothes—lay on the table. Bronza put it in his shirt pocket. "Please, Lars. Maybe leave me alone tonight."

Jorgenson shrugged. With even more exaggerated movements, he stomped off into Bronza's bedroom. Before Dilienko could realize what was happening, Lars had locked the door and jammed a chair under the knob. He knelt down right by the bed, folding his hands to pray and started in: "I'm so sorry, missy." He spoke loud enough for Bronza to hear. "Your man left me to take care of you, because he needs to get some serious shit done. Alone, in the other room. Some shit with his tape recorder. It has something to do with his Dick Moe."

Bronza was fighting with the door. "Lars. Lars!"

"I'm so happy for a moment with you, missy." He reached out and pressed her thigh, surprised by the warmth of her body. "You see, I have this problem in my head. Wish I could explain...it's that I don't know who I am. I'm confused. Shell shock, it must have been the war. Total amnesia. I'm this walking daydream. But I'm so happy you're available for me, missy. I can tell you all my secrets."

"Lars, leave her alone!"

"My book's a life with mixed-up pages. Funeral dirge. Now that my old lady's dead, we can run away to your Luganland, boil horse livers and worship elms. Me and you. You see, I don't know who the fuck I am. And I didn't want to tell you I'm sick."

"Shut up! You shut up!"

"I am so fucked in the brain. Need a mistress badly." Lars reached under the blanket and rubbed Gaja's belly. "I've got seeds to plant, and your pot's so right for my flowers. How about it? My Willy and your Wendy?" His hand was slowly rising up her torso, although Lars couldn't bring himself to touch her breasts. "I have a confession to make, missy. I've been going through your purse."

Bronza had given up fighting with the door and was listening to Lars carefully. Lars kept making references to Victoria, the stolen mirror and tea in a typewriter. Bronza had no key to the door and no tool large enough to break in. In the dining room, he shot down the glass of cognac and paced, wide awake, his thoughts clearing. Wondering if he should break the window from the outside, he drank another. Then he heard Gaja shriek out loud.

Lars backed away from her immediately. She retreated to the bed's corner, wrapping the sheets and blanket around herself. "What do you want? Who—don't touch me! Don't."

Lars stood up. "I want a drink." He kicked the chair away and unlocked the door, expecting Bronza to hammer it open and hit him. But Dilienko was waiting with the bottle in one hand and two glasses in another. They stared each other down. "You win," Bronza muttered. "Let's sit, have it out."

"I've already had it out," said Lars, slapping the glasses out of Bronza's hand and taking the bottle. In the front room, he took two expensive champagne flutes and filled them to the brim. Bronza sat at the table, his arms crossed, the flute in front of him. "What do you want from me, Lars?"

"Hate to break it to you, Dick Moe. You've got nothing anyone needs. A dingbat wife, a dead baby and a son who hates you. Fuck you."

"I didn't do anything to her."

Lars smiled painfully. "Cheers." He raised his glass and Bronza joined him—they knocked back the flutes and Lars threw his across the room, shattering it against a window. Bronza threw his over Lars who didn't flinch. Their eyes locked again until Lars broke away to find more glasses. "What was the best part of it?" he asked, pouring. "Maybe we can compare notes."

"I didn't do anything to her."

"Yeah, to, I like the word to. Not to her, no." He waited. "What was the best part?"

"It's nothing anyone's proud of."

"Me least of all. Drink." They did and Lars poured. Bronza was coughing from the pace, but the cognac only gave Lars energy. "Let me ask you," he said. "What did you want from her?"

Bronza didn't answer.

"An alternative to your Jesus freak? Or...you liked...you believed she's a little naïve...a little gullible. Could tell her your bullshit stories. Make her feel sorry for you. You'd twist her all around yourself with your bullshit sob story."

"She wasn't naïve. And she felt sorry for you," said Bronza. "That's why she stayed with you."

"Drink." They did and this time Bronza handled it. Lars said, "I didn't know human beings were your type. Surprised to find out, actually."

"I didn't do anything to her."

Gaja had been listening from the other room, still unsure if the bald priest who had been touching her was really Lars. When she recognized his voice for certain, it oddly calmed her. She put on a long sweater and pulled a thick robe all the way around her throat to come and join the men. Lars said, "Sit with us, missy."

"Stop calling her that."

Gaja took an empty glass. "I want water."

"Make it yourself," said Lars. "There's a bucket in the shitter."

"I never insulted or hurt Victoria."

"Oh...what do you call it? What do we call it, then? You massaged her heart. Stuffed her Christmas stocking."

Bronza shook his head, retreating. The men now pulled back into their own worlds, quietly drinking at their own pace. Gaja had never seen Lars as crazed and foolish...she grew frightened to be near him and went to the kitchen.

Her illness had gotten worse. It seemed her entire weight had risen to her shoulders and pounding head, and she had to hold the counter to keep her balance. When she heard Lars start playing the piano, the music immediately affected her. Every note was concentrated hatred, fury coming from a gentle, naïve child. She began crying so naturally, large tears, but managed to keep it silent. Gaja dipped her fingers in water to wipe her eyes. None of the kitchen rags were clean enough, so she dried her face with the skirt of her robe. Soon enough, Lars stopped the music, and she sat by herself to let the feelings settle. As the quiet persisted, she felt monstrous rage with Lars, both for touching her in bed and for playing the piano that way, so much hatred. Gaja came to the table to drink cognac as well, the first bottle almost finished.

"Not to fear. I've got another," said Lars, going to the front door. "Don't say I never gave you anything."

"What is this?" asked Bronza, trying to read the bottle.

"Genteel Franco Swanko."

Bronza was now visibly altered by the drink and coordinated his hands with difficulty. They drank the next bottle from shot glasses that Lars had to rub clean with a blouse lying on the floor. He poured three shots and raised his. "Now, I'd like to propose a toast..."

Bronza stared out from below thick eyebrows.

"A toast to you two...to your wonderful marriage. May it flicker and burn like the brightest star. And may your days together be full of each other. I wish you both on both of you, for ever and ever, eternity, infinity, messiah, amen." Lars drank immediately, but Bronza and Gaja took some time. He slapped Bronza on the shoulder. "So...question of the night. Don't avoid it, stallion. Tell us both, what did you want from her? In the end."

Bronza leaned on the table heavily. "I have always just wanted some calm."

"No...in the *end*. In the god damn end."

Gaja spoke up. "Lars. What do you think? She wanted him. That was enough."

"She didn't," said Bronza.

"Wanted you?" Lars muttered. "No. But what did you want? From her, in the end?"

"Are you stupid?" asked Gaja. "It's sex. Just sex. What more...it's all they ever want when they cheat." She drank by herself. "He was with her. She wanted him, it's finished. Can't change it."

"I didn't," said Bronza.

Gaja laughed. For a moment they all desperately waited for someone else to speak. Gaja said, "If she did it once, with him, she'd done it before, with others. It's always that way. You're another fool, Lars, just like me. Join the club."

Lars stood, "To fuck her...that's all? That's all."

"Lars," said Gaja. "Just drink. It's over, all over. There's no other answer for you."

"I didn't do anything with her," said Bronza, now speaking only to Gaja. "Nothing. All of it was in your head. Your paranoid, hypocrite head."

"You did it," she said. "Were doing it for years. So was she."

"Why lie?" shouted Bronza. "Gaja's sick. Lars. With Victoria. I shared with her. I tried to explain." Dilienko stood and his chair fell backwards. "It was almost a friendship. Two people who tried to understand each other."

"Was it in my house? In my front room?"

"Yes." Gaja had almost no emotion in her voice. "Front rooms and floors. Blankets and basements and the clinic. You thought different? He comes in your house when he doesn't even know you, follows you down the street. Sits in the dark and breathes when you're smoking. You run away, but he comes in your house, helps your uncle understand there's someone else to care for you now. So he can let go."

"Will you listen to me?" Bronza raised his voice. He poured the cognac and it flowed over. "I had the highest respect. Not like it was with you," he pointed at Gaja. "You didn't want Yuri. You're a Pharisee. You lie to yourself, every single person, your children. You're the one who wants to fuck. But you don't. That's the problem. You don't."

"I'm not an animal," Gaja said, now agitated, her eyes swelling. "No." She looked at Lars. "I'll tell you what I did," she said. "I broke down the door, and I took my wife. I broke and kicked in the door...go look at it. Go look at it...it's never been fixed. I broke in, forced my wife down so she couldn't move. He turned me into it."

Bronza drank his cognac and Lars grabbed him by the shoulders, trying to push him against the wall. "In my house? Mine?" Bronza stumbled backwards and tripped over the fallen chair, bumping his head on a windowsill. He tried to get up, but Lars knelt down on him. "In my house?"

"No."

"Yes," said Gaja. She had moved to the other side of the room to sit on the sofa. "I broke in. We fought."

Lars was kneeling on Bronza's stomach and pressing his shirt collar against his throat. "She didn't know. You tricked her. Trapped her." Lars felt a muscle pull—it stung and instantly stiffened in his back. He let Bronza go, rolling off his body—after struggling to get up, he went to the table. Dilienko lay on the floor for a moment longer, but finally sat, rubbing his throat. "Gaja's a liar," Bronza said. "She's lying to you."

She was smoking by the piano. "I lost her mirror," she said. "Think I left it in the rectory. I'm sorry."

Lars said, panting, "I want. You two to sit...down here." He tried to catch his breath, putting the fallen chair back upright. "Right here. And you," he pointed at Gaja. "I want to know the details, missy."

"We're created in a way we shouldn't be," said Gaja. "Look at yourself."

Bronza drank and Lars kept filling his glass. He continued pleading, "It's not what happened," but Lars had again returned to the piano.

Gaja came to stand uncomfortably close to him. She hesitated but reached out and gently pressed his shoulder. So soon as she had touched another person, she sensed the fever, a warm aura around her. She kissed Lars on the forehead and brushed the back of his head and neck, the way she would to her own child. Gaja said, "Everything they told you is true. I hurt Yuri." She sat next to Lars on the pianist's bench, pressing herself tightly to him. He tried to push her away, but she only gripped him tighter. "It's not a secret anymore," she whispered. "I'm so sorry for everything." She kissed his cheek and temple again, then brushed his ears. Gaja stood and he watched her walk to the bedroom, no way of understanding what the hell she was talking about.

It didn't matter. Lars played patiently and quietly. All he could see was Bronza and Victoria somewhere in his house...he couldn't picture where. And he couldn't see them together clearly, not embracing or naked or making love, but Lars could feel Bronza remembering her tonight. He could sense, deeply and fully, that they had found singularity together—Lars would never know what it was, only that it was different, wildly and painfully different from the space, the feeling of home he and Victoria had shared. Tonight he knew Bronza missed Victoria terribly, and this knowledge left Lars playing his fugues with unforgiving honesty.

Bronza listened to the music. He drank to put himself out of it for good, out cold before Lars came to smash the bottle over his head. He'd accept it—better to be numb from drink. Bronza said, "Don't hate her," getting up from the table. "Please, Lars. She was good t'you. Was good to you, Lars. And never betrayed." He stumbled to the sofa where he fell and passed out.

Lars remained patient. He looked around the front room, the beautiful hardwood floors, stained glass, archways, furniture—shadows falling crisp from the bright lights. He played until the swirling tornado within him had wound itself so tightly that it left his hands too stiff to make any music anymore.

He made sure they were both asleep, poking them in the bellies. The keys to the garage were in Bronza's pocket.

He was drunker than he thought he'd get and almost fell down the back stairs, catching himself on a railing. Lars pulled the white gloves tighter around his hands and let himself into the garage. He took the keys from the ignition and opened the trunk. The large red gas tank was still there, full and heavy.

He took it to the front room and poured it carefully around Dilienko's sofa, then made a trail to the den where he poured it over the bookshelves, the piles of paper, and over the desk. Pouring gas over the clothing on the floor, he pitied Gaja—for a split second he wanted to wake her and tell her to get out of the house. But no...she had seen him there; she knew he had shaved his head...to hell with her. To hell with them both. Lars poured the gas around her bed, onto her curtains, leaving a trail to the front room. The only thing he regretted was that the Steinway would burn. Lars actually sat down to play the piano one last time, improvising a melody, letting it glide out of him.

What the fuck...are you drunk! You'll wake them.

He took the can and poured gas along the curtains, splashing some onto the wooden doors, the windowsills, and over Bronza's legs. With the last bit of gasoline, he made a trail to the back door.

A wind-up alarm clock went off that instant in Bronza's den...it peeled incessantly, a loud and enraged shrill. Lars couldn't find the matches. Where were the matches? Had he left them outside? He stumbled out to look. When he found them, the small box lying in the grass, Lars panicked. The intense smell made him feel that all his clothes were soaked in gas. He'd ignite himself, burn instantly. Drunk and sweating, Lars thought he could feel his clothes wet, the gas against his skin.

He stood in the middle of the garden, the floodlight above the back door shining on him, the wind blowing hard through the evergreens, the box of matches in his hands. The whole neighborhood could see through these trees for sure. Now Lars remembered Benny, saw him and Gaja sitting in their front room together. She was his niece, after all. What had she done...poor girl couldn't help it if she married an asshole. Lars thought the sun was about to come up. He saw the streets full of people going to catch the L. And cop cars were driving around, up and down 19th. One went by with its lights flashing.

They could see him...he was caught. But there was a way out. He should relax and say, look, I came over to have a drink and found the whole place like this. Any second, a little spark in the house could blow it off the block. Maybe he could go inside and clean the gas somehow. Or maybe he should wake them, tell them to get out.

Something fell in the garage. Someone was there, watching—who the hell was it? Lars dropped the matches in the grass and stood petrified. Something metal fell and a cabinet closed. Lars ran straight for the gate, kicking it open. He did not turn to look back and could only hope no one had seen him.

It was Yuri in the garage—he had come to steal metal. He heard the gate slam and wandered out to see who it was. The garden was empty. He had heard the piano playing, Lars' angry fugue, had seen all the lights when he first came to steal, and figured Lars had come over to tell papachka off. He couldn't see anyone but still sensed that someone was there. Gazing at the intensity of the house's many glowing lights, Yuri felt terribly wrong.

He saw the matches, the box white against the blackish-green grass, and Yuri picked them up. The back door to the house was wide open, and now a heavy feeling, cold and dark blue, had taken hold of the night. Yuri struck a match and threw it into the grass. He played with another one, lighting it and licking his fingers to pinch the flame out. Then he approached the back door, not caring one way or another if his parents found him there. He struck one more match before looking inside, throwing the little flame toward the fence. The overwhelming smell of gasoline hit him and he found the empty can thrown on the bottom stair. Yuri backed off immediately, frightened to the core, a drum pounding in his chest.

He stared at the house from the middle of the garden and put the matches in his pocket. Yuri could actually see what was about to happen, and it filled him with such shattering grief that his whole body weakened. In his mind, he was pulling his parents out of the house, shaking them awake, screaming that they had to get out. Yuri did scream, "Ei! Ei, papachka! Mama! Ei!" but his voice faded in the night. He cried louder, "Papachka! Mama!" but the wind was strong and they couldn't hear him. Yuri gathered himself and approached the house again, determined to get them out.

He picked up the can with his naked hand and carried it to the back of the garden. What the hell was he doing—he turned to go back to the house and had taken only five steps when papachka's silhouette appeared in the back window. Yuri could see him clearly, a cigarette in his lips, and an odd, painful slouch to his shoulders. Papa didn't bother opening the stained glass, but broke it with a bottle, knocking out every last shard from the frame. He leaned out the window and said, speaking Ukrainian, "Hi. Hi. Hi." Papa did not seem like himself at all, a sleepwalker who didn't recognize Yuri. He said, "Тихо тихо тихо," lighting a match, bringing it to the cigarette. The ember glowed orange and he flicked the sliver of wood, letting it carry in the wind. "Hi. Hi. Hi. Тихо тихо тихо." Yuri was backing away, out to the garden's back fence. Papa exhaled smoke, flicked ash into the wind, and turned to head deep into the house.

Passage: Monsignor Kilba's Confession,
Early Summer, 1994

Kilba's caretaker, Brother Patrick, was preparing the patio table at St. Michael's home for elderly priests on the North Side of Chicago. The Monsignor was 94 years old. A partially paralyzed left foot and severe arthritis in his knees and hips kept him in a wheelchair. Macular degeneration had severely damaged his eyes—he could see only fuzzy shapes and smeared colors. He had lost all hearing in his right ear and needed a hearing aid in the other, but heard well enough when it was turned on. After a half dozen internal surgeries, the rest of his aching body pestered him, but his mind and memory were still sharp.

On warm days he liked to sit on the patio where he could feel the air and sun, see the gray, blue and green smudges that were Lake Michigan, and smell the water in the wind. He'd listen to music or news radio, almost always demanding to be left alone.

Since Yuri's trial and conviction, Kilba had been to confession only once. He told a bishop all his sins, how he had not kept the promise to Benny. He had failed to see the signs, the extreme feelings that had driven Yuri to violence. The bishop told him he had done nothing wrong—there was nothing to absolve—and the Monsignor finally gave up on all of them. He refused to attend mass, receive Holy Communion or have any part of the Bible read aloud. If Kilba ever found a book left in his room, without checking with anyone to see what it was, he'd throw it off the patio or out a window.

In the warm and the pleasant lake breeze, Kilba listened to music on a tape player. When Brother Patrick pressed his shoulder gently, it stung with a bit of pain, and Kilba lifted his head. "What?"

"Monsignor. I'm sorry to bother you."

"Yes, why? What's wrong now?"

"Unfortunately, he refuses to leave. A man says he needs to see you."

"No visits. Tell him I'm asleep. I'm in the bath. I'm asleep."

"Monsignor, please excuse me. He's making a scene and says he'll wait till you're up. I've already made every possible excuse. Just to calm him, I promised I'd at least mention his name."

"Who is it?"

"He says he's Lars Jorgenson."

Kilba set the tape player aside.

"Shall we have him sent away?"

The Monsignor motioned with his hand as if to say *follow me*. He said, "I know him. You'll have to...you'll have to send that man up."

Kilba had not seen Lars since Yuri's trial and had no idea what may have happened to him. When Lars came out to the patio, the Monsignor grabbed Jorgenson's forearm to feel the dry, chapped skin and the warm metal of the wristwatch that shimmered in the sun. The parasol squeaked as Lars opened it and Brother Patrick brought out a pitcher of ice water. Smaller waves broke and hushed on Lake Michigan. Lars sat at the table and said, "Hello, Monsignor."

"My bad ears, sit closer."

Lars pulled a chair right up alongside him. "It's amazing," he said. "You haven't changed at all. You're still the same."

"I don't understand."

"It's so easy to sit with you. I was afraid. Afraid maybe it'd be different now. But it's not."

Kilba said, "I'm mostly blind. I can't see your face."

"I've lost most of my hair. Don't need to shave it. Falls out on its own."

When Lars said this, it became obvious to Kilba that there was not much to talk about. He did not want to know where Lars lived, what had happened to him, although he did ask about Alina. Lars only said she was fine, married and had two boys, had spent some time in Russia. Kilba asked for descriptions, but Lars described the kind of boys anyone could see at a random park. After this the men grew quiet—Lars was tapping his leg nervously and the vibrations tinkled the ice in the pitcher. The lake still hushed. Kilba asked, "Is this only why you've come? Only to see me like this?"

"No, Monsignor."

"Why, then? You are different, Lars. I don't know how, but you are different."

"A lot has changed. Many things have changed."

Kilba didn't want to hear about them. He insisted: "Why are you here?"

When Lars reached out and pressed Kilba's arthritic knee, pain shot through his whole skeleton, and he grimaced. Jorgenson yanked the hand back. "I'm sorry. Bad knees?"

"It's fine. Fine. Just talk, in the end. What brings you?"

"Monsignor. I'll understand if you say no. But I thought maybe you could listen to me. Maybe I could tell you mine. Let you know what's mine."

"What? Speak up..."

"My confession, Monsignor. I want to confess."

"Confess? What?"

"I'm hoping you'll hear me confess."

"No, Lars...no!" He shook his head as briskly as he could. "No. I don't do that anymore. I don't listen to people, not that way. Forget it. And you're not Catholic, anyway. You're not baptized."

"Does it matter? It shouldn't matter."

"It matters. If you want, go to someone who doesn't know you. No. There's a rectory down the street. Whatever you've done, forget it. That's not my business anymore."

"But I have to tell you, Monsignor."

"That's not what I'm for."

"Monsignor." Lars touched him as gently as he could. He did not say anymore and hoped Kilba could understand what was inside him all on his own. But the Monsignor didn't. Lars spat it out. "I've just come back from the doctor's. Just two days ago. Can you hear me?"

Kilba's face tightened.

"She told me. She said it's very serious now."

Kilba heard him. He pressed the joystick of his chair and rolled it all the way to the patio's little fence. "I'm very sorry," he said. "But there's nothing I can do. I can't cure you."

"But will you listen to me?"

Kilba thought about it. "Listen?" He sighed. "You want my ears, to unload your stones, dying friend. You go ahead and dump whatever you've got, but I won't absolve you. And I cannot pretend that God will forgive you. If you want forgiveness, you need to go to another priest. There are plenty around."

"Monsignor, I want you to know."

Kilba backed up and the wheelchair bumped into the table, rattling the pitcher. Lars brought his chair right up to Kilba's side and spoke, leaning on the wheelchair's armrest.

He told all the details from the night at Bronza's house. To disguise himself while walking down the street, he had stolen a shirt and collar from Kilba's closet, and to keep from leaving fingerprints, he had taken pallbearer's gloves from the sacristy. Lars had shaved his head to complete the disguise. Kilba listened to all he had done in Dilienko's house. "And Yuri," Lars said. "When he testified how he'd heard someone playing piano just before it happened. It was real. It wasn't just music in his head. It was true."

Kilba sat with one hand covering his mouth, the other on the wheelchair's control stick.

"But I didn't light it up. Not my spark. I don't know who lit it up. Maybe Yuri did do it in the end. Or maybe his story, that Bronza did it himself, maybe that's real. But when he said he found the house that way, it's true. He found it ready to spark...and he heard the music. Because I played it."

Lars stood and leaned right over Kilba. "My story, that I was with Alina that night, was lies. She lied for me, Monsignor. She said I was with her that night, at her place in Wicker Park. She hates me. Ever since then. Now I'm sick and she hates me, Monsignor."

Kilba brushed one eye with a tense pinky, but then set the hand down in his lap. "You come to me with this? After all this time."

Lars drank water straight from the pitcher.

"Why would you tell me this?"

"I'm telling you. Because. Monsignor...because—"

"Idiot!" Kilba shouted. "Why would you tell me!" Lars had prepared for this reaction. He pulled back, leaning away. "What?" asked Kilba. "You can't carry it? Now that a doctor's said you're dying? Well, go to the cops. Unload where it matters. Are you going to the cops?"

Lars said nothing. Kilba only felt the awkward and foolish energy of Lars' cowardice. He pushed the button to summon Brother Patrick who came immediately. "Brother Patrick. We're finished here. Please escort this man out of the building."

Lars said, "Monsignor..."

Kilba turned to him, reaching out to grip his shirt so tightly that it hurt every joint in his hand. "Listen to me. At the last moment, no one will forgive you," he said. "There won't be anything for you but hell. You will always be a coward," Kilba muttered. "Thank you for telling me, Lars. Good bye."

For several days afterward, Kilba did not talk to anyone. While eating at the table, he wept heavily without regard for who was around him. At first he found new questions for God...stupid questions that sank like hunks of lead to the bottom of a muddy pond.

He could not stop remembering the round yellow leaves on the blue carpet in his study, Benny's amber eyes and callused hands, the figurines of the fisherman and the napping boy, the way the man used to cover his fist with a palm. Kilba remembered the intense longing he had felt, his wish that Benny could have stayed alive, the confusion during the funeral. But now Kilba believed he understood and knew the kind of despair Benny had felt.

One night the Monsignor was listening to the news. It was a report about a Catholic priest, defrocked for molesting a host of children. These kinds of stories were becoming more common now and they angered Kilba terribly, made him hate it all even more. The story was typical...the man had been friendly, a good-hearted priest whom no one had suspected, no one would have imagined it and everyone had trusted him. So many parents and neighbors were shocked, and many of his closest parishioners were still in denial. Had one victim never come forward, no one would have ever known.

The next day, Kilba had it arranged. Brother Patrick contacted detective Salerno from the Cicero Police Department. Salerno had originally investigated the fire and knew the details.

The meeting had to be one-on-one and face-to-face, Kilba insisted, because he couldn't hear people properly over the phone. On the morning when Salerno could come, they met on the patio. And the Monsignor started his confession:

"Detective Salerno. I'm going to tell you about it, in 1981, in autumn, early November. On the night when the house burned down. That night, I had come to Bronza Dilienko's house a few hours after nightfall. It was to help settle a dispute—his wife had learned he was cheating on her. We drank heavily. She was sick in bed. From the stress, Dilienko wasn't well and the fool drank so much that he passed out on the sofa. When I knew they were both asleep, I went to the car's trunk where I knew he had a can of gas. And I poured it throughout, around the sofa and bed where they slept.

"Then I heard an alarm clock. It was the old kind, with those metallic, incessant bells, and they rattled me up. I couldn't find the matches. I went to look for them in the garden, but when I found them, I panicked. I wanted to think it was my conscience...but you'll know, detective. You're a man who's heard confessions all your life. What stopped me was nothing more than base human cowardice. I heard a sound...it was someone in the garage...I stood still, convinced someone had seen me. But when I heard it again, I left out the gate."

Kilba could not see that Detective Salerno was sitting poker faced. "Really?" he asked. "Just out the gate?"

"That's right."

"Just like that." Salerno clicked a ballpoint pen. "You were able to get away? That's interesting. So tell me, Father. What would...if you don't mind me asking. What was it would motivate an old priest, one like yourself, to burn two people alive?"

"He was collateral damage. It was Gaja Laputis, really. I wanted Gaja."

"The wife?"

"His, yes. Because before, she had always been mine. Especially her. She was abusive, you'll remember. What she did to her boy. She was always on the edge of her nerves. And she was getting more and more talkative, more and more unstable. It had become clear to me. She was going to tell. She was already hinting it."

"Tell what?"

"When she was a child, detective Salerno, I used to babysit her. When her uncle—he used to work for me—when he was unable to. You won't understand what kind of purity it was. You're not in a position to see. But she was a little angel. A perfect and complete angel, the most delicate, like you've never seen. These were only a few instances, I'll explain, only a few years' worth. But they are enough, detective. They are enough."

"What did you do?"

Kilba was surprised, almost repelled by how much pleasure it gave him to lie this way.

"Detective. She was always a quiet little girl. Always so quiet, obedient and unblemished. She was the kind of child who never grows up, never changes, and everything you do together remains pure. I kept it pure, detective. At the quietest moments, when she sat with me obedient, I could believe it, that she would always remain that way. Always there, mine. Frozen, pleased with me, no one else's.

"But, of course, she grew into this anger—into a dirty woman. Filthy. On the edge of her wits. Ruined herself with that marriage, and then he disgraced her with pregnancy, ruined her completely. She hurt her children and soon enough she was wandering around town babbling. I could already see where it was heading. Gaja wanted to pin it all on me, tell them about what we had shared. No one would understand how it had really been. Because you're not in a position to see. She would have told you about our privacy, our pleasure, and it would forgive her everything. Make me the cause of it. Make me out to be the evil one."

403

Summer, 2001

1

On the seventh anniversary of Kilba's death, Father Cruz was still getting phone calls and occasional letters. A few old parishioners, most of them elderly Lithuanians, still remembered Kilba and wanted to buy masses in his honor, but Cruz never allowed anyone a dedication. "I'm very sorry, Mrs. Dobilas," he said. "But every single dedication is already bought up. Yes, for all of August and September. Well...I'm afraid I can't make any exceptions. You might try calling back in the winter."

Cruz couldn't take any more phone calls that afternoon. He had to visit the house of a woman in her final days. It was a small three-room house on 49th Court, right between 18th and 19th streets.

The inside had been paneled in wooden planks, some of them already warped. The obese woman lay on a hospice bed near the front window. When Cruz anointed her, only the woman's elderly brother stayed to witness—the son and daughter-in-law went to the kitchen, disinterested, possibly upset with the Catholic rite. They thanked Cruz politely when he was finished but made clear that he could leave.

The house was less than a block from the street corner where Gaja's bungalow had once stood. Cruz approached the corner casually, had not been to the site in years. A new house had been put up, wooden with light blue aluminum siding and a steep roof. The tan and green garage in the back stood as a kind of relic, separate and alone. The people who had moved into this property were pigs, their garden overgrown, stacks of boards and tires by the fence. The front lawn, just a patch of dirt and weeds, was left littered with plastic bottles and trampled pages of coupons, their colors faded from sunlight and rain.

Cruz clearly remembered the putrid smell of the burnt-out brick hulk and the black puddles of water, some kind of bluish oil floating on the surface. He had come the very next day after the fire when the house still radiated heat and the whole block stunk. He remembered the sight of her remains—he demanded to see them and had arranged the funeral—thin bones charred black, a skull without a jaw, and the tiny ribcage.

Cruz noticed Lita walking back from the L stop—she was passing underneath the old oak on 19th. Her electric guitar was strapped to her back and she carried a heavy book bag on her shoulder. He said, "Lita," and squeezed her fingertips.

"Hello, Father."

"Coming back from the college?"

She didn't want to talk to him. "*Si*. Back from the college."

"Classes, already?" His body swayed. "How's Yuri?"

Lita managed to smile. She knew Father Cruz hated that she lived with him. "He's okay."

"That's good."

Lita lifted her bag up higher onto her shoulder. Her eyes seemed to point to the house behind him.

2

Reikel was helping Yuri build a coal forge in his new studio, a long and narrow room in the back of an abandoned auto shop. Yuri had saved enough for a down payment and had bought the crumbling building, dirtied by squatters, for cheap. Reikel had helped spruce the place up and convert part of it to storage lockers. Renting them provided a bit of income and helped Yuri pay the mortgage.

The shop's old furnace room was now his studio. The walls had been stripped down to crumbling, moldy brick with a block glass window, some of the cubes smashed out. The wiring sagged between exposed pipes in the ceiling and pigeons cooed somewhere, able to get in through holes in the roof.

Yuri had drawn up crude plans for a large forge. The room's far end was a natural place with a brick chimney, level ground and power supply for a blower. They knocked part of the chimney out to build the forge right into the wall. A bricklayer from the Corner Billiard Club came around to help correct some of their mistakes, but after only four days of work the forge was starting to come together. "You'll bake a big pizza," said Reikel. "Barbecue whole damn side o'beef."

It was hot and humid when they finished working, their faces dirty and clothes soaked through with sweat. Reikel joked, his face dripping, "You got some coal? Blower's workin'. Fire this sucker up." Yuri imagined the coals burning green. "I'll get coal tomorrow," he said. "Bright and early, if you want to come around and see."

Reikel left Yuri alone to organize the place. He put his tools away and lay down on the cracked concrete to feel his property against his body. A feather floated in a shaft of late evening light and pigeons cooed from the corner. When a truck rumbled outside, Yuri felt the vibrations through his heels and the back of his head.

He had bought a motorcycle, a Honda with an orange gas tank, the seat's foam showing. He rode down to Aunt Sonia's and parked in the gangway, covering the bike with a dark green tarp.

Even though she had been dead for over a year, Yuri still called the house Aunt Sonia's. Lita had inherited it, and now that Yuri lived with her, the house was also his. He was almost used to the feeling even though he often expected Sonia to be drinking lemon water or Jarritos in the backyard, or watching Univision in the kitchen when he came home.

Lita was there reading from a textbook, her face covered in a pale facial mask. "Ono," she said, trying not to move her jaw or lips. "Y'ilthy. M'ask. Y'irty. Ono."

"The forge's ready to go."

"Owny-tuch. Nokiss. Ono. Y'stink."

Yuri grabbed her arm, his hand rough from dried cement. He laughed mildly on his way to the bathroom. Under the shower, he watched the red and brown brick dust darken the water flowing down his legs into the drain. Lita came to wash off the mask, and she put his clothes in a plastic bag. He was wearing only towels around his waist and over the shoulders when he came to eat rice, warm tortillas, stewed pork and sliced garden tomatoes.

Lita said, "Found out the music librarian at UIC sells hash."

"You mean your boss?"

"He's a grad student. Supposedly, he plays vibraphone. Wants to smoke with me on Friday, out on the roof of the architecture building. You ever been there?" She grabbed some of the meat with a tortilla. "Was kinda slow today. Almost nobody comes there, I think. I just messed around on the internet."

"Download some new music?"

"Wanna show you something." She had left a blue folder on top of the microwave. Lita reached over and laid it next to his plate. "Look in there."

The folder contained computer printouts, a music magazine and a schedule of concerts in Chicago. Yuri couldn't see what was so special about any of it. Lita pointed to a headline *Composer Hospitalized* above a very short article. "I googled Lars Jorgenson," she said. "There's more than one article about it."

Yuri read very carefully. Lars had been listening to a performance of *The Magic Flute* at the Civic Opera House, sitting right in the first row, when he had collapsed from a heart attack. The performance stopped for a short time to get him an ambulance. The article's short paragraphs said more about the fugues Lars was known for composing and about his position on the faculty of The Chicago College of Performing Arts than about his health. "A heart attack," said Yuri.

"Did you know about the cancer? He beat cancer. I had no idea."

"Didn't know." Yuri shoveled food around with his fork. "I didn't know about any of it."

"Totally weird karma, how I found that," Lita said. "I was stacking CDs. By accident, came across his *Second Fugue*. Thought, what the hell, google him. And this came up."

Yuri mashed his rice with a slow hand. "The Magic Flute."

Daydreaming and eating only half his food, he wasn't fun company for the rest of the evening. After dinner, he dressed in his blue slacks and shirt to go to work—he was still the night janitor at the Cicero Stadium. He took his large headphones to listen to music while waxing the basketball court and mopping the showers.

Tonight he sat at a computer in a back office and read about Lars on several websites. He looked up customer reviews of his fugues, most of them written by people who totally misunderstood the music. Yuri toyed around with his own review but deleted it.

The search engine's cursor blinked at him impatiently. He took a red and white piece of peppermint candy from a dish on the desk. The crackling plastic wrapper sounded like a campfire of bone-dry wood. Yuri typed *Alina Jorgenson* and looked at the shapes of the letters. He put the candy in his mouth, his molars crushing it, and clicked *Search*.

3

Alina checked into a high-rise hotel only one block from
Michigan Avenue. The delayed flight from New York and traffic on
the Kennedy had tired her boys, eight and ten years old. It was
only the middle of the afternoon, but they passed out without any
talk of games or ice cream.

Alina sat at the window with a vodka tonic in her lap and
her tired feet lifted onto a chair. She had not been to Chicago in
over ten years. From the 21st floor, she couldn't see if anything
had changed. Under overcast skies, Lake Michigan had turned
warship gray, and the few sails in the distance had been dabbed on
with the edge of a brush. On the balcony of an adjacent building,
an asshole in a blue shirt and red tie was speaking on the phone.
Alina imagined the balcony cracking and falling to the ground, this
man, a hollow clay statue, shattering on the sidewalk right where
limousines waited to pick up greater numbers of assholes.

Her room faced the north. One of the taller buildings in the
distance could have been St. Joseph's hospital. Lars was twelve
hours from a quadruple bypass and Alina was sure nobody was
with him. As she finished her drink, she didn't feel any
apprehension or fear or anything, really, beside numb malaise.
She mixed another vodka tonic and stirred it with her pinky,
looking down on the massive ant farm of the city.

After the second drink, she wrote her boys notes in
Russian:

Viktor,

Make sure your brother takes his medicine when he wakes up. I'll be down at the hospital. Call me if you want to come, or ask how to get there at the front desk. ~~You can come if you want~~. ~~Take a taxi.~~ *No! Call me when you wake up. Here's twenty dollars if you're hungry. Don't charge any films to the room! Love you,*

Mama

Mitya,

Make sure you take your medicine when you wake up. Remember to drink your juice. If you go outside, wear your jacket but don't go too far anywhere. It's better here in the room. If you don't feel well, stay and sleep. You'll get to meet your grandfather later. I promise. Love you,

Mama

Alina taped the notes to her boys' backpacks and placed a twenty-dollar bill on the floor next to Viktor's shoes. She left the room very quietly, twisting the handle to keep the door's bolt from clicking.

Between the elevator's polished brass walls, she was surrounded by infinite reflections of herself, tracers of her body curving into dense greenish-gold, thick as wax.

Outside it had begun to drizzle. Alina didn't even know where she was going and ended up flagging a taxi two blocks from the hotel.

Waiting to speak to someone on her dad's floor of the hospital, she twisted and pressed the ring around her finger. A chubby, very young black nurse led her to the sparse, gray and pink room where Lars lay asleep by himself.

He was gray, bald and thin. She had only been there a few minutes when he woke up and started talking, his eyes wide and intensely blue. Lars didn't recognize her and babbled something about clusters...or cloisters...the ticket window, Pergolesi. Alina said, "Green pepper. Seeds all over the floor." When he passed out again, she watched the drops dripping from the IV bag and made herself a vodka tonic from a stash she had brought in her purse.

4

The powerful thunderstorm had come from nowhere. Huge chunks of hail bounced off the expressway, tapping and clacking off the hoods and trunks of cars. A nervous system of white lightning splintered across the green sky, and the thunder cracked loud, rolling and rumbling. Lita had to pull the motorcycle under a bridge. When she cut the engine, Yuri drove his point again: "I said a storm's coming." Water was gushing from an overhead drain.

"You did not."

"I said we should take the L. Fuckin' you could've wiped out back there."

"So what," said Lita. She flipped up her helmet's visor. "We're just wet. It'll pass."

"We're stuck under a bridge. Who knows how long it'll be."

"Now you're impatient? Before you didn't even want to go."

"I didn't want to go with the bike," he said. He pointed to the train in the highway's median. "*Let's* take. *The* L."

"Don't talk that way to me."

"You just wanted to drive the bike. Now look. We're under this shit bridge breathing diesel exhaust."

"It's a storm. It's romantic."

"And this." Yuri kicked something toward her. "That's a syringe."

"Holy shit," she said. They were both laughing. "Don't fuckin' touch it."

Thunder cracked again and the storm intensified, the rain driving and billowing in surges from low clouds. Yuri and Lita leaned against the concrete wall, their shoulders touching. Cars crawled past them. Lita heard the hailstones beating amazing rhythms on their hoods.

A few hailstones rolled near their feet. Yuri took one, tossing the clump from hand to hand. Then he watched it melt in his palm.

"Are you rehearsing what to say to him?" asked Lita.

Yuri shook the water from his hand.

"He might not even be able to talk," she said. "Maybe there's cops around him and shit, since he's kinda famous."

"He's not famous."

"Do you think he knows where Alina's at these days?"

Yuri looked at Lita. A strobe light of lighting went off as the L rumbled through the torrent, bursts of electricity at its wheels. Lita said, "You're wondering where she is." She also reached for a hailstone. "Probably. Right? Aren't you?"

Yuri crushed the syringe with the heel of his boot. "I doubt Lars knows where she is," he said. Yuri kicked the plastic shards out into traffic. Then he stood with Lita again and they watched the storm as a good gust picked up and sprayed their faces with cold mist.

5

Under anesthesia, Lars thought he heard voices, someone muttering from the other end of a long hall.

A singing choir, in a church.

The first alto couldn't hit a note if Lars taped it to a punching bag. Frustrated, he stood from the organ to get away from the woman and to gather his papers, wrapping up the composition on which he'd been working.

In the alley, he lit it on fire and stared at the burning paper until the glowing outline of the last flake of ash, bending and curling to a restrained rhythm, died and left nothing but gray dust and smoke. He was seeing this as he returned to the hospital and came out of the anesthesia.

His hospital room was empty. Some idiot had plastered the sign *Towels* on the chrome towel dispenser. Above the bed, a massive television showed tasteless images of landscapes and white water crashing over rocks. The curtain was drawn, but Lars could hear the rain.

The drugs had reduced him to a pair of hands that touched a heavy, detached body. He could only reach his hips and stomach—Lars somehow understood not to touch his face. When the nurse came in, he remembered he had been under the knife, although he wasn't sure if the surgery was over. "Well...look who's up," the chubby girl said. Lars had a plastic tube in his mouth and couldn't talk. "It's over," she muttered. "You did fine and should relax."

For about a day, he lapsed in and out of consciousness, sometimes seeing the nurse, other times sure that a young boy was near him. Lars believed he was late for piano lessons. Someone wheeled the grand piano into the room so he could play music for the children, two young boys. One was staring through the chrome guardrail. The other one, a bit taller, was talking. "You've got staples in your chest."

Lars wanted something cool to drink.

"Don't talk that way. I'll take you back to the hotel."

"He can't hear, mama."

"You don't know that."

Lars was definitely not well...he was sick of the drugs and wanted to feel the true damage to his body, think his own thoughts. "My hearing things," he said. His hand found the catheter. "It's a tube. All these hoses." He wanted to pull the curtain, but it was too far away.

During that first day after the surgery, the intensive care unit only allowed close family to visit, and only for fifteen minutes at a time. Even though his room was usually empty and quiet, Lars believed he had many visitors who came in a constant stream. People from work—another composer he admired, orchestra conductors, violin teachers, a few better students. The director of the opera had sent a card, and random admirers of Lars' music waited in line to wish him well. He told Victoria to make them wait outside. "I'm ashamed," he said. "Tell them, I'll come and visit them as soon as they unhook me."

At some hour he awoke to see his room full of sunlight. Someone had left a half empty glass of orange juice on a little tray right next to a small toy car, blue with tinted glass—it recalled Alina's old Datsun. Lars pushed it gently with a finger and the car rolled to the tray's edge, stopping next to a thin pink coffee straw. A little boy sneezed in the corner.

Lars had never seen him before, not even in a photograph, but he knew this was Alina's son. His resemblance to Victoria, the green eyes, dark hair and the tone of the boy's skin struck him powerfully, a rush of heavy heat in his throat, and a dense, painful glow in his chest. Lars and the boy shared eye contact for a good while. Sometimes the little man pulled on the stings of his brown hooded sweatshirt. He glanced at the door often and faced the wall when he had to cough or sneeze, covering his mouth with tissue. When he had gathered enough courage, he came over to take his toy car and introduced himself, "Доброе утро. Меня зовут Митя."

"Oh," whispered Lars. "I don't. I'm sorry. I know only some words. *Pani mayu. Spasiba. Harasho*. But I don't speak."

The boy looked at him skeptically. "I'm Mitya," he said. "You slept for a whole day. Are you better now?"

"Not really."

"You see these plastic bags?" He pointed to the IV. "This one, it's just sweet water. That's why you're not thirsty. But, by this little tube here, they put medicine." The boy had the slightest Russian accent. "I saw nurse put it. It's also to make you sleep. It goes right in your hand and in your blood. Against pain."

"They think." Lars struggled to push out the words. "Of everything."

"You're my *diedushka*," said Mitya. He put the car in his sweatshirt's front pocket. "*Mamachka* went with Viktor to bring some breakfast."

"Your brother?"

"Да, да. Oh—yes." He climbed back onto his stool. "*Mamachka's* tired. She's staying awake. In the hotel, our window's higher than this one here. We can see how storms develop. She said she had dreams about flying."

"What time is it?"

Mitya took out a cell phone. "After eight, sixteen minutes."

"Morning?"

The boy nodded. He pushed some beeping buttons and put it away. They shared the same eye contact again. "Come closer?" Lars asked. "Could see you better."

Mitya stepped right up to the chrome guardrail. He bent down below the bed to cough in his sleeve...the coughs hammered out of him, an impossible sound from such a small body. When Mitya straightened himself again, *diedushka* cautiously reached out and brushed his greasy and uncombed hair.

Mitya was a bit uncomfortable: the dry veiny hand and the rugged wrinkles of *diedushka's* face. He went back to his stool. Now *diedushka* was looking up into the silent television monitor, its gray reflection of the room. Mitya said, "You write piano music."

Lars was quiet.

"*Mamachka* played it me for the first time. A CD. It sounded like mice running everywhere. They were scared of footsteps." Lars looked over at the boy. Mitya said, "Did you think of a cat chasing mice? Or footsteps?"

Diedushka breathed out once and scratched his upper lip, shaved smooth. "Call your *mamachka*," he said. "Tell her I'm awake."

6

Yuri and Lita had been refused entry into Lars' room. Wired on sugary, creamy coffee, they had been up all night, sitting in a diner filled with aging frat boys and scruffy *Sun-Times* readers. Lita burped up her dinner of deep fried pierogis, little bits of undigested meat and bacon rind in gross juice. She was too hazed to dig around her purse for the cherry antacids buried somewhere at the bottom.

Yuri was using a pocketknife to shave his pencil onto a napkin. He was inventing a crossword puzzle and had been quiet for many hours. It surprised Lita when he sighed and mumbled, "When it rains, what *good's* a fallen star?"

"Hum? Wait, what?"

"The muzak." He pointed to the speaker in the ceiling, a tan circle peppered with holes. "Catch a falling star." His hand rolled awkwardly to the rhythm. "Put it in your pocket. Save it for a rainy day. Everyone knows the words. What does it mean?"

"Never heard that song. Dunno."

He picked inside his ear with a pinky. "Everyone *knows* it," he said, annoyed. "Everyone."

Lita looked out the window, down Clark Street to the traffic signal. She burped up more pierogi juice mixed with coffee and Diet Coke. She chased it with water, and a small piece of ice almost went down the wrong pipe. On her way to the bathroom, her heart pounded from caffeine; in the chrome stall, she felt claustrophobic, packed in a tin. Lita had a toothbrush in her purse and brushed her teeth without toothpaste while sitting on the toilet. She searched for the antacids but found only lint-covered M&Ms.

Back at their table, Yuri was still shaving his pencil, his fingertips dirty with lead. Lita said, "I feel nasty. Think I'm gonna take a walk." She pressed his shoulder. "I gotta get some air."

He nodded and, without ever looking up at her, dumped his shavings into an ashtray. Lita slung her purse over a shoulder and grabbed a fashion magazine from a rack by the front door.

The diner wasn't too far from Lincoln Park. She was able to find a place under a tree to throw down the mag and use its surface to roll a hash joint, hardly concerned that the wet ground was soaking her ass. The smoke relaxed her heart rate and intensified a clear sky full of crisscrossing vapor trails, queues of little sheep. The crisp shadows cast by so many blades of grass seemed to be multiplying, and she noticed how many bugs were zipping and fluttering around. Her head grew too heavy for her neck and she lay back, inhaling the smell of the lake.

She could still smell the rain in the grass and remembered the storm, that rush of water from the drain above them, the rhythm of hail on the cars. Yuri had seemed perfectly normal once the rain had stopped, and he had held her tightly as she drove the motorcycle. But then the receptionist had said, "I'm sorry. Only immediate family's allowed till tomorrow."

Lita had no way of preparing herself for Yuri's withdrawal—he hadn't had one like this in years. But the receptionist's words had stoned him deaf, and Lita felt the heavy anxiety in him—it left him unable to plan, respond or understand what to do. He struggled to thread his jacket's zipper and finally gave up, telling Lita, "Just go in and see him on your own, then." Yuri wandered down the hall until he came to column of pay phones—he picked up a receiver and dialed.

"Who're you calling?" Lita asked, seeing if she could recognize the numbers.

"I can't remember." He listened to an automated voice, pressed the receiver with both hands, then set it back gently. "I'm hearing things."

"Hey..." She touched him, taking his hands and neck, but he froze up even more. Lita could feel his lungs turn to lead, the shell around his center harden as he finally zipped up the leather jacket. He turned down random corridors, found a flight of stairs and left the hospital out a side exit.

She had followed him to a yuppie cocktail lounge and drank a glass of beer while he stirred ginger ale. The bartender wasn't pleased when Yuri dumped salt onto the bar and, using his knife, shaped it into a jagged, sharpened snowflake. Lita followed him all around Lincoln Park's cafes and pubs. They took one break to smoke hash in an alley. "Please smoke some...it'll settle your nerves," she said. "I think we should just go home. We'll come back tomorrow. If you want, I mean, only if you want."

The hash didn't seem to affect him at all. They ended up in an all-night diner where Yuri sketched over a dozen sculptures—injured birds, violent shapes—and had started writing the crossword. After so many hours of exhausting silence, the sun already up and morning traffic lumbering along Clark, Yuri finally sighed. "Anyway, when it rains, what *good's* a fallen star?"

The simple melody—it seemed a sentimental children's song—was still in her head when she sat up in the lawn at Lincoln Park. She had napped, and now felt a bit of panic, checking to see if she had her purse and things. While the nap had rested her, she was still wired and stoned all at once, her legs and arms rubbery, clothes sodden. She rushed to Clark but found Yuri gone.

Stepping into the elevator at St. Joseph's, Lita knew she should just go home. Along the pink and white corridor to intensive care, she tried to remember where she had parked the motorcycle. Even if she found it, was she in any shape to drive?

The ICU reception was a thick window in the wall, similar to a gas station in a ghetto. A Philippine woman with bleached hair asked if she needed help.

"I'm looking for this guy," Lita said. "Did you see this guy go in here? He's tall. He's got a white and yellow shirt, kind of blue jeans and boots."

"I'm sorry?"

"His face is kinda round." Lita's hands formed a circle. "And he's got a bald spot right here. Would be visiting Lars Jorgenson."

The woman looked at a series of monitors. "Well, there's a visitor with Mr. Jorgenson now. You want to go in and see Mr. Jorgenson yourself?"

"Um, you know, let me. Lemme see for a second. Yeah, put my name down. Wait, no, because I'll...you know? I'll sit down and wait, see if he shows up."

Lita sat near a plant by a coffee table covered in news magazines. The cheesy gray and red speckled paintings matched the hideous chairs and carpet. Her eyes still stung.

Lita saw Alina come into the waiting area. She was surprised to recognize her so easily. Alina's face was rounder, bigger than in pictures, but she was still strikingly beautiful, dressed in foreign clothes, a flowing light blue skirt, the thin leather strings of her shoes wrapping around her ankles. Even though she wore tasteful makeup, delicate touches of eyeliner and expensive foundation, she could not hide her exhaustion.

Virtually every seat in the waiting room was empty, but Alina stared at them, unable to decide where to sit. When her phone rang, she plopped down a few seats from Lita. Alina spoke Russian, saying little besides yes and no, Да and Нет. When she hung up, Lita asked her, "Excuse me. Is that Russian?"

Alina nodded.

"Wow, that's cool. You speak Russian."

"Yes."

"I like Russian." Lita nodded like an idiot, no idea what to do now. Alina was staring at her blithely. "Like, where'd you learn it? Did you go to Russia or something like that?"

"I lived there. For a short time."

"I heard it's nice to visit. Not like Siberia or anything, or some dangerous part. You know, Moscow." Lita knew the names of many Russian cities but couldn't think of any at the moment. "Or Poland."

"I've never been to Poland."

"Sure. You're lucky. Because Chicago's kind of like mini-Poland. There's a damn statue of Copernicus by the Planetarium...I mean, what's he got to do with Chicago, right? And in this diner down here, down Clark." Lita pointed a thumb over her shoulder. "They have pierogis. Different kinds, some with meat, some with mushrooms or cabbage. I think with fruit, too."

Alina struggled to smile. She caught Lita looking curiously at her jewelry: a simple but graceful silver pendant, a narrow brown gem mounted into a thin silver ring. Some kind of half-circle clipped to her loose blouse; it created the illusion of an asymmetrical buckle that held the blouse together. "Did you make all that?" Lita asked.

"All that?"

"Your jewelry." Lita realized her mistake. How should she have known that Alina made jewelry? She stuttered briefly. "Or did you buy it? It's from Russia, or something?"

Alina didn't say anything else. She set a magazine on her lap and tucked her phone into her black handbag. She clipped open a small mirror and had a look at herself, wiping under her eyes, brushing her plucked eyebrows, and turning rigid with tension. Alina poured vodka and tonic into a travel mug, leaving the very small can of tonic on a table where everyone could see. To stir the drink, she capped the mug and sloshed it around. She drank, and then browsed through the magazine, pressing a knuckle into her eyebrow.

Lita was embarrassed for her. The longer she looked at Alina, the weaker she seemed, unable to accept so much, unable to rest. Yuri's description, that Alina was capable of listening—she was the kind of person who calms you, allows you to tell her the worst things you've ever felt or done—it seemed impossible to believe. Alina drank without pleasure and folded down the corners of a magazine that wasn't hers.

What would happen if Lita introduced herself? *I'm Angelita Avila. Yuri's told me all about you. I love your dad's music, and I'm sorry he's sick. Though I'm happy to meet you, finally.* Was that true? And why *finally*? Why had Lita assumed they'd meet one day? *I lost my dad, too. So I kinda know how it feels.*

She remembered Aunt Sonia telling her, "Your father's been killed." After the funeral, she had taken her favorite guitar to the alley and smashed it up with her dad's crowbar, the hollow reverberations dying with each blow until nothing was left but wooden shards and coiled wire, strain in Lita's wrists. When Aunt Sonia had died—Reikel and a hospice worker in the room with Lita—the blood poured from Sonia's mouth, running down to her neck and staining the sheet. Lita touched the blood and rubbed it on her hands because she wanted to admit it: she had been hoping for so long that it wouldn't happen, that a miracle would come, and now she was too tired of hope. But when she wiped Aunt

Sonia's dead face with a soft towel, she did it gently and carefully, afraid to wake or disturb her.

Alina was talking. "Who're you here to visit?"

"Me?" Lita perked up. "No one. I'm waiting for someone. My friend's visiting." Lita watched Alina finish the last bit of the drink and set the travel mug down on the floor. "What about you?" Lita asked. "You waiting for someone?"

"Just for someone to get out."

"Released from the hospital? Today?"

"No. Someone's visiting my dad. They have to talk." Alina flipped through the magazine, tearing into the corner of a page. "I'm curious what they're saying, actually. They're talking about me, probably. Or maybe they're just sitting together in hospital silence. You know the kind, I'm sure. But it's been over an hour now." Alina yawned through her nose. "Do you know what he said to me?"

"Your dad?"

"No. The guy. I knew him when he was a boy. Just a sprite. It would be like one of my children. It would be like the ten-year-old teaching you how to read."

My God, thought Lita, she's so drunk.

"I haven't seen him in twenty years. Do you know what he told me? The first thing he said was, *When I came back to Cicero, I found a cane just like your mom's. I still have it.* Word for word."

"What shudda he said?"

"You don't say anything to someone after twenty years. Not after you've taught them to read. Don't accuse me with that look, okay...I mean Russian. He taught me to read Russian. I went there to live, because...you're too young to know this. What are you, twenty? It's all an illusion." She pointed all around herself. "You leave all this. But there's no way to leave your head behind. It comes right with you, cobwebs in the skeletons, mouse shit in the attic. You fly and fly and fly, over oceans, over mountains. And then you run right into yourself. It's like someone leaves a spotless sheet of glass in the middle of the sidewalk where you're bound to walk."

After a moment, Alina continued: "You know what happened? I was walking down a street out there one day. One of my favorite streets by the university. At one of the tram stations, there was a poster for a concert. A piano player, you won't know him, he was going to play Bach, Sibelius and Jorgenson. *The Second Fugue?*" Alina smiled. "*The Second Fugue.*

"I went to that concert, a masochist. I stayed for every single note, for the pianist's final exhale. For the first time since I could remember, I heard something my father had written...exactly the piece he wrote when I told him I could read." She set the magazine down by the can of tonic. "Do you know what those stupid Russians did? All around me? They applauded. I looked around—every single one of them was applauding. Like they hadn't even heard the music. They didn't even understand what it was about.

"It would be easier," said Alina, "if people understood. If they could see the whole picture. All the curves and lines. All the naked and dirty colors. That's what I wish. I wish people could hear and see."

Lita asked, "Are you able to?"

"Listen to me. People don't want to see. They just want to unload on someone."

"Who?"

"What do you mean, *who*? People. People who ask *who*? They always think it's someone else who's blind. They never think, *maybe I'm the one who's spun this web*. Your hands gain weight, but the ring won't expand."

"What?"

"I'm sorry. I have nothing to explain," Alina rambled further, speaking more to the can of tonic than to Lita. "Turns out, my dad's the one with the answers. Yuri wants to talk to my dad, not to me. What am I supposed to tell my kids about my dad? I'm the idiot who brought them here. But where was I supposed to put them? I've already had to explain that their father's left us. My ex left me and our children for a travel agent with peroxide hair. A last-minute discount. So don't think I don't know how it feels."

"Excuse me?"

"It actually happened to me. My mom just imagined doing it, wondered how it would be. But Sergei didn't just imagine, write poems about it while sitting near a window. The travel agent is real, she's—"

"Alina," Lita interrupted, managing a tactful tone. "I'm really very sorry. I don't mean to change the subject, but I gotta question."

"You?" Alina's cheeks and neck flushed slightly. She leaned toward Lita, as if she only needed a better look to recognize her.

"What good's a rainy day when the stars are falling?"

"Excuse me?"

"Oh, fuck," Lita giggled. "I messed it up. It's something like, what good's a rainy day when your pocket's...I mean, you probably know it. It's a kid's song about a rainy day. And falling stars and pockets, or something. Yuri asked me about it just before we came over here."

"Who are you?"

"I didn't know the words," said Lita. "But Yuri said it's a famous song. Everyone knows it."

7

Yuri was sitting in the chair by the towel dispenser. Lars wiped his face with a moist cloth. A nurse came in and left them a white pitcher of water and a tray with two very clean glasses. Yuri continued speaking after she left.

"The first two, maybe three years were the worst. I had some guys protecting me, these guys from Cicero—they knew my story before I even showed up. It's weird. I never told anyone, not even Lita, about what it was like in there. I got hurt and bullied. But really not so much. In a way, I could rest in there. It's weird when you're among so many men. A lot don't have families at all, or what they got is completely wrecked. But they tell these delusional stories. All of them have dedicated girlfriends waiting for them to get out when their own mothers are on crack and their sisters are in gangs. It's a family of liars in there. I don't have another word for it—it was *familial*. Squabbles and fights, jealousy. There were a few murders and suicides. But just like in the outside world, people mostly left me alone.

"You think about the outside in there. Really a lot, every day. A lot at night. Could sleep pretty well there, often, but I had a lot of crazy dreams. I used to remember Reikel's shop a lot—the sound of the saw cutting frozen bones. That smell of bone dust, if you know it.

"Cruz came to visit me twice. Besides Reikel, he was the only one who ever visited me. It seemed he wanted to tell me something but could never spit it out. Father Cruz asked me these fucked up questions, if I missed my mother more than my father. Can I still find room in my heart for God? I imagined killing him, real violence, like Jack the Ripper kind of thing. I knew mama confessed every single thing to him and he forgave her for it. And he'd just stare at me with this veneer any time he saw me. I mean, I had fuckin' confessed it to him myself when I was twelve years old, but Cruz didn't even talk to me about that on his visits. When he came to prison the second time, I asked him if he could ignore it all because he secretly loved mama. Bastard never came back to visit me again.

"The thing about prison, in the daytime, it's noisy. Guys can't shut up and they're all pent up, so they bang things around and yell. I started hearing things. I actually wished Cruz would visit, just for variety...so I could imagine putting a sickle in him one day. I started hearing voices, people talking to me. And music. I heard so much music in my head...all those Ravel records papa played before bed. And Mozart and Bach. It terrorized me, because it's so beautiful in your head but you're actually in hell. It almost makes you feel like the work of every artist in the world is pointless. People think art is beautiful, but they don't understand it's actually begging them to be beautiful, too. A simple guy makes something beautiful with his hands...well, why can't I make something beautiful with my life? They don't get it. And having it in your head, it's a humiliating curse. Had I cut my arms off, I'd still have been making that shit in my head. And hearing the sounds. And the voices."

Yuri was quiet for a long time. He poured himself some water and sat on the stool. "It's true, Lars. I started thinking that maybe it really *was* me," he said. "Maybe I really had thrown the match. I might have done it, and then my brain just invented a fucked up memory around it, with your fugue playing and papa shattering the window. Maybe I had some kind of amnesia too, just like he had. Because, I did imagine them dead, and I know I hated them, at least sometimes, even though it's hard to remember now.

"I took the plea bargain for the minimum twenty years, told them it was me. Soon enough, I started believing it really was me."

"You did it," said Lars. "You heard the fugue."

"They told me Kilba did it, that he had confessed to it, and I almost told them, 'No, you fools, you idiots, I did it.'" He took a paper towel from the dispenser and rolled it into a ball. "Now I don't know what to think. No idea."

"Yuri," Lars whispered. "I played it." Lars paused to see Yuri's face. It seemed he didn't understand what Lars was trying to say. He said, slowly, "My music," and kept staring into him. "I played it that night. Before I heard you in the garage."

"You played?"

Lars nodded, his wet eyes gray as fog. Yuri took the pitcher of water and was about to pour, but the other glass was upside down and he just held the water above the tray. He set the pitcher down and took a glass, gripping it tightly with two hands. His grip kept tightening even though his body had weakened, his shoulders heavy as lead, and his face empty, like he was asleep. He stuck his fingers inside the glass and Lars thought Yuri was trying to pull it apart from the inside out...he was going to cut his hands open. Then he just let it fall and Lars heard it shatter on the floor.

Now Lars was talking, although Yuri kept his eyes hidden, looking down at the elegant shards of glass at his feet. "I'm going to tell you," Lars said. "I remembered it recently, maybe a year ago." Lars took time to breathe. "Didn't understand it, really, at the time. The last thing your mom said, I think." He was gripping the washcloth. "She took my face, said, Everything you hear is true. I did it to Yuri. It's true." Lars folded the cloth into a square. "She kissed me. Completely different from herself." Lars wiped his lips. "I hold my right hand up to God, I'm not making this up. She said, I'm so sorry for everything."

Yuri's hand hung down to the floor and he picked up a bigger piece of glass, holding it up to the fluorescent light. Yuri knelt down on one knee to pick up the smaller shards with his fingertips, taking time to find every single piece. He took the wash cloth from Lars and wiped up the glass dust, making sure all of it was gone, looking to see that no small piece had flown to some corner of the room. Yuri stepped across the room to throw the whole cloth away.

Timidly, he came over to Lars and held the chrome rail. He pressed Lars' forearm. Lars could feel his callused palms and fingers, and he welcomed the pain from Yuri's strong grip. Yuri leaned over and took Lars by the head and gently pressed his thumbs into his temples. His grip let up, and he kissed him above the eyes, on the forehead and cheeks, holding his face softly. Yuri set his palm flat against Lars' forehead, leaving it there as if checking his temperature. He kissed him one last time, setting his lips firmly on the salty skin above Lars' gray and wiry eyebrow.

8

Viktor and Mitya carried their mother's bags down to the rental car. They were relieved to leave the hotel after being cooped up for so long. After her visits to Diedushka, Mama was also less worried now and easier to be around.

Their flight was going to leave in the evening, and Alina wanted the boys to see her old house and the organ their grandfather used to play. She drove their rental down a ragged highway with rusting green bridges and train stations in the median. In Cicero, the roads were all cracked and broken, just like in Russia, and traffic dragged down the cluttered streets, mirages of heat radiating in the distance. On the hot day, Mexican families sat out on their front porches or on lawn chairs under the shady trees.

The boys could tell she didn't recognize the place, and that the changes in her hometown angered her. They wanted to ask which house was hers, but when she stopped to look at houses, two different ones, both Mitya and Viktor remained quiet. They thought she was lost for a while, turning down narrow streets, creeping between the rows of tightly parked cars.

When they pulled up to a church, much smaller and shabbier than the ones in Russia, Viktor asked, "Is this where the organ is?" Alina nodded. The boys understood she was seeing something she did not expect, although they could not know what it was. Maybe it was the Mexican priest on the stairs showing a construction crew what he wanted done. It could have been the cracked stairway or the amount of garbage the wind had blown against a black metal fence. Mitya asked, "Мама, что это?" but Alina didn't answer him. She drove away.

Lita and Yuri had invited Alina and the boys to Sonia's house. Reluctantly, Alina drove to 14th Street. She didn't understand why she was scared to upset Yuri and his girlfriend—they probably wouldn't care if she didn't come. Alina was only mildly curious about how Yuri lived, and that girl Lita had probably only agreed to the invitation out of politeness. Alina had finally pulled up to the tiny house, rickety with chipping paint and slumping wooden stairs. Victor said it reminded him of a summer house: "Это как Дачия." Alina looked for a place to park.

She knew what they would talk about. I live in New York now. It's where I ended up. After their father left me, his cousin Katya felt sorry for me and the boys, and she invited us to leave Russia and come stay with her in Manhattan. By Battery Park, you don't know where it is. Yes, I did eventually track down some of my mom's relatives. They're useless moochers. But whatever.

"Boys, forget it," Alina said. Viktor and Mitya were used to mama changing her mind. "Forget it," she said. "There's no reason to visit them."

Alina didn't tell the boys they were driving past Yuri's new studio, but she got a good look at it while stopped at a red light. The building leaned hard to one side like it had been stabbed in the corner and had crumpled sideways from pain. Alina felt senses, all at once, of chagrin and poverty and jealousy.

It angered her. What the hell was she jealous of? She didn't want an abandoned brick hulk or a homemade forge, and she definitely didn't need a *dachia* on 14th, where Carry's Bakery had been demolished, and butchers like Reikel were now lording over the slums. Alina didn't want to spend nights in motels where she'd find canes under pillows. And she didn't want a lover young enough to be her kid.

At O'Hare, she returned her rental and asked for a Red Cap to take all of her things to the check-in counter. Thankfully, there was a bar right near her gate where she could drink vodka and tonic with limes and ice. The boys' conversation about planes, and their questions about the flight, tightened a ring around her head. Her tension remained until she sat in the airplane's chair and the boys, nervous about takeoff, quieted.

From the air, Alina looked down to the crisscrossing city lights and the dark blue expanse of Lake Michigan. With the plane banking slightly, Alina forced her jealousy down, now a mere pinprick somewhere deep in her guts, as if from a needlepoint she had accidentally swallowed, but that now was going to pass through her system. The city lights gone, nothing but blue fading to black below her, Alina felt the simplest pity, gray as the belly of a cloud. But for whom? She couldn't know.

9

The summer passed for Cruz the way summers always pass in Cicero: busily and with far too many weddings. He would never admit it, neither to himself nor anyone else, but he actually welcomed the chance to say a funeral mass. People seemed much more attentive at funerals—the church's message of resurrection and forgiveness meant more to people when someone had died. During weddings almost nobody listened to him.

In September, a young man, not twenty-two years old, had fallen while working on a neighbor's roof. From the church, the procession to the cemetery was very long, perhaps sixty or more cars. Cruz knew this young man and his family—he had married him to his bride only the previous summer. These young people who surround him in the cemetery—the same ones who had celebrated last year's wedding as if life had no end—now stood shocked and silent, many of them holding back fierce emotions, some numbed to silence, others weeping in disbelief.

When it was finished, the casket lowered into the ground, people moved about, most back to their cars. Some took the chance to visit other gravesites and had brought flowers. Whenever at St. Anne's, Cruz glanced in the direction of Gaja's grave and remembered her, but since the time when Yuri had told him to leave the site alone, he only ever walked past it with a silent prayer.

Today, a man was standing where Gaja, Anya and Benny had been buried. He was bald and needed a walker to balance himself. Some younger person had come to help care for him, no doubt also to drive the Oldsmobile parked near the grave. When the man let a hand fall to his side, Cruz recognized the lanky signature. It was Lars Jorgenson.

Cruz didn't want to talk, but Lars had seen Cruz notice him. And now Cruz was curious to see Lars up close, to understand how much time had passed, perhaps to learn something about his life. He strolled easily toward the grave. Lars told him, "Don't worry, Father. I won't be here long."

"I only wanted to greet you." Lars' skin had faded, his eyes pale from age, and his hands trembled even while holding the walker. Cruz said, "Those flowers there," pointing to the little vase by Gaja's grave. "Did you put them?"

Lars nodded.

"They're lovely," he said. "When's the last time you had a chance to visit this grave?"

Jorgenson shrugged. His tone was slightly mocking, "I haven't been here enough."

"It's difficult to return to grave sites."

"Before today, I had thought it would mean more than it does. I'd learn something," said Lars. "To put flowers down, it would feel good. But it really doesn't mean a thing to come here, does it? You don't learn any secrets in cemeteries."

"Where do you live now, Lars?" he asked.

"Flying to New York today. Am actually flying out tonight."

"Success with music, I take it?"

Lars shook his head. His caretaker took a few steps closer to him and Lars leaned hard on the walker. "Not really," he said, his eyes falling softly on the gravestones. "Just found some family there." Then Lars coughed hard into his shoulder. "Have you set up a dedication mass for this whole family? Especially for Anya, the little one. I'll give your organist something to play on that old stack of pipes."

"We don't use the organ much anymore. But I'd be happy to do that."

"And one for Kilba."

"Sure," said Cruz. "Go ahead and call."

Lars looked at him. Old parishioners had visited Lars in the hospital and told him Cruz didn't allow the dedications to Kilba. The lie angered Lars a bit. His caretaker now whispered, "Mr. Jorgenson. It really is time to go." Lars patted the young man on the arm and then turned the walker to face Cruz. "Old man," he said.

"Lars..."

Jorgenson pressed the walker into the soft sod. "Good pal. Wish I had somethin' smart to tell you in the end. But I don't. Wish I could tell you a story, something that would make everything," he breathed, "all of it a lot smarter than it is. But I don't have anything like that. Father Cruz, I won't call to ask you to dedicate anything. Not for Kilba or anybody else. Good luck out here, good health to you, and good-bye."

"Yes, good-bye."

The caretaker opened the car door and helped Lars sit down. Cruz watched the car drive away, and he waved even though he knew Lars wasn't watching him.

Cruz had a look at the modest flowers Lars had left, snowdrops clustered in a short vase, and thought about moving them to Benny's grave, but he left them alone.

After the stress of traffic and the customary funeral lunch, Cruz returned to the rectory and sat alone in his study. Power tools whined in the backyard and his phone rang, several of the lines blinking, but Cruz could only sit. He looked over his desk, the cylinder of pencils, the neatly folded newspaper, the crisp pad of yellow paper, the Spanish bible, and the calendar pad that showed Sunday, September 9th. Cruz realized it was the wrong day, and he pulled off the little paper square to reveal Monday, September 10th.

He still had the little mirror Gaja had given him, wrapped in a small cloth and stashed way in the back of a bottom drawer. The drawer was stuck, would not slide open easily, and the power tools agitated him, but Cruz soon found it, all by itself in the back of an otherwise empty drawer. Without opening it, he held the mirror gently in his palm. He squeezed it with all his force, then put it in his pocket and went for a walk.

He peeked inside Reikel's shop. Cruz had forgotten Reikel no longer worked on Mondays. He wandered east, then back west, past the empty lot by the Family Clinic, the liquor store, the busy supermercado, the man who from a cart sold mangos with lime juice and salt. Cruz entered the block where Reikel owned some buildings and approached the house where Sonia Avila had lived.

Smoke from a barbecue rose above the house. Cruz could smell the grilling meat and sweet barbecue sauce. Reikel's dominant voice boomed from the yard, and then Lita and Yuri laughed out loud, unable to stop.

Rage, red as charcoal, surged in Cruz when, able to peer down a gangway, he saw Lita seated next to Yuri and holding his hand on her knee. Yuri made a clownlike face, poked fun at something, and raised a forefinger to say, raising his voice, "Sculpt this." Lita's body shook from laughter as she pressed Yuri's hand, flattening her other palm on her chest. Cruz's anger still surging, he took out the mirror, only vaguely aware of how hard he pressed it as he walked.

Down where 14th Street ended at Laramie, where some poor women were waiting for the bus, a thin dog was lying in the shadow of a pick-up truck. Cruz thought about tossing the mirror into the truck's bed. He knew a pawnshop down 22nd where he could get a few dollars for the silver mirror, donate the money to the poor box. He walked past a grease dumpster by the side of a taqueria and could have thrown the mirror there. Or into the sewer, under a passing bus. He could have given it to one of the thin girls waiting in line at an ice cream van. But Cruz returned the mirror to his pocket. It didn't matter what he did—Gaja's mirror didn't change a thing. He could keep it, give it away or destroy it, but no feeling, action or memory would ever change.

His pace increased on the way back to the parish, and he excused himself to the receptionist, asking one of the construction workers to wait just one moment, he'd be right back. Cruz went up to his study where he found the little cloth on his desk to wrap Gaja's mirror carefully and place it back in the bottom drawer. Now it slid freely—it must have aligned itself during Cruz's earlier struggle—and as he tested the fluid movement, Cruz noticed some pencil shavings in the drawer. They must have been there for years, yet how could they have fallen to a drawer that was always closed? How could they have escaped his careful effort to keep his desk tidy, surpass his relentless attention to all things that fell out of the place where they rightfully belonged? Cruz wiped the drawer clean with a dry cloth, making sure to get every corner, shouting "Just one moment!" to the construction worker calling him from downstairs. "One moment, please," he said. "I just have to tidy up."

Answer: Cicero, Illinois, November, 1981

Orest awoke on the crooked sofa, piles of clothes scattered through a room in a strange house. A piano stood near him, some chairs had been knocked over and he caught a whiff of a dangerous, acrid smell.

Petrol?

His face was wet. He licked his lips and had to spit, so violently that he almost threw up. He unbuttoned his wet pants because they felt a bit tight at the waist, but when he saw his old hairy hands, the expensive watch on his wrist and leather shoes on his feet, he knew something was terribly wrong.

Orest wandered through the large house, a labyrinth of long corridors, beaded glass doors, and a slippery waxed floor. He had the strong feeling that he had wanted to find something before falling asleep, though now he couldn't remember what it had been. In a room he saw a sleeping woman breathing heavily. Maybe she had taken him here? He asked her, in Ukrainian, Де я? Де я? to tell him where he was, but she remained asleep, and he was afraid to shake someone he didn't know.

A long mirror hung on the opposite wall. Orest came right up to look at himself. He was old with rough facial hair, and some of his teeth had chipped. His eyelids were swollen, chin thick and manly, and he realized he had been drinking. He was drunk, but he couldn't remember drinking anything.

Orest wandered into the other room—it was littered with unwashed laundry—to sit.

He remembered his family's flight. He had been away from the monastery for a short time, visiting his mother and grandfather in the village, when he learned that all the young men and priests from the monastery had been deported east into the Soviet Union. And his father, a professor of history at the University, had disappeared along with many of his colleagues, all of them most likely deported. Then the village just west of theirs, not fifteen kilometers down a dusty road, right near the Bug River, saw everyone removed in the middle of the night, deported east. Orest's grandfather had decided they would flee, head west, and on their first night he believed it made sense to seek shelter in a village where everyone had already been deported.

Orest had been holding his brother—now he remembered—they were down in the cellar. And the fear had locked his whole body, his hand tight around his brother's nose and mouth so that the infant couldn't breathe. Then he was piling the rocks and his hands had grown so cold that he could barely feel them. Now he was seeing a nightmare, his hands old, large and fat, wrinkles in palms dotted with white crescent scars.

He remembered he needed a shovel. It was true—yes, he had to return to the vacant farm with the shovel, bury his brother properly. It had been cold outside, but now it was warm. Orest could feel that winter had passed, and the ground must have thawed for sure. Orest could dig the dirt, then kneel down and pray properly as well. But how should he return to that place? Around him he saw nothing but piles of clothes, an empty bottle of cognac on the table, the label written not in Ukrainian or Russian or Polish but French. Someone had been fighting. Someone had thrown a glass against the wall.

He remembered the gunfire, how it had woken him, and how he had found himself in darkness.

He saw the last thing that would happen in his life: men knocking the trap door open to flood his eyes with terrible light. Faceless shadows moved toward him as a prayer poured from his body—he could see the land outside, the gray and brown winter plains, and the sun shimmering off the river, underwater grasses swaying in the gentle current. He saw the cherry trees that grew in his grandfather's yard and the log table where his mother sat spitting pits into a cup, her fingers purple from cherry juice.

He had to quiet his brother. They'd hear. The infant kept whimpering, but Orest tightened up and whispered, in Ukrainian,

Не роби цього! Тихо тихо тихо. *Don't. Don't. Don't. Quiet quiet quiet.*

He desperately craved a cigarette and found a pack in his shirt pocket, a box of matches. Hi. Hi. Hi. Тихо тихо тихо. Presently, he shouted the words because it didn't matter if anyone heard. He knew they had taken him here, to this place, and they were only preparing to finish him.

With the empty cognac bottle, Orest stormed to the back where it smelled even more horribly of petrol. In the back room, he pushed the bottle through one of the stained glass windows, knocking every remaining shard out of the frame.

He stuck his head out to breathe fresh air. At first it was only dark, but then he saw the young man, a frozen white apparition. Hi. Hi. Hi. Orest lit a match. Тихо тихо тихо. He brought the flame to the cigarette and inhaled deeply. The young man stood petrified before him, and his paralysis frightened Orest, but he repeated Hi. Hi. Hi. Тихо тихо тихо. As a great wind blew through the evergreens of that yard, Orest recognized, in a flash, who this young man was. It was young Orest staring back from the darkness he had left, a ghost in a nightmare. And he couldn't look. He couldn't look at himself.

Acknowledgements

The Fugue is a project that took almost fifteen years to complete and publish. Many people aided me along that path.

I must begin by thanking my wife, Maria Storm, whose support makes life as an artist possible, and whose violin is my greatest inspiration.

Early inceptions of The Fugue were supported, critiqued and aided by my classmates at Columbia University, whom I thank from the bottom of my heart, though in no particular order: Julia Holmes, Jessica Lamb-Shapiro, Gretchen Ernster-Henderson, Wells Tower, Dinaw Mengestu, Christina Saraceno, Sean-Michael "Turk" Robinson, Mark Binelli, Manuel Gonzalez, Hillery Hugg, Nadine Kavanaugh, Owen King, Animesh Sabnis, Marcela Valdes, Anthony Hawley, Nadia Aguiar, Jessica DeStefano and Kirsten Denker.

I am endlessly thankful to my writing teachers: Arabella Lyon, Mike Barrett, Michael Shapiro, Richard Howard, Maureen Howard and Ben Marcus, and I owe special thanks to David Plante for convincing me that Yuri Dilienko belonged in a novel about a family, not a short story about a neighborhood.

The champions and friends who guide and push me when I begin to wonder if I'll ever write another word are Kerri Smith Majors, Daiva Markelis, Mark Litwicki, Milda DeVoe, Rene Vasicek, Chantal Wright and Dan Vyleta.

Two writers, RP and SD, remain inspirations, and lessons they offered continue to guide my every word.

I offer incense and humble thanks to my Roshi, Robert Joshin Althouse, who showed me a much bigger mind. My sangha at the Zen Life and Meditation Center has offered invaluable support.

My in-laws, Ludmila Kasjanenko and Vadim Mikhailavich Perevoznikov, offered me a table and comfortable chair in the dacha outside Kiev where a large portion of this book was written.

This book would never have reached an audience if not for The Chicago Center for Literature and Photography and Jason Pettus, my original publishers and editor.

Obviously, Tortoise Books and Gerald Brennan breathed new life into this project, picking it up. With them, I feel resurrected and enormously thankful

Ir, pagaliau, ir kaip vis, kaimiečiams KLAK.

ABOUT THE AUTHOR

Gint Aras (Karolis Gintaras Žukauskas) lives in Oak Park, Illinois with his family. He's a community college instructor, photographer, and has worked as an editor, columnist, interpreter and translator. Learn more at gint-aras.com.

ABOUT THE PUBLISHER

Slow and steady wins in the end, but the book industry often focuses on the fast-seller. **Tortoise Books** is dedicated to finding and promoting quality authors who haven't yet found a niche in the marketplace—writers producing memorable and engaging works that will stand the test of time. Visit us at tortoisebooks.com.

Other titles include:
Resistance
The Last Good Halloween
Ninety-Seven to Three
Project Genesis
Zero Phase: Apollo 13 on the Moon
Public Loneliness: Yuri Gagarin's Circumlunar Flight
The Dark Will End The Dark
In Lieu Of Flowers

Printed in the USA
CPSIA information can be obtained
at www.ICGtesting.com
JSHW022203140824
68134JS00018B/833